Fields of Clover

Connie stared at her brother.

'An auction? You mean to sell this bakery in order to keep the bank at bay? You would do that, rather than cross Janine?'

'But Connie, surely you can't expect me to give up a smart house to save a shabby little bakery in a scruffy back street? That's not the way to move up in the world.'

'You were never a social climber, Jamie. It's your wife I hear talking, not you. Anyway, all you're doing is buying a respite. You'll still be in debt when this place is sold and she'll still be spending. Can't control her, can you, Jamie? She's more than you can handle, always was. Janine and her fancy house, her car, her clothes. First, last, before everything and everyone else. By God, if Mam had only known. She never dreamed you would marry a squanderer.'

Elizabeth Ann Hill was born in London in 1952 but grew up in South Wales and Cornwall where she now lives. She is the author of five previous novels.

Also by Elizabeth Ann Hill
*available in Mandarin

The Eve of Clancy Fair
Gypsy Hollow
The Hidden Spring
Pebbles in the Tide
*Bad Pennies

Fields of Clover

ELIZABETH ANN HILL

Mandarin

A Mandarin Paperback
FIELDS OF CLOVER

First published in Great Britain 1994
by William Heinemann Ltd
and by Mandarin Paperbacks
imprints of Reed Consumer Books Ltd
Michelin House, 81 Fulham Road, London SW3 6RB
and Auckland, Melbourne, Singapore and Toronto

Copyright © Elizabeth Ann Hill
The author has asserted her moral rights

A CIP catalogue record for this title
is available from the British Library
ISBN 0 7493 1876 7

Phototypeset by Intype, London
Printed and bound
by Cox & Wyman Ltd Reading, Berks

For my mother

One

She was sorely out of place in this fine shop, a drab figure in clumsy shoes and an old brown woollen coat. Her dark-red hair was lank, chopped off just below her ears, and held by grips at either temple. She was only twenty-two but she was frumpish. And she looked poor, too humble by far for this expensive establishment with its carpets and gilded mirrors and rails of evening gowns. The only pretty thing she possessed was her name. She was called Janine.

For a minute or two she walked slowly around, seeming spellbound by the sight of so many lovely dresses. At last, however, she paused and picked a frock from one of the racks, held it up against herself and smoothed a hand yearningly over the folds of plum silk. Then she took it to the nearest mirror, gazed at her reflection, day-dreamed for a while.

The salesladies watched her, thin-lipped. There were two of them, clothed in plain black skirts and high-necked white blouses. They were vaguely affronted that she had dared to come in, for this was the most exclusive shop in Plymouth. Needless to say, their regular patrons were women of style and means.

After a while, Janine replaced the dress. But almost at once she chose another, returned with it to the mirror.

The senior assistant felt obliged to make an approach. She advanced upon the young woman, pausing briefly to adjust the plum frock on its rail and inspect it, as if for signs of soiling.

The dress Janine now had in her hands was green satin with black beadwork on the bodice. She was looking closely at the delicate work, lovingly fingering the beads, when a voice at her shoulder informed her:

'That one is six guineas, madam.'

Startled, Janine turned around.

The saleslady folded her hands. A twitch of her mouth just passed for a smile, but her eyes were unfriendly.

What are you doing in here? they asked. Places like this aren't for you.

'We've nothing under five guineas, you know,' she added loftily.

For several seconds the young woman stared at her, with eyes which were dark and somewhat narrow. They were also unexpectedly shrewd, and a glint appeared in them now. She took her time in answering. Neither cowed nor apologetic, she seemed to be debating, considering something.

A fleeting discomfort removed the assistant's pale smile. But then, to her amazement, the dowdy creature nodded and said affably:

'I'm prepared to spend ten if you can show me something I really like.'

The assistant was taken aback. 'Ten?' she repeated faintly. It was more than she earned in a month. 'You . . .?'

'Hmm.' And from the left hip pocket of the shabby coat, Janine pulled two five pound notes. She held them up between finger and thumb.

'Oh,' the saleslady simpered. 'Well . . .'

Janine's cheeks dimpled and the dark eyes danced.

'Perhaps while I'm trying this little green one you'll bring me a few others?' she suggested. 'I'm size thirty-six.'

She spoke well, both tone and accent telling of education. It suddenly occurred to the saleslady that this might be some eccentric landed type. If so, she could be wealthy and worth cultivating. Even if she were not rich, even if this woman had saved for a year to amass the ten pounds, or simply stolen the notes, there was still a five per cent commission in the offing.

Helpfulness came oozing forth. 'Why, of course. Will madam please come this way?'

She showed Janine to the fitting room then bustled off to find something more costly to offer. The junior assistant, also scenting commission, volunteered to be of service too, but was shooed away by the older woman.

The senior assistant continued to bustle for over an hour, scurrying to and fro with concoctions of lace and satin and muslin, armfuls of floaty fabrics trimmed with sequins and feathers and fringes. She fetched alternative sizes and colours, and willingly brought back ones Janine had already tried and discarded, then asked to see again. She offered madam the best of the stock and generally ran about clucking and fussing as if her life depended on it.

Janine was appreciative, all smiles now. She asked opinions and advice on the care of the garments, and allowed the saleslady to flatter her. Time and again she seemed on the brink of making a choice. But then she would frown and dither and finally shake her head, joking that she really was a dreadfully indecisive person.

The assistant smiled till her cheeks ached, but the

3

smile grew harder and harder to hold each time her five per cent seemed all but in her grasp, only to be snatched away by yet another change of mind.

She had never worked so hard for a commission and in the end it failed to materialise, for suddenly, with regretful sighs, Janine said she could spare no more time just now. She put on her own dress and coat, thanked the saleslady sweetly for all her trouble and left the shop without buying a thing.

The assistant's knees were buckling. She stood in the middle of the shop, her arms full of frocks and her mouth indignantly open as she watched Janine go sailing out. Then, forgetting herself, she said something very ill-bred. The junior assistant tittered.

For a while Janine was gleeful as she walked homeward, exhilarated to think she had bested that awful woman. Before long, though, her sense of triumph wore off.

Because it wasn't her ten pounds at all. She would have to hand it over to her father when she got home. Janine had merely been to collect it that day in payment of a bill. Ten pounds, the price of a good headstone in this year of 1920. Her father, Matthew Jordan, was an undertaker, and far from being country types, the Jordans lived a few minutes' walk from Plymouth city centre. They and the funeral parlour occupied a spartan seventeenth century house in Bretonside.

Despondency settled upon her as she left behind the hurry and glamour of the shopping streets and dawdled through the narrow ways of the much older part of town where she had been brought up. Looking around the big shops was Janine's sole joy in life. And looking was as far as it ever went; buying was out of the question.

Janine never had any money. Her father said she would only spend it on finery, which went entirely against his belief in austerity. An intensely religious man, he accounted self-denial among the highest virtues. For Janine, it had meant a childhood and youth deprived of fun and treats and nice clothes. If she had shared her father's principles, of course, it would not have mattered. But despite his best efforts, Janine was not religious and within her there seethed a host of fierce, materialistic desires. Resentment, too, for the Jordans made a fairly good living. Much of it, however, was donated to Mr Jordan's church and its missionary endeavours overseas. Far too much, in Janine's opinion.

Her footsteps dragged as she approached her house. Gabled and dating from 1618, it was one of the largest in the street, whitewashed, with black paintwork and leaded windows, the panes diamond-shaped. Over the front door hung a sign, gold lettering on black announcing: M. L. JORDAN, UNDERTAKER AND EMBALMER.

Janine loathed the house. It seemed to embody everything she hated about her life. It was stark, uncomfortable, oppressive. She always thought of it as 'the family vault'.

Sighing heavily, she went in. Just inside the front door was a vestibule. A sign on the wall said 'Enquiries' with an arrow indicating another door on the right. That was where people called to do business. And had they but known it, this, the undertaker's office, was the most festive chamber in the house, being somewhat more nicely furnished and carpeted than any other room.

She opened the door and there behind his desk sat Mr Jordan, writing something in a ledger.

Pausing, he blinked up at his daughter through small, round spectacles. He was quite a large man, balding and bearded, sombrely dressed. He was instantly recognisable as a pompously respectable sort, an abider-by-the-rules.

'Ah – Janine. Did you collect the payment?'

'Yes, Dad.' She pulled the money from her pocket, put it on the desk.

'Good, good.' From the drawer came a cash box. Janine watched the notes disappear.

Her father peered at her over his spectacles. 'You've been a long time, haven't you?'

'I met an old schoolfriend. She kept me talking.'

'I see. Well . . .' he glanced at his pocket watch, '. . . best make a start on the dinner, don't you think? It's twenty past five and I don't like to eat later than seven, as you know.'

No, he always wanted a good two hours after the meal to digest his food and a chunk of the Bible before bed at half past nine.

'It won't take long, Dad. I'm doing chops tonight.'

'Ah, very nice, very nice.'

His face was pleasant when he smiled. She knew he wasn't a bad sort, well-meaning, albeit not especially intelligent. Not at all the kind of man one could hate. She could have been very fond of him, were he not so stuffy and frugal in his ways. He was one of those people who would use the same tea-leaves three times over, have things mended again and again until they finally fell to bits, and always buy second-hand rather than new.

Janine left him and went up to her bedroom to change her clothes. The house had a pole staircase, pointed-arch doorways and cumbersome oak furniture. Voices and footsteps echoed, startling in the heavy hush.

She had occupied the same room ever since she was a child, but had not been able to improve it much in all those years. A potted fern, a framed embroidery of a crinoline lady and a poster cadged from the Theatre Royal, advertising *The Magic Flute* were the only touches of gaiety she had managed to collect. There was one small rug beside the bed and the rest of the floor was black-varnished. Plain, tidy, bleak, that was the Jordan house. Everything in shades of beige, stone, black and brown. The Puritans would have felt entirely at home.

She hung her coat in the wardrobe, then sat down on the edge of the bed. From her bag she pulled a packet of cigarettes and a box of matches. Cigarettes were the one little treat she managed to scrounge for herself out of the house-keeping. Janine lit up, then kicked her shoes off. They hit the bare boards with a clunk. Putting her feet up, she laid her head back against the brass bedstead. She was watching the cigarette smoke curling upwards but seeing again in her mind that beautiful shop.

Her memory dwelt on the frocks she had tried that afternoon. There had been one in particular – satin, trimmed with swansdown, in aquamarine . . .

Oh, she had wanted it so much. It had actually crossed her mind to try and steal it, just to possess it, so that she could touch it, see it whenever she wanted, put it on from time to time and pretend that she was going somewhere special.

But of course she was not fool enough to try a thing like that. Her conscience would not have troubled her much, but it wasn't worth the risk.

Her thoughts moved once more to the sales assistant, and she saw again that subtly derisive expression on the woman's face, that coldness before the money worked its magic.

Janine scowled. She knew what sort of a figure she presented. People like that were always looking down their noses at her. Women who were nobody themselves. She made a little spitting sound and flicked the ash from her cigarette into the water glass on her bedside table.

The clock said ten past six when she finished a second cigarette, dropping the stub in the glass, where it expired with a tiny hiss. Rolling off the bed, she went to her cupboard and exchanged the shapeless woollen dress for an even older cotton one. Before she went downstairs she peered at herself in the mirror on the wall.

By the standards of current taste, she was not pretty. Certainly no Mary Pickford. Her mouth was too broad, the lower lip much more full than the top one. Her nose was upturned and spattered with freckles. It was a very knowing face, an intriguing face when she smiled, but not pretty. No wealthy man was likely to fall in love with Janine and carry her off to a life of opulence and ease.

Opening the window, Janine warily tipped the contents of the glass out into the street, then wiped it clean of any trace of ash. Mr Jordan didn't know she smoked. Nor did he know that she sometimes swore with frustration when she was alone in the kitchen, or that she often told him minor lies. She cherished her little sins and deceptions as tiny victories.

The dinner was overdone that evening. She charred the chops and boiled the cabbage and potatoes to a pulp, because her thoughts kept wandering, picking unhappily over her situation. When she set it down in front of him, Mr Jordan eyed her reprovingly over his glasses, but spared her the critical comments which sprang to his mind, for he was never deliberately unkind. Abhorring waste, of course, he girded himself to eat it.

The dining room lay right next to the Chapel of Rest, where the dead were laid out when Mr Jordan had finished preparing them. Accustomed to it, Janine seldom gave the fact a second thought. For sure, it had never spoiled her appetite for her late mother's good dinners. Still, meals were not lively affairs in the Jordan household. They were eaten slowly, in a silence broken only now and then by brief remarks which rarely led to much of a discussion. This evening, in the yellow glow of gaslight, to the tap of knives and forks on thick china, Janine and her father dined as usual, each wrapped up in private musings. Mr Jordan had his mind on matters of business. Janine, as she nibbled at her food, was remembering her mother and reflecting on an irony.

Mrs Jordan had wanted better things for her daughter than the suffocating existence she had known. Yet, her early death had condemned Janine to just that. The trap had closed as firmly as the coffin lid. The assumption had been immediate that Janine should look after her father. There was never any talk of marriage or career for her once her mother had gone. In

9

Matthew Jordan's view, the commandment 'Honour thy father . . .' included becoming his cook and house-keeper when he was widowed.

Janine had talked vaguely of taking a job, but he was against all that. He wanted his daughter at home every day to make his lunch and see any clients who called when he was out at a funeral. In any case, instinct told Janine that employment would not take her very far. To be a cog in someone's else's wheel was not her desire. What she wanted was something of her own.

Of course, as his only child, Janine would inherit the house and business one day. Still, Mr Jordan's demise was probably a long way off – twenty to thirty years, perhaps – and his was hardly a suitable or appealing trade for a woman.

The stuff of Janine's dreams was very different. Glamour, extravagance – how she craved them. And lively company, too. Friends with whom to chatter and visit, guests to entertain. Janine had acted out dinner parties in her mind a thousand times, and liked to imagine herself at dances, the centre of attention.

At length the main course was finished. She rose and went to the kitchen, returned with baked apples and custard. As they made a start on them Mr Jordan offered the first remark he had made for fifteen minutes.

'I hear that Mrs Sayers at the Barbican Bakery is not expected to live for more than a day or two longer.'

Janine was scarcely interested. 'Oh?'

'Poor woman,' said Mr Jordan, working his top lip over his bottom one, collecting a stray drop of custard. 'Such a long illness, so much suffering. What a mercy it will be when she is finally taken.'

His daughter made no response.

'One sometimes wonders,' he went on, 'why the good Lord visits such afflictions on harmless souls. Ah well, whom the Lord loveth he chasteneth, I suppose.'

She shot him a glance from under her brows, and irritation snapped in it. Matthew was always saying fatuous things like that. He wasn't even excitingly religious. He never went in for passionate denouncements or thrilling descriptions of hell. He was just banal and smug. Whenever her father was at his prayers, Janine felt certain that God must be bored stiff. Unhappier than usual this evening, she felt like giving him a jolt.

'From what I've heard, I don't think Mrs Sayers is any saint. I believe if you asked her neighbours they'd say she was a rather nasty woman.'

Mr Jordan's jaws stopped working. He coughed. His spoon, arrested by shock half-way to his mouth, dripped runny custard back into his dish. He stared at her, appalled, and then he breathed: 'Janine!'

'What's wrong with telling the truth? She's widely disliked and there must be reasons for it.'

'For shame, Janine, she's dying.'

'As we all do. And death doesn't change the facts about us, does it? If someone's been a tartar all her life, she doesn't acquire a halo just because her time is up. "Never speak ill" often means never again tell the truth once a person's gone.'

'If you could hear yourself,' gasped Matthew. 'Daughter, that's wicked talk.'

'It's the plain, unsentimental truth. Anyway, it's business for us, Dad. Don't pretend you're not thinking of that.'

'Janine, we have to live, but we don't profiteer. I don't rejoice in anyone's passing but I needn't rebuke myself

11

either for gratefully accepting trade. Remember how much of our money goes to our church to further God's work.'

'How could I forget?' she muttered testily.

Her father bent forward, earnest and distressed by what she had said.

'Faith brings comfort, Janine. So it's right, don't you see, that the proceeds of our doleful profession should help to propagate faith.'

She sighed. 'Yes, Dad.' As ever, Matthew's motives were benign. There was a broad vein of goodness in him which always made her bite back the more hurtful comments she could have made upon his religion.

They attended again to their food, but Mr Jordan eyed his daughter covertly, sadly, as he ate. He felt that he had failed with Janine. She was not a good sheep for the fold. He knew her cynicism and her discontent, and they dismayed him.

He had made mistakes, of course, in her upbringing. The first had been to indulge his wife and allow the child that name, that fancy, French-sounding name. All the other Jordan women for generations past had been given biblical names. He had wanted to call her Deborah.

And then, again to please his wife, he had sent Janine to that smart school in Mannamead. She had picked up 'ideas', not to mention a few unsuitable friends. When his wife died he had seized the excuse to take Janine away from the school at once. Still, it had left its mark. He'd never managed to cleanse her of the influence.

Janine's unsuitable friends had simply been girls from more prosperous and liberal backgrounds. And she hadn't needed them to plant a desire for the primrose path. Had he but realised it, her father had done that himself.

Janine had always lived cheek by jowl with death and decay. She had grasped her own mortality far earlier than most children. There were always bodies, coffins, in the house. Infant corpses, aged corpses, people mangled in accidents or retrieved after weeks in the sea. Janine had seen many a pitiful sight, and sometimes her father even permitted her to watch him at work when he was embalming, out in that cold, stone room at the back of the house. His plan had been to impress her with the brevity of earthly life, the frailty of the flesh, and the need to cultivate the eternal soul instead.

All it had done was to give her a stomach as strong as a battlefield surgeon and fill her with a desire to gather rosebuds while she might.

With poor appetite, Janine picked at her apple, chasing a stray pip round the bowl. Her thoughts were still on Mrs Sayers. Janine hadn't seen her for a long time, but remembered her well from the days before she fell ill. A proud, good-looking person. But not popular. Janine had not been making any judgement of her own – or overstating the case. Local people said that Ada Sayers was a bitch. Janine, who often shopped for groceries on the Barbican, had heard a number of sharp remarks about her over the years.

Mrs Sayers had a grown-up son and daughter. The son was called James. Janine had often seen him about; he was really quite handsome, except that he had a scar on his face.

Wondering about it, she broke the silence again.

'What happened to Mrs Sayers' son, Dad? How did he

13

get that mark on his cheek? It isn't a birthmark, is it? Looks more like a burn.'

Matthew sat back in his chair and his forehead crinkled as he summoned a memory. 'Yes, a burn, that's right. I don't know much about the incident, but there was a fire at the Sayers house – oh, more than ten years ago.' He ran his tongue around his teeth, dislodging bits of apple. 'It was just after Christmas. The talk was that decorations were somehow set ablaze one evening. I believe the children were home by themselves – I don't know why. Anyway, the little girl escaped unscathed, but the boy was not so lucky. That's all I can tell you.'

'How old were the children?'

'I should think a little younger than you. Yes, you were at Mannamead school at the time.'

'Perhaps that's the reason Mrs Sayers is not well liked, because she left them alone.'

'Perhaps it is,' allowed Mr Jordan, 'but I don't care to pass judgement. I dare say the poor soul's endured a great deal of remorse.'

'Mm.' Janine pushed her dish aside. 'Still, it would have been worse if the girl had been scarred.'

'In a way,' agreed Mr Jordan thoughtfully. 'But you know, as luck would have it, the boy was the beautiful one. It must have broken Mrs Sayers' heart.'

Two

Through a haze of morphia, Ada Sayers watched her daughter move about the room. Not that she could see her very clearly. The opiates were being given in massive doses now and Connie was just a fuzzy figure, a long shape in a white bib-top apron, with a yard of brown hair hanging down her back.

It wouldn't be long now. Ada could feel the life seeping out of her. Today or tomorrow she would be gone and she wouldn't be sorry. The disease had taken two years to kill her, and she was more than ready for the end.

The figure came to the foot of the bed. There was something in Connie's hand – an enamel bowl, Ada thought.

Oh yes, of course, she'd been sick again a little while ago.

'Would you like a drink, Mam? Some milk or orange juice?'

The voice was low and rich, warm with West-Country vowels.

'No,' breathed Ada with a weak sideways turn of her head. 'No, thank you.'

'The doctor's coming soon,' said Connie. 'Shall I prop you up?'

Another almost imperceptible shake of the head. Ada didn't really know why the doctor troubled to call any more. There was only one thing left for him to do and that was write the death certificate. And she didn't want to be bothered with him, with anyone, except . . .

'Where's Jamie?' she whispered. 'Where's my boy?'

'He's down in the shop, Mam. Shall I send him up to sit with you for a while when the doctor's gone?'

Ada nodded, smiling, and closed her eyes. For a minute Connie stood looking at her. The bowl in her hands reeked of vomit, but she was all too used to that by now, just as she was used to chamber-pots and blood and septic ulcerations.

It was hard to credit what had become of her mother. Stately Ada, gone to feeble skin and bones, shrunken, lined and grey. Dominant Ada, robbed of power – even to perform her natural functions without assistance. Accusing Ada, critical Ada . . .

Connie's face was calm and grave. She was twenty-one, tall and somewhat lean. Her bearing was digni-fied, as her mother's had been before the disease struck her down. Fine eyes, large and blue, were Connie's best feature. A gentleness about her mouth, a sympathetic tilt to her head, said she was the kind who would always listen to people's problems and help if she could. Beyond doubt, she was one who would always do her duty.

As she certainly had for Ada. It wasn't that she loved her mother. Connie didn't pretend that, even to herself. She knew full well that Ada did not love her. These years of nursing hadn't changed that. One had a duty to a parent, that was all.

Very soon now, Connie too would be released – from this particular burden, anyway. There were still others.

'You'll look after Jamie, won't you, Constance? You'll always help him if he needs you? Promise me you will.'

That was what Ada had asked only yesterday. And

Connie, of course, had said yes. But then, she truly did love Jamie. If taking care of her brother was a burden, it was one she carried gladly. Connie would always stand by James. She felt she owed it to him.

The clock said twenty-five past three and the doctor had promised to call around four. Connie went downstairs to empty the bowl.

As the door closed behind her, Ada's eyes opened, fixing blearily on the ceiling. Was everything in order? she asked herself for the hundredth time. Yes, it was. It was all arranged. He would be all right, her darling. As far as it was in her power, she had seen to that. Her James would have a comfortable life. Sinking gratefully into the blessed stupor of the drugs, Ada wondered idly if she would live another night.

'Jamie,' she murmured again. 'My dearest son.'

The mirror over the wash-stand reflected a handsome face. James Sayers, nineteen and six feet tall, flicked a last patch of lather and stubble from his right cheek and rinsed the razor in his shaving mug. He dried his neck with a towel and considered himself for a moment, his head still turned to present his normal side to the glass.

He would have been a heart-breaker, if not for his accident.

He stared, unsmiling, at the neat, straight nose and chiselled mouth which nature had given him. And the strong dark brows and deep blue eyes.

He should have been able to pick any girl he wanted.

But no. Slowly, he moved his head around to examine the great puckered scar on his other cheek. He'd done the same a thousand times, more and more often as he grew up, studying it from every angle, trying to picture what others saw and imagine how it affected them. He had read somewhere that you could never see yourself properly, not even using two mirrors. You could never get the full effect, as other people did, of expression and the constant movement of facial muscles.

James looked at himself full-face. The first hint of the mark was a tightness of the skin high up on his cheek, then more of a dragging, and little tucks, and finally, as he turned his head, the whole blasted thing. He often used that word, and deliberately. Blasted, that was how it looked, torn up like Flanders' fields.

Connie told him he exaggerated, but it seemed a fair enough comparison to James. Other people sometimes informed him that he was a rather lucky young man. He had missed by one year the duty to serve in the Great War. So many other local boys had been less fortunate. James didn't think himself all that lucky when he saw himself in the mirror. He might not have been at the front – but he looked as if he had.

Turning away from the glass, he put on a clean shirt, a collar and tie and flannel trousers. He was always very well turned out – fresh clothing every day. His chest of drawers was full of jerseys, mostly home-knitted Fair Isle or diamond-patterned V-necks. The women of his family took good care of him. His mother had always doted on him. From the day he was born he was Ada's little prince. And his sister loved him just as much. She had never resented the fact that he was the favourite child.

It was Sunday morning now, just after nine, and still Ada lingered. In truth, she had lasted far longer than the doctors had believed possible. At first they had given her just eight months. They said these last two years had been a terrible drain on Connie. They had nothing but praise for her unstinting care.

But then, thought James, Connie was like that. It was just what you'd expect of her.

He went across to Ada's room and sat on the chair beside the bed, taking the scrawny hand from the coverlet, squeezing it in his own. Ada looked up groggily, smiled and mumured something to him. Then she reached up, drew his head down, kissed him long and warmly on that patch of shiny, purplish skin which blighted his face.

'I've seen to it you're well provided for,' she whispered weakly. 'And I've told her she must look after you. She knows her obligations, I made sure.'

He gave a small frown. 'Now, Mother, be fair. There wasn't any need for that.'

Ada ignored his mild reproach. She subsided into her pillows, but her eyes still roved over the scar. 'I've done my best to make it up to you,' she murmured. 'Done my best . . .'

'Ssh, ssh, I know all that. Don't tire yourself.'

She went quiet, still holding his hand. She could feel herself sliding away, going down bit by bit, but her precious son was with her and that was all she wanted now. Just Jamie at the last. She closed her eyes. The clock ticked gently and pale spring sunshine lit the room, but Ada's awareness had narrowed to the firm, warm flesh of Jamie's hand. If that was to be her last sensation, she would be content.

But then, suddenly, there was intrusion. Connie's footsteps, Connie's voice: 'How is she, Jamie?'

And Ada found she still had strength enough for anger. Her eyelids lifted, her gaze fixed on her daughter, and Connie almost recoiled.

Go away, it said. Go away, I don't want you here. Get out, be gone. Just leave me alone with my son.

And Connie went, backing out of the room as if she had been physically shoved. Hostility seemed to strike her like cold air and throw a protective barrier round the loving little scene at the bed.

She closed the door and went downstairs, her throat tight. She wasn't going to be there at the end, she wasn't welcome.

Ada died soon afterwards, at twenty to eleven. Connie was sitting in the kitchen, drinking tea, when her brother came down to tell her. He was tearful but his sister received the news without emotion. Jamie was the one who was going to miss Ada.

He sat down and helped himself to tea. After a minute, he said: 'I saw the way she looked at you just now. I'm sorry, Connie.'

A dry laugh came from his sister. She held the cup between her hands and the steam rose gently to touch her face. 'I shouldn't have been quite so surprised,' she said, sipping and breathing in the fragrance. 'Nothing was really changed by these past two years. I felt it all along. Oh yes, there were smiles and there were grateful words sometimes, but I always knew what lay underneath. She needed me when she fell ill, but she didn't soften towards me, not in her heart of hearts. I've been useful – essential – but it didn't make her love me any better.'

Awkwardly, he ventured: 'Mother was always a bit irrational about my accident, Connie. You know I've never blamed you for it, don't you?'

'Yes, I know.'

'That was hard of her this morning, and I told her so.'

Connie shrugged. Hot and sweet, the tea seemed to send a bracing strength right through her frame. 'Very much in character,' she said wryly. 'A parting shot.'

He knew the truth of that and offered no argument. After a while, he asked vaguely: 'What do we do now? I have to go and fetch the doctor, do I?'

There were only two years between them, yet she was far more the adult. When uncertain or distressed he would look to Connie almost as if she were a parent.

'Yes. You'd best go straight away, I think.'

He stood up, took his coat and hat from the back of the kitchen door. Then he hovered.

'What about . . .? You know . . .'

'I'll take care of that.'

Yes, she would see to the funeral, the obituary notice and all the glum details. It would upset James too much.

She rubbed a hand over her forehead as he went out, sweeping back an untidy lock of hair. All she felt at Ada's passing was a sense of deliverance. She would not be able to mourn for her.

The funeral – whom to hire for that? Connie wondered. There had been no deaths in her family for so long now that she found herself unable to summon to mind the name of any undertaker. She thought about it for a while, then recalled that her neighbours across the street had buried a parent just a few months before.

Connie went out and across the road to knock at the door of Jack and Millie Chope, who lived right opposite. It was Millie who answered. She was thin, with a pallid oval face and very fine blond hair which lay flat to her head. Connie had no special liking for Millie, a two-faced, envious type. But then it was Jack Chope she really wanted to see.

'Ooh,' said Millie, 'hello, dear. Anything wrong?'

'Mother's just died, Millie, within the past hour.'

Another 'Ooh', very hushed and grave. 'Come in, Connie, do. You'll have to excuse Jack not being dressed.'

Connie followed her inside to the Chopes's tiny parlour, where Jack was sitting with his feet up in front of the fire.

'Jack, here's Connie. Poor Ada's passed on, just a short time ago.'

The man stood up. He was middle-aged and stout, a metal worker at Devonport dockyard. He was in his vest and pyjama bottoms, his customary condition on a Sunday morning. Connie took no notice of that. Jack was always the same, any old how.

For a moment he looked intently at her, then he said: 'So your mam's gone at last. How are you feeling, maid?'

'Wrung out, that's all.'

'We're so sorry, Connie,' Millie said. 'So sad, isn't it, Jack? Poor Ada.'

He let that pass unanswered. 'Is there something we can do to help you, Connie?' he asked.

'Yes, there is. I came to ask you the name of the undertaker you used when your father died, Jack.'

'Oh . . .' he scratchd his ear, '. . . it was Jordan, up in Bretonside. Did a good job, too, all went off very nicely.'

'Jordan,' repeated Connie. 'Do you have the address?'

'I have his bill around here somewhere, I'll find it.'

'Sit down, Connie,' Millie said. 'Like a drop of brandy? I expect you're feeling shaky.'

'No thanks, I'm all right. After all, it was far from a shock.'

'Yes,' crooned Millie, 'you've been expecting it so long, haven't you? I'd hate to linger like that. Poor Ada, it was cruel. I've always said I'd rather drop down dead in my tracks one day than go slowly, bit by bit. But there it is, we never know what's in store for us, do we?'

She went on, trotting out the usual platitudes and clichés, with a few tactless observations thrown in which would have upset Connie deeply, had she been fond of Ada.

Jack Chope returned with the undertaker's bill and gave it to Connie.

'There you are, maid. He's as good as anyone, I reckon, and better than some. Can't go far wrong with him.'

'Thank you, Jack.' Connie read the address, then gave the paper back.

'Very reasonable, he is. Won't overcharge.'

'I'm sure Connie isn't concerned about the cost,' reproved Millie. She bridled, adding proudly: 'Jack's dad had walnut, you know, with solid brass handles.'

'It was you wanted that, not him,' grunted her husband. 'He wouldn't have cared what he had.'

'And a granite kerb with marble chippings,' smiled Millie, ignoring him. 'Oh, it was lovely.'

A show-off, Millie, always anxious to go one better than the next person, always keen to impress.

'Sounds very smart,' obliged Connie, knowing what Millie liked to hear. 'All right, well, I must go. Jamie will be back with the doctor any minute.'

'Give him our sympathies,' Millie said, seeing her out. 'Tell him how upset we are, won't you? Poor Ada.'

If she says that once more, I'll clout her, thought Jack.

Still in the parlour, standing by the window, he watched Connie cross the street and go into her house. Such a tall figure, such a grave, good face she had. A solemn little girl grown into a kindly woman. Jack remembered that little girl very clearly, that quiet, unfortunate child. And as he gazed at the front of the Sayers' house this mild morning, he recalled a scene from twelve years before.

The same house, in the dark, with fire and smoke belching from the parlour window, the glass having cracked and fallen out in the heat. Himself, dashing over and pounding at the door. Connie answering, coughing, her eyes streaming. Connie, nine years old and panic-stricken. He could still see that little figure in pinafore and button-boots, and hear her weeping:

'I can't find Jamie. Help me, I can't find him.'

Pulling her out and leaving her in the street, he had plunged inside. Had he not located Jamie quickly, the boy would have suffocated where he lay, curled up behind the parlour door.

The image faded and Jack found he was scowling. Out – she was out that night, Ada Sayers. She had left her kids and gone out for some selfish reason. He forgot, now, precisely what, and it didn't matter anyway. She had no business being out, but had never accepted blame.

Another memory deepened his scowl. Screaming from the Sayers' house in the small hours that same night. Ada screaming, yelling her head off at the little girl . . .

Millie came back in and her twittery voice drove the memories away.

'You might have said you were sorry, Jack, even if you're not.'

He sniffed, went back to his chair and sat down.

'We must go to the funeral,' Millie went on. 'I wonder if they'll have a big tea after. I expect they will.' She poked him in the shoulder-blade as she passed his chair, and chirped: 'I'll need a new outfit.'

The Sayers family had owned their bakery for four generations, together with the slim, three-storey house next door. The frontage of the property stretched for forty feet along a sloping side-street of the Barbican. The bakery, stores and shop occupied a converted warehouse – one of many in this ancient harbourside area.

Almost every street on the Barbican was cobbled and narrow, for this was the Tudor quarter, Elizabethan Plymouth, a labyrinth of courts and alleys and gabled dwellings, quays and wharves. Everything here was built of rough granite, windows were small, and the height of the buildings – often four storeys – kept the slender streets always in shadow. A place of grey stone and brown paintwork, it was nevertheless a square mile drenched in the colour of history, a history huge and romantic.

Here in bygone times the press-gangs had raided the waterfront taverns. Here, lurking thieves and cutthroats had once made it madness to walk alone at night. Here, explorers, pirates and adventurers had lodged, caroused and laid their plans for the next voyage. The smooth old cobbles had felt the tread of Drake and Captain Cook and the Pilgrim Fathers. From modest little Sutton Harbour, mere yards from the Sayers' front door, ships had carried emigrants to every corner of the world. Scruffy, beaten about by centuries at the hub of great events, the Barbican echoed all the time to the cries of gulls. And in the mornings when the boats came in, it smelt of fish, a light, sharp scent of catches freshly landed from trawlers, drifters, crabbers, Devonshire and Cornish vessels with black-painted hulls and rust-brown sails.

The Sayers' house was a place of steep staircases and very few modern amenities, still equipped with gas lighting, an old-fashioned kitchen range, and a washhouse in the back yard with a copper for boiling the laundry. It was a house which had always demanded drudgery from the women who lived in it. The fact that it was clean and pleasant, cheerfully decorated and furnished, was a testament to the hard work of all those women, of whom Connie was the latest and perhaps most conscientious.

When they heard the news of Ada's death, most in the neighbourhood agreed that it was at least a mercy for her daughter. In respect of gossip, the Barbican was very much like a village – there weren't many secrets. Everyone knew that Connie's life had long been a thankless slog. Ada, what was more, had endeared herself to few of those who knew her. People hereabouts were mostly plain and forthright types – dockyard workers, fishermen – who had never liked her lofty manner.

A short walk from the bakery lay Southside Street, where the grocer, the butcher, the dairy and the ironmongery might be found. There was also a bookshop, a toyshop, a haberdashery and Blackfriars' distillery. A number of the Sayers' customers and fellow shopkeepers from the Barbican attended the funeral, mostly out of consideration for James's and Connie's feelings. A few said Ada had paid her debts in suffering these past two years, but most were of the view that she was neither chastened nor changed by it.

The owner of Southside Dairy was a widow named Cynthia Hardin. She had fat red cheeks, big front teeth, and popping eyes behind thick spectacles. A snob, she was scarcely more popular than Ada Sayers had been. She knew all about everybody and hadn't a shred of tact. People referred to her as 'the dairy cow'.

'I'm only stating facts,' she would say, if challenged. 'You know I'm a great believer in telling the truth.'

She boasted particular knowledge of the Sayers family, because her courtyard backed onto theirs and she had a good view through their kitchen window. Cynthia considered herself a student of human nature, and one morning just after the burial she was airing her opinions to the sweet-faced Mrs Paul from the haberdashery next door.

'I just hope Ada had the sense to give Connie control of the business,' Cynthia was saying. 'I know Jamie's the boy and all that, but he really doesn't have a lot of gumption. Ada spoilt him, brought him up soft, and he isn't a worker like his sister.'

'They'll own it jointly, I dare say,' said Mrs Paul.

'Mmph, even so, I bet I know who'll be putting in all the effort.' Cynthia ladled half a pound of thick, golden-crusted cream into Mrs Paul's basin. Handing it over the counter, she added: 'Jamie's a nice enough lad, of course, but he isn't capable of much, if you ask me. It's my belief he would still have been pampered, even without his accident. You know what Ada was like – queen bee. Women of that sort always treasure their sons – and they don't have much room for other females in their domain, you mark my words.'

'Jamie may change now she's gone.'

'Hah!' exclaimed Cynthia. 'It's too late for that, I'll bet a bob. You know what the Jesuits used to say – "Give me a child until he is six years old . . ." '

'You never allow anyone the benefit of the doubt, do you?' reproached Mrs Paul, who considered Cynthia callous, self-righteously cold and clean like the gleaming tiles of her dairy, the spotless china bowls of eggs and gleaming steel churns of milk. She was always glad to leave Cynthia's premises, return to her own little nook among the bright embroidery silks and knitting wools and coloured buttons.

'I don't delude myself about people,' Cynthia sniffed. 'If ever I saw an unhealthy situation, it was in the Sayers family. Can you imagine Ada's reaction if Jamie had ever brought home a girl? Possessive, my dear, that's what she was. I sometimes wonder if she didn't have mixed feelings about his scar. Deep down she might have felt it was a blessing in disguise.'

'Oh Cynthia! That's outrageous!'

'Is it? Well, I hope I'm wrong. But as I say, he was her darling boy.'

Mrs Paul didn't want to listen to any more of this. Cynthia could be hateful sometimes – not least because she had a disturbing habit of being right. Kindly, straightforward Mrs Paul never imagined dark motives and twisted emotions in people. Glimpses of such things frightened her, as if she had peered down into a pit full of rats and black beetles.

'I have to go,' she muttered, 'there may be someone in the shop.'

I suppose she thinks me nasty-minded, reflected Cynthia as her neighbour hurried away. Perhaps I am, but at least I'm sharp enough to look beneath the surface of things and see that there are many hidden layers. It's a pity poor Connie doesn't have the same capacity.

Three

'To my daughter Constance, the sum of one hundred pounds. To my dearest son James, the remainder of my estate.'

For long, dragging seconds, the words seemed to hover in the musty air of the solicitor's office. He had paused, glancing over the top of his spectacles at Miss Sayers and her brother. James simply registered wide-eyed surprise. On Connie's face was a look more complex – wry, but also shaken, perhaps even a little frightened.

In truth, Connie had never given much thought to what would happen to the family property when Ada died – until today. Up to now, such matters had scarcely occurred to her, busy as she was. Home was home, and taken for granted. Questions of ownership, of her own future security, had never troubled her.

But now – the house, the shop, everything to James. For Connie, a sum of money that would last no time at all if she had to live on it. And Connie was qualified for nothing other than domestic work and serving behind a counter.

The solicitor went on reading a few last details, then James was full of eager, excited questions. How long would it take for the necessary paperwork to be completed? What was the property deemed to be worth in total? When would he have control of it?

Connie sat in silence. She had nothing to ask. She

recalled her promise to 'look after' James. It seemed like a bad joke now.

The solicitor, fielding James's questions, kept glancing sadly at the pale young woman beside him. She was faintly old-fashioned, her hair pinned up in a coil at the back of her head, her choice of clothing plain and careless. Not at all like Ada Sayers had been in her youth. Always a vain woman, Mrs Sayers. And a vindictive one, too. The solicitor sighed. Oh, he had seen this sort of thing many a time before. This kind of treachery was nothing new to him.

Finally, James had all the answers he wanted. Chairs scraped back and everyone stood up. Hands were shaken and then they were leaving.

Detaining Connie at the door, however, the solicitor murmured: 'A moment, Miss Sayers. If I might have a word . . .'

James looked round. He hovered briefly, curious. Then the solicitor added: '. . . in private.'

James made a face of indifference and went out.

'You could contest it, you know,' the old man said gently. 'I'm aware that you've nursed your mother these past two years. It is, if I may say so, a staggering injustice that you should have nothing more than this paltry sum of money. If you were to appeal against this will, I believe you'd receive a sympathetic hearing, and perhaps . . .'

Connie interrupted. 'It was what she wanted. There was nothing wrong with her mind, she knew precisely what she was doing.'

'Indeed she did. We discussed it when I drew up the will. But I tried to talk her out of this, you know.'

'And you couldn't. So what more is there to be done?'

31

'Possibly a great deal. I'm sure you have a moral right to far more than she has given you.'

'Do I?' queried Connie numbly. 'Oh, I don't know, I just . . .' She made a helpless gesture, shaking her head and spreading her hands. 'I can't decide anything now, I have to think about it.'

'Well, when you've finished thinking, come back to me, Miss Sayers. I must confess, I've found this a most uncomfortable occasion today and I'm very sorry for you.'

Connie smiled weakly and bid him goodbye.

One of life's sacrificial lambs, he thought, as he closed the door after her.

She found James waiting outside on the pavement, leaning against the railings at the front of the house. The first excitement over, he had realised at last that his sister had been short-changed. Less bouncy now, he eyed her awkwardly as she came down the steps.

'Look, Connie,' he said, falling in step beside her. 'I'd no idea Mother was going to do this. You do believe me, don't you?'

She nodded.

'I suppose it was pretty unfair, after all you've done for her. But it doesn't really matter, does it? I mean, it won't make any difference. We'll just carry on in the same way. We'll run the place together. Just because it's in my name doesn't mean it's any less your home.'

'I hope you'll always feel the same way, Jamie.'

'Well, why ever not? Lord, you don't think I'd turn you out, do you?'

She laughed nervously. 'No, I suppose not.'

'Anyway, it's all in trust until I'm twenty-one. Listen . . .' He stopped and turned to face her, grasping her upper arms. '. . . Mother left it to me because I'm the man of the family and it's up to me to manage the finances. That's tradition, pure and simple. And another thing, Connie – with Mother gone you're free. You might start courting now. You might marry and have some children. If so, you'll have a home of your own and no time for anything else. It's only right that I should take full charge of the business.'

She stared at him. Start courting? The suggestion was amazing to her. That had been something for other girls, girls with spare time, girls who primped and knew how to flirt. Ada had never encouraged Connie to dress herself up or go with lads. Ada had kept her very busy throughout her adolescence. And then, of course, Mam had fallen ill.

Courting? What chance for Connie? Visions paraded through her mind of endless ministry to the frail figure in the bed, of countless evenings spent reading to Mam, innumerable broken nights, of stomach-turning sick-room chores, of holiday outings and social events missed, of confinement at home, at Ada's beck and call. It was true that James had sat with his mother some of the time, but Connie still had to be ever available in case something unpleasant had to be done, the sort of personal, bodily thing that a woman would hardly ask of her son.

Still, as James pointed out, all that was over now.

'Well,' she allowed, 'I suppose it's possible. Though, you know, I don't have any friends of any sort.'

'Nor do I. But at least you're not . . .' He broke off. 'I mean, there's nothing wrong with you. You'll meet somebody who'll want you.'

Connie glanced sideways at him and the sight of his disfigurement hit her like a hammer. He always wore a trilby when he was out, carefully set at an angle which was jaunty and served as well to hide part of the scar. Even so, it caught the eye, that livid patch extending from his cheek-bone down over his jaw. There were little ridges and tattered edges, and a shiny maroon area just below his ear.

James had very great difficulties with girls on account of his scar. Whenever a pretty one came into the shop, he would redden and lift a concealing hand to his face. He would pull at his ear or make a pretence of scratching it. He would tilt his head towards his shoulder or half turn away as he spoke. He believed they must be staring at it, and generally they were. The worst ones, however, were those who carefully steered their gaze away in a pitying effort to be kind. Poor James would start to stumble over his words, or drop things, and the prettier the girl, the greater his anguish and confusion.

It never failed to arouse guilt in Connie. *Mea culpa*, she always thought. Through my negligence, my disobedience . . . If I had done as I was told, there would never have been a fire.

Still, James made no effort to overcome that self-consciousness. Occasionally, in a more hard-hearted moment, Connie told him so. Such a moment came now.

'Jamie,' she said, 'I wish you'd try to help yourself. What's the alternative? Are you going to shun women all your life? Do without a wife and children? I don't think girls would take half as much notice if you didn't behave so awkwardly. Your embarrassment upsets them. If you could relax, then they would too.'

'It's no good. I know what they're thinking when they look at me. "Poor thing" or "God, what a fright" or "How repulsive".'

'Some may think that way, of course – the ignorant ones, the cruel. But there are plenty of kinder girls.'

'I don't want kindness, thanks all the same. Allow me some dignity, do.'

'Perhaps if you could make a joke or two about it . . .'

'Be a clown as well as a freak,' he muttered bitterly.

'You're not a freak and you know it. You had an accident, that's all.'

'Doesn't matter how it came about, the result's the same.'

'There are plenty of men around who came home from the war with injuries far worse than yours. Men who lost limbs or eyesight, or had their faces torn by shot and shell. I've seen men like that out walking with girls. They found the nerve to ask, Jamie. You'll have to do the same.'

'They must have thicker skins than mine, that's all I can say.' He looked wretchedly at her, then bowed his head. 'I can't, Connie. I'm ashamed of being afraid, but I just can't. I'd find it easier to jump off a cliff, and that's a fact.'

She gazed at him a moment, despairing, and then they walked on. James, she feared, might very well spend his life without wife or children. So perhaps it was right that he should have the property in compensation. The little surge of spirit and commonsense ebbed away, and guilt returned triumphantly to rule her. No, Connie would not contest the will. Ada had known that when she made it. She had done a fine job with Connie.

'By God, I call that evil!' Nell Colenso punched the bread dough as if she had a grudge against it. 'Ada always was a bugger, but I never thought she would do a thing like that.'

Her husband Harry shrugged and muttered: 'Oh, nothing surprises me – except that it was stupid of her. I shan't feel so safe in my job with Jamie in charge.'

The woman went on fiercely kneading. Both were dressed in white overalls and round, starched caps. Harry and Nell had worked at Sayers' bakery for fifteen years. Harry was short, with a face like a Toby jug. His wife was sharp of nose and sharp of wit. She missed – and forgot – very little. From six in the morning till three in the afternoon, the Colensos laboured amid the heat and the flour and the sugar, and brought forth from the big brick ovens fragrant breads and pies and confections which sold at a halfpenny, a penny, threepence, and so on up to half a crown for a truly elaborate cake.

'If I were Connie, I'd get out,' said Nell. 'I'd take that money and make my escape. Little though it is, it could buy her a chance in life. She should go away somewhere, find a room and a job and a nice young man, and let her brother get on with it. For as long as she stays at home, he'll lean on her, and she'll be so busy propping him up that she'll have no time for herself.'

Harry skimmed the pastry brush over a large tray of sausage rolls, glazing them with beaten egg, then hefted the whole thing from the table and swung it into one of the ovens.

'Oh God, don't wish that on us, woman. She's the capable one.'

'It would be better for her,' Nell insisted. 'As long as she's here, he'll make use of her. I don't say deliberately, but he'll go on in the way he's accustomed. That's how he's been raised, seeing her put upon and seeing nothing wrong with it, as if it were a law of nature that she should get all the hard work and dirty jobs, and always be the one to make sacrifices. There are factories paying decent wages. Or she might find a post as a nanny with a nice family. Why should she care about this place now? And what does she owe him? Nothing, despite what Ada drummed into her all those years.'

'She won't go,' said Harry quietly. 'She's strong and self-reliant, but she won't leave him.'

'No,' sighed Nell, 'I'm very much afraid not. Sometimes it's no good thing to be too strong, because the weak will batten on you. The weak will let you carry them until they break your back.'

'Only if you're foolish enough to let them.'

'Love and foolishness often go together, and Connie has too soft a heart, my dear.'

Always on the go, that was Connie Sayers. She was generally up at six in the morning with a full agenda for each day: cook, shop, dust, sweep, make the beds, fetch in coal – these were the daily basics. On top of this ran a weekly rota. On Mondays she cleaned the shop window and ground-floor house windows. On Tuesday she would blacklead the kitchen range and polish its brass handles and pot rack. Wednesday was the day to take up all the rugs, carry them out to the backyard, hang them over the clothes line and beat them. Thursday saw her changing the beds and scrubbing the kitchen floor. On Friday, by way of light relief, there were sit-down jobs such as polishing silver or darning or sewing on buttons. Saturday was laundry day – the worst – four hours of sweating and sloshing in the outhouse, dragging steaming linen out of the copper, hauling it from one tin bath of cold water to the next for the rinse, and finally forcing it inch by stubborn inch through the mangle. Sunday always meant a stack of ironing. There was no such thing as a genuine day of rest for Connie. Some were a bit less arduous than others, that was all.

Nell Colenso had hoped that Connie would slacken off when her mother died. Indeed, she had suggested it from the day Ada finally took to her bed, never to leave it again. But to no avail – the pattern was set. Connie could no more shrug at a film of dust or a stained table-cloth than she could step over an injured man in the street. Forever taking down curtains and putting up fresh ones, constantly shifting furniture to get at cob-webs and fluff, she was driven all the time by anxiety to be useful. The thought of being lazy, neglectful or selfish appalled her.

It wasn't praise from those around her which Connie sought. Indeed, from James she rarely received a jot of it, simply because he hardly noticed what she did. It was just what she had always done, what mothers, sisters, all women did, he assumed. If asked to think about it, he would probably have concluded that Connie liked to do it, since he never asked her to. Only if, one day, he had suddenly found himself without a clean shirt or socks or underwear, only if his dinner had failed to appear on time, or his bed had greeted him one night in the same rumpled state in which he had left it that morning – only then might James have realised her worth. But such things never happened, and Ada's little prince strolled placidly through his days while Connie scurried through hers.

What Jamie did in the business was keep the accounts – he was good at that – drive the delivery van in the morning and serve in the shop for the rest of the day. Ada had never tried to make a baker of him. She was no great cook herself and had hired the Colensos as soon as her husband died. Except when faced with an attractive female customer, James had grown to feel secure behind his counter. He saw the same people every day, mostly middle-aged or elderly women who had known him all his life, remembered his accident and were used to the way he looked.

Meeting anyone new, however, was an ordeal and so he never socialised. The business and his home were Jamie's world, a relatively safe one. He had learned very quickly after the accident just how uncomfortable he could be outside it.

One of the memories which haunted him most was that of his first day back at school after the fire.

The school – a grey granite Victorian building with pea-green paintwork. The playground – and his school-mates clustering round him that morning, peering at him, asking questions. He could take himself back and be seven years old again, standing there in his coat and cap and buttoned leather gaiters, in the very centre of a gawking crowd. Everyone staring at him, some with sadness but some with open repugnance. Some of them asking if it hurt. A few of them pulling faces. The realisation coming to him that he was now set apart. Not the same any more, not like the other children, because there was something 'wrong' with him. His erstwhile playmates treating him like something odd, a person somehow diminished.

Then, being bullied, hearing raucous voices:

'Let's see your face, then, Jamie. Haven't had a proper look at it.'

'Aw, he's shy, I do believe.'

'Come here, I won't hurt you if you let me see.'

A hand grabbing his jersey. The bigger boys standing over him, taking him by the hair and jerking his head around. Thick, rough fingers feeling the scar.

'Coo!' A whistle. 'Look at that! It's horrible!'

In his mind he would always see and hear them, bending over him, discussing him, as if he were something nasty they had found in a pond.

From that day on he had steadily withdrawn, gradually retreating into solitariness and the refuge that was home and Ada and Connie. And here he was still, with no plans to go further. Oh yes, he had dreams about girls, but dreams they always remained.

Ada had never minded one bit that her son had no friends – especially females. Young women, rivals for his affection, girls who might take him away from her. She had always wanted him all to herself. Even now that she was dead she would still claim many an hour of his time, for he had pledged himself to take her fresh flowers every week.

Four

James stood looking down at Ada's grave and on his face was a frown. He felt the headstone his sister had ordered left much to be desired. It was far too plain, with nothing to distinguish it from all the others round about. His mother deserved something better than this simple granite slab inscribed 'Ada Winifred Sayers, 1876–1920. At Peace'. His father's stone, some forty yards away by the cemetery wall, was also very modest, but Jamie scarcely remembered him, so he had no feelings about it. Mr Sayers had died when his son was only four.

James glanced around at other monuments. There were many more elaborate than Ada's, many he would have preferred. He wished, as well, that she were buried somewhere less exposed than this particular site. Beside the wall like her husband, perhaps, or underneath a tree. Her final resting place was so bleakly central. James was somehow more aware of it now than he had been at the funeral, perhaps because today there was no group of people clustered round and no sun shining. Today he was alone in the cemetery and it was coming to rain.

Well, he supposed, he would simply have to accept the location. Her headstone, though, was another matter; something could be done about that. James determined to have it replaced. Connie, he thought, had simply no idea about some things. He would go and see about it straight away. Walking briskly down to the gates, he hurried to catch the next bus home.

James had never been inside the Jordan house before. No bell sounded when he entered and for a while he stood in Matthew's office, waiting. Finally, he loudly cleared his throat and called: 'Hello?'

Half a minute passed. Then, somewhere in the depths of the house, a door banged. Footsteps approached. They came from a corridor behind a curtain at the back of the room. They were quick and light, which was not what James had expected, since Mr Jordan was a ponderous man.

The curtain was suddenly whisked aside and a young woman came and sat behind the desk, wishing him good morning.

James's first instinct was to turn and go. Which was worse, though: to have her staring at his face or to let her see him fleeing like a scalded cat? There seemed little to choose. Anyway, he saw now that she was not pretty, and therefore not too intimidating. James was just as guilty as anyone of snobbery regarding looks; his own disfigurement had not taught him any particular sympathy for plain women. Clad in a white blouse and limp grey skirt, this one had no style to compensate for her lack of beauty. He noted, though, that her figure was good.

Briefly, she watched him, knowing she was being judged and probably found wanting. Still, he was not exactly brimming with confidence himself, guessed Janine. She had seen that reflex, that tilt of his cheek towards his left shoulder and the way his blue gaze flitted about like a nervous fly. She held out a hand, indicating the other chair.

'Please – sit down.'

Deciding he might as well complete his errand, James sat.

'I'd hoped to see Mr Jordan,' he said.

'My father's attending a burial just now, so I'm in temporary charge. You're Mr Sayers, aren't you?'

'Yes.'

Everyone hereabouts knew him by sight, he glumly assumed. Everyone knew the young man with the burnt face, just as everyone would know the village idiot. The bizarre never went unnoticed.

'How may we help you?' asked Janine.

'Well, Mr Jordan handled my mother's funeral recently, and . . .'

'All was satisfactory, I trust?'

'Completely – except for the headstone.'

'Oh dear.' Her eyebrows lifted.

'Don't misunderstand me, I'm not making a complaint.' Nervously he fingered his cheek. 'I just don't like the one my sister ordered.'

'Ah.' She pulled the ledger towards her, opened it, flipped through the pages. She had beautiful hands, he noticed, small and elegant. She wore no rings. 'Here it is,' she murmured, 'Mrs Ada Sayers.' Scanning through the details, she nodded and then looked up. 'It's a very popular style of stone.'

'Too popular. I want it replaced with something better. I don't mind the extra expense.'

'Very well.' Closing the book, she folded her hands on the cover. 'What do you have in mind? We use an excellent monumental mason. Nothing seems beyond his skill, so you can be as original as you like.'

Original? It seemed an odd, slightly frivolous word.

'I was thinking, perhaps, an angel.'

'Hmm. Would that be a seraph or just a cherub? Seraphs tend to be a bit pricey. Large wings, you see. All those feathers – a lot of delicate work.'

For a moment he thought she must be poking fun. Indignation rose in him, but her gaze was perfectly steady and her lips were without the slightest upward twitch.

'I don't think a cherub would be very suitable.' He paused, considering. 'What else is there? I'm able and willing to pay for a seraph, but I'd just like to know the alternatives.'

'Crosses,' said Miss Jordan, thoughtfully pursing her mouth. 'Little temples, open books . . .'

'What?'

'With verse inscribed on the pages. "Crossing the bar" is a favourite.'

James doubted he would be good at picking appropriate lines.

'Some years ago we interred a gentleman who'd been a great dog lover all his life. His wife commissioned a statue of an Irish wolfhound to stand guard over the grave. Did your mother have any interests of that sort?'

'No.'

She sought inspiration from the ceiling, her gaze travelling upwards.

'Then, of course, there are little obelisks. And urns,' she added dismissively. 'I take it you do want something serious?'

'Naturally.' James was shocked. 'Nobody jokes about death.'

'Oh, you'd be surprised,' Miss Jordan said. 'I recall an engine driver whose monument was formed in the shape of railway buffers with the word "Terminus" between them.'

44

'Well, I'm not the flippant sort. I'll have the angel.'

'Certainly.' From a drawer in the desk she took a pad of printed orders. 'Marble, I assume?'

'Marble,' confirmed James.

'About four feet high?'

'I should think so.'

'Hands clasped in an attitude of prayer?'

'That would be very nice.'

She wrote it all down and pushed the pad across the desk for his signature.

'How long . . .?' he asked.

'About a month.'

'You'll send a bill?'

'Yes.' She regarded him curiously. 'You haven't asked the precise cost. It's likely to be forty pounds at least.'

'I don't care. We can afford it.'

'You must have loved your mother very much.'

'Yes, I did.'

And after everything she had heard about Ada Sayers. Janine surveyed him thoughtfully and wondered if his sister felt the same – she who had ordered a gravestone so unsentimental. This brought to mind as well a practical concern and prompted a question.

'Forgive me, but I have to ask – you are empowered to place this order, I take it? Since your sister made the original arrangements, I assume she is the elder of you? Is her consent required for this outlay? Please don't think me rude, but family wrangles in the past have left us out of pocket when one member ordered something special and another, who held the purse-strings, refused to pay for it.'

James was indignant. 'Don't worry, you'll be paid. It's I who own the business, not my sister.'

She eyed him with interest. 'The bakery is yours alone?'

'Everything's mine,' bridled James. 'There won't be any problem. You send the bill to our solicitor, as you did before.'

'I see. I presume you're not quite twenty-one, then, Mr Sayers?'

'Nineteen, actually. But as I say, the property was left to me. My sister won't object to what I want. Still,' he conceded, 'I understand your caution. If you want to ask her, or the solicitor, first, then go ahead.'

She shrugged. 'I'll leave it to my father. He may or may not think it necessary. Either way, I'm sure it'll be all right.'

'Yes. Well . . .' James stood up, '. . . if that's all there is to do . . .'

Miss Jordan stood up too. 'We'll let you know when the monument is ready.' She walked with him to the door, even opened it for him. 'You must be looking forward to the time when you take full control of what you own.' A grin now, broad and friendly. It quite changed her face, lending it something special, making James look twice at her, seeing something in her after all. He noted that her teeth were excellent, and what a pity, he thought, not to exploit that rich red hair.

'Do you have exciting plans?' she asked. 'I'm sure I should if I were in your shoes.'

'Plans?' queried James. He thought it would sound better if he said yes. 'Oh, naturally I have a few ideas.'

Miss Jordan nodded, smiling. She was more disturbing at close quarters. There was something about her eyes – attentive, intimate – that alarmed and aroused him all at once. It was difficult to look away. James also detected a faint smell of soap on her now. Not

46

perfumed, though – nothing so luxurious – yellow, household soap. There was something peculiarly wrong about that. A sudden feeling overwhelmed him that Miss Jordan did not belong here. Her dreary clothes, the nature of her family business, the odour of kitchen soap were all at odds with her intelligent manner and the strange, black, narrow eyes.

'Well . . .' she said, the smile growing wider.

He seemed to come to with a start, realising she was waiting for him to go. James feared he must have been staring at her like a transfixed rabbit. He felt hot colour rising from his neck and hurriedly bid Miss Jordan good day.

She watched him stride off down the street, noting with amusement that flat feet were his only physical blemish, aside from his scar. It wasn't so very dreadful, she thought, now she had seen it close up. There were birthmarks just as bad, and worse. As for some of the things she had witnessed when her father laid out accident victims . . . Janine was not squeamish like some women. Of course, Sayers' face was sadly marred, there was no denying that, but it would hardly give her nightmares. From most angles he was still attractive. Only that left side was startling.

He was painfully conscious of it, though, and half afraid of her, that was obvious. Janine went inside, slowly closing the door and musing on the encounter. She felt pleased to think she had been woman enough to unsettle him. For most men she didn't seem to exist as a female at all. In the street they just looked through her, no reaction.

Five

A short walk from the Barbican and Bretonside was a
very different Plymouth, the Victorian and Edwardian
city of the big stores, the banking and other commercial
institutions, the covered market, cinemas, restaurants,
the stop-go squeeze of trams and cars. Here, too, were
expanses of classical elegance; white façades, colon-
nades and porticos, the legacy of the architect Foulston,
designer of the Theatre Royal, the Athenaeum, the
Royal Hotel and the terraces of imposing houses leading up to the Hoe. In all, the city centre was a peculiar
blend of homeliness and style. There were market bar-
rows in Cornwall Street, expensive shops in George
Street, a couple of minutes' walk from one another.
Everything seemed the more attractive for being so
clean. The city had no dirty manufacturing to lay a coat
of grime upon its buildings. Factories hereabouts made
things like soap, matches and biscuits. The single
heavy industry was the dockyard out at Devonport.

One day in May, James walked up into town to buy a
gramophone record. He went into Moon & Sons in
George Street and purchased a copy of 'Barbara Allen',
sung by Dame Clara Butt. His taste in music tended
toward the sad and sentimental. Irish airs, English
folk-songs of the tragic variety and laments of the love-
lorn formed the bulk of his collection, relieved by a
handful of nonsense ditties such as 'Wot, no spinach?'

While there in the shop, he asked if he might hear

two other songs. The man behind the counter obligingly played them for him. James wandered around as he listened, looking at the pianos, accordions and gramophones on sale, flipping casually through the piles of sheet music. They had a piano at home, but he had never learned to play. Ada had tried to teach him but he had no aptitude. Connie did, he seemed to recall, but Mother had never given her very much encouragement. Somehow she had always been too busy to coach her.

James decided he would buy these two records as well. They had the melting tone he most enjoyed, and he went to the counter to pay for them. He was waiting for his change when a voice at his shoulder enquired:

'What have you bought, Mr Sayers? Are you fond of jazz?'

A female voice. James looked round and there stood Miss Jordan. She was standing to his right, his unmarked side, so he kept his composure fairly well.

'Oh, good morning. No, I can't say I care for all that noisy, jerky stuff. A good melody, that's what I like. Is that your preference, then, jazz? They've a good selection here.'

'It's certainly what I'd buy if I had some money, and freedom to do as I pleased at home.' Janine smiled ruefully. 'But I haven't, so that's that. I'm here today to replace a couple of Dad's hymns. I broke them while I was dusting, so I'm in the doghouse.' She grinned at him. 'They were two of his dreariest, you know. His favourites.'

An image flashed into James's mind of Miss Jordan holding a record aloft between finger and thumb, then gleefully letting it drop. Something about her faintly comical face said that she was capable of it. Something about the shimmer of her eyes, the wide stretch of that full bottom lip.

'So I've been sent out to buy new ones,' she went on. 'I don't mind too much.' The eyes fairly sparkled. 'I do love a chance to look around town.'

James's suspicion grew a little more. But then she abruptly straightened her face and asked: 'Was the angel satisfactory, by the way?'

'The . . .?'

'Your mother's monument.'

'Oh – yes. High quality work, I'm very pleased.'

Indeed he was. Ada's grave certainly stood out now, no longer lost and obscure amongst its neighbours. The presiding angel could be seen from every corner of the cemetery. James thought the money very well spent. If anyone had pressed him on the point, he would have had to admit that he did not, in fact, believe in angels. None of the Sayers family was religious. But the monument was elegant, special, and that was the point of it. Nothing was too good for his mother.

'Splendid,' said Janine.

The man at the counter handed James his change. Turning to him, Janine passed the man a slip of paper with two titles written on it.

'Do you have these in stock?'

The man said he did, and went off to fetch them.

'Well,' murmured James, 'must be going.'

She opened her mouth to bid him goodbye, but then, on second thoughts, she asked: 'Are you in a hurry? I was thinking I might go for a cup of coffee in a minute. I wouldn't mind having someone to talk to for a change.'

For a change. Yes – he supposed she was probably alone a lot, just as he was. She would hardly be a social butterfly, would she? He was taken aback that she should request his company. James didn't think it quite a woman's place to do so, not entirely proper. Still, perhaps necessity drove her to it, looking as she did. A spot of pride made him ask himself if he wanted to be seen with a woman so shabby. At least he was smart in his sandy-coloured suit and brown waistcoat. As always, he was wearing a trilby, tilted just-so to shadow his left cheek.

Immediately, James was ashamed of himself.

'Oh . . .' He hesitated. 'Well, I suppose I could.'

'Why not, then? It's nearly lunchtime, after all. We'll each pay for our own, of course.'

He made a dismissive gesture to show that he hadn't been thinking of that.

The shopkeeper returned with Janine's records and put them in a bag. She handed him two shillings. James eyed her covertly, noting the worn brown coat and awful shoes. It was in his mind to back out and rush off, but he could think of no plausible excuse now. Curiosity tugged him one way, shyness and a certain caution pulled him another. There were moments when she was almost attractive in an unorthodox way and he had to admire her for making this first move towards a friendship. Yet, what if she proved desperate, hard to shake off? He wouldn't want to hurt her feelings, poor thing.

Then it was too late to dither any longer. Janine turned around, smiled up at him.

'Well, then, where shall we go?'

'I don't mind.'

'There's a nice little place around the corner,' she said. 'I recommend their sticky buns.'

'Suits me.'

51

They left the shop and walked a hundred yards to a café. James picked a table away from the window, sitting with his left profile to the wall. The waitress took their orders as soon as they sat down.

'Just coffee for me,' said Janine. 'A separate bill, if you please.'

James asked for tea and a doughnut.

Janine took her cigarettes from her bag. 'Do you mind if I smoke?'

Although surprised, he shook his head. She offered the packet to him.

'No thanks, I don't.'

He watched her light up and toss the spent match into the ashtray. The movements were very quick and natural, practised. Miss Jordan had been smoking for a long time, he could tell. The effect was odd, incongruous. Her appearance was so frumpish and yet that cigarette in her hand created a certain style in her manner. As once before, in her father's office, James sensed that she was something different underneath, a woman of another type, heavily disguised.

'Dad doesn't know I smoke,' she confided, smiling. 'He'd consider it a vice and a frightful waste of money. He's very religious, you know, and very thrifty. Pious, parsimonious Pa, I call him – though not to his face.'

'You sound as if you don't like him.'

'Oh, he has his good points. Please don't misunderstand me; I have a certain affection for him. He doesn't believe in spending on himself or me, though – as you see.' She waved a hand, indicating her hair, her clothes.

James wondered what he should say. Something reassuring? Was a false compliment required?

Just then the waitress arrived with their coffee and tea.

'It's all right,' continued Janine when the girl had gone. 'I know I'm a mess. I'm simply explaining why.'

He cleared his throat and ventured: 'I did wonder why you don't have your hair waved or something.'

'Dear God, the expense!' laughed Janine. She sipped her coffee and flicked her ash.

'It's a pretty grim trade, isn't it, your business? Doesn't it depress you?'

'Not in itself. I grew up with it, after all. The house depresses me, and so does the way we live.'

'Didn't seem a bad place to me.'

'The office is the cosy part. You haven't seen the rest.' She pulled a wry face. 'Anyway, you're a baker, aren't you? That's more pleasant altogether.'

'I'm not actually a baker,' corrected James. 'Father was, but I'm not. I employ one, with his wife as pastry-cook.'

'I see.'

She watched as he tackled his doughnut, turning it round and round in search of a place to bite. Choosing one, he sank his teeth in. Jam squirted out of the opposite side and plopped onto his plate. He sat back, glancing nervously at Janine. There was sugar on the end of his nose.

She sipped again at her coffee. He was terribly edgy, she thought, the way he fumbled with that doughnut and kept glancing at her to see if she had noticed.

James avoided her eyes as much as he could, but he could feel now that she was studying him intently. Her scrutiny seemed to pull at him, and when he could not bear it a second longer he looked up with a jerk and found his gaze locked with hers.

Miss Jordan's face was half obscured by her cup as she drank but the dark eyes were watching him over the rim. Her hidden mouth might be smirking into her coffee, or twisting in distaste at his appearance. For a while he was panic-stricken, caught in one of those terrible moments when pretence and defence are gone and another person can plainly see the consternation going on inside. In his confusion, his hand flew straight to his face. He might as well have screamed: 'Don't stare at me! Don't look at this!'

With a firm, brisk movement, Janine put her cup down. 'You know,' she said, 'it isn't half as bad as you think. You really shouldn't let it rule your life.'

'What?' His voice shook.

'You know what I'm talking about – that scar.'

'I – I don't . . . I don't let it . . . What nonsense!'

'Oh, I suspect you do. I bet you never go anywhere without that hat.'

'You're very personal, aren't you?' stammered James. He abandoned the doughnut, then looked helplessly around for something with which to wipe his fingers.

Calmly, Janine pulled a fresh handkerchief from her pocket and pushed it across the table to him.

'I'm sorry, perhaps I was a bit rude. But then, it always does sound rude if you mention something taboo. It's the same with death, you know. That may be why I have an aversion to what you might call "pussy-footing". I think it's more healthy if people face nasty things squarely and talk about them in plain language.'

'Do you?' said James coldly.

'Certainly. My father, for instance, never admits that anyone's dead. Nor do most of the relatives, come to that. They talk about "passing over, going to sleep, going before, finding eternal rest" and so on, but they can't bring themselves to say plain "dead".'

'Why shouldn't they console themselves when they've lost somebody?'

'They're fooling themselves,' said Janine.

'You're very unkind.'

'Well, I don't mean to be – and certainly not when I speak of your face. I only meant to tell you that you're making things worse for yourself.'

'Is that why you asked me to come here? So that you could play the wise owl?'

'No,' she said mildly. 'I thought we might be friends, that's all.' She took a deep pull at her cigarette, breathed the smoke in hard. James saw her bosom rise and subside again under the shapeless coat. 'I'm lonely, I don't mind admitting it. I suspect that you are, too. I never see you about with anyone. No girls, no pals.'

His gaze dropped, fixing on the tablecloth, specifically on a single daisy in the floral pattern.

'I'm not much of a mixer,' he agreed.

'Hmm. I take it they've done all they can? The doctors, I mean.'

'Yes.'

'I must say, it is a shame, good-looking chap like you.'

No strange woman had ever spoken to him like this before, spoken candidly of his disfigurement. He was rattled by it, horribly embarrassed and yet almost excited. Janine was so very matter-of-fact about it.

He finished wiping his fingers. 'I'm sorry I snapped,' he mumbled.

'That's all right.' She took the handkerchief from him and then, to his amazement, leaned across the table and dabbed at the tip of his nose.

'Sugar,' she said, sitting back with a smile. 'It's gone now.' Stubbing out her cigarette, she drank some more coffee.

'What precisely happened?' she asked, after a moment. 'How did the fire start?'

For a minute James stared absently at his plate and then he said quietly: 'I started it. Mother had gone to a whist drive. She liked a hand of cards. She'd been going every Friday for several months, as a matter of fact. She felt my sister was big enough to look after me. She used to say that Connie had an old head on her shoulders.' He sighed. 'But after all, she was only a child.'

Janine said nothing, and as she watched him he seemed to drift away, remaining with her in body only as he told the tale, for his mind had gone back to the Christmas when he was not quite seven years old.

He was once more little Jamie, standing in front of the Christmas tree, barefoot and dressed in pyjamas. Such a pretty tree. Glass baubles hanging from every branch, twinkling in the lamplight. At the top, a star made of cardboard, painted silver. Here and there, clipped to the ends of the branches, little tin holders, each containing a tiny candle in red or white.

James the adult was barely aware of Janine or the café now, hardly even aware that he was talking, recounting. The memory played like a film in his head, and he was taking part in it again, very quickly lost in the awful vividness of images which would never leave him.

Jamie the child was crossing now to the mantelpiece, stretching up on tiptoe. Edging the clock aside, feeling his fingers closing on the matchbox. Then, back in front of the tree again, trying to strike one. Success – a red candle sprouting a neat yellow flame. A white one gently growing a golden halo. Looking pretty, oh, so pretty.

But then, suddenly, something awful happening. Around the burning red candle, the dry pine needles curling in the heat. A series of tiny flashes – and all at once the lovely tree turning into a crackling, thundering torch. All of it occurring so fast, leaving him rooted with shock. The baubles splintering, shattering, melting, the silver star engulfed in a rush of fire. Then, flaming debris falling on the table, setting the cloth alight. Fire climbing the curtains, too. Smoke stinging his eyes and throat. And now a greater terror still – the ceiling decorations ablaze in a flash, chinese lanterns and paper chains and garlands of coloured tissue all flaring and breaking and falling around him, on top of him ...

The touch of Janine's hand brought James back once more to the present. Looking down, he saw his own hands gripped together, the nails digging into his skin. Sighing, he relaxed them.

'My sister was upstairs in her room,' he said, 'drawing with the coloured pencils Mother had given her for Christmas. Connie thought I was in bed asleep. It wasn't her fault. I'd been nagging Mother all over the Christmas to light those candles. They were only ornamental, of course, and she'd warned me to leave them alone. I knew I was doing wrong when I sneaked downstairs to light them. Anyway, it was our neighbour from across the street, Jack Chope, who got me out, then went back and doused the fire. I was in hospital nine days. Paid a heavy price for being wilful, didn't I?'

'All children are apt to get themselves into trouble if they're not watched.'

'That's what everybody said – the doctors, nurses, all our neighbours. Mother had an awful time of it, everyone pointing the finger.'

So, reflected Janine, her guess about Ada Sayers had not been too far out. Yet, was this alone enough to earn her such dislike? Perhaps there was rather more to it, but she could hardly ask James why the mother he adored had been labelled a bitch.

He was looking at her, shyly smiling. 'I've never told anyone that before – exactly, second by second, what it was like.'

'I felt I was there.'

'Be glad you weren't. And let's change the subject. The fire is something I think about too much.'

'All right. Do you ever go to the theatre, Mr Sayers?'

'Now and again,' said James. 'I like musical comedies.'

'Comedies of any kind suit me. There's not a lot of mirth at home.'

He realised suddenly that the way was open for an invitation. She was actually helping him out, making it easy for him. He was feeling by now that he would indeed like her for a friend, yet something still made him hesitate. Perhaps it was the very fact that she had made all the running. To James it seemed vaguely improper. What was more, he had swallowed the notion that worthwhile girls had to be pursued and won. It was the old human perversity of disdaining anything too readily accessible.

Recognising that, he chided himself. This was the thing he had feared so much, to ask a woman out. Now, precisely because she was making it painless, he was having doubts. Quite irrational, he reflected. Damned silly, in fact. Why, after all, should it have to be an ordeal? Because manliness demanded a challenge, he supposed. A challenge and a lovely prize to show off.

Poor Janine was hardly that. Other men were not going to envy him her company.

We all want the best, he thought, even when we're not the best ourselves.

His vanity recoiled from settling for someone as needy as he was. Still, he would be doing her a favour. Giving her a special treat – no loss of pride in that. James was very protective of his pride, whereas Janine knew just what an obstacle it could be.

He took a deep breath. 'There's a play by Oscar Wilde at the Theatre Royal this week. Called *An Ideal Husband*. You'd enjoy that, I expect.'

'I certainly would, if I could afford to go.'

'I'll take you – if you like.'

'Yes, please.' She beamed at him. 'Aren't I shameless, dropping hints?'

He laughed, relieved. 'I don't mind.'

'I get so bored,' sighed Janine. 'Sometimes I'd kill for an evening out. Occasionally I go to the pictures, but that's all. The theatre's simply beyond my pocket. I hope you don't think I'm a sponger? I'm sure you'll enjoy the performance as much as I shall.'

James relaxed. Whether on purpose or not, she was certainly allowing him to feel superior.

'When would you like to go?' he asked. 'I'll book the tickets today.'

Six

Friday evening. Cold meat and salad. Matthew Jordan frowned. His daughter usually made him fishcakes on a Friday night, with peas and boiled potatoes. Matthew always looked forward to his fishcakes. He had not been warned until the last minute that Janine was going out and that no fishcakes would be forthcoming. She had said not a word until six o'clock when the shops were safely closed. Apart from cheese, the larder contained no alternative to the cold roast beef and salad.

Mr Jordan nibbled at the meat and carved up a tomato. She hadn't even cut and mixed the salad. Three inches of cucumber and a solid head of lettuce accompanied the two tomatoes. She was upstairs now, getting ready to go out with young Sayers. Prinking — as best she could. Leaving her poor old father by himself all evening. In the parlour tonight, when he looked up from his Bible, Janine would not be there in her chair. He would even have to make his own cocoa before he went to bed. It was altogether too bad.

James Sayers. The lad was younger than Janine, yet she claimed he had boldly invited her out. Matthew had his suspicions as to who had really engineered this little excursion, and anxieties as to where it might ultimately lead. He was always made uneasy by any sort of break in the normal routine. Any deviation from it by his daughter aroused immediate fears that she was about to escape.

He had started on his cold rice pudding when she came downstairs. Matthew observed that she had her Sunday outfit on; a fawn skirt and jacket, a squashy black velvet beret with a pom-pom, and a pair of heeled shoes. Her very best things.

Matthew eyed her reproachfully. 'At what hour may I expect you home, Janine?'

'I'm not quite sure what time the play ends, Dad. No later than eleven, I dare say.'

'The middle of the night.'

'Hardly.'

'You'll behave yourself, I trust?'

'I can't imagine what you mean,' she said, bending to kiss his bald head. 'Must go, I'm late.'

'What have you done to your hair? It's hanging down over your eyes.'

'No it's not, Dad. I cut a fringe, that's all, and put it in rag curlers.'

'I don't like it.'

'Well, don't worry, it won't last the evening,' she said testily. 'It's dropping already.'

That was the worst of her type of hair, she thought bitterly. It was thick and heavy, but resolutely straight, very difficult to style at home. It needed either expert cutting or a permanent wave, neither of which she could afford.

'I don't know why you waited so long to tell me you were going out,' complained Matthew.

Because you would have brooded for days, she thought. Because you might have contrived some means to stop me.

'Well, it doesn't matter, does it?'

'Why the Sayers boy?' he demanded suspiciously.

Janine was sarcastic. 'Because no one else has ever invited me – for some unfathomable reason.'

Her voice had taken on that brisk, hard edge acquired at Mannamead School. Matthew hated it. It had a way of making him feel like a dolt.

He grunted. 'Mmph. Enjoy yourself, then.'

'Thank you, I shall.' Then, at the door, she paused and said more gently: 'I bought you some shortbreads to go with your cocoa. They're in the tin on the sideboard.'

Matthew managed a smile. 'That was thoughtful, my dear.' His gaze moved over her, top to toe. She had made a great effort to look nice – even he could see that. Perhaps he was being unreasonable, begrudging her this little treat. And perhaps it would come to nothing, begin and end with a single evening out. He bent again over his meal. 'Off you go, then,' he said.

Seven fifteen. She wasn't coming, James felt sure. Having pushed him into making a date, she had changed her mind. Seized by a last-minute attack of nerves, he almost hadn't come himself. It had taken an effort of will to shave and dress and walk down here, and now, as the minutes ticked by, he was wishing he had not bothered.

Still, at least he was not standing outside the theatre where people would notice him and guess he had been let down by a female. No, at least he was stationed across the road, loitering by Derry's Clock and pretending he was waiting for a tram.

Shoulders hunched and hands in pockets, he watched other couples go into the theatre. Two trams came and went, picking up the queue and leaving him conspicuously alone.

Twenty-five past seven. No sign of her.

He told himself it was just as well. Silly idea all along . . .

But then – there she was! Coming down George Street with that quick, assured step and looking – well, not too bad at all.

His heart jumped with fear and excitement. Janine. Not Miss Jordan if they were going to be friends. He would be calling her Janine. Such a pretty name.

James sidled round behind the little clock tower and hid until she had gone by. He watched her climb the steps to the theatre entrance, saw her peer through the glass doors into the foyer and then back up the street.

Wondering where he was, if he might already have gone inside. Unsure what to do.

A tram went by, passing between them, and James slipped smartly out from behind the clock. When Janine looked again, he was swinging along the street towards her, appearing nonchalant.

She lifted a hand in greeting and he did likewise, calling lightly:

'Sorry I'm late. Have I kept you waiting long?'

She smiled and the long eyes danced. 'I've only just arrived.'

'We'd better hurry and go in. You, uh . . .' He felt jaunty enough to plunge in with a compliment. 'You look very nice.'

'Thank you.'

'Have you changed your hair?'

'I tried.'

They went inside. So very grand, the Theatre Royal.

Gilt, red plush and chandeliers. A wide entrance lobby and a fine curving staircase to the gallery. It had the indefinable smell that went with theatres and cinemas everywhere, hard to describe but recognisable always. To James, the scent recalled childhood entertainments – picture matinées and Christmas pantomimes. It was a signature as distinctive as the smell of hotels or hospitals or railway stations. They went up the staircase to the upper circle and took their balcony seats in row A just as the curtain was going up.

James made sure she sat to his right, and did not remove his trilby until the lights went down. The play was of little interest to him but he had guessed correctly that it would appeal to Janine.

Half-way through, he went down to the foyer and bought her some chocolates. He was starting to feel a pleasant comfort with her, an ease almost equal to that he felt with Connie. He thought Janine wondrously improved by the nicer clothes and the fringe, and told himself that if she were his girl he would buy her a few new things.

As they watched the play, she whispered to him now and then – a comment, a question – inclining her face close to his. This, and the touching of hands sometimes as they delved in the chocolate box, seemed to James the most delicious intimacy. Once again he found Janine beguiling at close quarters, possessing something more powerful than good looks. There was great appeal in the husky laugh and obvious sensual relish of the chocolates. It made him acutely aware of her as flesh and blood. Pretty women never seemed quite that human to James.

After the play they strolled homeward through the city centre. There had been a shower and the roads still glistened, dark and shiny, reflecting back the yellow glow from the windows of the big stores. It was ten o'clock but trams were still running and many people were about the streets.

'I so enjoyed that,' said Janine. 'I lost touch with all my friends after I left school and it's very difficult to go out on your own if you're a woman. What's more, mine isn't the sort of home which people like to visit – for obvious reasons. The first thing Dad does with a new acquaintance is ask him about his beliefs.'

She paused to look at the window display in a hat shop. Her profile was very pert in the light shining out.

'What are you going to do with yourself when you come of age and have control of your property?' she asked, as they walked on. 'Any plans, or are you content?'

James was feeling expansive after this evening's success. Having cleared what he thought was a fearsome hurdle, he imagined in his euphoria that nothing was beyond him. He also felt a need to impress Janine.

'Oh . . .' He spread his hands and swung a foot forward in a playful, kicking motion. '. . . I've a lot of ideas for branching out, you know. That's why Mother left the property entirely to me, I think.' His hands went into his trouser pockets. He gave a little skip, another measured kick. 'In time, I'd like a second shop up here in the city centre. I quite fancy going in for home-made confectionery, too – having it packaged and sent all over the country. Sayers' Devon Toffee, Sayers' Fudge, Sayers' Mints, that sort of thing. Sounds good, doesn't it? Needless to say, I'd require larger premises and more staff.'

Her gaze was on him, somewhat calculating, but he failed to notice that.

'It all sounds perfectly possible, Jamie.'

Jamie – thrilling familiarity.

Spurred on, he waved an arm towards a smart little café over the road.

'Then there's the catering side of it, of course. I've often thought about a tea-room, with a musical trio and perhaps a small dance floor.'

'Tea dances,' murmured Janine, her imagination soaring further and faster than his. 'What a splendid idea!'

'Oh, yes, I've been giving it all a lot of thought since my mother died. I believe I've a good head for business. I can often spot a need and see how to fill it. Once I have a free hand, there'll be no stopping me.'

In truth, he hardly knew where the ideas were coming from. It was just his mood. He was carried away by optimism and a flood of fantasies. Until these last few minutes he had never even pondered on adding so much as a new kind of bun to the Sayers' usual array. But suddenly here were reservoirs of ingenuity, hitherto unknown. What an effect Janine had, to be sure.

'Biscuits, that's another thing,' he said airily.

'Heavens, you'd need a factory,' smiled Janine.

'Anything's possible, Janine. Given time, naturally.'

They walked around St Andrew's Cross and started down to Bretonside, passing from the night-lit centre into the quieter, darker part of town. James grew quiet now, reluctant to let the evening end. If he wanted to see her a second time, then now was the moment to ask. Now he would find out if she had really meant it, really enjoyed his company.

He cleared his throat. Their footsteps echoed now on cobbles and the houses around them clustered close as if eavesdropping, their gables pointed silhouettes in the moonlight.

'Will you . . .?' Another small cough. 'Would you care to come out with me another time?'

Not a second's hesitation. 'Yes, I would.'

Relief, delight. He was bouncy again at once.

'How about Tuesday?'

'Fine,' said Janine. Her house was coming up ahead and she felt a momentary gloom.

'About seven, then? Where shall we go?'

'I'll leave that to you. Come up with one of your clever ideas.'

'I'll put my mind to it.'

They had come to her door. 'You'll collect me from here, then?' she asked.

'Yes, if your father won't mind.'

'Not at all.' Janine did not care if Matthew minded or not. She had a fish on the line and meant to reel him in at any cost.

'Well, goodnight then,' she said. 'And thank you for a lovely evening, Jamie.'

She waited then, but he made no move. So she stretched up and kissed him quickly, lightly, on the mouth. Just as quickly she was gone, and the door clicked shut behind her.

James stood on the cobbles in the darkness and the silence and the chill of a spring wind, but his soul was full of song and golden light, and his heart was a fireball of joy.

Janine lay awake half the night, thinking over what he had said. She fancied that most of his talk was just that and nothing more. Nevertheless, her mind kept going back to the notion of a smart café. She pictured a large one, in the style of a grand hotel tea lounge. Phrases like 'tea at the Ritz' kept recurring in her head, conjuring images of gleaming silver, white napery and potted palms. Janine would opt for something slightly more modern, though, more lively.

He was very pliable, James Sayers, and vulnerable, of course, on account of his face. She found him rather touching, very obvious and a mite silly in his efforts to impress her. Janine had spotted him skulking behind the clock-tower, too, at the start of the evening. She shook with laughter in the darkness, remembering that. Poor Jamie, poor soul, she thought with sympathetic fondness. He was sweet, but too gauche to make any woman's heart flutter. Janine was no romantic anyway but could tell that he certainly was. Her driving desires in life were material ones and the more she thought about it, the more convinced she became that they could meet each other's needs.

She tried to estimate what he might be worth. A bakery, a bread shop, a house. Not a bad starting point. Commercially gifted people had turned mere shillings into great fortunes, but she doubted that Jamie, for all his showing off, would ever progress very far. Unless he was propelled and guided by someone enterprising.

Seven

Jamie had a girl! He had known her two weeks and this evening she was coming to dinner.

Connie could scarcely believe it. She looked around the kitchen and wished for the first time ever that they had a dining room. She had scrubbed and tidied and polished the house from top to bottom. The kitchen was as pleasant as she could make it – white linen instead of oilcloth on the table, a vase of flowers on the dresser, another on the window sill. No washing hanging around this evening, airing on the clothes-horse by the stove, no floor mop or rubbish pail in sight, no sauce bottles and salt packet left on the table. Place-mats tonight, serviettes, a cut-glass cruet. That first impression mattered so very much.

She had made a dinner of onion soup and rolls, braised beef and brussels sprouts and roast potatoes, to be followed by almond and apricot pie. A meal more elaborate than usual, but then, the occasion called for nothing less.

Jamie had a girl. Connie was filled with gladness and yet, at the same time, racked with terror lest her hospitality should fall short and upset this most important guest.

She had never met Janine, having dealt with Mr Jordan when she went to arrange the funeral. James described her as 'out of the ordinary'. She was due in just a few minutes, at seven o'clock.

Connie lit the lamps in the kitchen, parlour and hall. Everything was nearly ready. They could sit down to eat at half past. Going into the parlour, she plumped up chair cushions, smoothed the antimacassars and poked the fire. Pausing, she looked around her, wondering what more she might do. There was fruit on the sideboard, a tray with a bottle of sherry and glasses, and a dish of Nell Colenso's home-made Turkish delight.

Connie, on tenterhooks, laced her fingers together, squeezing just a little anxiously. Her best – she had done her best for Jamie and his girl.

He was upstairs shaving, changing his clothes. A moment's thought for her own appearance took her to the mirror over the fireplace. A tired face looked back from the glass and she noticed spots of grease and gravy on her apron. Quickly, Connie took it off. She would put on a clean one before serving dinner. No amount of laundry was too much.

She had pinned up her hair tonight, knowing how unfashionable it was to wear it long. Now and again she thought about having it bobbed, but somehow she never got around to it. Always too busy. No time to fuss with primping and hairdressing. It was effort enough just to keep clean and tidy with all she had to do.

Her dress was not bad, she felt. Sea-green, just below the knee, with a round white collar. She had a pair of high-heeled shoes to go with it. They were new and hard and hurt her feet but in flat ones she might look dowdy.

Mustn't let Jamie down in any way, she told herself.

There had been a panic earlier on, when she found the lavatory blocked – again. It happened at least once a week, something to do with the pipework being placed a shade too high. Connie had spent an hour between four and five, struggling back and forth across the yard with buckets of water, and kneeling on the floor in front of the pan, pushing and pulling with the plunger, appalled to think of Jamie's girl asking to use the privy and finding it clogged.

The clock said nearly seven now – and suddenly a memory assailed her. A mental image of this room, at about this hour, many years ago. Connie remembered all too vividly hearing the shrieks and running out from her bedroom onto the landing. Her mind's eye still pictured everything clearly – the hallway below full of smoke, the parlour door open and a horrid dancing glow within. She recalled her headlong rush downstairs and into this room, a hand pressed over her nose and mouth. Finding everything alight, seeing the toppled Christmas tree lying on the table by the window, burning. Searching for James, her vision blurred with tears.

A dreadful milestone in Jamie's life – but tonight this room would see a happier one.

The clock ticked on, the hand hit seven, and the door-knocker sounded, two short taps.

Connie gave a start and a final pat to her hair. Going to the foot of the stairs, she shouted: 'Jamie, come on, she's here.'

Then she answered the door.

Janine was not what she expected. Everything about her seemed older, more composed. This was a woman, not a girl, and certainly no little feather-head.

Janine held out a hand. 'Good evening. You're Connie, of course.'

Connie clasped it, smiling.

'My, there's a good smell!'

'We're having beef. Come in, take off your coat.'

Janine's beret and jacket were hung on the hall-stand, as James came thumping downstairs. His hair was smoothly brushed and he smelt of male cologne.

'You two go and sit by the fire,' instructed Connie. 'I must see to the cooking. We can have a good chat over dinner.'

Three details about Janine caught Connie's notice as she watched her brother usher the young woman into the parlour: her hair was poorly cut and haphazardly curled, her yellow blouse was not quite right with the fawn skirt, and her stockings were snagged in several places. By comparison, Connie looked the more stylish. What a turn-up that was!

Puzzling, she went to tend the food. She would hardly have thought the Jordans were poor.

Whatever the shortcomings in her dress, Janine was amusing company, self-assured, intelligent, and full of interesting information. There were no awkward lapses in conversation over dinner, and her manners as she ate were graceful. She praised the meal at every stage and James could hardly keep his eyes off her, looking to Connie with a great silly grin at Janine's every other remark, as if to say: 'How about that!'

Janine, too, was assessing this other woman who meant so much to James. Not that he realised what Connie meant to him – oh no. He took all her service for granted, Janine could see. Just as Matthew expected care from her. The difference was that Connie did it all without resentment – even eagerly, Janine observed. She was ever alert to Jamie's wants and needs. When she noticed a smear on his glass, Connie replaced it, full of apologies. When he found the salt cellar empty, Connie quickly got up and went to fill it for him. When he dropped his fork, she rose immediately and fetched him another.

Something about it set Janine's teeth on edge, something about the way Jamie never protested or made any move to do these things for himself, but just sat placidly while his sister scuttled out. Connie's automatic disregard for her own comfort, her own convenience, grated on Janine. She felt like saying to her: 'He isn't paralysed, you know. For heaven's sake, relax and eat your meal.'

Matthew Jordan was not half as fussy or spoilt. Once she had settled down to her food, Janine would not bounce up and down on errands the way that Connie did. If Dad dropped his knife or fork, he went to the sideboard himself for a clean one. If his glass was smeared he just wiped it round with his napkin. And he could find his way to the kitchen cupboard for condiments without any help from his daughter. Janine had never been the slave that Connie was, and Matthew's expectations were lower than Jamie's. The Jordan house was altogether less brightly polished than the Sayers' home. Janine only cleaned where it showed – and not too often, either. She suspected, though, that Connie searched out dust and fluff like a bloodhound, wherever it lay. Mr Jordan was always just a bit rumpled, because Janine detested ironing and tended to be slapdash. She could not be bothered with bleach or starch; if a garment was clean, then that was sufficient. The spotlessness of Jamie's clothes had not escaped her notice – the crisp whiteness of his shirts, the sharply perfect creases of his trousers. She had thought it the work of professionals – that he sent his things to a laundry. Now she knew better. Connie Sayers kept house with love and nothing was too much trouble to do for her brother. A contrast indeed to Janine's grudging, ill-tempered housework.

It was clear to Janine that James had not been brought up in the manner she would have prescribed and would need to be acquainted with standards more realistic by a future wife.

After dinner, he showed her all over the house and bakery.

Quite extensive, really. Probably worth a good bit more than Dad's place, Janine reflected, noting the generous size of the shop. Recalling Jamie's chatter about business plans, she thoughtfully sucked her cheek. Hot air, most of it, she knew that. He had been putting on a show for her, or at best only making half-serious speculations. But she had seen merit in some of the ideas. James might be all talk and no action, but Janine was not. There was indeed potential here for greater things. As for finance, well – one could probably raise a very respectable loan on a place like this.

They ended the evening by the parlour fire, over sherry and Turkish delight. The Sayers' home might not be grand, but it was certainly more comfortable and cheerful than her own. Janine was quite reluctant to leave, but finally, close to eleven o'clock, she made a move to go.

'Thank you again for the lovely dinner,' she said to Connie.

'Thank you for your good company, Janine. Come round whenever you feel like it, you'll always be welcome.'

James put on his coat to walk her home. Connie saw them to the door, then returned to the parlour, sat down by the hearth and poured herself a drop more sherry. She was still sitting there when her brother came back at twenty to twelve. James slumped happily into another armchair, stretching out his feet towards the fire.

'Well?' he asked, brightly. 'What do you think? Splendid, isn't she?'

Connie smiled. 'Very – entertaining. Very likeable. You wouldn't think it, would you, if you saw her in the street and judged her by the way she looks? I must confess I had a shock when she arrived. I'd pictured someone more girlish and I thought she must be thirty, at least.'

'Twenty-two. It's just those damned clothes – and they're her best. Some of the other stuff looks as if it came from a jumble sale. Her old man's tight-fisted, you know.'

'What a shame. She sounds well-schooled. She's certainly very bright.'

James folded his arms behind his head, gazing at the ceiling.

'I want to marry her, Connie.'

She wasn't surprised, but she said: 'That's racing ahead a bit.'

'I realise I haven't known her long, but I don't care. I suppose I'd better not rush into asking her – she might take fright – but I've already decided that I want her.'

'If you think she'll make you happy, I'm all in favour. But she is the first girl you've been out with, remember.'

He brought his arms down, started twiddling his thumbs. 'Why should I look any further?'

He might have added: 'Anyway, I couldn't stand the strain.'

He didn't say it, but Connie knew it was in his mind. Grab Janine, spare himself the nerve-racking process of approaching others, if he was able to do so at all. A bird in the hand, that was how he saw her, and not such a bad one, either. She could probably be – fixed up.

Well, thought Connie, he may be right. She seems a nice enough girl.

'Perhaps you're one of those lucky ones, Jamie,' she conceded. 'One of those who find the right partner early.'

'Yes, I think I am. To tell you the truth, I believe we were made for each other, Janine and I. She needs rescuing, you know. And I need someone sensible like her.' He closed his eyes, yawning. 'Lord, I'm whacked. Think I'll be off to bed.'

'Did you enjoy your dinner?' she asked, as he pushed himself up out of his chair.

'What? Oh, yes, it was fine. Janine was very complimentary, wasn't she? Good old Connie.' He reached out a hand and ruffled the top of her head. 'Good night.'

''Night, Jamie.'

She heard him plodding up the stairs, then wearily got to her feet. When she had done the dishes, banked the fire and locked up, she too could get to bed.

Janine's favourite fairy-tale was the story of the ugly duckling. From the day she first read it as a child, she had thought to herself: That's me, and I too should become a swan one day.

The first step in that direction was taken on her birthday, late in July. Jamie gave her six pounds to have her hair done and buy some new clothes. Thrilled, Janine rushed straight up to town and into what she deemed the best hairdressing establishment. There, in front of the mirror, she watched the ragged mess snipped into a perfect bob. Two hours later she emerged, crowned with lustrous copper locks which swung with the wind and fell back into shape of their own accord. She had bought some perfumed shampoos and lotions with which to keep it beautiful.

With the five pounds six shillings remaining, she headed for Spooner's store.

It was late afternoon when Janine returned home, weighed down with carrier bags. The rustle and crackle of them seemed to desecrate the doleful silence of the house. Someone, it declared, had been spending money, enjoying herself.

Upstairs, she tipped out all her purchases on the bed. Three blouses, a jumper, two skirts. They made a colourful jumble on the faded counterpane. Pink cotton, blue crêpe-de-chine, red tartan, grey and violet stripes, burnt orange, plain white. There was also a hat – green felt, with a big purple pansy on one side.

Janine put it on before the mirror, lowering it carefully over the shining hair. An excited, happy face looked back from the glass, the face of the 'other' Janine, the real one. She then spent an hour trying on all the garments again, matching some of them with the best of her old clothes. Amazing, the number of combinations one could achieve. She had thought all that out in the shop, of course, mind working nimbly to get as much as she could for her money.

Standing at last in the white pleated skirt and crêpe-de-chine blouse, she marvelled at her reflection. God, what a difference! How little it took. How close she had always been to looking, well, more than presentable.

For a moment she hated her father, hated him fiercely.

Then she remembered another little purchase and hurried to find it. A lipstick. She had bought a lipstick.

77

Going to her bag, she took it out, stood at the mirror and put some on.

A further transformation. Something was added to her face, a quality Matthew would not like, an extra wickedness, as if a rather attractive Miss Hyde were surfacing. Janine giggled softly.

After a while she hung up all the clothes and flopped on the bed in her underwear. Looking in her purse, she found she had ninepence left. Janine tossed the purse on top of the Bible on her bedside table. The Book was always there, but she never opened it.

Jamie was taking her out tonight. They were going to a variety show at the Palace Theatre. Stretching and smiling, curling her toes, Janine was content.

Eight

James was delighted by Janine's improved appearance. She truly was a credit to him now. He felt he was being rewarded for treating a plain girl nicely, rather as the princess was when she kissed the frog. Aware that Janine would now be more attractive to other men, he courted her with an energy he had never shown for anything before, and in October made his proposal.

They had been to lunch together that day, and James was all prepared to go home with Janine and inform Mr Jordan. To his surprise, however, she said: 'No, Jamie, leave it to me.'

'Why?' He looked at her worriedly. 'Won't he be pleased? Doesn't he like me?'

'He likes you well enough. It's just that he'll see it as my abandoning him.'

'Good God, you're entitled to your own life. Anyway, he must have guessed this was coming.'

'Yes, but it's definite now. Let me tell him, Jamie. It'll be less uncomfortable for him if you're not there.'

It was three o'clock when Janine returned home to find her father busy in the Chapel of Rest to the left of the hall. On the trestles stood a coffin, occupied by an elderly man. Matthew had prepared him to receive his last visitors. The curtains were drawn and Jordan was lighting the candles. The corpse looked comfortable and serene. Fifty-odd years before, he had worn the

79

same grey suit at his wedding. Janine cast hardly a glance at the bony white face as she entered.

'Dad,' she said, 'I have to talk to you.'

'Not now, Janine. The relatives are coming in a while. I wish to mark a few helpful texts for them in the Book.'

She ignored that. 'Dad, please listen. Jamie and I are getting married. He asked me today and I said yes. We're going to buy the engagement ring tomorrow.'

Matthew turned around, lighted taper in hand. Two little flames reflected in his spectacles, obscuring his eyes. For a moment he said nothing, then he blew the taper out. Behind his glasses, his gaze was troubled but not surprised.

'I see. I've been expecting it, of course.'

'Aren't you going to congratulate me, Dad?'

'Yes. Yes, I suppose I must.' The tone was anything but enthusiastic. 'Better advertise for a housekeeper, hadn't I?'

'No hurry. We won't be married until next April.'

Matthew went to the lectern in the corner, where the Bible lay open. He started leafing through it with the speed of one who knew it back to front.

'I had imagined that you would be company for my old age,' he muttered. 'Still, it was selfish of me, I dare say.' He found a verse he wanted and placed a silk marker on the page. 'I wish you happiness, of course. But tell me, Janine, do you want this young man for his lovable self, or for what he can give you? There have been a lot of presents, haven't there, my dear? Those clothes you're wearing, that handbag, that scented whatever it is.'

'That's not unusual between courting couples, Dad.'

'No, but you have a particular hunger for such things, don't you?'

'Whose fault is that?'

Matthew continued searching through the Bible. 'He talks a lot about greater ventures, doesn't he?'

'Certainly.'

'A lot of it strikes me as fanciful, I have to say.'

'Oh, I know what's possible and what isn't,' said Janine.

'Yes.' Matthew placed another marker. 'I'm sure you do.' He paused and eyed her keenly now. 'You want to be wealthy, don't you, Janine? You want the broad and easy way, to live your life in fields of clover. You need a stake to gamble with, and the young man has a bit of property.'

This was it, this was what she had feared for James to hear.

'That's not fair, Dad. I do care for Jamie. He was miserably shy, and I've made him happy.'

'That may be true – but you wouldn't have done so if he had been penniless, I suspect.'

'There's a lot of nonsense talked about love,' snapped Janine. 'As if nothing else were needed.'

'Your mother married me in the knowledge that I led a frugal life.'

'And was sorry for it in the end, though she wouldn't say as much to you.'

In the flickering light she thought she saw him wince. That little truth had slipped out the way things did in heated moments. Mrs Jordan had never wanted him to know of her regrets. Janine could have bitten her tongue off. She tried to lay salve on the wound.

'I'm sorry, Dad, I made that up.'

'No,' he sighed, marking a third passage and closing the Bible. 'You didn't. Why else did she want you sent to that fancy school? I suppose in many ways you have been deprived. I never thought them important ways, Janine. I still believe they are not, but we must agree to differ on that. I shall pray that you and James will be content together. I know you'll have a more comfortable life with him, one enlivened by a few pleasures, a few luxuries. I just hope, my dear, that you don't want too much. He's only a baker's son, remember. Of course, there will be children,' Matthew added. 'You may find they are quite enough for you.'

Best to agree with him. 'Yes, Dad.'

'Well . . .' he came across the room and put an arm around her shoulders, '. . . we'd better notify the church in plenty of time.'

She stiffened. 'That won't be necessary, Dad. We're going to have a civil ceremony.'

He stepped away, frowning. 'Oh, Janine.'

'We'd both prefer the registry office.'

'I see.' His mouth grew thin. 'It would be a safe bet, no doubt, that you will not be attending service any more, once you are married?'

'I only go once a month as it is, and that's just to please you.' She looked up at him starkly. 'I don't believe in any of it, Dad.' She jerked her head towards the coffin. 'That's how we all finish up, in a box, dead meat. All we have is the journey and there's nothing at the end. I don't believe the road leads anywhere, but seeing I have to make the trip, I mean to travel in comfort if I possibly can.'

There was a brief silence, then he murmured: 'My, it really backfired on me, didn't it? Everything I tried to instil . . .'

'I'm afraid so.'

'It's easy to talk tough when you're young, Janine, when you think you have prospects before you. The time may come, however, when you'll feel a need for faith.'

She looked away and was saved from further argument by the sound of people arriving. The deceased man's relations, no doubt.

'Customers, Dad.'

She always called them that, just as she privately thought of Matthew's work as 'the death business'.

Matthew made no attempt to talk James out of the marriage, knowing that opposition was apt to strengthen a lover's resolve. As for Janine, she was fully of age and had made her choice, however unsuitable he appeared to Matthew. In truth, it would have surprised Mr Jordan if his daughter had taken up with a pious man. He could have wished, however, that she had found one older, more masterful than James, and felt entitled at least to give the young man a word of warning.

A few days after the engagement, Sayers called to take her out for a dinner in town. While she finished dressing, Mr Jordan beckoned the waiting James into his little study at the rear of the house. A coal fire was the only saving grace of this plain room lined with shelves of dusty books. The undertaker stationed himself before the hearth, his backside receiving all of the heat. He motioned to James to sit down, indicating a Windsor chair without benefit of cushion. He was not deliberately ungracious, but nor was he versed in hospitality.

'Mind if I have a word or two, James?' he asked, thumbs hooked in his waistcoat pockets.

'Of course not, Mr Jordan.'

'I suppose you'd better call me Dad, and I must call you son.'

Jamie smiled.

'You love my daughter very much, I know,' said Matthew thoughtfully. 'I wouldn't have it otherwise, but I'm going to say something to you now which may surprise you. I believe you may find Janine a bit of a handful once you're married.' This with a glance from under the brows. 'I feel obliged to counsel you – start as you mean to go on.'

James laughed nervously. 'I don't understand.'

'What I mean is, she has a keen appetite for the good things of this world. Janine is not the contented sort. I think you'll have to keep a rein on her.'

A coolness appeared in Sayers' eyes, a downturn to his mouth.

'Keep her under control, eh?'

Mr Jordan worked his mouth, top lip over bottom, bottom over top.

'That sounds oppressive to you, I suppose?'

The silence meant yes.

'I'm merely advising you, James. You've known my daughter a matter of months. My experience of Janine exceeds a score of years. If I must be blunt, I'm bound to say that I believe her more forceful than you. You'd be wise to correct that. Stay in charge, whatever you do. That's a man's right, after all.'

James would not disagree there, but he could see nothing to fear in his fiancée's confidence and zest for pleasure. Of course, it was natural that Jordan the Bible-thumper would not approve of such things.

'Oh, I shall, there's no question about that. As soon as I'm twenty-one I'll be making all the decisions concerning our business.'

84

'Twenty-one,' repeated Mr Jordan with a slow shake of his head. 'That's still very young, my boy. How unfortunate that your parents died so early.'

'I can cope,' shrugged Sayers. 'It's not as if I'm going into something new. I've grown up with the bakery, after all. I know all there is to know about it.'

Again, Mr Jordan's lips wrapped one around the other. Then he said: 'But Janine tells me you do have certain plans – quite extensive ones, by her account.'

'Oh.' James fidgeted. 'Well, I was thinking years ahead.'

'I see. Yes, I'd say you'd be sensible to wait. Don't hurry into anything, my boy.'

'I've no intention of that.'

'Or let yourself be pushed before you're ready.'

'Are you saying Janine would put pressure on me?'

'She isn't over-endowed with patience, and I think your talk of future expansion has caught her imagination.'

James looked a trifle disturbed.

'What's more, she's older than you.'

'Only three years, and anyway, what difference does that make?'

'Sense of urgency, perhaps?' suggested Mr Jordan. 'She's keenly aware that life is short. You have me to blame for that.'

'I'm aware of it too, Mr Jordan. As you've just pointed out, neither of my parents reached old age.'

'True, true. Well . . .' the undertaker's hands lifted in a mild, throwaway gesture, '. . . I've been promising myself this little talk with you, and I feel my duty's fulfilled. No doubt there are ifs and buts and provisos, no matter whom one plans to marry. Having pointed out the dangers that go with Janine, I must also say in

85

her favour that she's clever and capable. Just be as strong as she is, boy, and it may turn out well.'

Nine

James and Janine were married just after the Easter of
1921. The honeymoon was ten days in Weston-Super-
Mare, which was not the stuff of Janine's dreams but
still the farthest she had ever travelled. They stayed at
a small hotel on the seafront. The weather was less
than perfect; chill winds almost every day and sometimes drizzle too, but they made the best of it. They
walked across the beach most mornings and around
the town in raincoats. Twice during their stay they
went to the pictures, once they made an excursion to
Bath, and on the single sunny day they took a bus ride
out to the Mendip Hills and had a picnic.

James enjoyed that day most of all, being fond of
lonely places. A wonderful day, he would always recall
– just Janine and him and the hills and the sky. The
two of them, the only people in the world. She was
all he wanted, no one and nothing else was required.
Janine, with whom to talk and laugh, Janine to share
his bed.

She, in truth, had considered the wedding night a bit
of a joke. Neither was experienced, but still they had
muddled through. Janine had more idea than he did of
how to go about it and she made allowances for Jamie's
clumsiness. After all, he hadn't the benefit of a father
to instruct him or a crowd of pals to offer tips. There
was no question of James taking masterful charge; it
was more of a joint experiment, with Janine by far the

more calm and less embarrassed. She had no special expectations of sex and was not disappointed. Her husband, in contrast, was mighty pleased with himself and lost in adoration of her once the feat was accomplished. Janine reflected with amusement that it sent him completely 'gooey'. She had found it nice enough, but hardly ecstasy. If asked for some comparison in terms of pleasure, she would have put it on a par with a chocolate ice-cream. It certainly didn't make her head spin or her heart thump. Only one thing thrilled her that much – money and dreams of spending it. Still, if love-making reduced Jamie to such a helpless pulp, it was probably going to be very useful whenever she wanted something.

They returned home in early May and took over Ada's old room with its double bed. It was soon settled that Janine's contribution to the running of the business should be to serve in the shop instead of James.

'She's very good with the customers,' he observed. 'Knows just how to get on with everyone.'

That was true. No matter what their temperaments, Janine could always charm them, slipping in and out of different personalities to suit each customer. Dignity to deal with this one, cheek and humour to please another. She would tittle-tattle with the gossips, complain along with the moaners, and gasp with admiration for the braggarts. James decided that Janine was good for trade.

The Colensos agreed that she was, although Nell had reservations.

'She's a fair performer, I must say,' Harry Colenso remarked one day. 'She gets around all the old miseries, even makes them cackle. Who'd have thought Jamie would fetch up with someone like her?'

His wife was non-committal. 'I don't know what to make of her. Very genial, I agree. I don't know if it's a good thing, though, to have so many different faces. You can't help wondering which is the real one, or if there's something entirely different underneath them all.'

'Connie likes her well enough,' said Harry. 'I don't know when I've ever heard her laugh so much.'

'Oh yes, she makes you laugh, all right, though sometimes it's out of pure shock at the things she says. I don't think Janine holds anything sacred, Harry. Perhaps that's what a bit of education does, or perhaps it's just her, but her attitudes are cynical, don't you think?'

The baker shrugged. 'If a touch of that rubbed off on Connie, it would be no bad thing. Connie's an innocent, God help her. Janine might do her good.'

Yes, Janine made Connie laugh with her bald remarks. But sometimes the things she said were shocking in quite another way. When she spoke out, for instance, on matters close to the quick.

The more she learned of her sister-in-law, the more Janine thought her a fool. Connie, such an unquestioning drudge. Connie, who took so much upon her shoulders and never sought help. Janine was fascinated and appalled to see the way Connie toiled, as if she were driven by some invisible overseer, or some internal mechanism jammed on full throttle so that she could not stop. She seemed to have a mania for doing everything herself, even tasks that were truly beyond her strength.

Coming in from the shop one rainy day, Janine heard

thumping from overhead and paused at the foot of the stairs. There were bumps, a crash, and then the sound of something heavy being dragged.

Quietly, Janine went up the stairs. When she reached the top of the second flight, she saw two buckets of water on the landing. The trapdoor into the attic was open and sloshing noises could be heard from within. Going up the short spiral staircase, Janine poked her head through the trapdoor and into the roof space.

Some of the slates were broken. One was missing entirely and the holes allowed in dim grey light and pouring rain. A busy plinking and plopping and spattering filled the air as water dripped in a dozen places, landing in tin baths and buckets and pans. And beneath the slope of the roof, in a cramped space only three feet high, crouched Connie. In front of her was a large tin bath, full right to the brim. Beside her was a bucket, into which she was ladling water from the bath, using a saucepan.

Janine stared at her for a moment, then she said:

'What on earth are you doing that for?'

Connie looked round and there was Janine's head in its white starched cap, seeming in the gloom to be growing out of the floor.

'I can't leave it,' Connie said. 'If it overflows we'll have the bedroom ceilings down.'

'I know, but that's no job for you.' Janine looked indignant. 'Let Jamie do it.'

'He's having his tea.'

Janine's face registered disbelief, swiftly followed by outrage.

'Bugger his tea! I'll go and get him.'

'It's all right,' panted Connie, 'I can do it. I always have.'

'Is that a fact? Well, not any more you won't.'

The head disappeared, footsteps receded downstairs. Five minutes later James came up, looking sheepish.

'Leave this to me,' he told his sister.

'Oh, no . . . Janine shouldn't have . . . Look, I'll help you.'

'Go,' said James. 'I'll finish my tea later on.'

Connie shuffled out of the corner on her hands and knees till she reached a point where she could stand up straight. But still she hovered. This wasn't right, Jamie coming up here, interrupting his tea, taking over this chore which had always been hers. It felt all wrong, not normal.

'I'll take the other buckets down, empty them and bring them back,' she said.

'No, do as I tell you. Have something to eat.'

He was sharp with her and that, too, was upsetting. Connie slunk away, feeling guilty. Poor Jamie, his tea would be spoilt. Of course she would cook him another. Connie failed to understand at all why her brother was testy. She didn't know that Janine had told him off.

She went down to the kitchen and found her sister-in-law sitting with her feet up on the fender of the cooking range. Janine had a cup of tea in one hand, a cigarette in the other. Her white shop overall was unbuttoned. The working day was over, she had very definitely finished. Through the curls of cigarette smoke, she eyed Connie with impatience.

'How many times have you done that, may I ask?'

A short laugh. 'I've lost count. As many times as we've had wet days like this. Whenever there's continuous rain, I have to go up and bail.'

Her skirts and apron were damp, her hair was undone and had picked up cobwebs from the roof. She looked exhausted and her hands were red-knuckled from the cold.

'That's a man's job,' said Janine. 'Anyway, why hasn't the roof been mended? This family isn't short of money for repairs.'

'Mam always said it wasn't necessary. I have mentioned it to Jamie since she died. He's been meaning to get around to it.'

Connie took his abandoned pork chops and finished them off herself.

'We'll get the roof done,' Janine said, 'don't you worry. I'll see to that.'

From the corner of her eye she noticed how unsettled Connie was, picking at her food and constantly glancing up at the sounds of Jamie moving overhead. Janine took a sip of her tea and then asked softly: 'Why do you do it, Connie?'

The other seemed puzzled. 'Do what?'

'Work as if the devil's at your heels. Why do you wait on Jamie like a servant? What are you expecting – a brighter crown hereafter?'

Connie stared at her. 'I only do what all women do in their homes.'

'Oh no.' A slow shake of the head, a flick of the cigarette ash. 'There's more to it with you. You never stop. A glutton for punishment, that's what you are.'

'There's a lot to do in this house.' Suddenly Connie was very interested in the chops on her plate. She studied them intently, avoiding Janine's dark gaze.

'And a lot that could be left undone, with no ill-effects. And a lot you should ask your brother to do for you.'

92

'Well, I know he would if I asked. He just doesn't think.'

'And you don't remind him. You just go and do it yourself. Like that up there today.'

'I like being useful. I can't bear sitting about idle, that's for sure.'

'You'd do as much for a husband, then?'

'I'm sure I would,' sniffed Connie. 'It's the way I was brought up.'

But even as she said it, she knew the driving force would never be the same for a man to whom she owed no reparation. Memory struck at her again, calling up the image of her mother's face on the night of the fire, when she returned from the hospital at half past one in the morning . . .

Ada, her pompadour coming undone, strands of hair hanging wildly round her face and down her back. Looking half-mad, her lips pulled back tightly over her teeth, a freezing glare in her eyes and the red of fury in her cheeks. Looking as if she would like to kill Connie. Shouting: 'What were you doing? Answer me, what were you doing?'

Mam, kneeling in front of her, fingers digging into Connie's shoulders, shaking her so hard that she grew dizzy and sick. Raging: 'You were told to watch him. So how did it happen, eh? Where were you?'

Connie, weeping: 'In here, I wanted to finish my drawing. I didn't know he'd gone downstairs. He was in bed and I thought he'd gone to sleep or I wouldn't have left him. I didn't hear him go downstairs.'

Ada, unimpressed and spitting: 'Drawing! You and your drawing! You were told to stay with him all the time! Was that so much to ask? Was that beyond you? Just a few hours while I went out? We're lucky the whole place didn't burn down. Did you see your brother's face? Did you? He'll be scarred. Do you know that? The doctor said so. All his life. All his life!'

The voice a scream now, blasted full into Connie's face: 'Damn you! Damn you, you worthless little . . .'

A calm voice broke in. Janine, saying: 'Well, if you prefer hard graft, that's your concern.' Then, with shocking bluntness, adding: 'But it wasn't you who struck that match, was it?'

From under her brows, Connie glanced at her. 'He's told you all about it, then? Yes, I suppose he would.'

Janine tossed the cigarette butt into the cinder tray of the kitchen range. Knowingly, she said: 'From all I gather, she was a first-class cow, your mother. But she's gone and you're not a child any more. If you don't see sense now and look out for yourself, it's nobody's fault but your own.'

That was Janine's opinion, and she said as much to Nell Colenso one day soon afterwards. She was quietly rebuked.

'You weren't here, you didn't see,' Mrs Colenso told her, as she cleaned off the work-tops before going home. 'The way that Ada went about it – insidious, that's the word. After she cooled down, the bullying stopped and she took up a subtler method. Perhaps even she was only half aware of what she was doing, so how could a child like Connie understand and be on guard?' Nell shook the wet dishcloth, folded it over and went on sweeping it, left to right, across Harry's table. 'She started calling the boy "poor Jamie", whenever she spoke of him to Connie. Never just "James" or "your brother", but always "poor Jamie". I remember the

94

little talk Ada gave her when James came home from the hospital. Very solemn, it was, very sorrowful.'

' "Poor Jamie's had a lot of pain," Ada said. "He will for quite some time, so we must all be especially kind to him, mustn't we? We must do all we can to make it up to him. And if he's naughtier than usual we must forgive him, because he's had a terrible ordeal and he isn't quite himself." '

Janine made no comment, but took it all in, silently piling the day's unsold goods onto a flat wire tray, to be sold off cheaply in the morning.

'Of course, Ada never said in so many words that Connie owed him service. She would merely ask her to do such and such for "poor Jamie", or refer in a hushed voice to "the cross he has to bear". That was how she did it, in the main, though sometimes she would speak more generally, telling Connie that she should always put others first. And in a hundred little ways, that was what Connie did. That was why she never objected to cleaning her brother's shoes for him, or picking up his toys for him and putting them away. Anything Jamie did was all right. If he came in with muddy feet and left a mess on the kitchen floor and down the hallway, well, it didn't matter one bit. Connie would just clean it up. He soon took in the idea that this was his due, because he was the boy of the family. Jamie didn't understand what was going on, I'm sure. No doubt it all seemed very natural and normal to him. After all, Connie had always loved him. She never resented James, never begrudged him the special attention he was given. In her own small way, I suppose she had helped to spoil him, letting him win at silly games, sometimes giving him her toys to keep. Oh, I remember it all very clearly. There's nothing wrong, of course, in training a little girl to a few household duties. Long before the fire, Connie was used to washing dishes and peeling vegetables and tidying up a bit around the house. And Ada was never harsh to her then, only a bit detached, lukewarm. But Jamie's accident brought a change for the worse. By the time Connie was eleven, she'd become a maid-of-all-work.'

Nell dropped the cloth in the sink and started untying her apron strings.

'More than once I heard Ada saying the best way to make amends was to be a very good girl,' she said wryly, peeling off the apron and hanging it up in a cupboard. 'Connie's been too damned good ever since.'

Janine picked a saffron bun from the tray and took a bite. 'It's in her nature, though, isn't it?' she shrugged. 'That sort of thing would never have worked with me.'

'Hmm. Well, you're a different kettle of fish, I know.'

For a moment their eyes locked. Janine half smiled and took a second bite of her bun. She knew Nell Colenso did not exactly like her. The fact did not trouble Janine a great deal – and Nell knew that. They maintained a civil arm's-length relationship with a certain balance of equality to it. Janine's was the authority of being Mrs Sayers. Nell, after many years of service, enjoyed the status of family friend and fixture and was also a highly proficient pastry-cook who would not be easy to replace.

'Of course,' continued Mrs Colenso, putting on her outdoor coat, 'Ada never could face up to the fact that she was the one responsible for it all at rock bottom. Ada couldn't bear the truth, never would look at it squarely. Her boy, her beautiful boy, mutilated because she had wanted an evening out. I dare say she shrank from acknowledging such a thing. She took a lot of criticism, too. Everyone hereabouts had something to say. As for the doctor – she went on for days about him and how rude he was. Said she'd never been spoken to that way in all her life. I think she was punishing Connie for her own rough time as much as for Jamie's face. I could have felt sorry for Ada, if she hadn't taken everything out on the girl.'

Janine picked a piece of peel out of her bun and threw it away. 'Fortunate, really, that she didn't live to be a great age,' she observed. 'Since we're being candid, I may as well say it.'

Nell was tying on her headscarf. Half turning her head, she glanced at Janine and there was a glint of humour in her eyes. 'Certainly lucky for you,' she said.

'Mrs Sayers wouldn't have liked me,' smiled Janine.

'By God, she'd have hated you, I reckon. If he'd met you before she died . . .' A grin spread over Mrs Colenso's face. 'But you'd have given her a fight, wouldn't you? It would have been something to watch, I think. All credit to you, I believe you would have been guns enough for Ada. Still, if Jamie had been caught between you, if he'd had to choose, I wouldn't like to bet that you would have won. They were that close, see.'

'Then it's lucky for Jamie, too, that she's gone. Now he has a normal life and a free hand with the business.'

Yes, thought Nell, picking up her basket and pulling on her gloves. He just fell in your lap, didn't he? Jamie and all the property you knew she'd left him. Ada never bargained for that. Fortunate, indeed, that she died when she did, but it's only Connie for whom I'm glad.

Aloud, she said: 'Well, I won't disagree with you. I'm very pleased that Jamie's married – for his sister's sake.'

Janine's eyebrows lifted, questioning.

'Oh, Connie would have looked after him until his dying day if he hadn't found a wife,' enlarged Nell.

'Ah, I see.'

'At least she's at liberty now to make a life of her own, and I hope to God she will.'

'Don't see the slightest reason why not,' said Janine, and popped the last fragment of bun in her mouth.

'Yes,' said Nell stoutly on her way out, 'well, after all, she has no share in this place, does she?'

Ten

January of the following year brought James's twenty-first birthday, and with it control of what he now owned. It was only a month after that when Nell Colenso's hopes for Connie took a step towards fulfilment.

In town one Saturday, Connie called at the covered market to buy a turnip. Under a high corrugated roof dotted with skylights, the market was a noisy, crowded place, a maze of stalls selling fruit, vegetables, dairy produce and cold meats. There were pets and live poultry too; rabbits in hutches, birds such as mynahs and canaries alongside mice and hamsters, ducks and chickens. It was always cold, even in summer, the light a little baleful. On this February day it was freezing. Some of the stall-holders worked in coats and scarves. The occasional whiff of a paraffin heater hung around those booths which dealt in old books or fabric remnants or kitchenware, but foodstuffs lay on icy marble slabs or tables well removed from any heat.

Connie, as usual, was in a hurry. Her shopping bag was heavy, containing soda crystals, a bottle of bleach and a new pair of sheets from Spooner's store. She wanted the turnip for pasties, then she intended to go straight home where a pile of washing awaited her. By the time she had lit the fire under the copper in the outhouse, boiled, rinsed and mangled it all, the day would be gone. It had always been the same – keeping everything clean and tidy, serving up meals, getting in supplies – these were the things which ate up her life and she wondered how others found time to go out dancing or visit the cinema, or even stand gossiping over back fences as most of her neighbours did. Connie lacked their happy capacity to let things slide. They allowed their menfolk to wear shirts for two or three days instead of just one. They dished up makeshift meals sometimes, and let the dust accumulate a bit. Unlike Connie, they showed themselves some mercy.

She made straight for her favourite greengrocer's stall. Connie never took time to loiter and browse. Even her route was planned to be the shortest and quickest her shopping list would allow. A creature of habit, Connie stuck with tradesmen who knew her and treated her well. As a 'regular' she would get a penny off from this one, twopence from another, an ounce or two extra from somebody else. Ada had taught her to be thrifty.

Today, however, Connie found herself unexpectedly dealing with a stranger. When she reached the fruit and vegetable stall it was attended by a man she had never seen before. He was young – no more than twenty-five – with fine grey eyes and well-proportioned features. Light brown hair curled out from under his cap. He had a scarf wrapped twice around his neck and his hands were sunk in his trouser pockets. He kept shifting from foot to foot and stamping a little to try and stay warm.

'Oh,' said Connie, coming face to face with him. Looking up, she saw a new sign hanging up above the stall. It said: C. NICHOLLS.

'Where's Mr Toy?'

'Retired,' the young man said. 'Three weeks ago.'

'Oh. Well, I haven't been up here for a month or so.'

'I reckon my stuff's just as good.' He rubbed his hands together, grinning.

She looked over the boxes and trays and nodded. Cox's Pippins, conference pears, clementines, bananas, all very plump and bright and unblemished. Beautiful sprouts and carrots, King Edwards, parsnips, big Spanish onions. Quite artistically arranged, she thought, a design in red, green and orange. He knew the importance of presentation, unlike old Mr Toy, who had piled up his produce any old how. She wondered wryly how much extra this prettiness would cost.

'What are you asking for the turnips?'

He picked the biggest off the heap. 'Penny-halfpenny.'

That wasn't bad. She took it right away. 'I think I'll have three of your oranges, too. And those – are they Guernsey tomatoes?'

'They are.'

'How much?'

'Sixpence a pound.'

'I'll have four.'

In the end she bought a lot more than she had intended, but his prices were very reasonable and everything looked so good. He gave her a paper carrier with the words 'Charlie's Fruit and Flowers' printed on each side. The only flowers he had at present were daffodils and narcissi, she observed, plus a few cartons of aster and dahlia bulbs. He noticed her looking at them and said:

'Haven't sorted out the flower side yet. Too early in the year for much, anyway. The daffodils are from the Scilly Isles.'

Suddenly, bending over, he pulled a little bunch from the tub and gave them to her.

'Here – for being a good customer.'

'Oh – I can't . . .'

'Of course you can. I shan't sell them all anyway, never do.'

'Well, thank you. Thank you very much.'

'Pleasure,' said Mr Nicholls. 'See you again.'

He watched her plod off, laden now, with a bag in each hand, the daffodils sticking up out of the paper carrier. Quite a nice-looking girl, he thought, but she didn't make the best of herself. A kind face and roughened hands, hair pinned up behind in a rather untidy knot – the air of an overworked wife and mother. And yet, no wedding ring. He wondered idly what her circumstances were.

A fortnight later, Connie encountered Mr Nicholls again. It was Saturday lunch-time. She had been to see her dentist in Phoenix Street. Something of an emergency, the visit had meant a filling and she didn't feel like walking home. She caught a tram in Union Street and took a seat upstairs. It was March now, still cool, a day of pale sunshine and passing showers. She was glad to sit in the open air after the smell of the surgery. Odours of disinfectant and medication, hospital smells, always disturbed her. They brought back memories of the milky, antiseptic fluid with which Ada used to bathe Jamie's face until the skin grew over.

Connie prodded at the new filling with her tongue as the tram moved off. It tasted salty, of metal, and a few gritty bits were still lodged around her gums. She was working her mouth to dislodge them when a man sat down beside her. Connie didn't even glance at him, but turned away, staring out over the guard-rail at the bustle of Union Street. Capturing a bit of filling, she slyly spat it out. The street below was milling with men in naval uniform and its many pubs were noisily busy, for much of the fleet was in port.

Her fellow passenger shifted a few times on his seat, as if the wooden slats were too hard for his behind. She had the feeling suddenly that he was staring at her, and her gaze slid round to find that indeed he was. The face was familiar from somewhere, but at first she could not place it.

He grinned. 'The market stall,' he said. 'I gave you some daffodils.'

'Oh – yes.' She smiled at him. 'They lasted very well. I only threw them out three days ago. Going back to the market now?'

'Me? Oh, no. Not on a Saturday afternoon. I like to go to the football, see. Big match at Home Park today. Argyle are playing Bristol.'

'I suppose that's why the town's so busy.'

'Certainly is.'

A big football match brought as much trade to the city stores as the ships gave to Union Street. An excursion train had brought three thousand people up from Cornwall that morning, the men to see the game, their wives to go around the shops.

The tram pulled up at Derry's clock to take on passengers, then lumbered on its way along George Street, stopping and starting with the jerky progress of the traffic. It turned the corner into Bedford Street with a mighty groan of complaint and squealed to a halt for another queue.

'You ever go to the football?' Nicholls enquired.

'Lord, no. Anyway, it's my washday today.'

'On a Saturday?'

'It's as good a day as any other.'

'To most people it's the day for going out and having a bit of fun.'

'Tell that to any woman who has a home to run.'

'No one's busy every waking minute.'

'I am, very nearly.'

Nicholl's gaze danced over her profile as the tram started off again.

'Who's all the washing for?' he asked. 'I see you're not married. No husband, no children. Why do you spend your Saturdays doing laundry?'

'It's for myself, my brother and his wife. We have a bakery and bread shop on the Barbican, but I just look after the house.'

His forehead wrinkled slightly. The answer left him somehow unsatisfied, but he pressed her no further, asking instead: 'What's your name?'

'Connie Sayers.'

'I'm Charlie.'

'Yes, I know, it was on your paper bag.'

'Well, seeing you know who and what I am, how would you like to come to the game with me today?'

By instinct, Connie quailed from that, closing herself in like a frightened sea anemone.

'I couldn't. It's very nice of you, but as I've told you, I must . . .'

'Do the laundry. Why can't your brother's wife do it?'

'Because it's my job, that's why. We have it all arranged, you see, who does what.'

For a while they fell silent and the tram creaked on. Then he asked: 'Do you have many friends?'

'I'm not the mixing sort.'

'Thought not, somehow. I can't pretend that I am, either – but I like your company.'

She glanced at him, met a smile and quickly looked away.

'Come on, it's only a football match, only a single afternoon.'

'I'm expected back! They'll think something's happened to me.'

He sighed. 'All right, I suppose it is short notice.'

Connie thought that was the end of it. But then:

'We could go to the rugby, though. That's next week. Plenty of time to arrange a free afternoon, eh?'

She shook her head.

'Don't you like me?'

'It's not that. It's just . . .'

In truth, she hardly knew what her objection was.

'Just what? Just that you're not used to going anywhere?'

'That's about the size of it.'

'This is your chance, then. A bit of excitement. What do you say?'

Her stop was coming up ahead. She gripped the handle of her basket.

'I'll think about it. Excuse me, I'm getting out here.'

'I'd rather you promised me now.'

She was on her feet, ready to push past him. 'I really don't know . . .'

'Please?' He gazed up at her, serious now.

He was very appealing, really. Furthermore, there was nothing to stop her, was there? Nothing but habit, nothing but the strangeness of it, the discomfort of breaking routine. Except, perhaps, the knowledge that a friendship with a man could be a door to an entirely different life. Here, cowardice came in, she supposed, a dread of the unknown.

Nicholls moved his knees for her to pass. 'Come on,

I'll bring you a few more daffs. You can wear my Albion scarf. How could any sane woman refuse an offer like that?'

She laughed despite herself, then, in renewed anxiety, dropped her basket in the gangway as the tram halted.

Charlie picked it up for her. 'Sayers, you said? The bread shop on the Barbican? I could call for you at half past one next Saturday.'

Two years had passed since Ada's death. It was probably high time to think of making her own life. Even Jamie had said: 'You're free.' Fearful but tempted, she wavered.

'Go on, be adventurous.'

In a minute the tram would carry her on to the next stop and she would have a long walk back. Anyway, he was only asking her to a rugby match, for heaven's sake. She dithered a few seconds more, then surrendered.

'Yes, all right. All right.'

Eleven

'Lipstick?' Connie glanced doubtfully at her sister-in-law. 'Me? I'd look like a clown.'

Janine came and stood at her shoulder, so that their faces were reflected together in the sitting-room mirror.

'I'm the one with the clown's face,' she said wryly. 'Look at it, and let's be honest, I have a funny face. But I don't mind it, especially when it's made up.'

It was one of the things Connie liked about Janine, that lack of conceit, that dry realism about her appearance. With its tilted nose and plump lower lip, her face had a comical charm, but no one could describe her as a beauty and Janine had no illusions about herself.

'Go on, try this one. It's not too gaudy, it'll suit you.'

Connie took the lipstick and ran it lightly over her mouth. A muted red, it flattered the fairness of her skin, enlivened her face and seemed to make it more complete – younger, even. She hadn't expected that. On other women, make-up often appeared to add a few years, but perhaps that was just because it was overdone.

'That's good,' said Janine. 'You keep that lipstick. The colour's not quite right for me. Now, how about a bit of powder?'

'I don't think . . .'

'Just on your nose. Noses turn red in the cold, and

I'm sure it's going to be damned cold out at the rugby ground.'

Connie dabbed the middle of her face with the powder puff. 'I feel silly,' she said. 'I'm not used to this sort of thing.'

No, thought Janine, you're not accustomed to anything except doing for other people. I like you, Connie, but you're such a mug. You haven't the sense to grab for your share of life. You have to be pushed into doing what's good for you.

'You're not backing out,' she said sternly. 'He'll be here in a minute. What's his name again?'

'Charlie.'

'Nice-looking?'

'Yes, he is.'

Janine smiled. 'You ought to have your hair bobbed,' she advised. 'It's lovely hair, but it's out of style.'

Connie fingered the tortoise-shell slide at the back of her head, then ran her hand down over the fall of shining brown waves. 'I know,' she said. 'I couldn't decide what to do with it today. Is this all right?'

'Yes, but – tell you what . . .' Janine snapped her fingers. 'Borrow my new tam. It'll give you a touch of dash.'

She went into the hall and returned with a mushroom-coloured angora beret.

'Here now, try it. No, not straight and flat like a pancake. You wear it at an angle, it's meant to look cheeky.' She reached up and adjusted the tam on Connie's head, stood back and nodded approval. 'Just right.'

Connie surveyed herself in the mirror, pleasantly surprised. 'He'll hardly know me.' She fastened the top button of her coat. It was dark blue and a bit too long to

108

be fashionable. Still, her height helped her carry it off. Janine, who was several inches shorter, quite envied her that lofty grace.

Connie had rearranged her whole weekly schedule to have the washing done by Friday. It had meant leaving the silver and brass unpolished, and a number of socks undarned. She felt uneasy about that, and disoriented by the change, almost as if a stitch had been dropped in the fabric of her life. Who knew how big a hole it might make, how fast the pattern might unravel? She didn't feel right at all, going out this afternoon.

'To hell with the socks and bugger the polishing.'

That was what Janine had said. She had not actually offered to do any of Connie's work for her, sticking instead by her own belief that half of it didn't need to be done at all. Janine's attitude to housework had changed not a jot since she married.

Connie, though, could never shrug off the neglected tasks. The thought of them nagged reproachfully at her even now. She appeased her conscience with plans to stay up late tonight and get them done.

'There's the fella,' said Janine, as a shadow passed the window and the rap of the door-knocker sounded. 'Go and enjoy yourself, for heaven's sake. It's about time you learnt how.'

It was bitter at the rugby ground. Everyone was well wrapped up, some in scarves and gloves and woolly hats in club colours. They hunched their shoulders against the cold and their breath made feathers in the air, while the teams on the field boiled with exertion in their shorts and jerseys.

'How would you like to tackle their laundry?' yelled Charlie over the bellowing of the mob.

Connie laughed and rolled her eyes. Down on the pitch a huddle of mud-caked Cornishmen were locked with Plymouth Albion in a scrum. A swaying, shoving mound of broad backsides and meaty thighs, they were three points all and nearing half-time.

'Enjoying it?' he shouted.

She was, though she barely understood the game. Still, the spectacle and the atmosphere were entertainment enough. The flying tackles, the diving trys, the headlong charges down the pitch, the scuffles and the wallowing in mud.

The scrum collapsed, the ball shot out one end of it, was seized by the Albion side and passed adroitly from man to man at marvellous speed. The crowd were beside themselves and Charlie started to bawl with the rest.

Watching him sideways, Connie began to notice little details about him. In sunlight his hair was the brown of a hazelnut, and darker speckles showed in the grey of his eyes. He had a small mole just above his right eyebrow, and the tip of his nose was slightly flat. His face was expressive, revealing all he felt. The smile was joyous when Albion had the advantage and the look became forlorn, desperately worried when things went against them.

By the time she looked to the field again, the Plymouth team had lost the ball. A lanky Cornishman was sprinting for the goal-line with it, dodging and weaving. To Connie's amazement, he jumped the back of a man who dashed in for a tackle – jumped clean over him.

Charlie whistled. 'That's Jago,' he said. 'He's well known for that trick. Some player, Jago.'

Moments later he started to boo, as a tussle

developed for the ball. Five men were tearing up the turf with their studded boots, dragging at each other's limbs and jerseys. An Albion man had a Cornishman's head locked under his arm. He appeared to be trying to pull it off and the referee's whistle peeped frantically.

The game went on to end in a draw and the teams trooped off, all spattered and tattered.

'There's a food stall out by the gate,' said Nicholls. 'Like a cup of tea and a bacon sandwich?'

Janine would have given short shrift to that, but Connie thought it a fine idea. But then, Janine would never have gone to a rugby match in the first place. The Theatre Royal and a restaurant were more to her taste.

Charlie and Connie sat down on a public bench to drink their tea and eat their sandwiches. A few yards away was the tram stop, and the food stall was doing good business as people filed out of the gate and waited around for their ride home.

Connie sipped at the scalding tea between mouthfuls of bread and bacon.

'Have you any family?' she asked.

'All gone. Mother died years and years ago. Both my brothers were killed on the Somme and the shock of that put paid to my father, I reckon.' He pulled a bit of rind from his sandwich and tossed it away.

'Where do you live, then?'

'In lodgings, up near Wyndham Square. Landlady's not a bad old stick. If I do well with the stall, though, I'll look for a flat to rent and I'll buy a van.'

'I don't see why you shouldn't. Your trade is like ours – a basic. Jamie, that's my brother, always says you can't go wrong with food. He says it's the sort of business that never goes broke.'

Nicholls gave a small snort. 'Any business can, if it's run the wrong way.'

She finished her sandwich. 'Oh, Jamie's very bright. He knows what he's about.'

Charlie leaned forward, forearms on his knees, steaming cup and sandwich in either hand. The peak of his cap sat low on his brow and he asked: 'Is he much older than you?'

'He's two years younger.'

'Yet he's the one who's married? How's that?'

'Just circumstances,' Connie said.

For a long, long moment he studied her. What he knew of her situation vaguely bothered him. Something wasn't right, though he could not pinpoint what. She was so nice, too, with her gentle face and voice, such easy-going company. Not a demanding sort, at all. He appreciated that, being as yet a bit hard up. Connie was no prattler, either. They irritated him, those gabby girls who went on and on, giggled like imbeciles and wanted to be taken to places Charlie could not afford.

Embarrassed by his stare, she muttered: 'What are you looking at?'

'You, of course. Will you come to the pictures with me one evening?'

Her first thought was: I can't. I have to cook dinner every night. Then she realised that a stew could be left on the hob.

'Well,' she said slowly, 'I'd like to . . . Yes, I suppose I could.'

'There,' said Nicholls, grinning. 'See? Gets easier every time.'

Connie's new friend caused a ripple of interest in the neighbourhood. Millie Chope lifted aside her front

112

room curtains one April evening and peered across the road at the Sayers' house.

'You know, Jack,' she said, 'I believe Connie's courting. That young man's at the door again.'

Jack Chope went on reading the sports page. His day at the dockyard over, he sprawled on the sofa in shirt-sleeves and braces, a mug of tea on the floor beside him.

'That's four times now I've seen him call at their place. Hard to imagine Connie taking up with a chap.'

A grunt from behind the paper. 'She's as entitled as anyone else.'

Millie tensed with interest. 'Here she comes . . . Ooh, she's got a new coat on! Here, Jack, come and look!'

Her husband declined to budge.

'Not a bad looking fellow, is he?' murmured Millie.

She watched the couple across the street. Connie had paused on the doorstep, tucking a stray lock of hair up under her pull-on hat. Millie's mouth formed another 'Ooh' as she saw the pair link arms and walk off.

'Wonder where they're going. Perhaps he takes her dancing down at the pier,' said Millie wistfully. Her head swivelled round and a momentary glint lit her eyes. 'Like you used to take me. I always loved going dancing when we were courting, but that's a thing of the past now, sure enough. Soon as you had the ring on my finger, it was goodbye evenings out. All you care about now is pie and mash and cups of tea and clean socks and the racing results.'

'Give it a rest. We're not young any more.'

'I wasn't young for long at all, once I'd been to the altar.'

'Don't know why you're so pleased for Connie, then.'

The couple were now out of sight, so Millie turned from the window and sat down in her chair.

'Well, it's a bit of magic for her – at least it looks that way when you see them together. She never had any real youth, did she? No carefree times like other girls, poor thing. All this must be such a treat for her.' Millie's eyes snapped once more towards Jack, all belly and baggy trousers. 'A few months, perhaps a year of romance before the let-down once she's married.'

Irritably, Jack put down the paper. 'Listen, I keep you, don't I? I bring home a wage, which is more than some can do now the dockyard's winding down. Another fourteen men got laid off last week and you moan to me because we don't go dancing.'

Indeed, it was 1922 and the huge dockyard workforce of the war years was being pared down. A certain prosperity had lingered for a while after 1918, but had drained away now. Jack Chope was fortunate to have his job, but Millie never compared herself to those worse off, only to those who had more.

'What you bring in buys essentials, but there's never much left over,' she said glumly. Casting another look at the Sayers' house, she muttered: 'I wish we could afford a few of the nice things they've got.'

'Who?'

'The Sayers. Good furniture, good linen. Ada always bought the best quality, never had to go round the sales and pick up seconds like I do.'

'Thou shalt not covet, Millie dear.'

She sucked her teeth. 'I wonder if that young man knows that none of it belongs to Connie.'

'Oh, you would think of that.' He took up the paper again, shaking out the creases.

'He doesn't look too prosperous,' Millie went on. 'Still, it wouldn't seem natural for Connie to catch someone well off. She never was the lucky kind.'

*

Connie would have laughed at that. As spring turned into summer it seemed to her that fortune had finally remembered her existence and was striving to make up for past neglect.

'Here's something for you,' it seemed to say. 'I had your share of life put by. I simply forgot to deliver it till now.'

At last she had her hair cut short, and in June her brother made her a present of three new frocks. Connie had always favoured little floral prints, but now she felt more adventurous, opting for stripes and polka dots. She was 'quite re-made', to use Janine's approving phrase. Janine took almost as much pleasure in Connie's transformation as she had in her own. But then, she enjoyed any exercise which involved fashion and shopping.

The new Connie hardly knew herself. She felt that wonderful prospects lay before her. They were modest enough in Janine's estimation, those simple desires for a husband, children, some little home. Hardly ambitious – no more than millions of other women took for granted. Yet Connie was thrilled just to think she could have her own niche in the world, be something more than simply an appendage of James and Janine. Once, so tied to her flesh and blood by a sense of duty, Connie had viewed a separate life as a pipe-dream. Even with Ada gone and Jamie married, a feeling of constraint had remained until she met Charlie, as if she were governed by a deeply embedded commandment: 'Thou shalt not go forth to seek thine own happiness.'

Now, at last, the fetters had truly broken open and fallen away. The door had unlocked itself, swung back. There in the brilliant light on the other side of it stood

Charlie Nicholls and she could just walk through to him.

Their relationship had seemed to grow, keeping pace with the seasons, becoming warmer and brighter week by week from that first civil meeting in February, through the novelty of learning about one another as April and May went by, to the sheer exhilaration of love by the time of high summer. It was like Charlie's market stall, which burgeoned with fruit and flowers, becoming sweeter and more varied as the weather grew hotter.

He grew confident as his little business thrived. Every morning at six he was at the market, taking delivery from the wholesalers and local growers, laying out the produce ready to open at eight. Often, among his early customers, there would be chefs from local restaurants. They would buy such things as artichokes and aubergines by the boxful. Peppers, endive, courgettes and garlic might find little favour with housewives, but professional cooks bought them in quantity and Charlie often had the best in town. His stand groaned under the weight of strawberries, raspberries, gooseberries, peaches, fragrant William pears, glossy blackcurrants, cherries, and blushing, orange-yellow apples. He sold button mushrooms, fat and white, and big field mushrooms with their brown pleated skirts swirled wide. Cauliflowers, crisp and knobbly, were lined up in neat rows in their cartons, like so many snow-white faces framed in green bonnets of leaves.

There was nearly always a queue at Charlie's stall. He came to know most of the women by name – Christian names, more often than not – and a lot of their personal business too, for they gossiped together as they stood in line. None but the busiest minded queueing at Charlie's. The atmosphere was sociable and the air was heady with scent from the tubs of flowers on display. From allotments and flower farms for many miles around came a riot of roses, phlox and freesias, spears of larkspur and delphiniums, a froth of fragrant stock and sweet peas, ranks of irises and lilies, posies of candytuft and anemones.

Whatever flowers he had left over, Charlie took round to Connie most days. She liked to put them on the kitchen window sill to relieve the stark view of the backyard. They would have a place with a garden, he promised, when they were married.

Already they spent nearly all their spare time together – all but the hours when Charlie went out fishing. The man who ran the neighbouring stall at the market was a butcher. He owned a small boat with an outboard and on occasion he lent it to Charlie Nicholls. Charlie never took Connie with him on his fishing trips. He thought it would be boring for her. However, there came a day in August when he had a better idea for putting the boat to use.

'Like to go up the river this afternoon? My mate says I can borrow the boat today. We could take it up as far as, say, Calstock, and stop there for a cream tea.'

It was Saturday afternoon. They had just come out of Cynthia Hardin's dairy and were ambling down South-side Street towards the quay. Both had strawberry cornets. Cynthia had actually topped the ice-creams with nuts and raspberry sauce at no extra charge. It was her way of showing approval that Connie had a young man. Despite her sharp and tactless tongue, she had her good points, Connie thought.

'I'd love that,' she said. 'Where's the boat tied up?'

117

'Just down by the Mayflower steps.'

They walked along the quay to the place where a gap in the harbour wall was surmounted by an archway. Beyond the archway lay a flight of ordinary granite steps down to the water. This place, however, was celebrated by an American flag, a bronze plaque set in the harbour wall, and a very worn stone in the pavement nearby, inscribed '*Mayflower*, 1620'. The legend on the bronze tablet was clear and sharp, easy to read. The words in the stone were already becoming faint with the passage of time and many feet.

Three small boats were tied up at the foot of the steps. Connie and Charlie went down and climbed into the red one in the middle. No great journey for them today, unlike the pilgrims three centuries past. For Connie and Charlie, just another day out.

She held what remained of his cornet while he untied the mooring rope and started the engine. The ice-cream was melting fast, sticky pink drips running down her fingers. The gentle plop of lapping water was drowned by a coughing roar which settled into a chug. Settling himself in the stern with his hand on the tiller, Charlie turned the boat to head out into the bay. Connie passed his ice-cream back and he polished it off in two bites.

Away to their right now reared the high granite wall of the Citadel fortress, while the blue expanse of the Sound stretched away on their left into a sunny haze. The wind was pulling at their hair and flapping their clothes, and their nostrils were full of the smell of brine.

Connie tossed the end of the cornet overboard and trailed her hands in the water to clean them off. Then they were passing the Hoe and she thought that it looked like a great broad welcoming bosom when seen from the sea. Certainly, the town was out to play on it today – all those who had leisure, at least. People were out in pastel frocks and cardigans and sandals, white flannels, boaters and blazers. They were out riding bikes and strolling in couples, or fishing or diving off the rocks. They were out on the Promenade Pier, feeding the slot machines to giggle at film star photos or 'What the butler saw'. They lay on the grassy slopes above Hoe Road and sunned themselves, or hung around the bandstand, listening to Bizet and Strauss and military marches. Holiday Plymouth, the city of the regatta, the seaside shows, the pleasure ferries, was out for another lovely summer day.

Past Millbay Docks and Devil's Point, they turned towards Devonport. Another Plymouth here, the war town, the vast naval arsenal full of barracks and military stores. All along this stretch of river lay warships, grey and stately, anchored alongside their jetties or out in deeper water. As the little boat passed among them, Connie craned her neck to look up at towering superstructures bristling with guns. Yet, motionless and silent, these great ships appeared more aloof than menacing, leviathans dozing in the sun.

The Brunel Bridge passed overhead as the boat moved on up the Tamar. Everyone called it that, the Brunel Bridge, never the Royal Albert Bridge, its proper name. Half-way across, you were officially in Cornwall. The boat continued up the river, broad and placid, and now came countryside full of fruit and flower farms. Pear and apple orchards, fields given over to daffodils in spring, acres of strawberry plots and cherry trees.

Finally, after many winding miles, a railway viaduct

reared before them, spanning the river. Calstock village.

It was still only three o'clock, too early for tea. They left the boat and decided to explore a path which wound away into the woods on the river bank. A tunnel of birdsong and stillness and green-gold light, the track ran for over a mile, to end at last at a gate.

It was marked 'Private Property. No Trespassers'. Beyond it lay an open field, overgrown with yellow flowers like clusters of flattened pom-poms waving gently on tall stems.

'What is that stuff?' Connie asked, leaning her forearms on top of the gate.

'It's called tansy. As I recall, it has uses in cooking and home remedies. I dare say whoever owns this field considers it just a weed.'

'It's lovely. I wish we could go in.'

'Well, who's to know if we do?'

'Some farmer with a shotgun or a dog, perhaps.'

'Ah, there's nobody about, and what harm can we do?' Winking at her, he added: 'There's a perfume to tansy, you know. Lovely aromatic leaves, it has, especially when they're crushed. See how tall it is, three feet high. We could lie down in it, no one would know we were there.'

Connie smiled, her chin resting on the back of her hand as she gazed over the gate. All was perfectly quiet, save for the swish of the wind. The tansy flowers danced in the breeze, nodding as if in agreement with Charlie's suggestion.

Why not? she wondered. She trusted him and she adored him so.

The field stretched away a long distance before her,

disappearing gently downhill. What a bountiful day. A little love, a little snooze, a cream tea . . .

Yes, why not?

She took his hand and together they climbed over the gate, walked half a mile and disappeared down in the tansy.

Twelve

They planned to be married by Christmas. They even found a basement flat to rent at a modest cost. The owner said he would hold it for them, on payment of a retainer fee. The flat was small and the bedroom somewhat dark, but Connie looked around it with delighted eyes which picked out all its possibilities. It was dingy now, but that was easily cured. They would paint the walls white throughout. They would put down pretty coloured rugs and have lots of lamps. A bit of effort and imagination was all it needed.

Sitting room, bedroom, galley kitchen, lavatory outside in a tiny patch of garden – that was the extent of it. Still, as Charlie said, it was only a start. Throughout September they busied themselves with plaster, repairing flaky, crumbly surfaces and sanding them smooth, covering brown-stained walls with coats of whitewash. They took up sticky, broken lino and threw it out. The empty rooms echoed to their voices and smelt pungently of paint, turpentine, putty. They went home with it on their old clothes and in their hair, and the flat grew lighter, brighter, week by week.

Moving in by Christmas. When Connie looked around the bare rooms, she saw a fire dancing in the sitting-room grate, pictures on the walls, a sofa, a gramophone playing carols, a sideboard laden with nuts and dates and oranges and port. She smelt the aroma of roasting goose from the kitchen, heard the bubbling of saucepans on the stove. She knew where the tree would stand and where she would put the holly. Here she would be able to enjoy the Christmas decorations. A new place, her own place, free of bad memories.

'Of course, it'll only do for a year or two,' Charlie had said, 'Once the babies start arriving, we'll have to move on.'

He was right, she supposed, but she doubted that any future home, no matter how nice, would hold the same magic for her. A first home, like a first love, was a special, memorable thing.

Connie never thought of her forthcoming marriage as an escape route, more of a reward. She was in a frame of mind to believe in happy endings, ultimate justice. She had been a very good girl, as Ada demanded. She had paid her dues and was now released with all forgiven. Connie had never felt so loved, so much at peace, so safe.

October came and the weather began to turn cold. It had been a very settled summer, but the autumn was to be unpredictable, swift changes occurring in hours.

Charlie Nicholls, being no professional fisherman, was not especially sensitive to the moods of the weather, nor was he well-versed in spotting its warning signs. Charlie was one who pottered about in calm waters, staying close to the shore. He always said he knew his limitations; certainly he would not dream of taking the boat out in winter. As soon as the dark evenings set in, he left off fishing until the following spring.

One Sunday late in the month he set off on a last trip for the year. He had been to lunch at the Sayers' house and at three o'clock he went out for a couple of hours on the water. The day was dull, but calm enough. He had missed the weather forecast on the wireless – but then, he wasn't going very far. Connie was expecting him back for tea around half past five.

There was almost no one around as he boarded the little boat. Shops and pubs were closed, fishermen were superstitious and kept the Sabbath. An elderly man out walking his dog noticed Charlie going down the steps with his fishing gear, but thought nothing of it.

Charlie squatted down to start the motor. The engine puttered and then sustained at a steady buzz. He loosed the mooring rope and headed out into the Sound. He would stay on the landward side of Drake's Island, of course. Charlie certainly never ventured beyond the breakwater, which rendered the Sound such a peaceful haven.

About half a mile out, he turned off the engine, took up his fishing rod and baited the hook with an angle-worm. Casting his line, he settled back. Two weeks before, he had landed a fair-sized bass just here and hoped to do the same again.

Time went by and nothing happened. He reeled in his line and cast it again. It was ten to four.

Half an hour later, Charlie had still had no luck and the afternoon was becoming very chilly. The boat was rocking somewhat, and on looking around him he saw that the flags and pennants of other vessels were shivering at the mastheads, pulled out straight by a very stiff breeze. Charlie huddled in his jacket and thought he might call it a day. No pleasure in this, and he sensed there was not even going to be a catch. He had drifted a bit, as well. Off to his right, Drake's Island lay some way behind him now. Slowly but surely he was moving out towards the breakwater. It was still a fair distance ahead, but he could clearly see the lighthouse, the beacon, and the hump of paving in between.

Too far out for comfort, Charlie decided. Back at Connie's place were tea and a warm fire. Winding in his line, laying his fishing tackle in the bottom of the boat, he pulled the cord to start the motor.

Nothing happened.

Well, it often took several tries. He made another attempt.

The engine coughed, droned, died.

Again he pulled the cord, and again, with the same result.

That was when he thought about fuel, recalling that he had not checked to see there was enough. Charlie's heart turned over. He scrabbled for the little locker in the bow, peered and reached inside. No spare can, nothing but a rope and a first-aid box. No flares, either, nothing to attract attention, and he was now a considerable way from any other boat.

Unsteadily, Charlie stood up, shouted and waved his arms in hopes of being seen. The movement caused the little craft to sway alarmingly. He nearly lost his balance and toppled out. It would not take much, he realised, to overturn a boat like this.

Charlie sat down, frightened now. He could swim, all right, but not as far as the shore. It was all of a mile and a half away, the water was very cold and he had eaten a big lunch, none of which was encouraging. The breakwater was now a lot nearer than the land and he toyed with the idea of trying to make it that far. It was a very large structure – people had picnics on the breakwater in summer. In fine weather he could simply have waited there until someone picked him up.

125

However, behind the breakwater now was an ominous darkness. Coming up from the south-west were storm-clouds like vast puffs of charcoal velvet. The wind was rising and the boat had begun to toss. Nasty squalls arriving late afternoon, the wireless had warned, but Charlie, of course, had missed the broadcast.

He tried to paddle the boat with his hands and get into Cawsand, but the wind was against him and he soon gave up, exhausted. As the first spattering of rain fell, he lay down in the bottom of the boat. The wind, in any case, was such that he could no longer sit up against it. Screaming, it forced him down flat. The boat was bouncing madly now, bobbing around like a little red toy in a wilderness of heaving grey.

He knew he was probably finished. Just three hours before, all life had lain before him. Connie, the flat, his business, children . . . Three hours before, he had sat at the table eating roast beef, treacle pudding and custard. Three hours before, he had been pondering whether to make a short fishing trip, could still have made the choice which meant life and stayed in with Connie instead. In despair he screwed his eyes shut and wept at the cruelty of what was happening.

Soaked and numb with the cold, he was already half unconscious when the boat turned over.

Connie was stupefied by shock for nearly a fortnight. The suddenness and brutality of it stunned her, so that she did not cry a lot at first, but was simply dazed, unable to take it in. All her practicality deserted her. She just sat around, white and bewildered, while Janine took in hand the formalities and arrangements. Connie went through the funeral service like a sleepwalker, seeming remote from what was going on. She was insulated by a feeling of unreality, but dimly aware as well that an ocean of pain was waiting beyond that protective barrier, ready to rush in upon her.

It finally broke over her when she went back to the flat. Connie still had a set of keys and felt she ought to return them. She took them around to the landlord one day and he told her how sorry he was. She was walking away when he called her back and asked if she wanted to take Charlie's tool box.

Oh yes, his tool kit. Connie went down to the basement to pick it up. The agony struck her as soon as she stepped inside. All her defences dropped away and now she felt the magnitude of her loss. Things were exactly the way they had left them the last time they worked there together. On the kitchen window sill, a ball of putty still showed Charlie's thumb-print. In a jam jar full of turpentine stood the brush he had been using the day before he died. There lay an overall on the floor where he had thrown it. There was the dried blob of paint he had dropped on the draining board.

Everything had come to a full stop, here, like this. In the time elapsed since they walked away from this scene, a whole future had been destroyed.

As Connie went slowly from room to room, the dam gave way at last and grief flowed free. The naked walls and stone floor gave back a hollow echo of terrible sobbing.

Thirteen

As if Charlie's death and the loss of a bright future were not strain enough, there was more to follow. He had been buried just six weeks when Connie realised she might be pregnant. The suspicion would have grown before, had she not been too distraught to notice a missed period or two. The nausea she felt on waking seemed more to do with misery than anything else, for as soon as she opened her eyes in the morning a ton-weight of depression fell upon her. Her heart thumped, her mind felt sick at the prospect of another day, and her stomach merely seemed to agree. Then finally, one morning as she bent, retching, over the lavatory pan, the penny dropped.

Connie made an appointment to see the family doctor that afternoon. Within three days she had confirmation.

Due in late spring, the doctor said. The middle of May. A little man with crinkly, greying hair, he studied her with sympathy over the top of his spectacles.

'How do you feel about it, Connie? I'm aware of your circumstances, of course, and very sorry for your bereavement, but how do you view this development? It will bring difficulties, of course, but is it entirely unwelcome?'

She stared at him dumbly, head reeling. Pregnant. Unmarried. The old, old disaster. She was 'in trouble'.

The doctor was still talking, asking if her family

would stand by her. Connie couldn't answer. No such thing had ever occurred in the Sayers family before. Mam, she thought, would have hit the roof, had she been alive and well. But Jamie? Connie could not imagine how he would react.

'Perhaps, if it's going to be too unpleasant, you could go away somewhere and have the baby. Is that a possibility?' the doctor asked.

She looked confused. 'What good would that do? Everyone would know when I brought the child home.'

'I was thinking about adoption, actually. There is always that choice, but is that what you want, Connie? You loved the young man, didn't you? He's left you something of himself, my dear.'

He was smiling, his brown eyes persuasive, and something seemed to open up within her, as if the cramps and knots of grief were loosening.

Charlie's child. Hers and Charlie's. Something could be salvaged after all.

'Of course,' the doctor went on more soberly, 'it won't be easy, even if your family offers support. People can be priggish, vulgar and vicious about such matters. One cannot be a doctor for thirty-eight years without seeing almost every facet of human nature. I've encountered the noblest and the nastiest sides of people, and situations like yours are apt to bring out the worst in many cases, I'm afraid. You'll have to contend with coarseness and stupid prejudice, Connie. If you decide to keep the child, you'll have to be brave and face them down. Can you do that? I'll understand if you say no. A good home could certainly be found for the baby if you would prefer it that way.'

Give it away? Her flesh and blood, all that remained

of Charlie? Impossible, of course. She looked at the doctor mutely and shook her head.

He took it to signal indecision. 'Well,' he said gently, 'think it over, my dear. I'd advise you to tell your brother straight away. If he's worth his salt, he'll take care of you.'

Whatever James might do or say, she was going to keep the child. If he threw her out, Connie would find some way to make a living. She still had the hundred pounds her mother had left her. She might secure a live-in job somewhere – housekeeper, for instance. She could move far away and call herself 'Mrs Nicholls', as she had, in truth, so very nearly been. In Connie's mind, she was Charlie's widow, wedding ring or no.

Still, it was a daunting prospect, packing up and heading off God knew where. Despite what the doctor said, the neighbours were at least the devil she knew. Connie hoped Jamie would rally to her side.

She told him next morning at breakfast. He was tinkering with his kipper, nibbling bits and piling up skin on the edge of his plate, when she tensely announced it.

'Bloody hell!' was all he said at first. He seemed, more than anything, to be amazed that such a thing could befall his sister, as if there were no sexual aspect to her at all. He was hard put, as well, to imagine Connie breaking any rule of conduct. Connie, such a good girl. Laying down his knife and fork, he surveyed her, top to toe, as if he had never seen her properly before.

Connie stood nervously, frying pan in hand, wondering how to interpret 'Bloody hell'. Her glance flicked across to her sister-in-law at the other side of the table.

Janine pulled her top lip down as if to suppress a smile. 'Oh dear,' she said delicately and went on with her breakfast.

'Well,' said James awkwardly, 'when's it due?'

'In the spring. It won't start to show for a little while yet.'

James blinked at her. 'God,' he said, 'what a pickle.'

'Yes, well . . .' Connie sat down, still clutching the frying pan. '. . . I don't want to be an embarrassment to you, of course. Naturally, there's going to be a lot of talk and if you feel that my – situation – will reflect badly on you or make you at all uncomfortable, there's a simple remedy for it.'

Janine cut down the length of her fish and deftly whipped the backbone out. 'What's that?'

'I'll go away.'

'Oh, don't be so damned silly,' said her brother.

'Well, I'm aware that some mud will be slung and it's hard that you should get spattered . . .'

'If anyone says a word out of place to me, they'll regret it,' sniffed Janine.

James took up his cutlery again. 'Quite right. It's no one else's business.'

Connie looked from one to the other. 'So – I'm to stay? I'm keeping the baby, you know.'

'House is big enough,' shrugged James.

'You're not shocked at me, either of you?'

'You only did what we do all the time,' observed Janine.

Now James did look shocked, but at his wife. A morsel of kipper went the wrong way and he coughed.

'People think it's different somehow if a registrar or some old fool of a vicar mumbles a few words over you,' continued Janine. 'Irrational, isn't it? Mind you, for a lot of women, being married and "respectable" is their biggest achievement in life and they like to polish the trophy by sneering at others who "give it away" instead of holding out for the standard price.'

Again, her husband looked disturbed. He had always regarded marriage as something hallowed.

'Well, Connie was near enough to being wed,' he said. 'She just – jumped the gun a little.' Turning to his sister, he added: 'Anyway, there's no question of you leaving us. The neighbours can jabber all they want. It won't hurt our trade, I'm sure of that. I can't think of anyone round here who'd be outraged enough to traipse up to town for their bread, just because you're . . .'

Frowning, he waved his fork, indicating her belly.

'In the pudding club,' supplied Janine merrily.

Connie laughed as well, 'Thank you,' she sighed, 'thank you both. I didn't really want to go away.'

'I'd be a very poor brother if I let you,' said James. 'You've been through enough.'

'Nevertheless, I'm grateful,' Connie said, and felt that all her faith in him was fully justified.

'You have to feel sorry for her, don't you, even though she's misbehaved?' said Millie Chope.

'Connie, of all people,' whispered Mrs Paul. 'I'd never have thought her capable of – that.'

'Oh, I would,' sniffed Cynthia Hardin. 'Not because she's a bad lot, but because she's the generous sort. Typical of Connie to get herself caught, being so soft.'

It was April now. They were all in the dairy. Connie had just been in for cream and eggs. She was heavily pregnant by this time, with a fine great bulge in her dress that tipped her slightly backwards as she walked. It was too big to overlook, and yet the three neighbours studiously ignored it, chattering too brightly with her of other things. As soon as she had gone, of course, they began to discuss her 'plight'.

'Makes everything so much worse for her,' was Millie Chope's opinion. 'Bad enough to lose her young man, but having a by-blow means she's lost her good name too. She'll have a hard job to find a husband now. Nobody wants soiled goods, let alone someone else's kid to bring up.'

'It's courageous of her to keep it,' ventured Mrs Paul.

'I always said she had no sense of self-preservation,' chipped in Cynthia. 'He was a nice young man, mind you. I was very pleased for her when she was going with him, and it's tragic what happened. Still, men are men and she should have kept him at bay until the proper time.'

'Which wouldn't have come; he was killed,' pointed out Mrs Paul.

'Granted. Even so, she'd be better off than she is now if she'd kept her hand on her halfpenny. I never let my husband touch me before the wedding night. I've always upheld strict standards. Nobody would ever catch me bending.' Cynthia pursed her mouth primly over her bunny rabbit teeth and her spectacles glittered.

'I couldn't go out like that,' said Millie Chope. 'Being so huge and unmarried and everyone knowing. I was shame-faced enough when I was carrying my brood, even with a ring on my finger for all to see. People didn't snigger in my face the way some of them do with Connie. And I didn't have men making coarse suggestions to me in the street, either. They knew they'd have Jack to contend with. He was handy with his fists when he was young.'

Cynthia tittered. 'I don't think Jamie would be much use in a fight.'

'I don't suppose Connie even tells him,' sighed Mrs Paul. 'Poor soul, I've seen the louts nudging each other when she goes past the pub. I don't know how she stands it, that's the truth.'

She stood it because she had little choice, and no regard for people who treated her so. They were base and therefore unimportant. She stood it because it was Charlie's child and because, after all, there were many among her neighbours who behaved more kindly. Mrs Paul gave her all the knitting wool she wanted, charging nothing. Buttons and ribbons and patterns, too. Mrs Paul never told Millie or Cynthia, though, in case they thought she was condoning immorality. And for every oaf who made a lewd remark to Connie, some decent sort would tip his cap or hold a door or carry her shopping for her. The best came out in even Janine, who took over the heavier household work, albeit in a sloppy fashion. For the first time in his life, James received a taste of inferior housekeeping and realised just what a boon his sister was. He looked forward to the time when Connie was able to carry on again. He would have missed her, he thought, if she had gone away, and so would Janine. It was a good arrangement, really, Connie remaining there. It was – convenient.

The baby, a daughter, was born on 16 May 1923 at ten past one in the afternoon. James and Janine were of no help whatever in this. He went out and stayed out, making the bread delivery last until after two o'clock, horrified by the business of labour going on at home. His wife pleaded ignorance and helplessness, considering childbirth grotesque. It was Nell Colenso who stayed with Connie through the last six sweating, straining hours until the doctor came.

Afterwards, when the gore was cleaned up and the baby was washed and pinkly presentable, James and Janine went in to see mother and child. Nell passed them on the stairs with a faint sneer which escaped Jamie's notice but not Janine's.

Connie was sitting propped up with the child in her arms, a picture of motherhood very pleasing to James. He thought of Ada holding him like that and his throat grew tight. He imagined Janine clasping his first offspring and felt very broody. Sentimental James liked babies, when quietly smiling or cooing or gurgling. The mess they made was no concern of his, of course, and women did not mind such things, he fondly believed. He had never actually asked Janine how she felt about it.

Janine remarked that the infant was large and looked very healthy. She congratulated Connie, but was hardly in raptures over becoming an aunt herself. Babies simply failed to excite or even interest Janine.

'She resembles Charlie,' she observed. 'Look at the nose and mouth – they're his exactly.'

'Yes,' Connie said, smiling down at the child, 'I saw that as soon as the doctor gave her to me. I hope she won't change as she grows. They sometimes do, but I want her to look like him.'

'Well, then? What are you going to call her?'

'Tansy.'

James looked up at his sister. 'Curious name.'

'I just like it,' Connie said. She had no desire to explain the reason, let her brother in on a private, treasured memory, but she calculated that the child had probably been conceived on the day when she and Charlie went up the river to Calstock. Conceived in that field of tansy flowers.

'I'll buy her a cot and pram,' said James. Glancing to his wife, he grinned. 'They'll come in handy for ours when they start arriving.'

Janine produced a smile but made no comment.

'You don't have to do that, Jamie,' Connie said. 'I still have the money Mam left me.'

'That'll soon go,' sniffed Janine. 'The needs of children are endless. You let Jamie help where he can.'

'You're both so kind to me. You will be Godparents, won't you?'

'Jamie will. I'm a backslider, remember?' laughed Janine.

'The doctor says I'll be able to start doing a bit around the house in about a week,' Connie said. 'I can't work properly until the stitches come out.'

'Take it easy while you can,' Janine told her. 'God knows, you never slow down unless you're forced to, so make the best of it.'

She was right – within a fortnight, Connie was back in harness, now with the added burden of the child. At last she was obliged to drop a few of the inessential chores she had set herself, not only because she could no longer fit them in, but also because she was exhausted by broken nights. A peculiar, guilty happiness lay upon her, a weary giving up of control because the infant allowed her neither the time or energy for meticulous cleaning. She could not dust because the baby had to be fed, could not polish because the baby constantly needed changing, or sweep because Tansy was crying and had to be cuddled. Connie looked around her at what she considered household chaos and found she was not too upset. When rocking or crooning to her daughter, she was too content to care about much else. By any other woman's standards, the neglect was mild, in any case, and when people saw Connie out and about she never looked a slattern as some young mothers did. So high had her standards always been that she could drop them quite a lot without becoming slovenly.

When first she took the baby out, most people reacted kindly. A child was a child, and Tansy was a very beautiful one, attracting many smiles and admiring comments. There were, however, a handful of women who turned their noses up at Connie Sayers's 'bastard', crossing the street to avoid her, or making spiteful comments to each other for her to hear. Most of the time she ignored it, but occasionally it got her down. When she was pregnant, the sneers had been aimed at her and she could take that. Now they were often directed at the child, which was harder to bear.

One day she came home in tears after such an encounter. Janine's response was typically shrewd and crisp.

'Oh,' she said, 'that one. I know her. Five kids of her own and all of them grubby and foul-mannered. And what's she like? Looks as if she's been pulled through a hedge. Can't you see it, Connie? She's jealous. You always look nice and tidy, and there's the baby with good lacy clothes and a pretty quilt. The woman resents it because she's a mess and so are her horrible family. So she calls Tansy a little bastard. What other way does she have to get at you? Laugh it off, Connie, and make sure the baby always looks lovely when you go out. Rub their noses in it – that's what I'd do.'

At times like that, Connie really admired Janine and wished to be more like her.

Fourteen

Janine was restless. It was late, past midnight, but she was alert and her mind was busy. She lay in the crook of her snoozing husband's arm and thought about changes. She had laid a clutch of ideas in her head and brooded on them for nearly three years. Now she felt the time had come for them to hatch. It was November of 1923; she was twenty-five and unwilling to wait any longer.

James had gone to sleep and left the lamp still burning. His wife gazed up at the corner where the ceiling met the wall and a frill-shaped brown stain announced a patch of damp. She fidgeted, tugging at the bedclothes James had pulled off her. He never spoke of big plans any more; he just drifted on from day to day and would continue to do so if she were fool enough to stand for it, if she took no action. It was time to turn the crank and get him moving.

Janine had seen an advertisement in the local paper that morning. She had been thinking about it all day, feeling it held exciting possibilities. There was a shop for sale in a prime position in the city centre.

She glanced at her husband, then slyly prodded him with a finger in the ribs.

'Uh?' slurred James.

Janine slipped a hand inside his pyjama jacket, stroking his chest. 'Jamie,' she whispered, 'I've been thinking . . .'

'What?' He blinked at her, dopey with sleep.

'I've been mulling over your ideas for branching out.'

'Oh, Janine, not now.' He made to roll over, away from her, but the hand on his chest gave a strong, restraining press and the fingernails dented the flesh with little crescents.

'No, Jamie, please listen a minute. I've something special to tell you.'

'Do you recall that we talked about having a tea-room? Well, I read today of a place that's vacant in George Street – used to be a tailor's shop. I thought at once that they would be ideal premises for us.'

As he turned towards her, his scar was buried in the pillow. His tongue passed uneasily over his upper lip.

'Oh, look Janine, it's no use to think of new ventures at present.'

'Why?'

He sought refuge in theory. 'It's not a good time for expansion, that's all. The financial pages aren't a bit encouraging. We'd be wise to wait until the outlook's healthier.'

'Oh, twaddle! I don't believe in consulting oracles and experts. I prefer to follow my instincts and they clearly tell me we ought to look into this opportunity. We're young, James, and there's so much we can do! If we don't strike out, we'll just spend fifty years or so in this awful old place, this narrow little routine, and I'm sure you're capable of much more.'

'This awful old place? It's not a slum, Janine.'

'I'm not saying it is, but surely you don't intend to settle for so little?'

'Aren't you happy here?'

'I shan't be if I'm stuck here indefinitely, and the trouble with putting things off is that it becomes a habit, and sooner or later everything begins to seem like too much effort – or else you grow timid and start to see nothing but hurdles and dangers.'

An echo of Mr Jordan's warning sounded in his mind. 'Don't let her push you, stay in charge . . .'

Easier said than done, now he was alone with her. So hard to refuse his darling anything, his adored Janine. Her eyes were black and brilliant in the lamplight, as if she had bathed them in belladonna: intelligent eyes with a powerful will behind them. Far more powerful than his own. When he looked in those eyes he couldn't think straight. Not a single cogent argument came to his aid.

'Let's be brave,' she said urgently. 'Whatever happened to all the vision you had when we were courting?'

Be brave. Prove yourself. Put your flights of fancy to the test, put them into practice. That was what she demanded now. She would think very poorly of him if he refused. Yet, face to face with the challenge, he realised just how little ambition he truly had, how modest were his wants. He would have been satisfied to paddle through life in the shallows, but she was determined to take him into deeper water.

'James, I've thought out all the details. We can raise the money, we can make it a huge success. The right atmosphere – that's half the battle with a café, and I'm sure I can create an air that'll bring them flocking in. If we dally, we'll lose the chance of that place. It's a choice location and sure to be snapped up quickly. We could at least go and look at it, James. When you see the possibilities, you'll be as keen as I am.'

Again, he heard Mr Jordan say: 'I believe she's more forceful than you.'

Would she respect him for making a stand – or think

him a coward, a stick-in-the-mud, a mere day-dreamer? She was the greatest prize in his life. He had to have her esteem, he had to please her.

He sighed. 'We'll talk about it in the morning.'

Janine snuggled down beside him, sensing she had won the first round.

They went to see the tailor's premises the following afternoon. Janine was more than ever convinced that it was perfect. The tap-tap of her heels echoed loudly in the big empty shop as she walked around, noting everything with calculating eyes.

'I like the wood panelling, don't you? That could stay. This dreadful linoleum would have to go, though. The floorboards underneath are very good, we could have them varnished. The plaster above the panelling needs to be smoothed off and painted, and those old ceiling lights could be replaced with nice modern wall fittings.'

James nodded, though in truth he could not imagine this staid and sombre gentlemen's outfitters being transformed into the pretty tea-room Janine desired. The place had a fusty smell about it, a peculiar odour suggestive of old age and camphor liniment, as if customers and staff alike had all been creaky, doddering.

Janine went across to the door at the back of the shop and opened it. The room behind had just one little window. There was bare brickwork with shelving running along three walls. Against the fourth was a small sink with a cold tap. Beside this and jutting half the length of the room was a large wooden table.

'This will need some work before it'll serve as a kitchen,' she said. 'But that's all right. It's not as if the baking will be done here. This will be used just for storage, making the tea and coffee and washing up. We'll have it whitewashed and get a swing-door fitted.'

'Will,' she was saying now, forgetting in her enthusiasm that James had the decision.

'No electric sockets,' he observed.

'I'll have some put in.'

'No lavatory, either.'

She consulted the property agent's particulars. 'Yes, there is, on the first-floor landing. The flat above is up another flight of stairs and has its own.' She clapped her hands, delighted. 'Oh, sweetheart, didn't I tell you it was ideal?'

How he loved it when she called him that. Indulgently he smiled and wondered if he might indeed be a bit too cautious. Glancing round the shop, he tried to estimate capacity.

'How many customers would you propose to fit in here?'

'Forty or so,' said Janine. 'A lot will depend on the size of the tables we buy. Then we have to leave decent gangways, room to wheel the trolleys back and forth easily. It's better to omit a few tables, I think, than annoy people by cramping them together. I know places where they pack them in so tightly that it really is a horrid squeeze and no pleasure at all.'

There was pensive silence as James surveyed the shop once more. He ran a hand thoughtfully over the mahogany top of an old glass-fronted counter.

'This could be put to use, I suppose,' he mused. 'Moved across to the window and filled with a display of cakes.'

Ah, he was interested at last. She jumped in quickly with questions. He liked to be asked for advice.

'Jamie, that's a good idea! And where do you think

143

the band should be? What about that corner over there?'

'Yes, possibly.'

'I can just picture it,' purred Janine. 'Couples swaying cheek to cheek.' She hugged him. 'Oh sweetheart, this place is a plum. All we have to do is pick it and make our jam. We're not going to let it slip through our fingers, are we? You have to spend money to make money. Every businessman knows that.'

One last hesitation and James capitulated. 'I'll make an appointment to see the bank manager. If he thinks the plan is sound, we'll give it a try.'

Janine rewarded him with a passionate kiss. 'I'll come with you,' she said dreamily, straightening his tie.

'There's no need.'

She tightened the knot a little and patted his chest. 'But I want to, my dearest.'

Because I'm a better talker than you, she added inwardly.

'All right, as you please.'

She looked towards the window, then up at him, her face glowing. 'We'll have the name painted on the glass – "Sayers Tea and Coffee House". An arch of gold lettering! What do you think?'

'Too long-winded,' differed James. 'An arch of gold lettering, yes, but I think it should simply say "Janine's".'

Her mouth popped open. 'Oh – but Jamie . . .'

'It's going to be your café. Anyway, it has a good ring to it. I can just hear people saying: 'I'll meet you at "Janine's" '.

She beamed at him. 'It is a bit more romantic than "Sayers Tea and Coffee House", I must admit. It has overtones of – well – an assignation.'

They returned to the front of the shop and stood at the window for a few minutes. Such a busy street. So much traffic, so many people with money jingling in their pockets. Lots and lots of money.

Janine pointed to the corner by the door. 'That's where we'll have the till,' she said.

The bank manager was more impressed with Mrs Sayers than with her husband. That air of certainty, that zest – he quickly perceived that she was the driving force. Very sharp, he thought, very go-ahead.

Still, it was the young man who was going to finance it all. The manager beamed at James across what seemed an acre of desk. He liked the sound of the scheme proposed.

'It seems a good idea, Mr Sayers. Where did you say these premises were?'

'George Street. It was a tailor's shop for many years.'

'Ah, yes, yes.' The manager's voice was very soft and very thoughtful. 'I know the place. Quite spacious, with a nice frontage.'

'That's what we feel. It'll be very handy for people who've been shopping and need somewhere pleasant to go and ease their aching feet. There's no other tea-room at that end of town.'

'Hmm. You're in the bakery business, so you have a certain amount of relevant experience.' The manager considered, tapping his fingers against his lower lip. 'Do you propose to buy or rent these premises?'

'They're for sale, leasehold – ninety-nine years.'

'Hmm, hmm.' A reflective nod. 'Of course, you'll also need a lot in the way of furnishings and equipment. What about staff?'

'My wife is going to run it by herself – although, of

course, we'll have to hire musicians. Janine has tremendous flair, you know. She's made some excellent suggestions about décor and atmosphere. Smart but friendly, that's the sort of place we want.'

Janine, in fact, had wanted to hire a waitress to do the serving, but James had made a stand on that. She would have to do it herself, at least until the volume of trade proved a need for more staff.

'I see. Well . . .' Elbows on desk, fingers steepled, still smiling. '. . . how much do you wish to borrow?'

'Six hundred and fifty pounds. The place needs a lot of work, you see.'

Another nod, but now the merest hint of a frown as well. 'That's a large sum. You must be very confident of success, Mr Sayers. If I may say so, you are rather young.'

'I have time and I have energy, and the full support of my wife.'

He took Janine's hand and pressed it. Both of them smiled at the manager. Janine was wearing her mushroom hat, a neat mauve suit and pearls. The manager thought her captivating.

'Indeed,' he said. 'Indeed. You do, of course, own some property already. And you have no other debts, you say?'

'Not one.'

The bank manager was wreathed in smiles. 'Well, Mr Sayers, we exist to lend money and I can tell you now that my instinct is to back you. I would like, before making a firm promise, to inspect the bakery's books of account and I shall require a valuation on your property to obtain an overall view of your financial condition and past performance.'

'Of course.'

146

'But as long as these things prove satisfactory, I'm sure that we can come to an arrangement.'

Fifteen

Everything went forward quickly after that. Loan agreement and purchase contract were signed and completed, and renovation began in January of 1924. Janine was at the shop each day to supervise, chivvying the workmen when they dawdled and pulling them up on carelessness wherever she spotted it. James was far too lax, too soft in that respect. If he noticed poor craftsmanship at all, he was weak in pointing it out, almost apologetic in his complaints. Janine knew how to deal with shirking tradesmen. They never dared try to hoodwink her in any way. Since the Sayers were paying for the best materials, she made sure they got them. Protracted tea-breaks drew sarcastic comments and those of the men who were apt to loaf declared her a tartar. The fast and efficient, by contrast, found her charming.

Week by week, the old tailor's shop could be seen acquiring a new personality and Janine looked ahead with excitement to the opening day planned for early spring. Everything, on the whole, was going like clockwork and she foresaw no hindrances in her path.

Then nature chose to remind her that she was a woman just as fertile as the next. In the middle of February, she learned that she was pregnant.

She was not in the best of temper when she came home from the doctor's that day. Slamming the front door behind her, Janine hustled into the sitting room, flinging her handbag, hat and coat across the sofa. For several minutes she paced the rug in front of the hearth. Her hands were balled into fists and she curled and uncurled them in frustration. After a while, she stopped and leaned with an elbow on the mantel, combing her fingers roughly through her hair. Finally, she went to the sofa, sat down and fumbled in her bag for a cigarette. Shakily, she lit it and pulled in deeply. She smoked it half-way down, then irritably stubbed it out.

'Blast it!' she muttered. 'Damn! Oh, damn!'

Pregnant, now, when she wanted it least. Pregnant, with all the constraints that implied. After two and half years of marriage with no sign of offspring, Janine had been lulled into thinking there simply might not be any children for her and James. Therefore she had made no provision for them in her plans. She needed freedom to run her new business. She had assumed she would have it.

Babies. She had never been able to understand what people saw in them. Since Tansy arrived the house had been filled with a distinctive, sweetish scent for which Janine did not care. There was that and the smell of nappies, and the bouts of crying at night. Connie said Tansy was a good baby, not much trouble at all. Janine hardly dared imagine how a 'difficult' baby would be.

If only this had happened later, after she had made some money. Having children was no great bother if one had money – enough, anyway, to afford a nanny. Janine could vaguely imagine herself kissing goodnight a child or two already fed and bathed and put to bed by someone else. She could not, however, welcome the vision of herself distraught and exhausted, mopping up vomit or emptying potties or shovelling some revolting purée into a bawling infant.

One of the worst things about babies and small children was the fact that one could never get away from them. There was no escape from their helplessness. Toddlers, in particular, appalled Janine by their very liveliness. Constant questions and demands, hands in everything. She knew the endless vigilance needed to keep them out of trouble. She knew the voracious need for 'Mummy', for Mummy's whole attention and all of her time. What happened to Mummy? She lost herself, Janine thought, panic-stricken. Her own personality, her adult interests, all would be overridden, submerged. She, Janine, would disappear. There would only be Mummy left.

Needless to say, her husband was going to be delighted at the news. James had frequently muttered with furrowed brow that there should have been children by now. He was bound to be thrilled when she announced this. Janine only wished she could feel the same. It was not that she hated children or anything like that. It was simply that they bored her and the sacrifice required to raise them had always seemed far too great.

Janine felt a prickling in her nose which signalled tears. Pulling a handkerchief from her pocket, she blew fiercely.

'Got a cold coming?' enquired a voice from the doorway.

Janine looked over the crumpled ball of linen in her hand and there stood Connie. She was holding Tansy, jigging her gently. A soft mewing and gurgling came from the blanket-wrapped bundle.

Janine forced a smile. 'It's just the snuffles.'

'Shall I make you a drop of hot grog?'

'No. Thank you, but I'm all right.'

So content, old Connie, Janine thought, eyeing her curiously. Just look at her standing there with that baby, wanting nothing else. She's happy whenever she holds that child, whenever she's even in the same room. Am I lacking something, missing something, feeling as I do? Will there be some magic change in me when mine is born?

Again, at that, she felt afraid. To lose control and be altered, even if the result was a happy state . . .

'You do look pale – and troubled,' Connie said. 'Is anything wrong?'

She came into the room and sat down beside Janine. The child's face peeped out of the blanket, blowing bubbles and smiling. Janine stared at it so worriedly that Connie asked again.

'Has something happened, Janine? Something bad?'

The gut reaction was to answer yes, but that would be unwise. Janine produced another shaky smile. 'Something unexpected, that's all. I've been to the doctor, Connie. I'm three months pregnant.'

'Oh! My dear! Congratulations! Aren't you pleased?'

'Yes,' lied Janine, 'naturally I am – but for Jamie more than for me.' She regarded Connie pensively and decided she could safely confide. 'It's going to make things difficult for me, as a matter of fact. Because of the café, you see.'

'Oh – yes, of course.'

'I was going to run it myself.'

'I doubt you'll want to when the baby's born.'

'I will, Connie. I'm not like you. This is very inconvenient for me.'

Connie's blue eyes regarded her with puzzlement rather than condemnation. She always accepted the differences in other people, even when at a loss to understand them.

'I suppose that sounds awful, but we've already spent so much on the tea-room and I was so excited about it.'

Connie laid a hand on her arm. 'Look, I dare say I can help if necessary. I can just as easily care for two babies as one if you're out during the day. I'm willing to bet, though, you'll feel quite differently when the time comes.'

You'll lose your money, then, thought Janine.

'Oh, Connie, would you? I can't tell you what a relief that is.' She gratefully hugged her sister-in-law.

'Assuming, of course, that Jamie won't mind,' said Connie. 'He may not like the idea. He's old-fashioned, you know.'

'He's also in debt for setting up the café. We can't just abandon the project now.'

Thank God, Janine added inwardly. It's a pest to be pregnant at all, but the timing could have been worse. What luck that this didn't happen six months ago.

'Tsk,' said James that night in bed, 'talk about bad timing. If only this had happened a few months earlier, before we went in for the café. Damned awkward now, isn't it?'

'No, not really,' soothed Janine. 'I've told you Connie's going to help. There won't be any great problem.'

'Babies need their mothers,' said James. 'They need to be – you know – breast-fed throughout the day. You're not expecting Connie to do that?'

'No,' Janine said wearily, 'and it isn't essential, you know. There's nothing wrong with a bottle.'

'I'm sure it can't be as good,' grumbled James. 'I've

half a mind to call a halt to this café thing and re-sell the lease, even if we take a loss.'

'Which we certainly would, with all the work half finished. Now Jamie, don't be silly. We're going to make money with that place, I know we are. Imagine what that prosperity will mean for our child. We'll be able to give him or her so much – good schooling, lovely toys and clothes. Hadn't you thought of that?'

No, he had not, and the argument gave him pause.

'Well,' he allowed, 'you do have a point there, I admit.'

'It's not as if I'll never see the child. Here I'll be every evening, every night. Here you and Connie will be all day long. I'd hardly call that neglect.' She cheerfully patted her belly. 'On the whole, I'd call this a very fortunate baby.'

Her husband sighed. 'All right, Janine, as long as you're not taking on too much. You may not find it as easy as you think to face a day in the tea-room after a broken night.'

'Why, Jamie dear, that's where you can help,' she said sweetly. 'I'll expect you to take your turn to get out of bed sometimes when the baby cries.'

His mouth dropped open. He looked amazed. 'Oh,' he said faintly. 'Oh – yes.'

Janine smiled winsomely.

So all was well, the child was not going to stand in her way. As her belly started rounding out, Janine smilingly accepted everyone's congratulations and said she was hoping for a girl. It might be quite fun, she thought, dressing up a little girl. Boys' clothing was so dull.

Spring drew on and the preparations for opening day would soon be complete. It was set for the last week in

April. Janine went down to the café one afternoon in the middle of the month when no workmen were there. The carpet-layers had finished their job the day before and she wanted to inspect the work.

She was pleased, very pleased with everything, on the whole. Above the polished wood panelling, the plaster was now painted a gentle greyish-mauve. Six brass light fittings arched from the walls, bearing shades of violet and green glass. A seventh and larger matching shade adorned the central ceiling pendant. Most of the floor was carpeted now in charcoal grey, leaving only one square area of varnished floor for dancing.

Next week they would take delivery of the chairs and tables. Everything else was in place – cooker, kettles, coffee-makers, trolleys, display counters, till, sideboard . . .

She looked twice at the sideboard, then softly swore to herself. She had thought there was something slightly amiss when she walked in the door. The carpet-layers had put it back in the wrong place. It was meant to go along the back wall beside the kitchen door, but they had left it facing the dais for the musicians.

Tradesmen – they simply were not to be trusted without supervision. Irritably Janine went over to it and tried to tug it away from the wall. It was heavy – mahogany – with bracket feet. Doubly difficult to move because it now stood on thick carpet. Still, it only had to be pushed a matter of three or four yards.

Grasping two end corners, she edged it out from the wall an inch or two. Changing to the other end, she did the same again, then repeated the process three times more, shoving with her hip and thigh.

After a couple of minutes, Janine was panting. Leaning upon the sideboard for a rest, she laid one hand unthinkingly upon her pregnant belly. Her mind was not on the baby at all, only the stubborn bulk of the sideboard and how to move it.

The carpet, that was the trouble. The feet sank down in the pile and so there was drag to contend with. She pushed the sideboard a further eighteen inches, then stopped again. Time to swing it round now, to have it parallel with the back wall. With all her weight and strength, she gave another heave.

The sideboard resisted, budging only slightly.

Oh, to hell with it, thought Janine. She went into the kitchen and made herself a cup of tea, wishing she had not bothered to try and shift the thing herself. She was sticky with sweat and there it now stood in the middle of the room, defiant.

Fool, she thought, settling down to drink her tea. That was the sort of silly thing Connie would do, hauling furniture about. She should have left it for Jamie. He could put it back where it belonged when he called to drive her home later on.

James was appalled to learn what she had done.

'God, Janine – in your condition!' he exclaimed. 'You must be crazy!'

'Oh, humbug. Connie went on working as normal right up to a month before she had Tansy.'

'Yes, well perhaps you're not as tough as she is.'

'Don't fuss, James, I'm all right.'

'This damned café,' he muttered, placing the sideboard where she directed. 'More trouble than it's worth, if you ask me.'

'You won't say that when the money starts rolling in. Now let's go home.'

'You're sure you're feeling all right?'

'Yes, yes,' Janine said testily.

Late that night, however, as she undressed for bed, a dreadful sensation came over her. She suddenly felt hot and weak. There was nausea and an airy, disconnected feeling in her head, then moments of blackout to her vision, like the falling of a thick, dark curtain stippled with golden specks. She was standing at the wardrobe in her slip, hanging up her dress, and as she swayed with giddiness she clutched at the clothes inside. Then there was pain, slicing through her insides as if they were being chopped up. Wave after wave of cramps followed after. Janine sank slowly to her knees, dragging down frocks and skirts off their hangers.

James had gone out to the lavatory, so she tried to call for Connie. All that emerged from her mouth was a wheezing gasp as she was seized by terrible contractions. She knew quite distinctly what was happening, or going to happen soon. Miscarriage. In a minute, an hour, any time, everything would come away. She was five months pregnant, more than half-way to term.

When James came in and found her several minutes later, she was lying half in and half out of the wardrobe, clutching her stomach as if she had been shot. By the time the ambulance came, she was unconscious.

White walls, a chipped enamel bedstead, the sound of brisk female voices, the feel of starched sheets.

Hospital.

Janine's eyes opened wider and she remembered. Her left hand lay on her stomach. She could tell the bulge was gone.

She lay feeling – how? She was not quite sure. Guilty? Yes. Frightened? Yes again. Bereft? Disappointed? Her brain would give no clear response. Neutral on that one, declining to comment.

But she felt guilty, certainly. For being foolhardy, thoughtless, impatient, and thereby cheating Jamie of his child.

Her head was turned to the right on her pillow, looking down the ward. Three other beds, each with an old lady in it. Flowers on bedside cabinets, a nurse and a ward sister talking at the door.

Janine wondered about the sex of the child. At five months, it must have been fairly well developed. She did not recall the actual miscarriage, or even the journey to hospital.

She closed her eyes again and that was when she sensed the presence of someone beside the bed, someone sitting to her left.

Instinct told her who.

What do I say? she thought wretchedly. How does he feel? Is he angry? I wish I didn't have to see him yet. He was so keen, so pleased there was a baby on the way. I could pretend I'm still asleep. Perhaps if I do he'll go away.

She kept her eyes closed but the presence remained, so at last she turned.

James was looking straight at her, his face very strained. Whiter than she had ever seen him. With shock? Or fury? Or both?

'Janine . . .' His voice was very small. 'Oh, thank God you're all right.'

She avoided his eyes. 'I'm sorry,' came the whisper. 'The baby . . .'

'Yes, you've lost the child.' She heard his voice catch. 'And might have died yourself. The doctor said the bleeding was very bad.'

'Do you hate me?' she murmured. 'I wouldn't blame you.'

'Don't be silly. Look, I've brought you some flowers.'

Her gaze drifted to the bedside locker. Primroses and violets.

'They're lovely, Jamie.' She reached for his hand. 'We'll have another one, I promise. I'll be much more careful next time.'

She meant it, too, at that moment, aware of how much he had given her and perceiving a duty to give something back.

But James seemed to flinch at the words. He moistened his lips. 'Janine,' he said slowly, 'the doctor feels it's going to be difficult. He went into explanations for me. I didn't understand much of what he said, but the gist of it was that you're probably the type who miscarries easily, even though you're otherwise healthy. Apparently some women do. He warned me it was questionable whether you could carry a child to full term – especially after this.'

Her face was unreadable. Relief and shame were at war within her. So, it might have happened anyway, it was not entirely her fault. It could occur again and again. She might always be without children. Free, and nature could take the blame. Janine felt a sense of sin for that relief, that gladness . . .

'I feel I've deprived you.'

'Nature's done that.'

'You think it's a coincidence that it happened the same day I did such a stupid thing as to move that sideboard?'

'The doctor says that may have contributed, but only because the baby was not secure in the first place. You said it yourself – Connie went on carrying shopping and doing the laundry right into the eighth month. Some country women are still out digging the fields in their final weeks. You have some sort of internal weakness, my dear, and you can't help that. I suppose your father would call it God's will. We'll have to look at it that way, too.'

She nodded but passed no comment. It had always annoyed her to hear Matthew parroting that. For once she felt quite grateful for the concept.

'Connie will be here to see you tomorrow,' said James. 'Will it upset you if she brings Tansy?'

Janine shook her head. Then a worry was born. Tomorrow. How many of those, how long would she be here?

'Jamie, when can I go home?'

'The doctor wants to keep you in for a couple of weeks to make sure there's no infection and no more bleeding.'

She frowned but said nothing. The café was due to open in less than a fortnight.

'I feel drowsy,' she said.

'All right, I'm going now.' He stood up, bent and kissed her forehead. 'Thank God you're all right,' he whispered again. 'I'm sad about the baby, but you come first, Janine.'

She lay staring at the ceiling, brooding, after James had gone. Why, she wondered bitterly, did she have to feel so wicked for being quietly grateful to escape an unwanted role? Perhaps she was unnatural, perhaps there was something wrong with her soul . . .

'Jamie, I'm so sorry for you both,' said Connie when he went home from the hospital that day. 'I'd been thinking your child would be such nice company for Tansy, too.'

She was sitting by the parlour fire, making a rag doll. Beside her lay a little basket full of cotton-reels, felt needle-cases, scraps of braid and cloth. Her fingers moved swiftly, jabbing stitches through the calico as she sewed yellow woollen tresses onto the doll's head.

Her brother slumped in an armchair, head in hands. 'We may never have any now,' he said miserably. 'God, I wanted children – and women need them, don't they? I don't know what she'll do with herself for the rest of her life without a family.'

Connie tweaked at the doll's curls. Round, vacant eyes made of felt stared up at her and the mouth was a smiling half-moon.

'Well, she'll have the café, Jamie. You know I was going to look after the child for her. She hadn't planned to be at home all day.'

'Oh, the café!' He was scornful. 'That's no substitute for a baby. She'd soon have found that out. I think she'd have lost interest in the whole scheme, once she had a child.'

Connie could not share his certainty about that, remembering that Janine had called child-raising inconvenient.

'That would have been awkward,' she said, 'since you borrowed so much money to get it going.'

'Mmph,' grunted James. 'Bloody place. I never really wanted it, you know.' He raked his fingers through his hair. 'Oh, perhaps you're right. It's a good job she'll have something to occupy her. It can't be just a hobby, though, we can't afford that. It has to show a profit.'

'You know I'll help you out in any way I can.'

James sighed. He looked drawn and his mind was only half on what she was saying. 'I expect Nell and Harry will need a hand,' he said absently. 'They'll have to turn out a few extra cakes, I suppose, when the tea-room opens. I'd rather not employ anyone else until I know how things are going.'

'Oh, of course, I'll pitch in and help with the baking. I can keep Tansy with me while I work.'

Suddenly her brother started blinking, and before he knew it he was crying. 'I was thinking only yesterday about a christening cake and how we'd have a toy soldier on it for a boy, or a ballerina for a baby girl. That was what you had for Tansy, wasn't it?'

Connie hastened across to him, knelt down beside his chair and hugged him, patting his back. 'No,' she said tearfully, 'it was a clown. Poor Jamie. Poor, poor Jamie.'

Sixteen

'Janine's' held its opening day just one week late. Excitement had given her strength to make a fast recovery and she was fit by the time that special Monday morning dawned.

The appointed hour was ten o'clock. At five minutes to, Janine was walking among the tables, inspecting everything. As she passed she straightened a menu card here, smoothed a wrinkled tablecloth there, or tweaked at a prettily folded serviette. The cloths were all white linen with a small square of lilac cotton laid on top. All the tables were round and the corners of the cloths fell down like crocus petals. In the centre of each table stood a small white alabaster vase holding sprigs of maidenhair fern.

Janine looked around her, satisfied. Every little detail spoke of her tastes, including the pencil portraits around the walls. All were caricatures of fat men – Nero, Falstaff, the Prince Regent, Oliver Hardy – gorging themselves on fancy cakes. Janine had commissioned the drawings at no small expense from a local artist, suggesting the subjects and humorous treatment. The result was jolly, witty and said everything about the atmosphere she wished to create.

The smell of coffee filled the air and the trolleys were laden with a host of gorgeous confections foaming with cream and studded with nuts and fruit: peach gateau, chocolate gateau, almond gateau, fresh-cream sponge and ginger cake, meringues, éclairs and coconut slices. In the alcove by the dance floor, flanked by potted palms and aspidistras, three chairs and a piano awaited the musical trio.

She glanced at her watch. Two minutes to ten – time to put some music on. Going to the gramophone, she wound it quickly and placed the needle on a jazz record – 'In the Gloaming of Wyoming' by the Savoy Havana Band. A surge of excitement seemed to burst around her. Like the first bars of an overture to a great show, or so it felt to Janine. As if her life were starting here, to a fanfare of jumping jazz. Unable to contain herself, she capered a few dancing steps. In her black dress, white frilly apron and cap, she looked like a stray from the chorus of a popular revue.

Then, outside the window, framed beneath the golden arch of her name, Janine spotted her first customers. A smart young couple, gazing and pointing at the cakes arrayed to tempt them in.

Again she consulted her watch. Dead on ten.

'Well, here we go,' she whispered.

Moving to the door, she pulled back the bolt and turned the sign around to say 'Open'.

In they came and she took their order for two coffees, one scone, two slices of toast, two portions of chocolate gateau. Her hands were shaking with nerves as she buttered the toast and the scone in the kitchen and filled the coffee pot. Later, she was completely composed as she wheeled the trolley up to the table and cut the wedges of cake, laying them on the plates with a shining silver cake-slice. Sensually dark and moist, encrusted with walnuts, cherries and whipped cream, the gateau brought forth a swooning 'Aah' from the girl and a whistle from her companion.

Janine went off to change the gramophone record and write out their bill.

Several more people had drifted in by the time she bid the couple goodbye and dropped their money into the till. Middle-aged women this time, carrying bags emblazoned 'Pophams' and 'Spooner's Store', followed by a trio of twittering girls in cloches, beads and short silk frocks. Janine took note of the accents and the chatter as she served them. The older ladies were both robust, committee types, the sort who organised church bazaars, while the three younger females were feather-heads with 'Daddies' and 'Mummies' who gave them allowances. They talked about tennis and weekends away with friends, and giggled together about their admirers. They were just the kind Janine wanted – women with money in their pockets and time on their hands. It troubled her not at all when others, in head-scarves and shabby clothes, paused curiously at the window, read the tariff, then shook their heads and moved on. Because this was no cheap tea-shop, this was 'Janine's'. She was offering quality and style, she was going to be known for it, and her patrons would have to be able to pay for the pleasure of eating here. So easy was it to forget that in her single days she, too, would have been discouraged by the prices.

Trade was steady rather than brisk – but then, it was just the first day. It was certainly as much as she could manage by herself to serve and clear and take the money and keep the music going. She promised herself she would not be coping single-handed for long.

By the end of the day she had served forty people and taken a respectable sum. Counting the money, Janine felt satisfied. Before too long the word would spread. Before too long she would be taking five times as much.

Her feet and legs were screaming for mercy, but the ache spelt success, the pain meant money, and she luxuriated in it. How complimentary people had been, and how they had enjoyed themselves. Closed now and silent, the café still conveyed to her a faraway echo of bouncing, romping music. In her mind's eye she could still see the sporty young man in the boater, unable to resist the jazz, who had taken to the dance floor with his girlfriend.

Just the start, Janine thought, pulling off her starched cap. I'm off, I'm up and running. Watch me now!

At twenty to six the squeak of brakes made her look to the window, and there was James pulling up outside in the van. Coming in, he glanced around, noting the trays of dirty dishes on the sideboard, the crumbs on the carpet, the remnants of once-proud cakes on the trolleys. Evidence of a fair day's business.

'It hasn't gone too badly, then? I see you've sold a bit.'

Janine was radiant. 'Jamie, I'm sure we're going to be a gigantic success. You should have heard the nice things the customers said! Just wait till all those people tell their friends. This place simply won't be big enough!'

'Now don't get carried away.'

'I'm not. I just know we're going to do well. I can smell prosperity coming, just as strongly as I can smell spring when it's in the air.' She started scraping the money into a linen bag. 'Lord, I'm exhausted. I must have a nice warm bath when I get home, and an early night ...' She was talking mostly to herself as she scrabbled for the last few coins at the back of the drawer. 'Because I must make an early start tomorrow morning. There's all the washing up to do, and the cloths to change and the carpet to sweep before I open. I'm much too tired to do it now.'

'Go easy, Janine, you haven't been out of hospital long.'

'Oh, tosh! I'm all right. Anyway, if you think I'm over-doing things, you should take my advice and hire a waitress to help me out.'

He wavered. 'Do you really think we're going to be that busy?'

'Yes, I do.' She knotted the neck of the money bag and thrust it at him. 'I'd stake my life on it, Jamie. We're on our way.'

Sure enough, in the weeks that followed they had to take on staff – two waitresses to clear and serve while Janine manned the till and played the music. She was mightily glad to give up such arduous work – not to mention the cap and apron. She was, after all, the proprietress and wished to dress accordingly. She bought herself a few new frocks 'for work', fashionable, well-cut and expensive. For the waitresses' uniforms she provided dresses in bottle green. They went well with the décor and somehow looked fresher, crisper than black. Anyway, this was 'Janine's', and she liked to be different.

The older girl, Pat, was pug-faced and frizzy-haired, a resentful type but efficient. The other, chubby Doris, was a milder soul, more grateful for her job. Her starched white cap sat low on her brow and made her look Neanderthal, while Pat's encircled her ginger curls like a cake frill. Janine paid them well, but they worked extremely hard for it.

The business grew at a startling pace. An empty table at 'Janine's' soon became a prize to be quickly grabbed. The mornings were lively with constant jazz. Janine had become a valued customer at Parker and Smith's music shop in Bedford Street, forever buying new records to swell her collection. She was always happy to play requests at the café.

The afternoons were somewhat different, for at two o'clock the musical trio took over. They were called 'The April Moons' and comprised a clarinet, violin and piano. They wore brightly striped blazers and hair oil. The pianist was quite handsome and vain; he smiled and winked all the time at women who caught his interest. Some of them fell in love with him and haunted the café constantly, stuffing themselves with too many pastries so that they could stay and gaze at him. Janine had known when she hired the trio that he would be a particular asset. He had that Latin look so popular at present.

'The April Moons' specialised in sentimental, droopy melodies. During their sessions the atmosphere was languid amid the potted greenery. Couples swayed and shuffled around the floor, or blinked dreamily at one another across the iced fancies and the watercress sandwiches.

No matter what the tempo, the place was always full. Each day, all day, the babble and hum of gossip mingled with the music. Lovers murmured endearments as sticky as the gateaux on their plates, the waitresses bustled around with their trolleys and the till rang merrily.

By the middle of 1925, Janine had raised the tariff twice, with no adverse effects on trade. She had never seen so much money. She was awed and thrilled and impatient to start spending some. These fistfuls of coins and notes were magic tokens and tickets to a dazzling world of lovely things. Bright things, new things. She wanted to go on a spree every day, but realised that the overdraft called for a measure of self-control. Nevertheless, she thought she might open a store account or two. No harm in that.

She would mention it to Jamie. It was not that she needed his permission – hadn't he said it was her café? But the shops with their tiresome, archaic rules, would want his signature. Still, it would only be a formality. Jamie never said no.

Spooner's and Popham's were first to be honoured with Mrs Sayers' custom. She set about building up a complete new wardrobe in the most up-to-date styles. Short skirts were flattering to her and Janine ceased wearing anything that came below the knee. All her old clothes, including the ones James had bought her, were cleared out of her cupboards and put in a trunk. She was going to take the hems up when she had the time, she said. Somehow, though, she was always too busy. Shortened or not, the frocks and skirts were outmoded, and Janine preferred to forget all about them. There was a limit, anyway, to what could be done with old dresses, and she was no expert with needle and thread. Furthermore, there was no escaping the staleness of fabric many times worn, however it might be chopped about and altered. It remained the same old pattern, the same old colour, one step from being a rag. She wanted freshness, novelty, all the time, and the stores never disappointed her.

Janine could while away hours among the racks and rails, up and down, back and forth over the acres of carpet, looking at tube dresses, cloches, crocodile shoes and Russian boots, trying skirts and blouses and coats, comparing handbags and poring over Egyptian-style jewellery. Content as an addict in an opium den, she felt at peace the moment she pushed open the big glass doors and walked into a shop. The smell of the place and the temperature of the air seemed balmy to her, welcoming, like water to a fish. Rarely did a week-day go by without a visit to some establishment she liked, and seldom did she leave without a purchase of some sort. If not a frock, then a scarf, perhaps, a belt, or a little purse. Something. She had to have something. She felt so alive and clean and young – even beautiful – in new clothes. The colours and textures were sensual pleasures enjoyed like foreplay. Consummation was the signing of the sales voucher and triumphant exit with her prize in a crisp carrier bag.

The sales staff came to know her well. They greeted her warmly. They noted that Mrs Sayers had taste, that they rarely saw her in the same outfit more than twice. They knew the symptoms of shopping mania when they saw them, and that only the limit set on her monthly credit held her back from real excesses.

The waitresses at the café knew, as well, what it meant when Janine said she was popping out for an hour or so, because she never came back empty-handed. Being of a jealous nature, Pat would sneer and say: 'She's been at it again,' when Janine returned with her spoils.

'I'm sure I'd do the same if I had the means,' remarked Doris one afternoon when Janine had come in with three large bags. 'She's entitled to the rewards of success, after all. She brings the customers in, that's for sure. You have to admire what she's done here.'

Pat sniffed as she watched Janine wafting among the tables, chatting to the customers and asking if all was satisfactory. Janine saw herself as their hostess now, and sometimes gentlemen asked her to dance.

'She's a bugger to work for, her and her "standards".'

'That's one of the reasons she's doing well, her standards.'

'Down on you like a ton of bricks if you let them slip, be it ever so trivial,' groused Pat.

'The April Moons' were playing 'Tea for Two', and the girls saw an old buffer kiss Janine's hand as she spoke to him. She made some smiling reply and everyone at the table laughed. Janine was always fun, always jolly for her public.

'A bit of a star in her own little way,' observed Pat wryly.

That was true. Janine was something of a person-ality about town these days. People congratulated her on the tea-room and remarked how smart she was, how charming. She was recognised everywhere and she loved it.

'Well, she has the most popular café in the city,' shrugged Doris. 'The most pre—prestee—'

'Prestigious,' grunted Pat.

'That's it.'

'And doesn't she know it?'

'She.' They rarely spoke or thought of James. He was a background figure, referred to by Doris as 'Mister', and by Pat as simply 'He' or 'Him'.

'Mister's shy, I reckon,' Doris would say. 'I believe he don't like coming in here where it's so crowded. Sad about his poor face, eh?'

Pat's response to that was typically cynical. 'Well,' she often said, 'I think it suits her very well that he stays away. I dare say he put up the money, but this is her show entirely and that's the way she likes it. I bet she'd be none too pleased if he wanted to be more involved.'

Seventeen

James's involvement with the café was limited to keeping the accounts. The success of 'Janine's' bemused him. It had been so fast, so unerring. He had wondered at first if it might be a passing fad, but as time went on and the takings went up and up, he began to realise that the Sayers had struck gold.

James sat back in his chair one evening, emitting a sound that was half a sigh and half a whistle. It was ten past nine and his wife was having a bath. On the parlour table in front of him lay the café's paying-in book. Each day's takings were banked first thing next morning, and tomorrow he would deposit as much for one day as the bakery took in three. 'Janine's' had been open twenty-two months and James could scarcely believe the prices people paid at the café – or his wife's nerve in charging them.

'This is a rendezvous, Jamie,' she would say. 'They like the music, the ambience, the fact that they can afford it when others can't. Don't you understand?'

No, he didn't, not really. The concept of 'snob value' was foreign to him, just as Janine's clientèle were people with whom he would never have expected to associate. It bothered him just a little that she mixed so easily with them. Still, she was happy, and what was more important than that? Without her café she would doubtless grieve and fret, as women did when denied their natural motherly role. James thought he under-

172

stood all about that. Janine had suffered a second, albeit less dramatic, miscarriage late the previous year, and it was considered virtually certain now that she would never bear a child.

James placed the money and the bank book in a leather bag ready for the morning, stretched and yawned, then went to sit in his armchair before the fire. Of course, he reminded himself, it was not all profit. The expenses at 'Janine's' were considerable, with the bank loan and all the usual overheads, including staff wages and the fee for the band. Nevertheless, the café yielded a thicker layer of cream than the bakery ever could. James wondered vaguely what he should do with so much money. He was not the sort of person who knew how to spend, having no vices, no desire for grandeur, no eye for style.

Janine did, though. She was more and more modish these days. She never made the mistake of overdressing or loading herself with too many trinkets just to show she had them. No one could sniff and say that she had a bit of money now but not a particle of taste. She knew what was classy and what was pretentious, vulgar.

James was proud of her, even if the transformation did make him faintly uneasy. It had pleased him, back in the courting days, to see the poor, shabby girl from the funeral parlour enlivened by a few pretty clothes and a hairdo. It had pleased him to have a nicely dressed wife who was a credit to him. It was good to see a grub become a cabbage butterfly. Only – now she had gone a stage further, and quite without his help. Now she was elegant, witty, and slightly strange to him. It was just a bit unnerving to plain, unassuming Jamie, who never altered himself. Still, it was all appearances, he supposed. Beneath it all she was just his Janine, just an undertaker's daughter.

He crossed his feet on the fender and fell into a doze. He did not hear Connie when she came in to put some more wood on the fire and take away his coffee cup. Even if he had been awake, James would not have noticed the pallor and the lines of exhaustion about her face, the weary sag of her frame as she trudged from the room. James was so used to seeing her tired that it never registered as being significant. It was nothing a few hours' sleep could not cure. Always, in the mornings, Connie was recharged and ready for another punishing day.

And more and more brutal had they become since the café opened, for neither James nor Janine had given thought to employing someone extra at the bakery. Connie had volunteered to help out, and almost two years on she was still doing so. It was quite forgotten that this was not her job. As always, once Connie undertook something she was stuck with it and, as always, she made no protest. Her purpose, after all, had always been to serve.

Each morning at five she was dressed and downstairs, getting a head start on the day's work to help Harry and Nell cope with the café's demands. After they left in the evening, Connie was still there, measuring out ingredients for the next day, running back and forth to the store rooms, doing anything and everything she possibly could in advance – because every day had become a race, a terrible treadmill.

'We've had a pay rise,' Nell Colenso said to Connie one day. 'What have you had, may I ask? All you get is the housekeeping. Where's your share of all this money, eh?'

Connie went on beating up the fat and sugar for yet another cake. A small burn blister was coming up on the back of her hand and her blouse showed stains of damp at the armpits. The margarine was hard and she pounded at it with the wooden spoon. Stubborn lumps of it slid around in the bowl as she squashed it into a paste. Her arm and wrist were aching horribly already, and later the mixture would be stiff with flour and fruit.

'Jamie's been good to me, Nell,' she said. 'I don't want to squeeze him for anything more.'

'More fool you, then,' came the reply.

Harry Colenso went to one of the ovens and threw back the door. A blast of heat blew out into the room, already stifling. He thrust a long wooden paddle back into the oven and drew out a fragrant fruit pie, then a second and a third. Lastly, he pulled out a large, spicy sausage roll and put it on a plate for Tansy, who sat at the table beside her mother. The child was now coming on for three, a quiet, good-tempered sprite who laughed at everything.

'You let that cool now,' Harry warned. 'Here, I'll cut it up for you.'

The little girl nodded and nibbled at flakes of pastry while the meat inside cooled down.

He shut the oven door with a clang. 'You look like death half the time,' he said to Connie. 'It's enough for you to run the house and mind the child without slogging in here as well. And to do it without payment – Connie, you're mad.'

'I don't know why Jamie can't come in here and help out,' added Nell.

'He has his accounts to do, the deliveries and the shop.'

'The shop's easy. He should let you do that. Sometimes nobody comes in for half an hour – and what does he do then? He reads the paper.'

'He reads the financial pages, Harry. That's important for a man in business.'

'Theory's all very well, but what about the graft? He's not so keen on that.'

'Jamie never had the knack for baking.'

'He was never brought to it, you mean. Doesn't like rolling his sleeves up, doesn't like the heat or clearing away the mess.'

'Nell, I know we're old friends, but don't speak against my brother.'

Mrs Colenso sucked her teeth, offended. 'Oh, well, you don't have to listen to me, of course. I'm only an employee, I know that.'

'I didn't mean it that way.' Connie tried to steer them off the subject. 'Look, it's twenty to twelve already and this has to go on the van by two o'clock. Just let me get on with it.'

Nell sniffed. 'The world won't end if Madam Janine is short of a cake today.'

'Connie thinks it will,' sighed Harry, dusting powdered sugar over the pies. 'Indispensable Connie, holding everything together, eh? Don't worry, maid, they'd soon get a woman in to cook and clean if ever you fell ill. They'd find somebody double quick.'

Connie put down the bowl and said with exaggerated patience: 'Harry, they took out a big loan to set up "Janine's". I know it's doing well, but we're not yet on such a firm footing that we can afford to dispense with economies. Another pastry-cook, for instance, could cost three pounds a week.'

'Hah!' exclaimed Nell. 'Janine spends as much as that – and more – on clothes for herself.'

'Yes,' mumbled Connie, 'well, I know, and it's wrong of her. Understandable, though, when you think of all those years her father kept her short. I'm aware that she's a bit extravagant these days and I'm not saying I approve of it. The excitement of it all has gone to her head, I dare say – but I don't think my downing tools would stop her. Anyway, as I said just now, she and James have been good to me and my child. I want to show a bit of appreciation.'

'Jamie should never have been in any position to dole out favours,' said Mrs Colenso stoutly.

'But he was, and he did. He could just as easily have told me to clear out. He had to put up with quite a few jokes and digs about me when I . . .'

She stopped herself, with a nervous glance at the baby. Tansy was conscious of nothing shameful surrounding her birth, nor of being charitably allowed to remain in Uncle Jamie's house. It was her home, to which she had a child's sense of full rights. Connie wanted no feeling of lesser status communicated to her yet. That sort of thing would come all too soon when Tansy started school.

'Jamie's been well rewarded,' grunted Nell.

'Does it not occur to you,' said Harry, 'that there was just as much advantage for them in keeping you here? Who do you think would be running this house if you weren't here? Not Janine, I'll tell you that. She's at the café all day long, being Lady Muck. In the evenings she comes home and puts her feet up, doesn't she? They both do. Can you see her coming in and putting the supper on to cook? Or doing a stack of ironing or cleaning out the grate? Of course not. She and Jamie are very content to have you here. They're not suffering any inconvenience, Connie, you're handy.'

She swallowed and frowned a little. 'That's a pretty unpleasant way of looking at things, and I think you're wrong. They stood by me because we're family, and I help out here for the same reason. It's not like working for strangers.'

'No,' he said wryly, 'strangers would value you more. An accident of birth, that's what being family is. You're given no choice, it's all pot luck. Relations can be good or wise or fortunate, or they can be weaklings, wasters, bullies, you name it. Whatever they are, a sensible person takes a cool, careful look at them and gets the hell out of it if they're no good. But a fool only sees that they're "family", and for that silly reason puts up with anything they do. There's no limit, is there, to what you can ask of "family"? Only, the trouble is, there's rarely equal give and take. Some do all the asking and others do all the supporting. Isn't that right?'

Connie fingered the blister on her hand and winced a little. 'I never knew you were such a cynic, Harry,' was all she could say.

The Sayers' neighbours were equally critical of James and Janine. In many quarters, their success had gone down badly. Janine, in particular, was not so popular among them any more. They recalled the days when she used to serve in the bread shop and gossip with them. They knew what sort of customers she chattered and joked with now. Prosperous merchants, professional people, the middle-class, even a few of the gentry. Some of the neighbours now called her 'jumped-up' and 'swollen-headed'. Oh, she still smiled and said 'Good day' when she breezed past them in the street, but she never stopped to talk any more and they guessed that she thought herself quite democratic for greeting them at all.

'Here she comes,' said Millie Chope one day, as she spotted a neat little figure in a mustard coat approaching. 'The Barbican clothes-horse. Ridiculous, I call it, dressing up like that round here. She looks so out of place.'

Cynthia Hardin agreed. Surrounded by plainly clad, often down-at-heel women, Janine stood out like a tropical bird among starlings. From under the droopy brims of shapeless hats, a dozen pairs of eyes took envious note of her outfit that day. Women paused and turned when she had passed, staring with resentment at her back before slogging on in their old flat shoes, with bags of groceries in their hands. Janine's step was sprightly, a cheerful click and tap, click and tap. She never struggled along with anything weighty. Today all she carried was a small leather handbag, and she swung it as she walked. Over her shingled hair was a brown pull-on hat. The brim stood out stiff and perky, framing her face and the curl of hair curved forward on each cheek. As Millie said, she looked out of place among the hard-worked, the unfashionable. She was galling to them, arousing discontent where there had been none before, and among those who could do nothing to change their situation.

'Look at me!' screamed her appearance, to those who could never hope to look the same.

'I wonder if she realises what an effect she has,' continued Millie sourly. 'She's a show-off. It isn't nice. You don't see Connie going around done up like that.'

Cynthia was standing in the doorway of her dairy, while Millie was out on the pavement. Cynthia's mouth pursed, bunching up her fat cheeks.

'Somehow, I don't think Connie is sharing in the pot of gold, my dear.'

'Ooh!' Millie was scandalised. 'How do you know?'

'Something Nell Colenso let slip one day when she came in here. She said that Connie would die a poor relation.'

'Ooh!' breathed Millie again.

'Well, that's what comes of loving too well,' snorted Cynthia.

They switched on smiles as Janine drew near.

'Morning, Janine,' they chorused. 'Lovely day.'

'Good morning, Millie, Mrs Hardin,' she said brightly.

'She must spend a mint of money,' Millie said when Janine was out of earshot. 'Nobody needs so many clothes. I don't know why Jamie allows it.'

'Hah!' Cynthia's teeth jutted out in amusement. 'Because he's too wet to object, I should think. Anyway, she's the one who's making the cash, isn't she? It's Janine who's made that café what it is. All he's good for is signing on the dotted line where and when she tells him.'

'True, he always was ineffectual. Lucky for him he married a clever woman, eh?'

'Yes . . . Except that if she makes a mistake – and she's only human, after all – he won't be able to stop her. Even if he has wit enough to see trouble coming, he won't be able to turn her aside.'

'You mean she might become too ambitious?' There was a hopeful lilt to Millie's voice.

'Perhaps, perhaps not,' said Cynthia reflectively. 'But

I always think quick success is a perilous thing. There are no lessons in it.'

Janine, as she walked on down the street, sensed that she was under discussion. She knew how they felt about her these days, but she didn't care. They were not her own, these pinny-clad women with their head-scarf turbans and hair-nets. She would wish them a pleasant 'Good day' because she had nothing against them and would never deliberately cut anyone dead. But if she had lost their affection on account of her success, if they begrudged it so much, well, that was a trifling matter to Janine. It only went to show how well she had done. As for her clothes, she wore her nice things because she enjoyed them. If they aroused envy in others, that was just incidental.

She was, however, concerned that she and the neighbourhood no longer blended well. Nowadays, when James collected her in the bakery van and took her home to the Barbican, she felt that she was stepping downwards, backwards. It was so unfitting to leave 'Janine's' and return to that terraced house, that narrow street. Lately she had been thinking more and more about getting away. Lately she had been scanning the property pages in the local paper and haunting the furniture departments of the stores.

Eighteen

Nearly all of the loan had been repaid. Absently, Janine put on another record. It was 'Margie' by the Dixieland Jazz Band. The café was packed as usual, and the time was nearly twelve. Janine had been thinking all morning about the bank statement which had come in the first post.

The Sayers were in a very healthy situation now, almost out of debt, with the café thriving. She had taken that statement as a green light. 1927 had just begun and 'Janine's' would soon celebrate its third anniversary. She wanted that celebration to take the form of a move to the suburbs.

Janine looked around the room with satisfaction. Busy, busy, busy. Busy all the time. Chomping, chattering mouths, a ceaseless clinking of teaspoons and cake forks, always the faint chuckle of tea and coffee being poured.

Some of the customers smiled at her, giving little waves. Covertly, she counted the notable faces. There was the Lord Mayor's wife and a friend at a corner table. Here the owner of a well-known chain of florist shops, there the leading actress from the current production at the Theatre Royal. By the window, the young artist who had an exhibition of hideous but highly-praised paintings at the Guildhall that week. Beside the dais for the band, the liberal candidate who hoped in vain to take Nancy Astor's seat at the next election.

Quite an assembly today, thought Janine. That was one of the things she loved most about her business. It attracted so many interesting types. She liked the theatre people best. On occasion they would do impromptu turns, singers joining in with 'The April Moons', dancers demonstrating the Charleston, comics telling a joke or two. Once she had lost some crockery when a juggler tried to keep too many plates in the air. She had laughed off the breakages. It was all part of the fun at 'Janine's' and did the café's reputation no harm at all.

Janine's clientèle, in the main, were the kind of people she wanted to know, the kind she wanted to be. If anyone had called her a social climber outright, she would have accepted the label without embarrassment. With some of the customers, Janine was on very friendly terms. Quite often now she received invitations from this one or that. Garden parties, fêtes and tennis games, that sort of thing. Even, once, an informal dinner.

She would have loved to go – if not for James. Naturally, the invitations always included him, but he shot back into his shell like a hermit crab at any sign of a social approach. Janine was peeved about this. Once or twice she had been tempted to accept and go somewhere without him, but so far she had resisted doing so. It was annoying, though, to be held back when she so desired to have friends. 'Janine's' itself was her social life, but she wanted so much more.

It had always been a dream of hers to give parties and dinners herself, but that would require a setting a good deal more grand than the house beside the bakery.

That would require a residence altogether smarter. She needed to live somewhere elegant, she felt, somewhere more in keeping with her new status as proprietress of a stylish, popular establishment. Somewhere at the top end of town, somewhere with leafy avenues, large gardens and driveways.

Janine's thoughts returned to that very encouraging bank statement. Suddenly the bank manager's face appeared in her mind's eye and he was smiling, saying: 'Why, yes, of course, I'm sure we can offer you a further loan. You're valued customers, Mr and Mrs Sayers. An excellent repayment record. Very, very sound. Lovely area you've chosen. I live there myself . . .'

A waving hand and a 'Coo-ee' brought Janine back from her little day-dream. The Lord Mayor's wife was calling her over to her table.

Did she have 'Smilin' Through' by Dame Clara Butt, the lady wanted to know. Would she play it? Oh, how kind.

Janine went back to find the record, and promised herself as she searched through the box that she would tackle James that very night about the new house.

The property on which Janine set her sights was a villa called Gardenia Lodge. There was a short, curved drive up to the front door and the house was screened from the road by a row of beech trees and a ten-foot garden wall. It had two bay windows to the ground floor. Behind those windows were sitting room and dining room, very spacious, with wide fireplaces and high ceilings. Every room in the house was large, except the study. The four bedrooms, the kitchen, even the bathroom, were all of a generous size. Along one side of the house ran a big conservatory, and on the other side there was a garage.

Janine particularly liked the garden. Camellia and rhododendron bushes clustered darkly round the lawns to front and back. Azaleas lined the driveway and a fine magnolia stood near the entrance gate.

The cost of this desirable dwelling made James feel faint, and of course it would require a lot of furnishing. He asked uneasily if they really needed such a big house.

'Oh Jamie, it truly isn't all that large! Anyway, it'll be a good investment. Property always is, the value goes up and up.' She hugged his arm with a rapturous sigh, smiling up at the front of the house. 'Oh, I love it, my sweetheart. I want it so much! Look, there are the gardenias!'

She pointed to the fanlight over the front door – a spray of gardenias depicted in stained glass.

James nodded, but then he said: 'I don't know, Janine. Going into debt again . . . God, it's a lot of money.'

'But we're quite secure!'

'You never know what lies ahead.'

'Oh tosh! Oh, Jamie, you will buy it for me, won't you? I was right about the café, remember. Trust my judgement in this as well. We'll be making a mistake if we let this opportunity go. Houses rarely come up for sale round here and it's not over-priced.'

He glanced at her from the shadow of his trilby and she gazed back expectantly. From under her black cloche hat a dark-red curl came down over her brow. She was smiling at him, snuggled up in the high velvet collar of her coat.

'Well?' she pressed, the plump lower lip out-thrust.

He lifted his head and looked again at the house. Bright sunlight picked out shiny pinks and purples in his scar. Hands in pockets, he mumbled: 'I'm not sure I'd feel at home.'

'That's because you've lived in the same house all your life. And because this one's empty now, so it seems as big as a barn. Wait until it's furnished, my sweetheart, you'll soon settle in. We have to seize the moment, Jamie. You know what I always say – fortune favours the bold.'

The bank was more than willing to make the loan. The manager had great faith in the Sayers. What flair they had shown, what industry and acumen in building up 'Janine's'. A fast, spectacular success. Of course they could have the money.

Janine was like a child given the freedom of a sweet-shop. Determined to turn her new home into a show-piece, she spent hour after hour with sketch-pad and pencils, designing layouts and colour schemes for all the rooms. Then in came electricians to wire the place, because Janine was not going to settle for the old-fashioned gas lighting and cookers that came with the house. Plumbers were called to install wash basins in the two largest bedrooms and a second lavatory just off the entrance hall. Next were decorators, followed by carpet layers. For weeks the house resounded to the noise of hammers, saws, and the grating of sandpaper.

She had an ornamental window put in the bathroom. It was octagonal, with pale blue and green glass panes in a geometric pattern. Out went the rust-stained old white fittings, replaced by a brand new suite. Janine had the walls covered with green onyx tiling and a number of painted panels depicting naked odalisques in a Turkish harem. James found it rather disconcerting to think these sloe-eyed women would be gazing inscrutably at him while he was in the bath or on the lavatory, but he had to admit the overall effect was splendid.

Fond of pastel colours, Janine had them in all the bedrooms – ivory, beige, mauve and pink. Downstairs she favoured shades of amber and burgundy, and once again there were painted panels – masked harlequins in diamond-patterned costumes round the dining-room walls, sad-faced pierrots in the hall.

The kitchen was equipped with every electrical gadget available. Stark white with the plainest built-in fittings, it would have looked like an operating theatre if not for the copper pots and pans. It was not a place where Janine meant to spend much time.

Once the house was dressed in its fresh new colours, she set about filling it up with all the things she had ever desired. She trailed around furniture stores, pored over fabric samples and scoured galleries and exhibitions for pictures. Janine adored the modern style; tub chairs, plump and curvy or with backs like scallop shells; inlaid sunburst patterns on the head and footboards of the beds; tables with strangely-angled legs. Gilded metalwork featured everywhere at Gardenia Lodge – fire-screens, room dividers, ornate mirror frames. Boxy chests and sideboards which might otherwise have been profoundly ugly, were offset by the prettiness of Tiffany lamps and Lalique vases, colourful cushions and rugs. Prints and posters of a romantic nature adorned the walls. Urns and balconies dripping blossom figured in them prominently, as did dusky evening scenes with stars and fireworks. Statuettes and novelties were perhaps Janine's greatest weakness.

187

She loved the ivory and bronze figurines of dancers, mythical characters and athletes, caught in graceful motion and often robed in exotic costume. Elegant bodies and fluttering folds of fabric, delicately painted in metallic colours – Janine collected them avidly. She had 'Salome', 'The Sorceress', 'The Skater', 'The Diver' and half a dozen more. Some of them were merely ornaments, others held lamps or clocks or cigarette lighters. All were lithe and young with streaming hair. They cost a lot of money. But then, nothing she bought was cheap.

The final effect when Gardenia Lodge was finished was overwhelmingly pretty, opposite in every way to Matthew Jordan's house. Gardenia Lodge was flamboyant, comfortable. It celebrated life and self-indulgence, whereas the Jordan house had felt like the ante-room to the grave, which of course it was.

James had an understanding of this, so he gritted his teeth and fought down his anxiety as the bills mounted up. They were, after all, doing well in business, and he so adored his wife.

Connie was impressed, if somewhat over-awed, by the house. Janine cooked a celebration dinner for the family the day she and James moved in. Used to eating in the kitchen, Connie thought Janine's dining room too grand for words and was in terror lest Tansy should break or soil anything. Janine seemed not to mind the little girl playing with some of the pretty knick-knacks. Nevertheless, this was no house for children – about as suitable as a china shop. It would take a good deal of labour as well, Connie thought, to keep it in its present pristine condition, and she knew all too well that Janine was not a domesticated type.

After the meal, while James read his niece a story,

Connie went into the kitchen to help her sister-in-law with the washing up.

'It's a beautiful house,' she said, gingerly wiping some delicate wine glasses. 'Going to be quite a task, though, to keep it so immaculate.'

'Oh, I shan't mind,' Janine said blithely. 'Modern houses are light work and I'll enjoy looking after all my lovely things. It makes such a difference, you know, when it's your own home, when you've chosen everything yourself.'

Connie smiled, but the phrase 'playing house' crossed her mind, and something told her the fad would pass. It was she who had the temperament, the patience and self-discipline for housework. Her own domestic burden would be very much eased by James's and Janine's departure, but she could not help feeling her sister-in-law might have taken on more than she could comfortably manage by herself.

Sure enough, just two months later, Janine declared that she could not cope with Gardenia Lodge alone. The house was so large, requiring such a lot of work, and she did have the café to run. Her presence was essential there, she was part of the ambience. To neglect 'Janine's' would be a perilous course, much as she loved Gardenia Lodge and wanted to care for it herself. She simply could not afford, she said, to spend her time cooking and dusting at home when the customers were asking for her, missing her. Anyway, the staff were in need of Janine's supervision. They were not to be trusted without it. Pat, in particular, was apt to be surly, if given the chance.

Therefore there was only one thing for it. A cook-housekeeper would have to be found. Janine, if the truth were told, was missing Connie's services more than she had expected. Gardenia Lodge's modern gadgetry was no substitute for a good domestic woman.

James made a token protest and then caved in. An advertisement was placed in the *Western Morning News* and brought seven replies. Janine interviewed them all, finally settling on number six. This was a fat little widow, Mrs Coade by name, as broad as she was long, with a hard voice and a hard face but a talent for serving up fine meals and maintaining order.

Mrs Coade moved in a week later, to become a dour but mostly unseen presence in the house. She contrived to keep out of the Sayers' way for most of the time by staying in the kitchen. They scarcely saw her except when she served their meals. When about her cleaning, she would slip into another room if she heard one of them coming, and generally moved about the place like a shadow. She was hardly the jolly Mrs Mop of popular films, but she had her good points nevertheless, being honest, and content with her meals and her room at the rear of the house plus a modest wage.

James, in truth, was uncomfortable with the idea of having a servant. He remained a plain and simple baker's son, and being 'sir' to Mrs Coade did not feel right at all. The work she did about his house was no more – indeed, rather less – than Connie had done for him all his life. That, however, was different; that had never made him feel awkward at all. That was just what his sister did, and had done for as long as he could recall. But this formal arrangement with a stranger? No, it didn't feel natural to James.

Janine, on the other hand, was quite at ease with the situation. She readily assumed the habit of command and was not in the least averse to being addressed as 'madam'. Anyone, in her view, could be 'madam', given the manner to carry it off and the money to pay. Unlike her husband, she had no sense of being 'ordinary', tied to humble origins.

Sometimes, when he looked around him at the furnishings, the décor, James would experience a strange sensation of unreality, as if he hardly knew where he was. These moments were fleeting but frequent, because everything had moved so fast in the six years since he had married Janine. She had pushed him – upwards, he supposed – into this fancy house with a servant, this house which was all Janine. It spoke very loudly of her personality, but there wasn't a whisper of his – although, thinking it over, James scarcely knew what his own tastes would have been in any case. Still, Gardenia Lodge was alien to him, elegant, pleasant, but not really home. It felt more like living in a hotel.

He never said as much, though, to Janine. The stride had been taken, so here they were. He could hardly drag her back to the bakery now. He supposed he would grow used to the new house in time, and then they would be settled, for she surely had all she wanted now.

And for the time being, so she did. That is, apart from the car.

When one lived in such a fine house in such a smart avenue, it was hardly fitting to come and go in a bakery van each day. They hadn't been at Gardenia Lodge six months before she started to wheedle for the car.

'Just a little runabout, Jamie,' she pleaded one evening at dinner. 'It doesn't have to be new, but it would be so handy, wouldn't it, if I had my own little car? Then you could leave the van down at the bakery where it belongs.'

He toyed uneasily with his pork fillet. 'The van's

pretty old, Janine. I shall have to replace it soon. If we buy a car as well, that's two vehicles to pay for.'

'Not beyond our means, though, is it?' she said lightly.

'It might be wise to pause for breath, don't you think?'

'Jamie, you're such a worrier!' she scoffed, laying down her cutlery on her empty plate.

James pushed his unfinished meal aside and as if by magic Mrs Coade appeared to clear the table. James sometimes wondered if she were telepathic or had a spy-hole somewhere between the dining room and the kitchen, so promptly did she arrive whenever a course was finished.

'Would you really use it all that much?' he asked. 'Back and forth between here and the café – hardly seems worthwhile.'

'Of course I would, my sweetheart. I'd drive for pleasure if I had a car. We could go out in the country on Sundays, for instance. Ride with the top down – wouldn't that be lovely?'

'I suppose it would be nice,' admitted James.

'Anyway, you know how difficult it is to manoeuvre the van through our front gate. It's such a squeeze. You've twice dented the wing, haven't you? And then the wretched thing's too high to fit in the garage, so you have to park it in the drive, cutting all the light off from the sitting room.'

'We can leave it out on the road instead,' suggested her husband.

'Oh Jamie, you know what people are like round here. They'll think it's an eyesore. And what a nuisance in wet weather to have to run down the drive to get in the van.'

James would hardly call that a gross inconvenience. He had always been obliged to park the van fifty yards from the bakery because the street was too narrow for anything more than a short pause while loading.

Padding round the table in her slippers, Mrs Coade was taking everything in. She glanced at Janine, so svelte and glossy in salmon pink with coral and onyx ear-studs. Want, want, want. She knew the type. Without a word, she removed their plates and waddled off to fetch the dessert.

'Cars depreciate so fast,' muttered James. 'They're not a solid investment like a house or good furniture.'

'We can't judge absolutely everything in those terms. One pays for the fun and convenience of a car. Why shouldn't we treat ourselves, spend our money? We've no one to pass it on to, no one for whom to save it.'

Mrs Coade heard that as she returned with the chocolate mousse. She had noticed how often Mrs Sayers used that one, and how effective it was. James had gravely told Mrs Coade of their childless state. More perceptive than he was, the housekeeper doubted that Janine was suffering over it. Placing his dish before him, she hoped against hope that Mr Sayers would not fall for this ploy again.

But he did. 'Well,' he said, 'that's very true. Life is meant to be lived.'

Covertly, Mrs Coade rolled her eyes as she made to leave the room. She was stopped on her way, however, by a smiling complaint from 'Mrs'.

'The mousse is rather too sweet, Mrs Coade. I should be a little more sparing with the sugar next time.'

The housekeeper bridled. 'Oh. Dear me. Well, I'm sorry, of course. I know Mr Sayers likes plenty, you see.'

'Then I should make two separate lots in future.

That will solve the problem, won't it?' purred Janine, still smiling. 'Oh, and would you mind putting some fresh towels in the bathroom? They haven't been changed since I had my bath this morning, and I'd like another before I go to bed.'

'I'll see to it.'

'Thank you so much – oh, and while I think of it, the sitting room carpet needs sweeping. Tomorrow will do.'

'Very well.' Mrs Coade's voice was quite toneless whenever she took orders.

'Do have a nightcap before bed, won't you?' beamed Janine.

Permission to tap the whisky bottle every night was one of the little perks which helped to allay Mrs Coade's resentment of criticism and Janine knew it. Since the relationship was not founded on mutual liking, sops were required to keep all smooth.

Mrs Coade retired to her kitchen, promising herself a treble tot that evening. 'Mrs', she felt, was pretty demanding. But then, the jumped-up ones were always the worst. Like the staff at the café, Mrs Coade found Janine pernickety. She also thought her shamefully wasteful of food and had never before met a woman who changed her clothes so often and made so much washing. Mrs Coade thought grimly that they had better not expect her to clean this new car, that was all. And there most certainly would be a new car, of course. She had never seen 'Mrs' lose a battle yet.

'So what shall we have, then?' Janine was asking, back in the dining room. 'Something sporty, Jamie, don't you think?'

'Something you can handle, Janine. I don't want you coming to grief.'

She leaned across the table and clasped his hand.

'Oh Jamie, bless you. When can I have it? Soon? This week?'

'We'll go and have a look around on Wednesday.'

Thus, she had her car. He bought her a Crossley, two years old, and taught her to drive himself. Again, the bank had been obliging, having utter faith in the Sayers – and the deeds to all their property. Janine lost no sleep over that, blithely suggesting that they put a few pence on the café tariff here and there.

Nineteen

Connie had found it strange at first, having the house to herself. Life was undeniably easier, though, now James and Janine had moved out. There was just herself and Tansy for whom to cook and wash and shop. Connie was glad of the extra hours she now had free to spend with the child. Tansy had passed her fourth birthday in May; another eighteen months and she would be starting school. Hard to believe, thought Connie that autumn, but Charlie had been gone a full five years. This little bit of him left behind, this child with hazelnut-brown hair, was growing as swiftly as he was receding into the past, so that Connie marked her progress with pride and sadness.

Nineteen twenty-seven sped towards its end, and with the approach of Christmas, Tansy became excited. Doubly so this year because they were going to spend it with James and Janine at Gardenia Lodge, and Tansy liked Uncle Jamie's big garden. For Connie, the prospect of Christmas meals laid on by Mrs Coade was a luxury beyond belief. Mrs Coade would set the table, and cook and serve and wash up. For five whole days, Connie would need do nothing. Such a holiday!

The shop and bakery closed on 23 December. Connie still had presents to buy and planned an excursion into town next day, Christmas Eve.

'Would you like to go to Spooner's caves?' she asked

Tansy that morning. 'Like to visit Father Christmas and see if he has something for you?'

An eager nod, a grin, a breathlessly excited 'Yes'.

Kneeling in front of her, Connie buttoned the little girl's coat and wiped a few specks off Tansy's shiny, black patent shoes. This was the centre of her life, this child. This was her all now, her joy. Virtually all of the hundred pound legacy from Ada had been spent on clothes and toys and outings for Tansy. Connie meant to give her as happy a childhood as she could, and had never forgotten Janine's advice to keep the baby looking lovely. Tansy always did, so clean and pretty that strangers on trams would point and smile and remark admiringly upon her.

Connie surveyed her daughter proudly. 'What do you most want for Christmas, eh?'

'Snow,' said Tansy promptly.

'Oh, well, I don't think Father Christmas carries that about in his sack. Never seen real snow yet, have you? Only in pictures.' She patted Tansy's cheek. 'Even when it comes, it doesn't last for long in these parts. Better to have a nice game or something, eh? Come on, let's go and see if old Santa's got one of those.'

They left the house and walked up through Breton-side to the city centre; Connie a stately figure in a green tweed coat, the child skip-hopping along beside her, dressed in royal blue with a white woolly hat and mittens.

Lights and garlands were strung across all the shopping streets and the Salvation Army band was playing at St Andrew's Cross beside a towering Christmas tree. 'Unto Us a Boy Is Born' exulted the brass and drums.

It was a dark day with a freezing wind that made eyes water and noses run. The town was in a furious rush. People were buying food and drink as if stocking up for a siege. Hasty, unwise purchases were being made in their hundreds in last-day desperation to find some gift or other for the awkward friend or aunt.

As systematic as ever, Connie consulted her list and took the shortest route to all the necessary shops. She was buying for James and Janine, and for a handful of neighbours – particularly Mrs Paul at the wool shop. Connie had never forgotten her kindness when she was carrying Tansy. Toys for the child were already wrapped up and locked away in a suitcase, ready to go to Gardenia Lodge after tea.

Spooner's store was the last stop on Connie's round that day. It was crowded and overheated, a mad babble and a wave of hot air striking her as she entered.

'Keep hold of my hand now,' she told the child as they headed for the stairs.

'Is it time to see the caves?'

'Yes, they're on the second floor. Won't be long now.'

The child stayed close beside her as they threaded their way through the press of people. Tansy kept being buffeted by shopping bags and large female backsides amid this shifting forest of people. Craning her neck, she saw paper chains and cardboard reindeer and cotton wool snowmen hanging high above her head. There was a constant ching of cash registers, and smells of bath salts, leather and – something else. The scent of 'newness', Janine would have said.

They reached the stairs and Connie carried her daughter up the four flights to the second floor. There, at one end of the china department, were the 'caves', a labyrinth of cardboard painted to resemble rough rock, shadowy tunnels with niches at every turn, eerily lit and peopled with elves, gnomes, witches and mermaids, automata, enchanted woods, dragons and fairy castles.

Meandering, doubling back on itself, the cave seemed to Tansy to go on for miles. She stopped and marvelled at every display and tableau, and Connie walked patiently behind her, following the little white bobble hat through these dim, magical corridors (which lay in a basement store-room the rest of the year).

Journey's end, of course, was the grotto, and Father Christmas attended by an elf. Father Christmas's alter ego worked in Spooner's accounts department. He enjoyed his role as Santa Claus and played it to the hilt. There was belly laughter, much twirling of moustache and long white beard. Tansy was taken onto his lap and kissed. From the sack came a present wrapped in pink paper with a white bow, which meant that it was suitable for a small girl. Asked if she was good, Tansy bit her lip and bashfully nodded. Father Christmas winked at the smiling Connie and handed over the package, plus a barley sugar stick.

'Well, how about that?' said Connie, when they emerged from the caves. 'Good, wasn't it? Wonder what he's given you, eh?'

'Can I open it now?'

'Oh, I shouldn't. Wait for tomorrow. Then you'll have lots of surprises in the morning.'

There was no argument. Such a good child, Connie thought. Never any trouble, right from the time she was born.

It was twenty past one when they left the store. The city was busier than ever as shop and office workers scurried for final items in their lunch hour. Connie felt she would be glad to get home, away from the noise and bustle. She was carrying quite a lot by now – three bags in one hand. The other kept a firm grip on Tansy's little right mitten as they walked up Bedford Street. The child was clutching her parcel as if it were made of gold.

The Salvation Army band had gone from St Andrew's Cross. In its place was now a barrel organ, churning out 'Jingle Bells'. A small group of people hung about listening, and a hot chestnut man had set up his stand nearby.

Tansy's footsteps started to drag as she and Connie passed by on the other side of the road. She pulled back a little, wanting to stop.

Connie looked down at her. 'What's the matter?'

Excitedly, Tansy pointed to the barrel organ. On top of it sat a monkey in a tiny red jacket and pill-box hat.

'Oh yes,' said Connie, laughing. 'Isn't he funny?'

They stood for a moment, watching as the monkey capered and chattered, taking off its hat and holding it out to passers-by for coppers. Tansy was fascinated. She had never seen a monkey before, never been to a zoo. She wanted to have a closer look, wanted to give him a coin.

In the road the cars flashed by, but Tansy paid them no heed. Between them she had tantalising glimpses of the monkey. She saw a man drop something in its hat, saw a woman offer it food of some kind. The creature took the titbit and ate it daintily.

Tansy's eyes widened with an idea. She still had the barley sugar stick in her pocket.

To the end of her days, Connie would recall the ghastly, bewildering swiftness of what happened next. One moment she was looking down the street, awaiting a break in the traffic and aware of Tansy's hand clasped in her own. Then there was a twist and a pull and the hand was gone, leaving only a white woolly mitten behind. Connie's head snapped round, but before she could even focus on the tiny running figure there sounded a blaring horn, an ear-splitting squeal of brakes and a dull thump.

Everything abruptly stopped. The traffic came to a halt, the barrel organ ceased grinding. People stood as if rooted, staring at the small, unmoving body in the royal blue coat. Connie, transfixed by shock, told herself it could not be real. She was surely having a nightmare . . .

Then there was movement again. The driver got out of his car, seeming dazed. A woman pushed through the mob, saying that she was a nurse, and crouched to examine the little figure between the front wheels. Tansy lay on her back, one arm flung above her head, the other thrown out sideways. She looked to be merely asleep.

The bags and mitten dropped from Connie's hands. She stepped off the kerb and came forward, trembling. Dread slowed her footsteps, as if she were dragging her legs against a current of water. She knew, she already knew, but shrank from seeing, being told. Her face was rigid with anguish, a staring tragedy mask.

The nurse looked up at her and the sight of that face brought tears of pity.

'I'm sorry, my dear,' she whispered, 'the child is gone.'

Am I evil? Am I cursed? Why should it be that everyone I love always comes to grief?

Connie sat rocking, hugging herself, perched on the edge of the bed. It was the day after the funeral, and here she was at Gardenia Lodge, in a pretty bedroom overlooking the garden. The strangeness of the house added to the sense of her life being fractured, normality discontinued. How bizarre that she was here in this bright and airy room, while her thoughts were all of death and darkness and decay.

And terror, because the only thing that now seemed certain about life was its cruelty. It had surely been so all her days; it would always be so. She would never dare again to have confidence in the future, because there would always be another vicious blow in store. She would always be afraid now, especially of anything resembling good fortune, since it would only be another trick, more bait to lead her into agony, like cheese on a mousetrap. The fear made Connie's heart pound constantly. It had not ceased to hammer for many, many days. The feel of it in her chest and the drumming it made in her head was exhausting and nearly enough to drive her mad. But worst of all was the other thing – most unbearable was the guilt.

Connie stared, unseeing, through the window. She hardly seemed to blink and her gaze was fixed on a point of sky above the magnolia tree at the gate. Distant clouds moved slowly past but her eyes never wavered to follow their movements. The scenes in her head were more vivid by far, images of all those around her who had ever met with disaster. Jamie, seven years old again, his cheek red-raw and blistered; Charlie at the hospital mortuary, cold and greyish-white, as if the sea had begun to turn him into one of its own creatures. Tansy between the wheels of the car, eyes wide and mouth half open in the blankly pretty expression of a doll. Even Ada, dying slowly. Perhaps she, too, had been Connie's victim. Perhaps some undercurrent of ill-will had passed to Ada, caused the growth. Perhaps there had been defiance, hatred in Connie, buried deep but travelling underground like a bramble root and digging with thorny vengeance into Ada, mutating her tissues.

In lucid moments, Connie thought she might be going insane, that she could entertain such notions. Yet she could not shake them off. The feeling of being bane to others or else accursed herself was too overpowering. She was fated to loss and misery and disaster, that was her role in the great playwright's drama and nothing she could do would make it otherwise.

The bedroom was cold but she scarcely felt it. She sat and sat and rocked and rocked on the pale green counterpane in the frigid air, while her mind was, as Milton said, its own place, a hot, red pit of pain. Connie didn't know how long she had been up here in this bedroom on her own. She had told Janine and James she wanted to take a nap. It was the only way to escape from their watchful, worried eyes, their useless attempts to comfort her. They had both been very kind, of course, but they could not reach her, couldn't come down here where she was, in this trench of despair. And all their arguments sounded so false, designed to give her absolution she did not deserve.

'If I hadn't kept Tansy, hadn't been so selfish, she would be alive today,' she had told Janine. 'If I'd only had her adopted instead of clinging on to her . . .'

'But Connie,' Janine had said quite reasonably, 'you can never know where any choice will lead. We all wonder about the alternatives we didn't take. There's no guarantee at all that they would have been better.'

Connie failed to see how things could have turned out worse.

The afternoon light began to fade. Her eyes grew tired and she closed them for a while. When she opened them again, they chanced to light upon her suitcase in the corner by the wardrobe. She had not unpacked it or even bothered to dress for most of the time she had been here. Only for the funeral. Janine had been down to the bakery and fetched the suitcase and her black coat – the same one she had worn when Charlie was buried. The rest of the time, Connie shuffled about Gardenia Lodge in a borrowed night-shirt and dressing gown. She never thought about combing her hair. Sometimes Janine combed it for her.

Eyeing the suitcase, Connie tried to remember what she had packed. A week ago now, seven days of – indescribable pain and turmoil. Periods of sedation, sleeping and waking, never knowing the time, being taken in hand by James and Janine, being brought here, crying hour after hour, being held by someone, offered meals on a tray, none of which she could eat. Seven days – a blur of flowers and cards, some of them anonymous, conscience-gestures from the name-callers who could not face Connie now. Seven appalling nights when she kept the light on and sobbed unendingly and Mrs Coade kept appearing with cups of cocoa and glasses of brandy. Yesterday at the church – hymns she could not sing, a reading she could not absorb. In the graveyard, wet earth, a cold wind and the cawing of rooks. Matthew Jordan and the vicar being very kind. A week of hell stood between Connie and the hour when she had packed that case. Now her memory stalled – perhaps because she was dopey still with some kind of drug. Or because her mind was shying away from something.

She hesitated, frowning, fretfully twisting her fingers, but at last she went over to pick up the case. It was still locked. She opened her handbag, found the keys, threw back the lid.

More than half of it was Tansy's stuff. Little dresses, little shoes. A special velvet frock for Christmas Day. Dry-eyed, peculiarly calm, Connie took the miniature garments out, brushing them off and laying them carefully on the bed. Looking at them, she switched her thoughts off, attempting to keep all feeling at bay. Like the parted Red Sea, they hung back, just waiting to drown her.

A layer of her own clothes next. Not many, just a change or two. And underneath . . .

Her hands hovered, shook.

Christmas packages, lovingly wrapped, the shapes betraying their contents. The flat one was a box of paints, the square one a clockwork rabbit. The one that rattled was a board game with dice and counters, the oblong one a wooden jigsaw, the lumpy soft one a Scotty dog made of felt.

Tansy would have loved the Scotty dog. Connie had made it in secret during the evenings when the child had gone to bed. She remembered cutting out the tab of red for the tongue, stitching on the tartan jacket and tweaking the silly little quiff of hair in front. She had been so proud of her handiwork, hard put to wait until Christmas day to give it to the child. She should have followed her instincts, not tradition.

Suddenly, Connie remembered the pink package from Spooner's. Where was that? Had someone picked it up at the accident, gone off with it? Well, it was probably nothing much anyway. But . . .

'Can I open it now?' she heard Tansy ask again.

And her own reply. 'Oh, I shouldn't. Wait for tomorrow.'

205

A terrible sound escaped her then, and the Christmas paper became a multi-coloured blur. Before she knew it, she was howling like a wounded animal.

Janine and James had sent for the doctor again.

'I've given her some tablets,' he said as he left. 'She ought to sleep for a good twelve hours now.'

'Did you talk to her at all?' asked Janine. 'We've tried, but it does no good.'

The doctor surveyed them over his glasses. 'What do you mean?'

'She blames herself,' said James.

'That's not so very unusual.'

'There's more to it than that,' said Janine. 'Connie's had so much tragedy . . .'

'I know. I've been her doctor since she was born.'

'But she's hatched some peculiar ideas, as if everything bad that happens to people around her is her fault. *Mea culpa*. I'm a jinx. That's what she's convinced herself.'

'She's bound to be distraught at a time like this. I'm sure it'll pass. Connie was never short of common sense.'

'I wish I were as certain,' snorted Janine when he had gone. 'God knows, what she's suffered would be enough to send any woman off her head.' She flopped down in an armchair and scowled at the burning coals in the grate.

'How can one person be so consistently unfortunate?' she muttered. 'Why is life so merciless to some?'

'Do you think it might help if she talked to your father?' suggested James.

'What? No! Oh, he'd love the chance to feed her a lot of pap about compensation in the next world. She

206

needs a change of luck in this one, and eventually another man and another child.'

'Somehow I don't think she'll have the heart for it,' sighed James, adding: 'God, I wish you hadn't brought that suitcase here.'

'I didn't know what was in it,' snapped Janine. 'I didn't think, I was just too harrassed. She was in such a state and I had to make all the arrangements again. You weren't much help.'

Both fell silent. The fire crackled, throwing fiery glints on the glass baubles of the tree.

Christmas again, thought James. Trouble and tragedy at Christmas. God, I hate this season.

Connie went back to the bakery in February. She was not the same person. She still worked as hard, she was still as kind, she ate and she slept, but she had not recovered. Purged of emotion by now she developed a passive attitude of endurance, refusing to think about past or future. Nothing excited or interested her, not money or anything it could buy, not entertainment of any kind. Her existence was a series of twenty-four hour compartments. She would go through them one at a time and one day, when a certain number had passed, she would die and that would be that.

The neighbours hardly knew what to say to her about Tansy. They would touch her gently, shake their heads and squeeze her hand, then hurry away. Her gross misfortune frightened many, as if they witnessed a flogging too relentless to stomach.

Even Janine was deeply shaken by what had befallen her sister-in-law. It had always been a belief of hers that one created one's good or bad fortune. She was no longer sure of that. It seemed that some lives were doomed – and they never appeared to be those of the rotten or selfish. Always the good and the generous suffered, as far as Janine could see. The devil surely did take care of his own. Wryly, Janine recalled her miscarriages, the way she had felt about them, recognising the irony of that in the light of Connie's loss. She, Janine, had flourished, had she not, like the green bay tree? Evidence, surely, that she was numbered among the wicked.

In truth, she was annoyed to discover just how often religious concepts cropped up in her mind at times of great distress, how difficult it was to forget Matthew's teaching altogether. It created an angry defiance in her, not least because of Connie's plight. If that was where goodness got you, Janine would just as soon be a thorough-going sinner.

Twenty

It was said that after seven years married people grew restless and started to think about affairs. Janine had no particular desire for another man, but she was certainly feeling bored with James. The trouble was that James never did anything much. He liked to stay at home and read, or listen to the radiogram. He would cut the grass or wash the car and that was just about all he did for leisure. Rarely, he took Janine out to the theatre or a restaurant. Never did he wish to socialise with his neighbours. Janine didn't push him too hard at first, but eventually they began having rows about it.

'Jamie, I've been thinking . . .' she murmured one night at bedtime.

'What?' He looked up warily. He knew by now those words, that slow and speculative tone.

With long, tapered nails, Janine picked a piece of skin off her pomegranate, extracted a single seed and placed it on her tongue as if it were a pill. She was lying on top of the bed in a silk night-gown, left foot dangling off the edge. A slipper with a pom-pom swung from her big toe.

'Now that the house is straight, we could ask some people round.'

His stomach suffered a nervous jolt.

'What people?'

'Oh, one or two I know.'

He was half undressed, down to his shirt and underpants and socks. He stood there holding his trousers, looking hunted and, Janine thought, rather wet.

'What for?' he asked weakly.

'For dinner. I'm sure Mrs Coade could manage it.'

James rolled the trousers into a bundle, which his fingers anxiously squeezed. 'I don't think I'd like that, Janine.'

'Why not?' Her eyes were on the pomegranate. She ate a few seeds in quick succession and daintily licked her fingers.

'You know why not. You know I don't want to be bothered with other people.'

'Mmm,' she murmured, 'all too well. We never accept an invitation anywhere, but I thought perhaps you wouldn't mind me bringing a friend or two here.' She flicked a glance at him and something cutting, scornful, was in it. 'I thought you'd feel more at ease, more secure on your own ground.'

Agitated, he yanked at the knot of his tie and pulled the loop over his head. 'I bought this house for us, just for you and me. I don't want a horde of outsiders here, strangers. I'd hate it, Janine, pretending they were welcome, trying to think of things to say. I'm just not the sociable type and I like my privacy.'

'God, you're a bore,' she muttered. Her hand was half across her mouth as she said it, just as she half wanted him to hear it.

'What?' demanded James.

'Nothing.'

He finished undressing and climbed into bed. As the mattress sank beneath his weight, she shied the pomegranate accurately across the room to land in the waste basket in the corner.

'Aren't you going to get into bed?' he asked.

'In a minute,' came the sullen answer.

He gazed up at her, sitting propped against her pillows, examining those sharp nails. She could look very hard indeed when she was displeased.

'Janine . . .' he was apologetic now, '. . . you know I'll give you anything you want, within my means, but please don't ask me to play the host. I can't bear—'

'You don't try.' The words were crisp, verging on tart. 'Just because a situation is unfamiliar, you take fright.'

'When we were courting you agreed it would always be just you and me.'

'Oh, for God's sake! People say all sorts of silly things when they're engaged. Look, Jamie, it simply isn't possible for any couple to be all things to one another. It isn't healthy!'

'I can't imagine what that means,' grunted James.

She gritted her teeth, fighting her temper. 'What on earth is the point of having a nice home if we don't invite anyone in to admire it?'

'I didn't buy it to impress anybody else, Janine. I bought it for you to enjoy.'

She thought for a moment, then became sweeter, recalling that most of her flies had been caught with honey. Sliding down on the silky quilt, she shifted onto her side to face him.

'Having guests is part of the enjoyment, don't you see? And you know, it would do you so much good to shed that awful shyness.' She began to play with his earlobe in the way she knew he loved. 'I want people to see my fine husband, Jamie. I'm proud of you.'

Abruptly, he turned away from her. 'Well, I don't wish to be put on display, and if you loved me you wouldn't ask it.'

'Really, James!' she flared. 'You make such a great dramatic issue out of that bloody scar! I know people with birthmarks, buck teeth, game legs and God knows what other afflictions who live their lives to the full in spite of it. Do you know what your real problem is, James? You're vain.'

'Vain!' He rolled over again, open-mouthed.

'Yes, vain.' She flung herself off the bed and went to the wall cupboard in the corner and poured herself a Scotch, adding a splash of water.

'How, in the name of God, do you make that out?' He was sitting up in bed now, flushed with outrage.

'Because all that's on your mind is what people are thinking of you – and not even you as a character, Jamie, just you as a handsome face.'

'Handsome?' The word was choked.

'Oh yes.' She swilled the Scotch around her teeth and swallowed. 'You think you're beauty blighted, that's why you've never come to terms with it. You do have a conceit about your looks, Jamie. You're like some self-obsessed actress who won't leave the house if she has a pimple!'

'I've never heard anything so ridiculous, so far-fetched.'

'Oh no, it's not. The principle's much the same. If I'm not at my glorious best, I don't want to be seen. What's that but bloody vanity? And by the way, I know how little you thought of me when first we met. I know you saw me as a booby prize.'

'I thought you were someone who understood . . .' spluttered James.

'Now I'm attractive, popular, and that bothers you even more.'

'Only because you want to push me into situations

where I'm uncomfortable. I never thought you would expect this sort of thing. I thought you would let me relax in peace.'

'By living like a hermit with you?'

'I'd no idea your life was so bleak.'

'I didn't call it bleak. I'm merely saying there could be more to it, for both of us. Other people are interesting, James. They have jokes to tell, experiences to relate. They can widen your narrow horizons for you . . .'

'That's what you think of me, is it? Narrow, limited?'

'Well, you haven't travelled, have you, James? Or climbed any mountains or blazed any trails? You don't study any subject just for pleasure. You don't play any games or get involved in local affairs. You're dull! You're stodgy!'

He was staring at her, as a man who had been knifed might stare at his killer before he dropped to the floor, and she saw at once that she had gone too far. Setting down her glass, she came across to him, climbed on the bed and hugged his head to her bosom.

'I'm sorry,' she said, 'that was wicked of me, and you know I didn't mean it.'

James was silent and still against the silk of her night-gown. She might be wishing she had not voiced them, but he knew some truths had come out.

'I only meant that if you took an interest in such things you'd soon forget about that wretched scar. You dwell on it too much, Jamie, I've always said that.'

'My interests have been you and what you wanted,' came the muffled reply. 'But I can't be other than I am. You married a homebody, Janine, and that's all there is to it. At the end of the day, I want to close the door and be with you. You're welcome to anything I can afford to buy you, but you can't turn me into the life and soul of the party. I want nobody's company but yours, and I'm no sort of actor, I couldn't keep up a pretence.'

After a silent moment, she moved away from him, slipped into bed and lay looking up at the ceiling. 'All right,' she sighed, 'it was just an idea. It wouldn't be any good if you felt ill-at-ease. Everyone else would too, people sense these things.'

James turned out the light and lay down again. Guilt began to assail him now, for denying his beloved something she desired. Fate, after all, had refused her children. No doubt if she had had some they would have been friends enough for her. Still, he could find no courage to face a social round. Once it started, he knew it would never stop, because Janine never did anything in moderation. She spent, smoked and drank very freely. If he gave in on this, he feared he would never know privacy again.

Beside him, Janine was coldly fuming. And worse, she was afraid. For stretching in front of her she saw forty years of being cooped up with Jamie. For the first time she felt trapped, however fine the cage. He had bought her the lovely house she wanted, but here she had reached a dead end. Now she was expected to live in it with him alone, and be content.

Out on the landing, Mrs Coade had paused on her way from the bathroom. A dumpy figure in dressing gown and hairnet, she listened and smirked, delighted that 'mister' was standing up to 'her' for once. Mrs Coade didn't relish the prospect of parties and dinners. She worked hard enough as it was. Nowadays, madam had some fanciful ideas about food which didn't sit too well with her cook. Nowadays Mrs Coade was asked to marinade things and serve them up with foreign sauces. It was all very fiddly and spoilt good food, in Mrs Coade's opinion. She thought of the unfamiliar dishes as 'that old foreign muck'. Oh, she could well do without Janine's friends, people dropping cigarette ash everywhere and spilling drinks on the carpets, people over-indulging and being sick, staying the night and making more laundry for Mrs Coade to do. It was bad enough picking up after madam, who dropped her clothes just anywhere and left them. Beautiful clothes, too, not cheap by any means. 'Mister' was far too open-handed, far too mild, so what a treat it was to hear him stand his ground. Perhaps 'she' would respect him more from now on, Mrs Coade thought, rolling off to bed.

It was a vain hope. Janine was simply resentful after that night. For the first time she had met with real resistance from James and was privately enraged. Outwardly, she let the matter blow over. Inwardly, she sulked. And whenever she felt especially frustrated, she went and bought something expensive.

Twenty-one

A year went by and the decade drew towards its close. For all the Sayers it had been tumultuous in one way or another. The twenties had given Connie little but tragedy, while Janine had seen most of her hopes fulfilled and James had been somewhat helplessly carried along with his wife like a cork on a fast-moving stream.

In the autumn of 1929, their financial situation was in a fair state of equilibrium. They were considerably in debt, but both 'Janine's' and the bakery were doing excellent trade. They easily paid off the interest on the loans and sometimes a chunk of the principal too – although that had a tendency always to creep back up to a certain level because of Janine's spending sprees. Still, everything was under control; the bank was not worried at all.

Then, in late October, the balance was unexpectedly tipped by a crisis across the Atlantic. At first the Sayers failed to grasp the significance of it. Certainly, it meant little at all to Nell Colenso and Connie when they heard it on the wireless one busy morning.

The music was interrupted for the mid-day news. In the bakery, scant attention was paid to what the announcer was saying. Harry had gone to the pub for a lunch-time pint, while his wife and Connie were making ready the goods for the afternoon delivery to the café. Neither woman understood much about finance or economics at the best of times, and, since the report concerned the stock market of America, there seemed no connection with the Sayers' livelihood. Nell Colenso was taking in odd sentences as she worked and missing others. The broadcast was describing a frantic selling of shares, a disastrous collapse of prices, and enormous purchases made in desperate efforts to stop the panic.

Connie threw open an oven door, peered anxiously in at the bread rolls and muttered that they should have gone in earlier. Nell was picking hot scones off the baking tray from the second oven, dropping them onto a cooling rack and shaking her fingers after each one.

'Where's Wall Street?' she asked, catching a phrase or two from the broadcast.

'New York, I think,' said Connie. 'Why?'

'Sounds as if there's a riot going on. Something about a lot of people losing all their money.'

'I expect there's been some kind of robbery, then.'

'No, it's to do with shares. They're saying people's savings are suddenly worthless. How can that be?'

'Fraud, I dare say. Somebody's worked a swindle.'

'I think there's more to it than that,' murmured Nell. She glanced at Connie from under her brows. 'Jamie and Janine don't meddle with that sort of thing, do they? Investments abroad?'

'Lord, no. They're not as well off as that, and Janine isn't given to saving. Whatever's happening over there, it can't hurt us.'

Janine and James paid slightly more attention to the news when they read about it in the paper next morning, but even they had little idea of how severe the shock waves of this catastrophe were going to be.

'Bound to have some effect on trade in this country,'

Janine observed. 'Still, I expect it'll soon blow over, and I dare say it's mainly large industries that'll suffer.'

James looked at her. 'Such as shipbuilding?'

A small frown creased her brow. 'Well . . .' she said slowly, '. . . the dockyard has the Navy as well as commercial trade. I don't expect it'll be too bad for Plymouth.'

She had no real conception of what the crash was going to mean, no proper understanding of the way in which the foundations of prosperity had been shaken, the way that key threads would be broken in the interlocking mesh of commodity prices and bank loans to business and international debts, the way one thing shored up another, the way the whole delicately balanced structure could easily and suddenly fall apart. Janine, for all her personality and flair, had only a superficial knowledge of such things. She recognised a degree of interdependence between countries, but failed to see the true breadth and depth of it. What she liked to read was *Vogue*, not the financial pages and so she did not comprehend how the foundering of America's far-distant boat could swamp her own.

James understood a little better, but had never experienced a serious slump. His notions of what it might be like fell short of the reality.

It was not until the late spring of 1930 that the takings at 'Janine's' began to fall. The drop was not dramatic at first, but it was noticeable. Cakes were returned to the kitchen uncut at the end of the day. Scones and rolls went back to the bakery to be sold off cheaply in the shop next morning. After a while the quantity of goods produced for the lunch-time delivery was somewhat reduced.

Business went on slowly declining throughout the year. There were not so many shoppers in the streets that Christmas, and 1931 brought no improvement. Takings even fell at the bread shop, making Connie and the Colensos realise that the ice beneath them was growing thin.

'I don't like it,' Connie said one day to Harry, carefully placing sugar violets round the edge of a cake. 'Janine's lost so many customers whom I would have thought secure. Professional types – solicitors, doctors, teachers, civil servants – not the sort to worry about the ups and downs of commerce.'

'When the wind blows cold, everyone becomes a bit more careful with the money. Depressions touch almost everybody, one way or another. Snip a few stitches in a piece of knitting and watch the fabric unravel, see how fast the holes appear. Nobody's immune. Even if their jobs are safe, you don't know what debts people have or how much they might have lost on their investments.'

Connie turned the cake around, arranging angelica slices and crystallised fruit in the centre. 'It's terrifying, Harry,' she said. 'How long do you think it can last?'

'I'm afraid it's going to grow worse before it gets better, maid. And you can't expect the café to escape unscathed. It's a luxury, after all.'

Her hands stroked uneasily at her thighs, making a faint dry swish against the fabric of her apron. 'My God,' she said, 'I dread to think how much my brother owes the bank. He can't afford a drop in takings, Harry.'

The baker shrugged. 'Oh, I dare say he and Janine can hold out – if milady curbs her spending, that is.'

Connie's look was eloquent.

'Well,' said Harry quietly, 'it's up to him to stop her. If he can.'

The drawing room table was covered with ledgers, files and boxes full of invoices. In the centre of it all lay the latest yearly balance sheet. James sat in his shirt-sleeves, collar undone, and rubbed absently at his left temple with the ball of his thumb. He had a headache coming and his thoughts were scrambled after hours of poring over the books. Leaning back in his chair, he lifted his gaze to the window and the drifts of roses blooming outside, thinking anxiously about 'Janine's'.

There were always empty tables at the café now. Not a great many, to be sure, but still it showed the trend. Even some of the well-to-do were watching the pennies, forgoing little treats.

James looked again at the figures. He supposed there was no cause to worry unduly, as long as they kept treading water. Business was sluggish but very far from dead. He would lose no sleep over it – if only they didn't owe such a lot.

It was the house which had done it. The house, and the car, and Janine's accounts. James looked around the elegant room. Janine's house. The deeds were in joint names, but in every other way it belonged to her. He had never grown to like the place himself.

The bald truth was that they had over-reached themselves. All they had, after all, was a bakery and a tea-room, however smart. Most of the people in this neighbourhood had larger businesses than that. But Janine adored Gardenia Lodge – Jamie's hand moved down from his temple to finger his cheek – and he loved her. He could not be sociable to please her; it was therefore important to give her whatever else he could to keep her content.

The price tag on her happiness was unnerving, though. He flipped through sheaves of bills from local stores, from garages. That damned car – always something going wrong with it. But once again, she loved her darling jalopy, as she called it.

James stood up and went to the sideboard to pour himself a brandy. He frequently felt right out of his depth, and this was one of those moments. His reason told him that his situation was no worse than that of many other businessmen, and considerably better than some. Yet something else within him, more intuitive, was afraid. Whenever that something stirred, he felt his heart turn over.

Ada had not brought him up to be a borrower. 'If you haven't the cash, then go without. Don't fall into the money-lenders' hands.' Those had been among her favourite sayings. Instilled in James, they yet retained a power to reproach and threaten.

He downed the brandy in a single gulp and poured another. He had gone against his nature to please Janine, gone even against the things his mother had taught him.

'Janine is stronger than you,' he heard old Jordan say again.

Stronger than Ada, too, he acknowledged, for a mother never had the power a wife could wield in bed.

He threw back the second drink and felt his uneasiness ebb as the alcohol went to his head.

'Your parents were old-fashioned, Jamie, too cautious. That's why they never went far.'

That was what Janine would say, and perhaps she was right.

Returning to the table, he gathered up the papers and the books. His wife would be home soon. He couldn't let her catch him fretting over money. It made her impatient and he couldn't bear it when she grew annoyed with him. Dumping it all in its cupboard, James locked the door and put on his jacket and tie, then sat down with the newspaper.

It was full of grim tidings regarding the situation in America, and on the leader page was an article concerning Germany. Opposite was a photograph, taken in Berlin, of half a dozen unemployed men crouched wretchedly around a fire in a shanty made of junk and corrugated sheets. Having read this account of that country's plight, James began to feel almost safe and affluent once more. How uplifting it always was to hear of those in a far more desperate condition.

When he heard the crunch of tyres on gravel and the slam of a car door, he folded the newspaper and tossed it aside, ready with a cheerful greeting for his wife. She bounced in, bearing the inevitable paper bag.

'Hello, my sweetheart! Look at this . . .!' She threw her handbag on the sofa, ripping the carrier open. A cream silk summer frock appeared and slithered down in front of her as she held it up by its shoulder straps. 'Suits me, doesn't it? See the buttons – aren't they pretty? I really think it's the nicest frock I've ever bought.'

'You say that about them all when first you bring them home,' he said indulgently.

'Oh Jamie, I don't! She pulled off her hat and flung it at him, giggling.

'As a matter of interest, how much was it?'

The question was light, not accusing, but a furtiveness appeared in Janine's eyes.

'Three guineas, I think,' she said vaguely, knowing the price had been five. 'That's not too bad, is it?'

A mere trifle, James supposed, when they owed the bank a thousand times as much. It pricked him, though, to think the frock had cost twice a family man's dole money for a week, particularly since he refused credit at the bread shop to such men's wives.

'You don't – mind – do you?'

'Of course not. I just wondered.'

'It isn't really extravagant, Jamie, I'll wear it a lot.'

Half a dozen times – that was a lot for Janine. There would not be days enough in a lifetime to get full wear out of everything she bought, even if fashions stopped changing – which, of course, they never did. From season to season items vanished from her cupboards because room had to be made for the new. Mrs Sayers was very well thought of by the organisers of local jumble sales.

Still, her husband just nodded, smiled and said nothing. She took such pleasure in her clothes.

Dropping the frock on the sofa under the window, she went to the mantel mirror and fiddled daintily with her hair. 'What time is it?' she murmured. 'Nearly two? I must get back to the café when I've had a bite of lunch. Have you eaten yet?'

'I don't want anything. Mrs Coade has made you a salad, I think.'

She wrinkled her nose at that. 'Oh, then I shan't bother after all. Jamie, should I have a permanent wave, do you think? My hair's been straight for such a long time and I'm bored with it.'

'I like it as it is.'

'But you've never seen me with curls. Anyway, now I'm past thirty, I need a gentler style.'

223

'What if you regret it?'

'I shan't. I know what'll suit me, I can always tell. I think I'll make an appointment this afternoon on the way to the café. Yes, I will! I'll have it done on Monday!'

Whether he approved or not. Like the house, it was going to be the way she wanted it. She expected no challenge from Jamie, and sure enough received none.

'As you please,' came the mild reply.

She bent and kissed him, then grabbed for her bag. 'Must fly. We're always so busy on Saturday afternoons.'

'We used to be,' mumbled James.

'Oh, nonsense, we still are! Not packed out, I grant you, but we still have a very good trade.' She paused on her way out the door and cocked her head, perky, teasing. 'You're not upset by all the gloom are you, Jamie? Don't worry, we'll ride it out. It would take a financial earthquake to topple "Janine's".'

With that, she was gone in a flurry of swirly skirts and tapping heels. He heard the car start and saw her back it past the window, swing it round. Its roar faded away as she drove off, and he was alone again. His gaze swivelled to the heap of cream silk lying on the sofa cushions. She hadn't even bothered to hang it up. He suspected she had forgotten all about it in her sudden enthusiasm for a new hairstyle.

James picked up his paper again and re-read the piece about Germany. This time it failed to comfort him at all, and he wondered how long it might be before Britain descended to the same piteous state. Every day he read of hunger marches and protests against the Means Test. Things were worse in the North and Midlands, of course. Nevertheless, when down at the Barbican, James was always encountering men of his own age with whom he had gone to school, or older ones who had been kind to him as a child, who were out of a job now and desperate. There was real want now, there were evictions, great queues of unemployed men. Every week brought lay-offs and sackings at the dock-yard. Lately there had been pay cuts too, and strikes in consequence of that. There were gaunt men hanging round street corners all the time, and round the dock-yard gates in hopes of casual work. The pawn shops were very busy these days, and certain women had taken to buying stale bread when they came into the Sayers' shop.

James hated the way they looked at him, pleading or sullen. He hated saying no when they asked if they could pay next week. Connie would have given them credit, but James had stopped her, saying:

'We can't start that, we daren't. You know what happens. Word gets round and before long they all want it. Do it for this one and that one asks, "Why her and not me?" We'd have shouting matches here in the shop, and some of them would never pay in the end.'

James knew his sister compensated where she could, slipping an extra bun or a little fancy cake or two into the bag as a bonus when she served a neighbour in dire straits. He turned a blind eye to that, but he had to endure their resentment all the same. In the end, though, it was easier to refuse them than Janine.

James had an uncomfortable sense of not belonging anywhere any more. His old neighbours thought him an upstart now, while his new ones over-awed him. Only with his wife and sister did he feel at ease. Connie demanded nothing, of course. But Janine? Well, he had to please her, and that cost money – which he told himself was Matthew Jordan's fault. It was too disturbing to blame his darling.

Sometimes, late in the evening, Janine would kick off her shoes, lay out on the sofa with a drink and a cigarette, and talk about how far they had come from the bakery on the Barbican, and how much farther they might go when things picked up. Sometimes she talked about opening a restaurant, a notion which terrified James. She lived in constant expectation of an end to the depression, confident that 'they' would surely do something soon.

James tried to share her optimism and summoned old sayings to comfort him: 'The darkest hour is just before dawn' or 'It's a long road which has no turning'. Janine might be right. Recovery might start any day, and so he elected to wait a little longer before gently suggesting that she might be a bit less careless with the money.

However, the following year, the worst of all, brought distress that not even Janine could overlook. The time came when it was no longer worthwhile to pay 'The April Moons'. In any case, their style was now passé. At any one time there were seldom more than twenty people in the café and often only a solitary couple shuffling round the dance floor. Pat the waitress was made redundant, having tossed a coin for it with Doris and lost.

Janine was neither philosophical nor brave about these reversals. She had bitter things to say about the politicians, bankers and industrialists whom she deemed to be responsible. James had finally been forced to tell her that she would have to close a few of her accounts in town, use the car less and do her own hair. With much grumbling, she made the economies, but it was rather too late. James could see no way now that they would ever get out of debt without selling off property. Simply in order to survive, they would need an upturn very soon. Something like a big contract for the dockyard would be of help. At times he guiltily felt that the city could do with another war.

Twenty-two

'Hitler now Führer' yelled the headline. Connie glanced at it, then flipped through the rest of the paper with just as little interest. Something tickled her bare shoulder. Absently, she brushed the fly away, and in so doing realised that she was starting to burn. Her skin was growing tender pink and the straps of her bathing costume were chafing. Discarding the newspaper, she threw a towel round her, thinking she ought to go home soon and put on some calamine.

It was August of 1934, and the day was still hot, even though the time was approaching five. A balmy wind stirred her hair as she squinted out across the Sound towards Drake's Island. The shimmer off the sea was almost blinding and she put up a hand to shade her eyes. Small boats with white and coloured sails were scudding round the bay.

Sunday today. No one at home for whom to cook. She would make do on cold beef and pickles. Connie had not done a Sunday roast since Tansy died. Sometimes she went up to Gardenia Lodge for a Sunday meal, but mostly she stayed at home or, if it was sunny, came here to the swimming pool under the Hoe. Connie liked to sit here and watch the children. She could bear it now, nearly seven years on.

The pool was large and circular, with a little fountain in the middle. All around it ran a concrete terrace crowded with deck-chairs. Away to the right lay the

Promenade Pier, its glass dome winking in the sun. Nearly all the deck-chairs were occupied, and boisterous screams and splashes came from the pool. The scent of brine was mingled with a sweet, biscuity smell which spoke to Connie of sun-oil and ice-cream wafers. People around her lounged in the warmth and looked content. Everyone seemed happier, more at ease this year. Trade of all kinds had been improving a little lately, and James had lost his perpetual worried frown. The Sayers had pulled through the worst and better days were on the way.

Connie had no deck-chair. She was sitting among the rocks up behind the terrace and her backside was starting to feel the discomfort. She had been for a swim and her costume was still somewhat wet. As soon as it dried enough, she would slip on her frock and walk home.

Looking out across the pool, she noticed a child, a little girl, climbing up the steps and out of the water. She had light brown hair, like Tansy's, and appeared about eleven years old. Connie's eyes followed her as she ran around the concrete parapet, a skinny little figure in a pink costume. Tansy would have been that age now, on the brink of maturing, filling out. Connie observed the girl with a placid sadness. Once, the sight of small girls had felt like a knife-cut. Now it was a gentler sorrow. It had to be; she could not have lived for long with pain of that degree. The deadness, the shutting off of emotion had helped Connie survive. The jagged misery, like grit in an oyster, had been wrapped up in numb acceptance before it could slice her to pieces. People seemed to worry about her, seemed to feel she had clung too long to her remoteness, but Connie was comfortable in it, she felt safe. Nothing happened, nothing changed in her world, day in, day out, and that was quite all right.

Connie rummaged in her holdall, searching for her comb. The pool was of seawater and her hair had dried out stiff with the salt. She started raking through it, tugging at the tangles. Other women nowadays wore marcel waves but Connie could not be bothered with anything like that. Her hair was cut at jaw level, with only the turn which nature gave it. Anyway, she thought it didn't look too bad.

A shadow fell across her as she pulled and flicked with the comb, and an unfamiliar voice offered a piece of unwanted advice.

'Ought to wear a cap when you go in.'

Connie blinked up at the dark figure standing over her. A man in shorts and open-necked shirt. He was not very tall and his accent was local.

'I don't like bathing caps,' she said flatly, and looked away.

Uninvited, the man sat down. 'I saw you here last week,' he said. 'You're the lady from the bread shop. Know me, do you?'

She had seen him about. He had been in the shop a few times. He was dark, with a wavy mouth and curly hair which was starting to show some grey. Not a young man – forty perhaps. He had what she thought of as a Welsh look about him, round-faced and humorous. Still, she said: 'No.'

'I'm Sam Tucker. I work at the dockyard alongside your neighbour, Jack Chope.'

'Oh, I see.' Connie went on combing. The hair at the crown of her head was matted.

'Shall I do that?' he offered.

She looked startled, then indignant. 'No, thank you.'

He was silent a moment and then he asked: 'Like an orange juice or something? Café's open down at the pier.'

Lord, he was trying to get friendly, start something! The idea appalled her, so long had it been since she gave up all interest in men. She was thirty-five now, and guardedly self-sufficient.

'I have to get home.'

'Why? You live alone, don't you?'

'How do you know that?'

'Jack Chope. I asked him about you.'

'Did you, indeed?' She was hurriedly packing her holdall now, stuffing in the towel and her cotton sunhat.

'I'm a widower, you see.'

Connie's mouth fell open. He certainly wasn't one to beat about the bush. Her gaze slithered quickly over him. He had chubby knees and his feet were broad in their leather sandals.

Smiling, he said: 'Sorry, that was clumsy.' His eyes were brown and apologetic.

Connie frowned slightly, but softened her tone. 'Look, Mr Tucker, if Jack suggested to you that I was a likely prospect, I'm sorry to have to tell you that he was wrong and he should have known better.'

'Oh. Well, he meant no harm. Nor did I.'

She switched on and off a brief smile. 'That's all right. I must go now.' Standing up, she dropped her frock over her head and buttoned the front.

Tucker liked her figure. She was taller by two or three inches than he was, a different physical type altogether.

'Mind if I walk with you?' he asked. 'I live near you, just off New Street.'

'I'd rather you didn't.'

'I won't talk about anything personal, I promise.'

'I should think not, you're a stranger! I don't mean to be unpleasant, Mr Tucker, but I'm truly not interested and I wish you would accept that.'

'I only said I'd walk with you.'

'You're pushing. Please leave me alone.'

'All right, all right.' He sighed and clasped his hands between his knees, staring out over the pool. Connie, with her native kindness, felt a mite guilty for being so sharp. He was lonely, she supposed. Pretty guileless, too.

'I, um – I'm sorry you lost your wife,' she said, by way of smoothing things over.

He nodded, then looked away again.

Connie hovered. It was on the tip of her tongue to say: 'I'm sure you'll meet someone else.' But it struck her as trite, so she simply bid him goodbye and hurried off.

Marching home, she thought she would have something to say to Jack Chope the next time she saw him. The nerve of him – match-making, interfering in her life and obliging her to snub the unfortunate Mr Tucker. It was too bad of Jack and she would tell him so.

Sam Tucker was a riveter. His wife had died in 1930, leaving him alone in the cottage he had bought only six months before. It was one of three surrounding a courtyard, closed off from New Street by a wrought-iron gate. In the centre of the courtyard was a patch of grass, and in the middle of that a sundial on a granite pedestal. The cottages were also of granite, two up and two down, with low ceilings. Sam and his wife didn't even have the place straight by the time she died, and once she was gone he had lost any urge to finish it off. The cottage was dark, half-painted, half-furnished, and Sam rattled about in it like a nut in an over-large shell. It was clean and relatively tidy, but without any comfort or atmosphere. For those things he went down the road to the pub in Parade Ope, by the quay.

Jack Chope had told him Connie Sayers was just the woman he needed. Jack had told him Connie needed someone too, but Sam had nothing good to report when the two men met in the pub that night.

'You'll have to persevere,' said Chope. 'I've told you what her life's been like.'

'Made a fool of myself,' grumbled Sam, sucking the froth off his beer.

'She's a good soul. Make a lovely wife. Don't give up so fast.'

Chope put down his empty glass on the counter and signed to the barmaid to fill it again. The pub was a cosy place of low beams and polished brasses. All its customers were either fishermen or dockers, mostly the latter in the evenings when the boats were out. In the winter, Sam came here for shepherd's pie or stew and a warm by the fire.

'What am I supposed to do? Go round there knocking on the door and ask her out?'

'Why not?'

'She'll shut it in my face.'

Jack paid for his second beer. 'Keep knocking. Make a nuisance of yourself.'

'That's easy for you to say.'

'Want to spend your life alone?'

'No, but she does.'

Chope sank his mouth in his pint and gulped. 'Get

away, she only thinks so. Nice-looking maid,' he wheed-led, licking the froth from his top lip. 'Know of a better one around here?'

'No,' admitted Sam.

'Like me to put in a good word for you?'

'Oh, that'd be helpful, I'm sure. You're a real diplo-mat, you are.'

'Do it your own way, then,' shrugged Chope. 'But don't you give up, Sam. If any woman's worth the effort, Connie is.'

Keep knocking. Make a nuisance of yourself. Despite initial misgivings, Tucker decided to try it.

Connie answered a knock at the door one evening to find him standing on the step in his best brown suit and his 'social' cap (which was fawn and clean, whereas his work cap was grey and grubby).

'Oh,' said Connie warily.

'Come to the pictures with me?' he asked. 'There's *Grand Hotel* at the Gaumont.'

She shook her head. 'Thank you, but . . .'

'Or *Jekyll and Hyde* at the Palladium. I don't mind.'

'I don't often go to the cinema, Mr Tucker.'

'Well, I'm offering to take you, aren't I?'

'I really can't. I'm busy.'

'Would you rather see *Frail Women* at the Savoy?'

'No,' said Connie, harassed. 'I'm sorry. Good evening to you.'

The door closed. He stared at the knocker, tempted to rap again. No sense, though, in making her angry, he supposed.

'Tsk,' he said, and moped off to the pub.

Connie, skulking behind the net curtain in the

parlour, saw him pass the window and breathed a sigh of relief.

On Sunday morning, however, there came another tap at the door.

'Hello,' said Tucker cheerfully. 'Coming to church?'

She was briefly speechless, then she tartly informed him: 'I'm not religious.'

'Then you're missing a lot. I'm Methodist, you know.'

'How nice for you.'

'You can make a lot of friends at church.'

'If so, why are you in need of my company, Mr Tucker?'

'Sam.'

'I've no desire to come to church.'

His bounce subsided. He eyed her a little sadly. 'Nice morning,' he pointed out. 'We could go for a walk instead.'

'Oh, for heaven's sake! If you think you're going to wear me down, you're badly mistaken!'

This time the door slammed hard.

Tucker sighed and turned away. Across the street, he saw the curtains twitch in Jack Chope's front room. Despondently, Sam trailed off to church. It crossed his mind to go to the pool that afternoon to see if Connie was there, but then he thought better of it. Perhaps she was even now regretting her sharpness. He would wait a while before tackling her again.

With many an anxious backward glance at the door, Connie had retreated into the kitchen. She sat down at the table and nibbled her nails with a worried frown. She had planned to go to the pool that afternoon, but now she felt she had better not, in case he followed her there. It was too bad, she told herself again. Connie had not seen Jack Chope in the past week to chide him, but knew he would be at home just now, awaiting his Sunday lunch. In a sudden access of temper, she got up and marched down the hallway, bustled across the street and hammered at his door.

Unshaven, with his braces hanging down, he opened it a crack and peeped around it.

'Jack, your friend Mr Tucker was around here just now, as I'm sure you know.'

'Eh?' he said. 'Oh, Sam. Was he? Know him, do you?'

'Please don't play innocent with me. You put him up to it, I'm sure.'

'Don't know a thing about it, Connie.'

'He's pursuing me!' she flared.

A smile. 'Well, he's not a bad sort. Not afraid of him, are you, Connie? Good as gold, old Sam.'

'He's being a pest and I don't want to be bothered. You tell him, Jack, you tell him to let me be.'

'I don't carry messages,' said Chope.

'No, but you try and engineer things, don't you?' She levelled her tone and fixed him with an accusing blue stare.

Letting the door back farther, Jack pulled his braces up over his shoulders and scratched his stomach. 'He asked me if you were unattached and I told you were. He asked me why and I told him that as well. What else was I to do?'

Her voice became pleading. 'I'm sure he's a very nice man, but I wish you would put him off.'

'I don't do his thinking for him. He's met you now, he likes you.'

'Well, don't encourage him, anyway.'

'Shan't say another word about you,' lied Chope.

For a moment she gazed at him helplessly. Then: 'Jack, I've been through enough, I couldn't face any more. I'm settled now, I'm on an even keel. I don't want to be involved with anyone ever again. Don't make mischief, please.'

He was staring soberly back at her now. 'Settled?' he said softly, at the end of a thoughtful pause. 'Half-dead, Connie, that's what you are.'

'Be that as it may, it suits me,' she hissed. 'It's painless, and if you have any regard for your friend, you'll advise him to look elsewhere. I'm not exactly good luck, am I, Jack? Think of that.'

'Ye Gods,' he called as she walked away. 'I never guessed you were superstitious, Connie. Bad medicine, is that the idea?' he mocked.

'Oh, shut up!' she flung back over her shoulder.

'I'll tell Sam that, I surely will. He'll be glad to know it's not that you dislike him.'

What a treat, he thought, to see her angry for once.

Routed, Connie fled indoors. She felt on the verge of tears but they didn't quite come. It would sound silly to others, she supposed, that conviction of being somehow destructive, a carrier of calamity, just as Typhoid Mary carried sickness. No one could understand without living in Connie's head, Connie's skin. Only she could feel the reality of her curse.

Reaching across the kitchen table, she pulled towards her the plate of bread and cheese and salad set out for her solitary lunch, sat down and tried to eat. But her appetite had completely gone and after a couple of bites she unhappily thrust the plate away.

Three days later came the bouquet. James brought it into the bakery one lunch-time.

'Look,' he said, sounding amazed, 'for you. There I was, outside loading up the van, and this man taps me on the shoulder, tells me to give you these flowers. I asked who I should say they were from and he reckoned you would know.'

Wearily, Connie took the flowers. Delphiniums, of all things. Huge delphiniums.

'Why, they're beautiful,' said Nell.

Glancing around her, Connie cleared her throat. Everyone was staring, waiting, Jamie and the Colensos.

'Well?' prompted Harry. 'Who is he?'

'He's called Sam Tucker,' mumbled Connie. 'He's chasing me.'

'Fancy that!' exclaimed Nell, delighted. 'Flowers like those must have cost him a bit.'

Another mumble. 'I daresay.'

'Shy, is he?' enquired her brother. 'He could have come in and presented them himself.'

'Shy?' snorted Connie. 'Not him! He wanted you to see them, I don't doubt. He's looking for allies.'

'Why should he need allies? Don't you like him?'

'I've nothing against him, I'm simply not interested, but he's being very persistent.'

'Oh?' They were all intrigued.

'What did he look like?' Harry asked of James.

'Just a pleasant working man like any other. Thick-set, middle-aged.'

'That's him,' muttered Connie.

'How long has he been after you?' asked James.

'About a fortnight. I wish he would leave me alone, but he won't take no for an answer. It's Jack Chope's fault. They're workmates.'

'Ah,' said everyone.

'You ought to feel flattered,' Nell declared.

'Hounded is how I feel.'

238

'Bachelor, is he?' asked Harry.

'Widower.'

The Colensos exchanged eager looks.

'Why don't you give him a chance, then, maid?'

'Don't you start on me too!' She appealed to her brother. 'Jamie, perhaps if you warned him off . . .'

'You're a grown woman, you can deal with him.' James was plainly tickled.

'He's after a wife.'

'Has he said so?'

'Not in so many words, but it's obvious.'

'Perhaps he only wants a bit of companionship.'

'It's more romantic than that to send flowers.' A flash of perception made her add: 'If I were to marry, I'd have to leave here, you know.'

James took the point and his grin disappeared. Still, he repeated: 'It's not for me to see him off. You'll have to do that for yourself.'

He was not so amused now, disturbed by the thought of Connie leaving the bakery. He had come to rely on her so much. Well, he reassured himself, this Mr Tucker's flirtation would probably come to nothing. Hoisting a last tray of flans for the café, he went out, carrying it in front of him.

'You know,' Harry said as they heard him drive off, 'we don't get endless chances in life, Connie. This could be your last.'

'Well, I don't want it.' Connie thrust the flowers at Nell. 'You're welcome to these, if you like them.'

'I'll put them in water for you,' said Mrs Colenso stoutly. 'I couldn't possibly take them. It isn't like you, Connie, to be unkind.'

'The man's been making a damned nuisance of him-

239

self. Anyway . . .' she looked from one to the other, begging understanding, '. . . you know my reasons.'

Harry and Nell were expressively silent.

Twenty-three

Thereafter, Sam Tucker took to calling into the shop for a pasty every Saturday. If James was having his lunch or out with the van, Mrs Colenso served him, with the result that Nell came to know him quite well. Such an agreeable man, she would say at every opportunity. A thoroughly decent sort.

Somehow or other the word had spread around the neighbourhood that Connie had an admirer. The tattler was probably Millie Chope. Whoever had put it about, the result was a gentle, if unsubtle, pressure on Connie. When she called in at the dairy, Cynthia Hardin would often find some means to mention 'that nice Mr Tucker'. At the butcher's the man would ask point-blank, 'How's Sam?' as if they were already related. The ironmonger joked when she went to buy picture hooks, 'Get Sam to put them up for you. I hear he's handy.'

Beset on all sides, Connie was vexed. Everyone seemed to be rooting for Sam, recommending him. No one appeared to comprehend her reluctance at all. For the first time ever, Connie wished she lived elsewhere in the city. The Barbican, being small, close and nosy, was the sort of neighbourhood where everyone knew everyone else's business. What they did not know, they were busily trying to find out, and everybody felt entitled to meddle.

As for Tucker, he had warmed to the challenge,

seeing in it now an element of sport. Rebuffs no longer made him feel foolish, they simply put him on his mettle. He was ever on the look-out for Connie and would always make a point of stopping if he met her in the street, always insist on saying something, even if he could only detain her for a minute. Occasionally, he sent her a fond little letter, always ending with an invitation to go out with him. She never answered them.

If Sam was sometimes daunted, he never let her see it. Connie found him as bothersome as a bluebottle and was driven to snap at him on more than one occasion. Since harshness never came easily to her, she was doubly vexed that he forced her to it.

One Thursday afternoon he spotted her on her way home from the shops and seized the opportunity to carry her grocery bags.

'Shall I take those?' he offered, falling in step beside her.

Connie paused and frowned at him. 'Why aren't you at work?' The question was indignant – she expected to be safe from him on weekdays, during shift hours at least.

'Had a bit of bonus owed to me. Took time in lieu of the extra pay.'

He reached for her bags, but she snatched them away.

'Mph,' she said. 'Are you that well off? Most men need the money.'

'Most men have wives and kids.'

She walked on.

'Give me those bags, come on.'

'I can manage.'

'I'm stronger than you are.'

No reply.

242

Suddenly, he grabbed at them, tugged, and the dragging weight was gone from her arms.

'There, that's better, isn't it?'

'If you're trying to make me feel obliged to you, you're going to be disappointed.'

'I'm not after your gratitude, just a few minutes of your company.'

Irritable silence.

'Funny sort of woman, aren't you?' he continued. 'Determined that you don't need anybody.' He started swinging the bags slightly, dawdling along the cobbles and thereby forcing Connie to slow her pace. 'I mean, here am I, not unpresentable, not unintelligent, with no vices to speak of, keen to take you out and spend a bit of money on you, but you'll have none of me.'

'Then why waste your time?'

'I love a challenge.'

'You'll fail at this one.'

Mr Tucker chuckled and started whistling through his teeth. He paused outside the gate before his courtyard. 'That's where I live, look, in there. Not a bad little place. Like to come in and see?'

'No, thank you.'

Sighing, he walked on. 'You're your own worst enemy,' he said.

'You don't know . . .!' She exploded – then clamped her mouth shut. Because he did know all about her, from Jack, from the neighbours, even, she suspected, from Nell Colenso.

'I know you're a lovely woman going to waste, I know that, all right.' A sparkle came into his eyes. 'I'm very affectionate, Connie. Imagine what you're missing.'

'Keep it.'

'You'll grow old and dry up and turn sour.'

'What's it to you, if that's my choice?'

'Well, see, I look at it like this – for every woman who shuts herself off, there's a lonely man deprived. And the other way about, of course. Every poor old bachelor creates a poor old spinster. Ever thought of that?'

'Can't say I have. Can't say I care, either.'

'But look at me – a good man gathering cobwebs.'

'Find someone else with a duster, I don't want the job.'

'But it's you who've caught my fancy. Where's the harm in coming out with me? No shady motives, I promise. No dire intentions. We could go to the Palace variety show, if you like.'

She shook her head.

For a moment he was at a loss. Then: 'I've a good job, you know. Well paid, secure.'

A snort. 'No one can ever be sure of that – not that it makes any difference to me whether you're in work or out of it.'

'Oh, I'm sure enough,' said Tucker wryly. 'This country's going to start re-arming, you know. We'll have to.'

They had almost reached her door. She stopped again, stared at him. 'Why?'

'Germany.'

'Oh, tosh! They won't want another war, not after the last one. Nobody will.'

'Don't you read the papers? Don't you know ambition when you see it? That's a dangerous bugger they've put in power over there.'

'He's pulling his country out of the doldrums, seems to me.'

'Oh yes, and making it fit and strong enough to over-run its neighbours.'

Her gaze shifted uneasily. Another war? It hardly seemed credible that such a thing could happen twice, that anyone would instigate a second orgy of carnage. Who in his right mind . . .?

'That's alarmist talk, Mr Tucker. Mind you, I've nothing against the building of new ships. It means jobs and overtime, as you say, and it's better to be safe than sorry, I admit. No sense being complacent or weak, but I can't see us having another war like the last one.'

He pushed his tongue thoughtfully into his cheek. 'I didn't say it was going to be the same.'

'What could be so different?'

'Everything's new-fangled nowadays, so why not war as well?'

He was just blethering, Connie decided.

'May I have my bags, please?'

He handed them over. 'Come out with me tomorrow night. We'll do anything you like.'

'Please, Mr Tucker, give this up. You're driving me mad, I confess it, but I'm not going to change my mind.'

'I've told you and told you to call me Sam.'

Turning on her heel, she went into her house and banged the door.

Five weeks later, on her birthday, a little parcel arrived in the post. Inside was a card with roses on it, and a bottle of 'Devon Violets' scent. She sat on the edge of the parlour sofa, wrapping paper and coloured ribbon strewn around her, helplessly looking down at his gift.

'Love from Sam,' said the card.

After a time, Connie took the stopper from the bottle, sniffed, and smiled with pleasure in spite of herself. It was her favourite, 'Devon Violets'. Nell Colenso must have told him that.

The smile faded and she gazed unhappily at the little bottle. Oh God, he simply would not give up. He was such a nice man, really. And Lord, what patience, what determination. Connie had never encountered anything like it. Picking up the ribbon with its little bow, she twirled it absently round her fingers, examining the card again. The writing was large and somewhat awkward, and suddenly she found it touching. His notes had never had the same effect. Something about this hopeful offering moved her. 'Devon Violets', a card with roses – obvious, unimaginative choices, but ones which had seemed right to Sam. It was almost a child-like present. Connie felt her eyes prick. He wanted her so earnestly, but she could not, dared not respond.

She would have to be less rude in future, though, she decided. Being abrupt had failed to work, in any case. Connie could not think how she was ever going to shake him off.

She used the perfume, though. She put some on that day and both the Colensos remarked approvingly on it. Their present to her was a new crêpe blouse. No one mentioned the fact that James and Janine had forgotten her birthday.

Winter came and late November brought an outbreak of influenza. Connie escaped it, but half of her neighbours fell ill and a number of old people died. It was while on her way to the greengrocer's shop that she met Sam Tucker and learned that he too had caught the virus. Once again it was a weekday, when normally he would have been at work. She saw him coming down the road, muffled up in a scarf, clutching a bottle of whisky and looking miserable. His footsteps dragged and his shoulders sagged. He stopped when he saw her, but kept a couple of yards between them. Connie could see at once what was wrong with him.

'Got the flu, Mr Tucker?'

'Yes, maid,' he answered, coughing.

'Going home to bed with a drop of hot grog?'

He nodded.

'I must say, you're looking rough.'

He was – pale with livid feverish patches on his cheeks.

'Can't keep anything down but liquids,' he said. 'Haven't eaten a solid morsel in days.'

'Oh dear. Have you got a temperature?'

'I'm sweating now. Other times I shiver.'

'Seen the doctor?'

'They can't do much for flu. It has to run its course.'

'Well, I hope you'll be over it soon.'

'Nice to see you, Connie.' He coughed again and trudged on his way.

Connie walked on a few paces, then turned and watched him for a moment or so until he disappeared round a corner and up a sidestreet leading towards his home.

Poor soul, she thought. I wonder if he has a fire lit. Some men know how to look after themselves, but most don't.

Carrying on to the greengrocer's, she bought her vegetables and was about to leave when a memory from childhood bobbed into her mind. Ada's cure-all, brewed up every winter when James and Connie were children. A very simple remedy and general protector of health. Mam had always sworn by it, even though other people laughed, calling it countrified and cranky.

Ada had made her children take it throughout the winter months each year, and it had to be said that Connie and James had been less prone to sickness than most of their peers. Furthermore, when they did go down with something, it was seldom severe. They had weathered throat infections, colds and all the childhood fevers with relative ease, and Mam had always said that the reason was leeks.

Simple garden leeks, cleaned, roughly chopped and boiled in a couple of inches of water, which was then strained off and drunk. The children had hated the smell and taste. Connie could recall her brother whining and throwing tantrums because he didn't want his leek juice. One day he had spat a mouthful all over Ada's best blouse. He had been forgiven, of course, and to make the potion more palatable, Mam had taken to adding beef stock.

So many years ago. Connie had quite forgotten until now about taking leek juice. Ada had let the habit lapse as the children grew up. But there was something in it, Connie was sure. Mam, for all her faults, had known a thing or two.

Turning to the shopkeeper, Connie said: 'I'll have two pounds of leeks as well, I think.'

It was Sam Tucker's turn to answer a knock at the door. On the step he found Connie, bearing a large white basin. It was covered with a cloth, through which there seeped a thin steam smelling of onions. Sam had hastily pulled on his overcoat, for beneath he was clad in pyjamas. He stared at Connie as if she were some sort of apparition.

'Don't just stand there, let me in. I have something for you.'

He stood back and she brushed past him.

'Where's your kitchen?'

Slowly closing the front door, he waved an arm towards a room on the left.

Connie went in. Cupboard doors opened and closed and the clatter of dishes was heard. A moment later she re-emerged with Tucker's largest mug.

'Drink this.'

He sniffed at it. 'God, what is it?'

'Something to do you good.'

'Smells beastly.'

'Don't exaggerate. Down it quickly, come on.'

'I'll bring it back up.'

'Not this you won't.'

'Tell me what it is.'

'Leek water.'

He looked at her as if she were mad.

'I know, I know,' said Connie impatiently. 'No one ever believes it's any good. But take my word for it, Mr Tucker. Try it, will you please?'

A glint came into his eyes. 'I will if you call me Sam.'

'All right.'

Still he hesitated.

'I'm waiting.'

Tucker gulped it back and screwed his face up. 'God's truth,' he spluttered.

'Well done, Sam. Now you'd better go back to bed.'

She glanced around his dwelling and frowned. There was a fire in the sitting-room grate, but it was feeble. The whole place was about as comfortable as a waiting room at a railway station. She had already seen that the kitchen cupboards were all but empty. No supplies to speak of. How typical of a man on his own.

She followed him to the door of his bedroom and waited while he climbed between the rumpled covers.

'Why don't you straighten your bed out, Sam? You'd sleep a lot better.'

'I'm all right.'

Connie glanced down at the floor – cold lino. One of the curtains was half torn off its hooks and flapped despondently, betraying a draught.

'I don't suppose you possess such a thing as a hot-water bottle?' she asked.

He shook his head, eyeing her piteously over the blankets.

'I thought not. Look, Sam, I've left some more leek water in a saucepan on your stove. Heat it up and drink it this afternoon, and I'll bring you some stew this evening. Agreed?'

'I appreciate it, maid, but I've told you I can't keep anything down.'

'Take the second dose of leeks as I tell you and we'll see. Will you do that? Promise me you won't chuck it out?'

He didn't believe it would work, but still he promised. She had come to his house! That was progress indeed. She would come back this evening and bring him hot food! She was taking it upon herself to look after him a bit. This had to be some sort of turning point and the last thing he wanted to do was discourage her – even if it meant drinking more of that foul stuff.

'I'll see you later on, then.'

Before she left she stoked the fire. It could be nice, this cottage, she thought. Pity he had never made a home of it.

Sam was sitting up when Connie returned that

evening. He had honoured his promise and drunk the leek juice.

'How are you feeling?'

'Not too bad.'

'Been sick again?'

'Not once.'

'Hmm,' said Connie wisely. 'Here, you'll be ready for this now.' She handed him a bowl of stew and a spoon. The stew was thick with beef, potatoes, carrots, split peas and, he noted, a good deal of chopped leek. Tucker was ravenous and dug into it eagerly.

'Perhaps your onion water did some good,' he allowed.

'They're a natural antiseptic, leeks. People scoff at the notion because they're just commonplace vegetables, but I believe they have a special virtue. By the way,' she added, 'I've brought you this.'

It was a hot-water bottle in a home-knitted cover.

He grinned at her over his spoon. 'I'd rather have you in bed.'

'Don't be so saucy,' said Connie, smiling. 'Anyway, I don't want your flu.'

He went on eating, but after a minute he stopped and asked: 'Does this mean we're going to be friends now, Connie? Are you going to give me a chance?'

Sitting on the edge of his bed, still with her coat on, she twisted her fingers anxiously. 'Look, Sam, you're a nice man and I'm flattered that you're so interested in me, but I only came round here today because you're ill and I thought I could help. Please don't read anything more into it.'

'But it was the gesture of a friend.'

'A good neighbour, perhaps.'

'Nobody else has called, not even Jack.' A pause,

then: 'Look, I shan't ask too much. Can't we just have a few outings, Connie? I swear to God I'll behave myself. How about it? Let me thank you for your kindness when I'm over this. Let's go to the pictures, eh?'

Her hesitation was long and troubled. Finally: 'I'll think about it, but I can't promise.'

She was doubtful about the wisdom of it, but she went with him in the end. Thereafter, what had been an energetic pursuit and a sparring match turned into a gentle companionship as both modified their positions. Since he knew it disturbed her, Sam ceased to harp about marriage, while Connie allowed him little inroads into the solitude she had guarded so fiercely for so long. Now and again they went out together. Sometimes she cooked him a meal or made him a batch of scones, and he, in his turn, could be called upon to do little jobs for her around the house. Sam would fix a cupboard door or a window sash for Connie. Connie would sew on a button or mend a tear for Sam.

Millie Chope called it an arm's-length affection, somewhat unsatisfactory in her view, but better than nothing at all. Jack, when he talked to Sam about it, found his friend both hopeful and frustrated, stalled half-way to where he wanted to be, unable to move ahead or abandon the quest. The more he saw Connie, the more he grew to love her, but she, never having seen the kindlier face of fate, kept a degree of detachment for safety's sake.

Twenty-four

Nineteen thirty-five brought a glorious spring. On a brilliant, warm Sunday morning in May, James and Janine were sitting out in the garden. The magnolia tree was in full bloom, the azaleas frothed with red and pink blossom and the avenue trees were decked in sharp new green.

In white cotton shorts and a blue low-backed blouse, Janine was lounging in her garden chair with a gin and tonic. James was in a panama hat and shirt-sleeves. Between them was a wrought-iron table, painted white and occupied by a tray of bottles, but he wanted nothing to drink. His wife often had a few before lunch, but early drinking always made him feel ill.

The grimmest days of depression were past, and trade at the café was fairly healthy again. Healthy – but not as exuberant as it had been before the depression. Changes of fashion, changes of mood had occurred, and 'Janine's' could not accommodate them. In style and atmosphere, it had been a thing of the twenties and felt dated now. Janine could buy the latest gramophone records, it was true, but she could hardly replace 'The April Moons' with a big swing band. She had tried a couple of jazz quartets, but they had never been popular, so there was no live music now in the afternoons. Still, a lot of the old customers remained faithful. Many had drifted back when the economic fear started to pass. If there was cause for concern, it was just that 'Janine's' no longer seemed to attract the young. No new generation of giggly girls and smart young men had appeared at the tables. Janine, in response, was wondering if it might help to redecorate.

'Gold and cream would be nice,' she was saying. 'I think we should get some estimates, don't you? People like something fresh from time to time. I'm a bit bored with the old colour scheme myself.'

Her husband shifted uneasily in his chair. 'What if it does more harm than good? The regulars obviously like it the way it is and there's no guarantee that a fresh coat of paint will pull in any new customers. I'm afraid it'll never again be the way it used to be. You have to accept that. We were lucky to survive the way we did. We need to be realistic now, and more cautious in future.'

'Defeatist.'

'It was touch-and-go, my dear. Another year of poor business would have seen us in the bankruptcy court. We're still very much in debt, you know.'

'And I'm proposing a means to improve trade.'

'I don't think it'll work.'

'That's your expert judgement, is it?' Irritably, she set down her empty glass, snatched up her cigarette case and lighter. He winced at the scorn in her tone.

'I'm entitled to an opinion, I suppose?'

Like a genie from a bottle, smoke streamed from her lipstick-red mouth and billowed into the air.

'What else do you suggest?'

'Leave well alone.'

'Jamie, that's typical of you. Do nothing. Stagnate.' Her gaze flicked down to fix for a moment on the grass beneath the table. Then she said: 'If you really believe we can't make the café buzz again, then we ought to sell it and go in for something else. You know I've thought about opening a restaurant.'

His heart did a somersault. 'Oh, Janine, we can't . . .'

'Why not?'

'It's such a risk. The café is a natural extension of the bakery business, but a restaurant . . . We don't know anything about that sort of catering, and think of the staff we'd need. Think of the hours involved. It's too big a step, Janine.'

'I've talked about this before and you never raised objections. Why now?'

Because now it was more than mere talk, now she was ready to do it. He knew what kind of restaurant she would want – licensed, with a menu in French and dishes cooked at the table on flambé lamps. It would mean exchanging Doris for liveried waiters and a chef. It would mean larger premises with a proper kitchen. It would mean another jump in debt, even if the café fetched a good price.

'I didn't want to dampen your spirits, but I never really thought it was a sensible idea.'

'Indeed,' Janine said coldly. 'Humouring me, were you?'

James looked away. For a while there was silence, broken only by the chirruping of birds. Finally, he offered a concession to placate her.

'If you want to have the café redecorated, go ahead. Perhaps it does need a fresh look.'

'And that's the lesser evil, eh?' Janine said wryly.

'Yes,' admitted James.

'Mmph.' She nodded and said no more. How timid he was, how weak. If the truth were told, Janine was becoming a little tired of the café now. Nothing would have delighted her more than to push him into a brand new venture, something she could start from scratch and build up into another success. Bored as she was with her husband, she longed for a fresh enterprise, something stimulating to fill her days. But Jamie was being obstructive again, he was not going to sign for any more loans. Throwing her cigarette butt on the ground, she darted him a less-than-loving look.

Spotting it, her husband cringed inside. After a moment, as further appeasement, he said: 'By the way, I've been thinking, if you want to re-open a couple of your store accounts, it should be all right now. You can't have such big credit limits, though. We mustn't let the bills get out of hand again.'

Well, that was something. Yes, that was a big consolation. Unfolding her legs from beneath her, she breathed: 'Oh Jamie, may I? Thank you, my sweetheart!' Treating him to a smile, she added: 'I'm sorry if I was a bitch just now, but these last years have been so frustrating.'

'I know.'

The thought of shopping mollified her greatly. She moved across to him, sat on his lap and wrapped her arms around his neck. 'I'm dreadful sometimes, aren't I? And you're so good to me. I wish I could make it up to you.'

'You're my wife and that's enough.'

Such adoration in his eyes. For a moment she felt quite ashamed.

'I'd like to give you something,' she said, 'to prove how sorry I am. What would you like, Jamie? Think of a present. Come on, there must be something.'

Fondly, James gazed up at her. Her hair was the red

of a beech tree in autumn and the black eyes were dancing now.

'There's nothing I need.'

'Think harder.'

He looked away towards the house, seeming baffled. Then suddenly, smiling, he said: 'A photograph.'

'What?'

'A portrait of you.'

'Oh, go on!'

'Yes,' he insisted, 'it's what I want. Do you realise we've nothing but our wedding photographs, and precious few of those. I'd like a head and shoulders portrait in a silver frame.'

'Just that?'

'Yes. Go to a really good photographer.'

'Oh, all right,' she shrugged, 'if you're certain. I'll see what I can do.'

In his basement studio in Westwell Street, Clive Bridger, photographer, was waiting for his ten o'clock appointment. The client was a woman and she was late. A Mrs Sayers. He knew who she was, of course. He had been to her café a dozen times with various fluffy girlfriends. Mrs Sayers had always impressed him with her poise and her nice low voice – such a contrast to the shrill and idiotic babble he often endured from his female companions. Mr Bridger was looking forward to this morning's session with Janine. He was very much hoping to strike up a friendly acquaintance.

She wafted in at almost a quarter past and was charmingly apologetic about it. Mr Bridger was equally charming, dismissing it as nothing. As always, Janine was an elegant figure, dressed today in a white frock and jacket, both trimmed with black braid and large black buttons. Her white hat had a turned back brim and the auburn curls fanned out daintily across it. Mr Bridger surveyed her with frank admiration and said it was a pleasure to have such an interesting subject for a change.

'Interesting?' queried Janine with a smile, as she sat where he directed.

'You have an unusual face,' he said. 'Very striking, individual. I get mightily tired of photographing women who try to look like little girls or vamps. They're all alike, all a copy of someone else – usually someone they've seen on the cinema screen.'

'Oh, I seldom go to the pictures. Should I take my hat off?'

'No, it's very flattering. Let's dispense with the jacket, though. You do want the portrait informal?'

'Yes, it's for my husband.'

She took off the jacket and sat down again, while he fussed with lights and tried a variety of backdrops, finally settling on plain drapes.

She watched him, patient, amused. He was very attractive, she thought. Dark, and wearing grey flannels with a slate-blue blazer and a red and black striped tie, he was somewhat younger than Janine. But then, she rather favoured younger men. His face was good-looking, yet hard. An exciting, sexual quality, that – something James had always lacked. Regardless of his scar, Jamie's handsomeness was soft and not arousing.

'I've seen you at the café,' she remarked, as he went to his tripod and squinted at her through the camera lens. 'You have a lot of different lady-friends.'

She had noticed that, then, had she? He raised his eyes and smiled at her over the camera.

'Just casual acquaintances. I meet a lot of actresses and music hall players. Some of the photos you see on the billboards are my work. You know, the ones taken in costume for the current play or show.'

'Ah, yes, of course. Good business for you.'

'I do quite nicely, when you add in all the other work – dogs and brides and babies, that sort of thing.'

He was peering down the lens again, fiddling with the camera, making adjustments.

She looked around her. 'Is this your house?'

'No, I rent. I've a flat on the second floor.'

He straightened up and came across to her.

'Would you mind . . .?' he murmured, turning her head slightly one way, then another. 'Yes, just keep it there and . . .' he stood back, considering, then bent close again, '. . . lift your chin a little for me, will you? No, that's too much.'

Here and there his fingers touched her face and he paused to place a curl just so against the brim of her hat. So close, she felt his breath and could see the tiny pinpoints of stubble still flush with his skin at this early hour. There was a brief quiver of intimacy, the same face-to-face nearness experienced with doctors, dentists, opticians, but somehow less detached in this case, more lingering and personal. He was wearing some kind of cologne with a heavy, smoky odour, like something aromatic being burned.

'Could you drop your shoulder slightly, too? I think you're tense.' His palm closed over the point of her shoulder, bare in the sleeveless frock, and pressed a little. 'Now, let's have this hand here, just toying with your necklace.' He took her forearm, posing her as he wanted, and again the warmth of his grip gave a *frisson* of pleasure. 'There, that's lovely. Don't move, now,

just stay like that for five seconds and we've got it.'
Hurrying back to his camera, he called: 'Look happy.'

There came a flash.

'That's good, that should be nice,' said Mr Bridger.
'How about a couple more?'

'Another four. I'd like a few to choose from.'

'Let your husband pick his favourite, eh?' He was
round her again, turning her this way and that. She
found herself uncommonly obedient, making no objections, no suggestions of her own. Janine, so fond of
taking charge, was enjoying being moulded and posed,
gently pushed and pulled like a mindless jointed doll.
He was a professional, after all, she told herself. He
knew his business and how she'd look best. And
anyway, she liked to have him touch her.

Several clicks and flashes later, he said: 'There, that's
fine. I don't think we'll be disappointed with any of
those.'

She reached for her jacket, sorry the session was
ended. 'Shall I pay you now?'

'No, when you collect them.'

'When will they be ready?'

'Thursday morning time enough?'

'That'll do very well.'

Smiling, he showed her out. 'I'll look forward to
seeing you, Mrs Sayers.'

She skipped up the steps and out onto Westwell
Street, disturbed by a kind of fluttering elation. She
had planned some other errands for that morning, but
suddenly couldn't remember what they were. Janine
had never been one to need lists. She normally carried
it all in her head and forgot very little. This morning,
however, she found herself oddly disoriented, her
thinking vague and disconnected, because her mind

kept going back to that basement room. She could swear she could still feel Bridger's hands and smell that musky cologne.

On Thursday morning she returned, and wandered round the ante-room to his studio, looking at the portraits on the walls while he fetched her photos. They were mostly of children and young girls, but there were a few group shots too. One, inside the Guildhall, recorded a banquet attended by town dignitaries. Another was of Plymouth Argyle football team. A third, evidently taken at Millbay docks, showed a glamorous couple disembarking from the *Mauretania*. The woman was blonde, the man all grin and moustache in a sharp suit and spats. They looked extremely rich.

Janine was still studying it when Bridger emerged from his tiny office, bearing a brown envelope. He jerked a thumb at the photo.

'Americans,' he said. 'Made a fortune in cookies.'

Janine's brows lifted. 'Really?' she murmured, impressed, and recalling Jamie's idea of producing biscuits, wondering if perhaps they should have tried it.

Bridger opened the envelope and Janine took out her purse. She was wearing a cool green cotton today, and a shady straw hat. Mr Bridger's gaze was on her face, intent, as she glanced at the pictures, approved them, and counted out the money. He didn't even look at what she handed him to see if it was right. He simply thanked her, staring at her all the while. She felt the pull of that stare as a pin feels the magnet, looked up and found herself held by it in a kind of pleasant confusion.

'Do you recall we talked about my contacts with the theatre?' he asked.

'Why, yes.'

'Well, I get a lot of social invitations, you know.'

'And?'

'There's a bit of a party this coming Saturday night at one of the houses up on the Hoe – Elliot Street. It crossed my mind that you might like to come.'

Excitement flared in her, then died away.

'Oh, my husband hates going out. He's a bit reclusive.'

Bridger's gaze didn't waver a jot. 'Well, he can please himself – but what about you?'

That heady, spicy smell of his, that tough, dark face. He was in a charcoal-grey suit today and the sombre colour lent him a shady air. She liked it better than the blazer and gaudy tie. For a moment she eyed him, yearning for what he offered. A party. With theatre people. And he'd be there. He'd dance with her, touch her again, longer and closer. She'd find out more about him.

Her tongue darted over her lower lip and a hard shine came to her eyes. It would serve James right for being such a bore.

'Would he mind, do you think?' queried Bridger lightly. 'Some couples are quite independent of each other, aren't they? Others are like book-ends, only function as pairs.'

'I'm perfectly free,' she hastened to say.

'How about the party, then?'

Calculations were going on in her mind, he could clearly see it. How to contrive it, what to tell the spouse. Free, was she? Mr Bridger doubted that. Certainly not free enough to do what she wanted openly. Subterfuge would be required, discovery could lead to trouble, little or much. Mr Bridger didn't care. Husbands were merely a minor annoyance to him.

'Won't matter if you don't know anyone,' he coaxed. 'I'll take care of you.'

He grinned and his teeth were healthy, neat, the canines sharp. The grin was different to the smile. The smile was bland, agreeable. The grin revealed more of what he was – unprincipled.

But it caused Janine to catch her breath. She had always felt the appeal of badness, felt it strongly. It made her feel languid and desirous.

The corners of her mouth twitched up. 'I must admit, I'm tempted.'

'Wouldn't hurt, would it? Just a few hours. Do you good, I expect. All work and no play, as they say.'

'I'll bet you don't go short of play, do you, Mr Bridger?'

'Please, call me Clive.'

What the hell, she thought, and made her decision. 'What time shall I be there?'

'Say, eight o'clock? If you like, I'll pick you up – somewhere.'

Not at home. Oh no. He already understood that.

'No need. I have a car.'

'Of course. Saturday, then. I can hardly wait, Janine. Here, I'll write down the address.'

Twenty-five

Going to see poor, neglected old Dad, that was what she told Jamie, and what he believed when she left Gardenia Lodge on the evening of the party. Conscience, claimed Janine, had been chafing her a little. Mr Jordan, after all, was into his sixties now.

Her husband saw her going out in the plainest of her coats, the flattest of her shoes, as if to reassure her father that she hadn't changed so very much. Jamie never guessed that underneath she wore a brand new frock – maroon silk, backless, sleeveless, with a fluttering gored skirt and cross-over bodice. She had bought it on Thursday afternoon, smuggled it into the house and hidden it from him. The fact that Janine was made up did not alert him, either. She was always made up from morn till night. Not even for Matthew Jordan would she compromise on that.

'Don't worry if I'm a bit late back,' she said. 'Haven't seen the old man for such a long while and I dare say he's a bit lonely these days, so I ought to spare a few hours.'

James looked up from his armchair beside the radiogram where he was spending the evening with the BBC and a murder novel.

'You could always ask him here, you know. Make it a regular thing. I shouldn't mind.'

'Lord, no,' Janine said hastily. 'He wouldn't feel

comfortable here. You know he doesn't approve of the place – all this sinful luxury, as he considers it.'

James nodded. 'True enough.' He yawned. 'I might turn in early tonight. Have you got your key?'

'Of course,' Janine said brightly. 'See you later.'

Couldn't be better, she thought as she stepped outside and closed the front door. She drew in a deep breath of spring-perfumed air and shivered with anticipation. Night, and she was going out, down among the city lights, going to a stranger's house where there was drink and dancing and a man she was impatient to see again.

The crunch of gravel under her feet sounded loud as she walked to the car, and the street lights along the avenue were sharp yellow stars against the black sky. Wrongdoing somehow seemed to heighten the senses, she observed.

Once in the car she changed into different shoes, her favourites – black patent with ankle straps and a slim high heel. A strutting, dancing style of shoe she sometimes wore at the café. From her bag she pulled gold drop ear-rings and a bracelet and put them on, then she was ready.

The car slid down the driveway, went slowly out through the gate. Then with a roar and a whoosh she was gone and the avenue was quiet again. Deep in his armchair and his thriller, trusting Jamie turned a page, content.

The house in Elliot Street was already pulsating with swing and jazz when Janine arrived. It was hard to find a place to park, for the road was lined with partygoers' cars. In the end she had to pull around the corner into a side-street and walk the fifty yards back.

Standing outside, she hesitated briefly, looking up at

the windows. Three storeys and every one ablaze with light. She wondered if Clive were already inside. She wondered, too, if she ought to turn around and go home while she still could. Before . . .

Before what? It was only a party, might not lead anywhere.

Yet she knew that it would. If not Bridger, then perhaps someone else in there was going to make an impact on her life. This was a fork in a road which had run too straight for too long, and she had to take the unknown way.

Going resolutely up the steps, she rang the bell. There might be people inside who would know her. Still, she didn't care. She had lied to James, she could lie to them, say he was indisposed. If he didn't care to mix with people, he wouldn't hear their gossip.

Noise came pumping out as a young female opened the door. She was only about sixteen and decidedly drunk. She babbled a giggly greeting and waved Janine inside, not knowing or caring who she was. It was open house. She took Janine's coat and scampered upstairs with it. From the thumps and screams of laughter from overhead, it sounded as if someone was being chased around a bedroom.

The party was everywhere – in all the reception rooms and in the hall. There were people sitting on the stairs and revelling in the kitchen. The guests numbered probably sixty or so, more than half of them women. Talkative, flamboyant women, all brightly dressed and dramatically made up. Janine suspected there were few fully professional performers among them. Most were arty amateurs who enjoyed playing at being Bohemian.

At first she felt lost. Against expectation, she

recognised no one, and so she drifted through the crowd in search of Bridger. In the lounge the carpet was rolled back and several couples were shimmying to an old jazz favourite: 'Somebody's crazy about you, crazy about you . . .' A man waylaid Janine, trying to introduce himself above the din of the gramophone, the wild guffaws and the chatter. He was asking her to dance but she pulled away from him and wandered on into the dining room. There, a woman who might have been the hostess, greeted her, thrust a glass of wine into her hand and bade her enjoy herself. Even at this early hour there was a good deal of party débris. The buffet was already half demolished, and empty bottles, dirty glasses and overflowing ashtrays were everywhere. Janine could imagine Mrs Coade's reaction if asked to clean up such a mess.

Finally, in a small side parlour, she found Clive, surrounded by women. He was sitting cross-legged on the carpet, a cigarette stuck in the corner of his mouth, showing them a card trick. When he spotted Janine in the doorway, however, he promptly tossed down the cards and bounced to his feet with a careless: 'Excuse me, girls.'

Trouble incarnate, thought Janine, grinning as he approached her.

'Well,' he said, 'I see you managed it. Any problems making your escape?'

'No, it was easy.'

'My, you do know how to dress. That's a splendid frock and there aren't many women here who could wear it so well.' His hand went to the flesh of her bare back, laying hot and flat against it, urging her once more out into the hall. 'Come on, I want you to meet a few of my friends.'

They were all of a type, Clive Bridger's circle. Most of
the women were giddy creatures with silly nicknames,
who greeted Janine with much squealing and pressing
of cheek upon cheek. The men were jolly, back-slapping
individuals with loud voices. They all played tennis
and golf, tore about in overloaded cars and were always
au fait with the latest dance, slang expression or style
of dress. A very great deal of adultery went on between
them. Every one had had almost everyone else. They
were a club, a clique, but would have been very willing
to recruit some new blood like Janine.

For a while they were a novelty and she enjoyed herself. Glass in one hand and cigarette in the other, she
flirted with the men and teased them, laughed at all
their jokes and told some good ones of her own. She
skipped and hopped and swayed with them to synco-
pated tunes, and promised she would come to so-and-
so's dinner next Friday evening, or someone else's midnight swim and picnic at the beach.

She promised – and yet she quickly realised that she
did not really want to see these people again. Not one of
them, except for Bridger himself. It was odd, she
thought, retiring to the bathroom for a break, but the
fun of the party very quickly palled. She hadn't
expected that. All her life she had imagined this to
be her element. Experience of it, however, taught her
something about herself. She was too intelligent for so
much silliness, and it wasn't long before her companions began to get on her nerves, before the laughter
began to sound a mite demented, before she tired of
listening to fools who thought themselves immensely
clever, or removing from her backside the unwelcome
hands of unattractive men.

In the relative peace of the bathroom, she stood at

the mirror, tinkering with her hair. Social life, she supposed, was like everything else – desperately desirable when out of reach, a trifle disappointing once it was sampled. She very much wished that Clive could have taken her out to dinner instead, somewhere quiet, intimate. That morning in his studio had been far more exciting than this noisy shindig tonight.

Going downstairs at last, she found him waiting for her. He was leaning on the stairpost at the bottom, and a shrewd smile hovered round his mouth.

'Don't really like them very much, do you?' he said. 'Not your type. Too empty-headed, eh?'

Janine looked sheepish. 'I must say, I've had enough.'

'Well, you've tested the water. Now you know.'

'I suppose I'd better go home soon, it's nearly eleven o'clock.'

'All right, but shall we go out for a breath of fresh air first? We could walk up on the Hoe. The *Normandie* is out in the bay tonight and she's quite a sight.'

'That would be a good idea. I've had far too much to drink and I have to drive home.'

And I'd love to be alone with you, added the inner voice.

He fetched her coat and they slipped away with a few brief goodbyes. The peace was blissful as they left the house behind, strolled up past the war monument and onto the wide, breezy promenade. Behind them the white-painted houses and hotels rose like tall ghosts in the night.

'It's funny,' she said, 'I'd thought that I would want to stay till dawn. Not that I could have.'

'Parties are generally mindless affairs.'

'Then why do you go to so many? What do you get out of them? Oh – don't tell me. Assignations.'

'What an old-fashioned, disapproving word.'

'I'm sorry, it wasn't meant to sound that way.'

'Never mind, you're right.'

For a time they walked on without speaking and the echo of their footsteps carried far. At length they stopped to gaze at the great French liner anchored in the bay. The *Normandie* was strung with lanterns and bunting from stem to stern. Light streamed from the portholes and the dining rooms and salons of the upper decks. The water all around her scintillated with reflections.

'What a show,' Janine said. 'Have you ever been aboard a ship like that?'

'Not as a passenger, couldn't afford it. I saw around her once in Millbay dock. She was much more grand than any hotel in town. Got a picture of the new American ambassador, sold it to the *Western Morning News*.'

'I'd love to travel,' sighed Janine. 'No chance of it with Jamie, though. He's such a stick-in-the-mud.'

Bridger was thoughtfully silent for a minute. 'Don't you have any diversions at all?'

'Shopping,' said Janine.

Beside her, a low chuckle. 'What about games? Play tennis? Or better still, golf? Now, you'd enjoy that – not too energetic. I play golf.'

'Do you?' She was surprised. 'I can't quite see you in plus-fours.'

Another laugh. 'You ought to let me teach you, Janine, take you down to my favourite course one Saturday.'

'Where's that?'

'Cornwall – a place near St Austell. Only about an hour's drive and right beside the sea. There's, um . . .'

He paused as if weighing his words. 'There's a good hotel there, too. We could have lunch or – something.'

'Or something,' she repeated.

'Hmm. Sound good to you? Does it, Janine?' His arms were creeping round her and the musky scent was overpowering. He was hot and muscular, all-enveloping like a playful python, and she had not the slightest urge to object. 'You could arrange it, couldn't you?' murmured the nuzzling mouth against her throat. 'Your husband doesn't keep a check on your whereabouts during the day?'

'No.' She smiled to herself. 'I'm often out from breakfast until dinner.'

'And will you be at large next Saturday?'

'I don't see why not.'

'Could you be at the hotel by ten?'

'I think I could.'

'I'll ring ahead and make arrangements, then. You won't change your mind now, will you? You'd be missing such a lot.'

'Is the game that good?'

'The game and what comes after.'

Janine could well believe it. He kissed as if he meant to eat her alive.

The hotel was quite a grand establishment – flock paper and friezes and chandeliers, à la carte menu and *en suite* bathrooms. Nicely situated, too, for secret meetings, being several miles from the nearest town. Built on a cliff-top, it was one of Bridger's regular haunts and he was well known to the staff. They liked him because he always gave good tips.

His lady-friends were generally all cast in similar moulds, decorative and brainless, so the latest one caused a stir of interest, since she was clearly not his usual type. For a start, she arrived in her own car instead of Clive's passenger seat. She was late, as well, breezing in at twenty to eleven, while he had been waiting since ten. Older than the giddy girls he normally brought, the receptionist noted. A mature, smart woman, very self-possessed and not a bit over-awed by this fine hotel. A humorous, dark-eyed woman with red hair and considerable style. This one commanded respect instead of the amused contempt aroused by the nitwits Clive had favoured up to now. When he saw Janine, the porter reflected that Mr Bridger's taste was improving.

She calmly registered as 'Miss J Jordan'. Clive had booked two rooms, but everybody knew full well that one of them would not be used. They allocated him a room he particularly liked – sunny and spacious, looking straight out over the sea. Although officially a single, it had a four-foot bed. The management were very advanced and understanding, and always eager to please a good customer.

The golf course ran across the cliffs, two miles of rolling, carefully tended green, broken by clumps of gorse and swathes of heather. Down below it lay a broad white beach with calm bathing waters.

Janine looked quite the golfer out on the turf that morning, dressed for the part in slacks and jersey and a jaunty cap. Clive, who was no great player in truth, gave her a few token demonstrations as they strolled from hole to hole, but it was all a prelude to the proper business of the day, which was lunch and then bed. The pretence of golf, an excuse for more and more touching, to build anticipation for the coming afternoon.

At one o'clock they had avocados, crab and salad,

with white Bordeaux. By half past two they were both in Bridger's roomy bed.

Almost frightening, almost violent, ever on the edge of cruelty, that was how he was. But never quite crossing that borderline, never going that step too far. Only just the beginning, the hint of pain – the bite that narrowly missed being hard, the scratch that never quite drew blood. Most wicked, the long, tormenting pauses. Again and again he would wind her up like a spring, then stop and make her wait while he had a drink or a cigarette. Tireless, he was always over her, all around her, dark and powerful and tight, utterly in charge.

Not like Jamie. Not like poor, mild Jamie who loved her. Jamie was plain gruel, a harmless mush. Bridger was something highly-seasoned, something which, once sampled, could not be left alone. And what a novelty for Janine, the boss, to feel so helpless. What a gorgeous, lewd and writhing struggle. How fierce it was, how all-absorbing. No woman lay under Clive Bridger and thought about something else.

In the late afternoon, the sunlight filtered through the curtains onto a well-tossed bed where they lay still at last. The top sheet was all but tied in knots and the rest of the covers trailed to the floor. Bridger lounged beside Janine, expansively naked and drinking Scotch. Her hand reached up from beside him for the glass and he let her take it.

'What's your husband like?' he asked as he watched her sip.

'Very easy-going. Shy.'

'I suppose he loves you?'

'Yes.' Janine swilled the whisky round her teeth. 'Oh yes, he does. He's given me almost everything I've ever wanted.' After a brief consideration she added: 'But we

273

seem to have reached a dead end. At least, I feel that I have. He's content enough.' Taking a swig from the glass, she went on: 'I married him largely to get away from home. Not that I didn't have any feelings for Jamie, I was fond of him. Before all else, though, I was being practical. He had some property, you see, but he'd never have put it to use, and I'd always wanted my own business and a nice house.'

Bridger smiled in the dim gold light and toyed with the line of black hair running down to his navel. 'So you're the enterprising one. I guessed as much. What are you going to do about your boredom, may I ask?'

'I suppose this is it, seeing divorce would cost me too much and I'm not in any position to start a new business project.'

'Affairs,' he murmured.

Handing back the glass, Janine settled with her cheek upon his chest.

'They're your hobby, aren't they? Why shouldn't they be mine?'

'Never thought of it that way. Truth is, none of them ever lasted long enough to be called a proper affair.'

Janine cocked an eyebrow. 'Do you think this one might?'

'Well, I've been sitting here thinking about that.' His hand sought her head and his fingers wound absently in her hair. 'It depends what limits you want to set, precisely what you're looking for. I think we ought to get that clear between us straight away.'

She looked up at him and the dark, hard face looked soberly back.

'I've had scenes and tears and tantrums when I've finished with girls in the past. I've been involved in one divorce case and very nearly a second. I've taken a couple of punches from angry husbands, and threats of suicide from one demented little chit who expected me to marry her after a single afternoon here. I tell you these things so that you'll have no romantic illusions about me – or us. I want sex, Janine, I want amusing company, but that's all. I've never cared if my women were married, but if there's talk of leaving husbands for me, I call an immediate halt. If you can be adult about it – cold-blooded, to be more frank – then we can be friends and have good times together. But if you try to turn it into *Wuthering Heights*, then I'll put an end to it, fast.'

'My, how forthright. I wasn't thinking of leaving my husband, Clive. As I said just now, divorce can be expensive. The last thing I want is to risk my security. It's just a bit of adventure which is lacking.'

'In that case, we can get along. I give no guarantee how long it'll last, Janine, and I ask none from you. If you start to feel nervous about it, I'll understand. By the same token, you'll have to accept it gracefully if I want to call it off.'

'Don't worry, Clive, there won't be any suicide threats from me. Did she do it, by the way?'

'Of course not,' he grunted. 'The little bitch took revenge instead. At least, I'm pretty sure that it was her. Somebody threw a gallon of yellow paint over my car one night soon afterwards. Worse luck, the top was down. She wouldn't admit it – but what a coincidence, eh?'

'Could have been one of the others,' chuckled Janine. 'Hard to be sure when you've had so many. Vengeful women bide their time, you know. So sometimes you do pay the price, eh?'

'Most sports have their dangers.'

'Speaking of which . . .' she reached for her watch on the bedside table, '. . . I'd better make a move. It's nearly five.'

Bridger lightly pinched a nipple and kissed the end of her nose.

'Drop in and see me during the week,' he said. 'I'll make an hour or two to show you round my flat, such as it is.'

'Lovely,' purred Janine. She rolled off the bed and stood up, presenting her back to him. 'You haven't marked me, have you, Clive? No scratches, no bruises to show?'

'I never leave any clues. I'm just as careful as you are.'

Clive's work took him all over the place in pursuit of local happenings. Thereafter, Janine very often went with him, especially if the event was out of town. A garden party at Saltram House, the Devon County Show, the Flora Day at Helston, Falmouth regatta – such were typical days out for Clive and Janine during that first year of their affair. And always, of course, there was that favourite hotel, not to mention his poky but convenient flat above the studio. It was only just five minutes' walk from the café. Often, when Doris thought Mrs Sayers had gone out shopping, Janine was paying a visit to Clive.

There was no particular day when she fell in love with him. The addiction grew gradually, steadily, over a span of months. The sex had gripped her right away, but what entranced her even more was the realisation that she and Bridger were so very much alike. They enjoyed the same things, scorned the same things, looked at life the same way. Janine felt she had found a spirit in tune with her own. There was little on which they disagreed and neither had any criticisms of the other.

This romantic experience was something quite new for Janine, and she had no more defence against it than a sixteen-year-old. At thirty-seven, she should, perhaps, have been immune to the worst follies of 'love', but Jamie had been her only man up till then, and her feelings for him had never been more than warm. Making money, acquiring possessions, that was what had obsessed her for most of her life. Romance was a whole new world, and discovery of it elated her beyond all expression. This was what all the songs and the cinema fantasies were about. Hard-headed Janine had sneered at such things in the past. Now, as if a missing faculty had been slotted into place, she understood the silly, soppy feelings portrayed on the screen and crooned on the wireless. From waking to sleeping, thoughts of Bridger filled her head each day. She would think his name over and over, mentally repeating it with a shiver of inward pleasure. A spriteliness was in her soul and she thought the sensation would never end.

Since uncertainty served to keep it alive, she was justified in expecting the thrill to continue. Bridger had meant what he said and she knew it. No talk of leaving James would be allowed, no shackles were to be tolerated, no demands. The fine, sharp edge stayed honed because she knew she could never be sure of him. Janine had to play the nonchalant lover; she dared not ever abandon the semblance of being casual about it all. Thus, a tormenting element of restraint was required. Never before had Janine been so tightly strung with emotion. Nothing had ever compared to this for excitement.

To Bridger it seemed she was being as good as her word, being mature about it. It was quite a relief after so much hysteria in the past from babyish girls, and some desire for continuity made him glad of a congenial woman friend. All his relationships had been short-lived and shallow, and although the thought of marriage still appalled him, he found it rather agreeable to have an amusing mistress like Janine as a feature of his landscape.

One day the following May, she presented him with a gold cigarette lighter. He was pleased – albeit slightly embarrassed by the fact that it had obviously cost a lot of money. His income was modest and, unlike Janine, he lived within his means. Unsentimental as he was, Clive did not recall precisely when they had met, and so he failed to realise that this was the anniversary of that photographic session.

The lighter never appeared on any bill from any store, as nearly all her other purchases did. Janine had paid for it in cash, taken out of the café till. When she bought him a tie-pin a few weeks later, she did the same again. She was not concerned that Clive was unable to respond with equally expensive gifts. What he gave her was better, priceless. He made her feel young.

Twenty-six

Lines, very fine but unmistakable, underneath her eyes. Connie gazed placidly at her reflection and noted without distress these first hints of ageing. Taking her new spectacles from their case, she put them on and considered herself again.

Like some old schoolmistress, she thought dispassionately. Behind the round lenses her blue eyes looked even larger, more sad, her soul displayed under a magnifying glass. But there it was, she needed spectacles now – could not see well enough to sew or read without them. They felt hard and heavy; she was terribly aware of them on her face. The sensation made it difficult to concentrate on whatever else she was doing. The optician had promised her this discomfort would wear off, that she would soon forget they were even there. It was hard to believe just now, but no doubt he was right.

She sat down on the sofa and picked up her darning. A fire burned silently in the grate and the clock ticked gently. Around her, the rest of the house was cold, empty, dark. Sometimes she could feel it, the two storeys overhead, the hall outside, the kitchen – gloomy spaces surrounding this one lit room. The house around her, the night around that. No one else in the universe, it sometimes seemed, except when footsteps and murmuring voices passed the window. Within, there was the fire, the lamp, the needle and thread moving rhythmically. For Connie, a typical evening. It was like being buried, but she was used to it.

In the morning she was going to church with Sam. He had finally coaxed her into attending a service. She thought she would go just the once to stop him nagging.

Laying down her darning, she thought about him with a fondness mixed with worry. They had known each other eighteen months – been friends now for over a year. A new kind of self-reproach was troubling her lately. Perhaps she was tormenting him, keeping him hopefully trotting along by being on good terms. He needed more, of course, he needed a wife, and Connie would not fulfil that need. He was wasting his time on her and perhaps it was unfair to let him do so.

Yet, it was by his own choice. She had certainly tried to stop him. She still reminded him frequently of where the boundaries lay. There could be no question of marriage or even . . .

A rogue thought suddenly arose in Connie's mind, a momentary doubt and a stirring of mutiny against the fear-filled isolation she had imposed on herself. Something whispered to her: 'Why? Why not abandon caution, accept him? Have one last stab at life, however perilous?'

Connie's eyes blinked nervously behind her glasses. He was willing. Sam was not afraid. What if she were wrong? Perhaps she was not protecting either him or herself, but merely depriving them both of a priceless chance to be happy. What if compensation was being sincerely offered on a platter? What if life was making amends, reparation was being laid before her, and she would have none of it? What if she were choosing emptiness for herself – and for Sam as well?

Connie's hand crept up to her throat as an awful

confusion filled her mind. She shook her head help-lessly, pulled off her glasses and clasped a hand over her eyes.

After a moment, however, the agitation passed. Cheese on a mousetrap, Connie reminded herself. A morsel of bait, another trick. She wasn't going to fall for it. No, indeed. Fate was not going to injure her again, she would see to that. As for Sam, he was quite at liberty to look elsewhere for a wife. If he chose to cry for the moon instead, that was his look-out.

Thrusting on her spectacles, she briskly resumed her sewing, mouth pursed tight. She had learnt her lesson. Yes, she had.

Only . . .

Once more a flicker of doubt beset her, a wistful moment of weakness. He made her laugh, Sam Tucker. She enjoyed the sound of his voice and the sight of his chubby face. She could do wonders with that cottage of his, make it lovely. With an ache, she remembered love and cuddling and sex, how good it had been. Untouched for so long, sleeping alone – she could easily put an end to that, avert all the years of it stretching ahead . . .

Fright and anger reclaimed her mind. 'Damn it!' she muttered. 'I must be losing my wits!'

Flinging her work aside, she went and made herself some tea. She had a good mind not to go to church with him after all. She had a good mind to shut him right out of her life again. She certainly would, if plagued by many more such fits of foolishness.

Next morning, however, calm once more, she ac-companied him to the service. As she had expected, though, the sermon made little impression on her, and going through the motions of kneeling and singing felt like a farce.

'Don't want to go again, then?' sighed Sam, as they strolled homeward from the King Street Methodist church by way of the Hoe. It was spring of 1936, a dull day with a light wind.

'I don't think so. I'm sorry, Sam.'

He pushed his hands in his trouser pockets. 'Most people need some sort of comfort, Connie. You've nothing, and by your own choice.'

'I just can't swallow religion. It feels too much like wishful thinking. The stuff they tell you – people aren't really dead, everything's going to be wonderful one day, there's a holy reason even for dreadful things and so on and so on.' She shook her head. 'My sister-in-law is right, it's too good to be true.'

'That's become your real tragedy, I think. You'll say the same of anything hopeful that comes your way.'

Irritation flared up in her, left over from the previous night.

'Don't start lecturing me, Sam. Don't start again, telling me what's wrong with me.'

'All right, all right.' The round face folded into smiling lines.

'Tell me instead what you're doing at work,' she sighed, regretting her temper.

'Maintenance job on a cruiser.'

'Plenty of employment now?'

'Fair bit, and there will be more.'

'Still expecting trouble?' she teased.

'Herr Hitler's gone into the Rhineland, hasn't he?'

'We haven't challenged him.'

'Precisely. Therefore he'll go further still, and further again after that. Sooner or later – well, I'm just glad I haven't got a son to go and get killed . . .' He stopped himself short. 'Oh, Connie, I'm sorry.'

A faint smile. 'It's all right, you're not calling up anything I'd forgotten. I think about my daughter every day. I expect I always shall. She'd be nearly thirteen now. I try and imagine how she would have turned out, what she would have looked like grown up. Like Charlie more than me, I'd guess.'

Connie paused by the harbour wall below the Citadel, and her gaze turned back towards the bay.

'It was a similar day to this when he was drowned,' she murmured with an absent look. 'At least, it was when he went out, before the weather changed. We were going to live in a little flat not far from the market, you know. I was so excited to think I was leaving home for a place of my own.' A short laugh. 'But I never went anywhere, did I? Here I am after all these years, and here I'll always remain.'

'I can offer you a move – at least around the corner and up the street.'

'Now, Sam . . .'

'You know you can always come to me, Connie.' He leaned his forearms atop the harbour wall, but his face was turned to her and his gaze was intent beneath the peak of his Sunday cap. 'The minute you change your mind, you'll be welcome in my house. I'm not ashamed to tell you that it bothers me, growing older. The cottage is lonely. It makes me think of a cold grave.'

Something about that sad admission brought her uncertainty back yet again, and she tried to dispel it by being brusquely practical.

'I couldn't leave the bakery, Sam. Jamie needs me there.'

'Your brother doesn't need that house, though, maid.

283

The shop and bakery, yes – but the house? If you were out of there he could sell it and take a slice off his debt. She's a spender, isn't she, that Janine? And your business fell off badly during the depression. Your Jamie must be well and truly in the red.'

Annoyed, she eyed him sharply. 'Who have you been talking to? Nell Colenso, I suppose. My brother's finances are none of your concern, Sam.'

'Since you're dependent on him, I feel that they are.'

'Then you're very presumptuous.'

'I love you, Connie, that's why.'

'Oh, please don't.'

He looked away, down at the water lapping at the granite wall. A film of oil from a nearby boat spread swirls of iridescent mauve and silver over the green.

'If he did sell your place . . .'

'He wouldn't.'

'If he had to . . .'

'Don't talk nonsense.'

'Don't you be complacent.'

'Would you have me marry you because I needed somewhere to go? I don't use people, Sam.'

'Believe me, I wouldn't feel put upon. I'd dearly love to have you live with me.'

'I'm too afraid, for both of us. I often think I shouldn't see you at all, for fear you'll come to some harm.'

'That old superstition again. Well, Connie, I'm willing to take the risk. In fact, I so love to live dangerously that I'll even come to lunch today, if you ask me.' He grinned at her and his face was ruddy-brown.

'All right then, if you don't mind bubble and squeak and bacon.' Smiling again, she took his arm and they walked on. 'You know, you're the first real friend I've ever had – purely a good, kind friend. Charlie was my love and that's something else. Nell and Harry care about me, but I never see them outside working hours. I think, in the early days, Janine tried to be my friend, but we're just too different. Anyway, she became madly involved in all her exciting plans, and once she had money to spend she couldn't think about anything else.' The smile faded and Connie added more soberly: 'Sometimes, you know, I get the feeling she's outgrown Jamie, and that worries me. Sometimes when I go to lunch with them on a Sunday I'll hear a brittleness in her voice as she speaks to him, or catch her looking at him as if he were an idiot. She seems to go on changing all the time. Perhaps it's simply a ripening of what was in her all along, or maybe it's the effect of being indulged too much. Whatever the reason, she's grown harder over the years and it makes me fear for Jamie.'

'Your brother's a man of – what – thirty-five or thereabouts?'

'Yes.'

'Old enough to take care of himself.'

'That's what Nell and Harry say, but somehow to me he's always . . .' She spread her hands, at a loss.

'Baby brother. Connie, take a tip from Janine. Harden up a bit yourself and look out for number one.'

She chuckled. 'By marrying you, for instance?'

'Can't think of a better way. Consider it, Connie, my cottage is all paid for. I don't owe a bean to anyone. I'll bet your brother wishes he could say the same. I'll bet he doesn't sleep too well in his fine house.'

Hers, not his, thought Connie to herself, though she made no reply. It was always Janine's place, every stick and stone of it, every ornament and potted plant. Jamie never wanted it. If ever he has to sell anything off, it'll be Gardenia Lodge.

Twenty-seven

Janine wandered through her conservatory, pruning shears in hand, snipping off dead flower heads here and there. It was mid-September. The pelargoniums were past their best but still put on a pleasant show of purple and shocking pink. The Star of Bethlehem's cascade of white flowers was spectacular this year, and the fuchsias kept blooming bravely. In this gentle southern climate, summer ended late and spring came early. Often a few last roses lingered outdoors right into December. Within Janine's conservatory there was colour all year round. Placidly she walked between the potted palms and rubber plants, cutting off shrivelled bits and humming happily to herself.

Then, abruptly, the peace was shattered by clumping male footsteps and puffing and panting, accompanied by an agitated rustle of paper.

'Janine, can you explain this?'

Turning, she eyed her husband calmly. 'Probably, James, if you show me what it is.'

'A bill.'

'Ah. And what about it?'

'A hundred and six pounds,' he breathed. 'For clothes. In one month. How the hell did you manage this?'

Warily, she ran her tongue around her upper teeth. 'They must have made a mistake, my sweetheart.'

'Everything's itemised, look for yourself.' He handed her the paper. 'Tell me where the error is.'

She put down the clippers, frowned for a moment at the bill. 'Yes,' she said slowly, 'well, I suppose . . . I mean, I hadn't realised . . .'

No, she had not, obsessed as she was with Clive, thinking always and only of the next time she would see him and what she would wear when they met.

'Janine . . .' he moistened his lips and swallowed uncomfortably, but found the courage to take the plunge, '. . . it's got to stop.'

Just for a second she thought he knew. Her glance flashed up to meet his.

'Must I insist you close your store accounts again? We've been through all this before. I thought you'd learned something, but it seems you're worse than ever.'

Her eyelids came down. She looked contrite. 'Yes, yes, all right, I'll be more careful, I promise.'

'Will you?'

'I've just said so.'

He eyed her uneasily. 'Perhaps I should ask, can you?'

'Oh, for heaven's sake!' She spread her hands, the fingers stiffly straight. 'Yes, yes, don't keep on.'

He surveyed her for what seemed a long time, and in her discomfort she snatched up the shears, started cutting briskly at the plants. James fancied there was something slightly odd about her these days, an edginess coupled with rapid swings from gaiety to bad temper. Troubled, he had gone to the library, taken out some medical books and looked up such things as the menopause and manic-depression, but nothing he read had quite seemed to fit her behaviour.

'For God's sake stop staring at me,' she snapped at

last. 'I've promised to cut back. I'll do so. Now, leave me alone.'

'After I've told you what else arrived in the post this morning.'

She paused. The dark eyes were nervous. From between the fronds of a palm they regarded him tensely.

'What was that?'

'I've had a sharp letter from the bank.'

Nothing to do with Clive, then. Relief. She had half feared someone might know, might have written to tip off her husband. The black eyes blinked, then she gave a small sniff.

'Really? What do they say?'

'I've been summoned for an interview on Thursday. I don't think they're going to congratulate me on our performance, Janine.'

'I'll come along with you,' she said. 'I see I shall have to charm our nice manager again.'

'They have a new manager now, my dear. The tame one's retired and this one's far less sympathetic. He knows from the cheques where the money goes, and he's asked to see me alone.'

'What?' She was affronted.

'And I think I'd better comply.'

'Well, I like that! Bloody men! Here we are in nineteen thirty-six and nothing's changed. Money matters aren't for women . . .'

'Specifically, not for you, Janine. I'm afraid that's how the bank feels, anyway.'

She started hacking savagely at the parasol plant and half a dozen large leaves plopped to the floor.

'I see,' she said through gritted teeth. 'Well, I shan't

forget this. In fact, I really think we ought to take our business elsewhere.'

'Banks exchange information, you know,' her husband said quietly. 'Quite frankly, I doubt we'd easily find another willing to take us on in our present condition.'

'Fair weather friends,' she grunted.

'Well, naturally, Janine. What else could we expect? They're in business, just like us. How could you lose sight of that? You know, these days you don't seem altogether down-to-earth.'

'I thought you said we were out of trouble, holding steady?' she demanded pettishly.

'Redecorating the café set us back a bit, and it hasn't brought in any more trade, that's certain. But the problem is mostly you and your spending, as ever. I don't know what the outcome of this interview will be, but I'll tell you straight, I'm not looking forward to it.'

Thursday morning. The town was busy. The Sayers were sitting in the car around the corner from the bank. Janine stared through the windscreen at the bustling pavements, and her face was blankly disbelieving. James had just received an ultimatum.

'They can't mean it, Jamie! Surely it's not as bad as that?'

'They don't joke about these things. We're not among their favourite clients any more.'

'Well I know we've lost the first impetus and all that,' she snorted, 'but we're not exactly failing, are we? Damn them, they were oozing around us like oil when the business was flying high.'

'That's the nature of the beast,' sighed James. 'That's banks all over. Mother was right about them.' Distractedly, he drummed his fingers on the steering wheel. 'But you don't understand, my dear. They haven't said the café is failing, just that we're far too deeply in debt for our size. The overdraft has to come down substantially. Some of our property has to be sold.' He swallowed hard before delivering the blow. 'They recommend we get rid of Gardenia Lodge.'

Briefly there was silence beside him. Her shock was almost tangible, a shiver in the air. Then, a harsh and vehement whisper: 'No! No, Jamie, not my house. Anything but that.'

'It's a practical suggestion,' he ventured. 'The place was always a luxury, and luxuries have to be sacrificed first.'

'No!' A snap this time. 'I will not give up my house. Never, never, never!'

'If we don't comply I'm afraid they'll call in everything we owe.' He bowed his head, screwing his eyes shut and pinching the bridge of his nose between finger and thumb. 'Look, the debt has got to the point where we couldn't pay it back from the takings, even if "Janine's" were packed out seven days a week. But if we take a big chunk off it now by selling Gardenia Lodge, and live more modestly in future, we may be all right.'

He met her gaze again and she was glaring at him now. James had never seen her look ugly before. It made his heart quail when she scowled at him like that. It made him feel cold and ill.

'Janine,' he begged, 'I'm so sorry, but I don't know what else we can do.'

She eyed him for a moment, calculating. Then she announced: 'I can see an alternative. We'll toss the hounds a different bone.'

'What?'

290

'The bakery will have to go instead.'

'The bakery?' he repeated faintly.

'And the bread shop and the house, of course. That should satisfy them.'

'Janine, we need the bakery! It's the foundation on which we've built everything else! If you take the bottom tin from a stack, the whole damned lot collapses.'

'That's not a very good analogy, James. It doesn't apply here. The café can manage perfectly well without the bakery now. We can simply order our cakes and bread from elsewhere. Plymouth isn't short of bakeries, you know.'

His mouth was open, working soundlessly.

'I don't think . . .' he stammered. 'I mean, it mightn't work as well as you believe. It wouldn't be the same, Janine. People would notice, make no mistake. Our cakes have a special something, they're distinctive, extra good.'

'Twaddle.'

'And imagine the expense.'

'What expense?' she demanded. 'You're not thinking straight. What we save on wages, supplies, overheads – and the interest on the overdraft – will more than pay for the stuff we buy.'

'Wages,' murmured James. 'Oh Lord – poor Nell and Harry.'

She slumped back in her seat, picking at a thumbnail. 'Yes, well, I'm sorry about that, but needs must when the devil drives. Do you really want to go backwards, James? Is that what you'd prefer? To give up all the progress we've made and return to living on the Barbican? I have to tell you frankly that I will not do that. I just cannot. We must hold on to the best of

291

what we have. I . . .' she hesitated, weighing her words, seeking a delicate way to deliver the threat, '. . . I could never resign myself to losing so much. I'd sooner die or – well, I'd have to do something about it, that's all.'

He raised his head and his eyes were glassy with fear.

'What do you mean by that?'

'Oh . . .' her tone was unconvincing, deliberately so, '. . . nothing. Nothing, really.'

'Leave me?' His voice shook. 'Find a wealthier man? And a better-looking one into the bargain?'

'No.' Again that uncertainty, that quaver which belied the word. She glanced away from him in a manner she knew to be shifty. 'I didn't mean anything, James. I was just upset. I forgot myself.'

It was meant to frighten him, and it did. For a space they sat saying nothing. Despite the traffic noise outside, all seemed deathly quiet within the car. The air was oppressively stuffy and smelling strongly of the leather seats. James had a sense of being enclosed within a capsule of woe, shut off from the world of the carefree outside. The ground had been dug from under him today, not so much by the bank, for that was half expected, but by the suggestion that his wife might abandon him if they lost Gardenia Lodge. Now he knew the nature and the depth of her devotion. Yet, still he could not contemplate being without her.

Finally, his thoughts turned to Connie. Connie, last of all.

'What – what about my sister?'

Janine blew out a heavy breath. 'She'll have to come and live with us at Gardenia Lodge. There's plenty of room. She'll have an easier time of it, won't she? We'll all be cosily together once again and that ought to suit you. She always was more like a mother to you than a sister. Between the two of us, you'll have the best of both worlds – sex and coddling.'

A surge of bile rose up in him. 'If I had to choose one or the other, no doubt I'd be better off without you and the sex.'

'But could you choose that way?' Her voice was softly mocking.

'I might. You've been less than lukewarm lately.'

'I don't know what more you expect after fifteen years.'

The rancour left him and suddenly he was wrung-out, choked. He could have cried.

His wife watched him coldly for a moment, then her own contempt and anger ebbed away.

'Jamie,' she sighed, 'forgive me. Couples say awful things when they have a row. Extravagant, silly things.'

'Or spit out truths they can't utter at any other time. It's happened like this before, hasn't it? You lose your temper and show your true colours. Anyway,' he said stiffly, 'I know where I stand now, that's for sure. All right, my dear, we'll do it your way, if the bank will wear it. I'll try and arrange to keep your precious house.'

The bank, after some hesitation, agreed to go along with the plan. To James's dismay, it was his sister who took it badly.

When he went home that day to tell her, he found her about her chores as usual.

Standing at the parlour door, James watched Connie clearing out the grate. She was kneeling, vigorously riddling down the dust and coke and clinkers. Beside her lay newspaper, kindling and a fresh scuttle of coal.

'Connie, could I talk to you?'

She twisted round and a lock of hair fell in her eyes. In brushing it away, she smeared her face with ash.

'Oh – Jamie, I didn't hear you come in. You made me jump.' Stiffly, she rose to her feet, wiping her hands on her apron. 'What is it, then?'

She smiled and he very nearly lost his nerve. Guilt overwhelmed him at the sight of her. Connie – always, it seemed, in the middle of some dirty job. Connie, who had nothing because he had been given too much. Now he had to tell her that he could not even hold onto it.

Coming in, he sat down in an armchair, while she, being none too clean, perched on top of the log box by the hearth. In his dark brown suit and red waistcoat, he made her think affectionately that he looked just like a robin.

'I, um . . .' he picked at the brown silk band of his hat, '. . . I have to tell you something.'

She gazed back at him, calm, receptive. He moistened his lips, not meeting her eyes.

'The overdraft has got out of hand again lately.'

'Oh? I thought everything was all right?'

'Well, obviously we're still afloat, but you know the café never fully recovered after the slump.' He waggled his shoulder to straighten his jacket, and tugged at his collar as if his Adam's apple were trapped.

His sister bent and picked up a few chunks of half-burnt coal from the grate, then tossed them into the scuttle. Economical Connie always saved them. But the action was unthinking, automatic, for her mind was on her brother's words.

'How serious is it, Jamie?'

He could not look away from her now, but he blinked a lot. 'I'm under pressure from the bank.'

She pushed her hands in her apron pockets, then took them straight out again, wringing the fingers anxiously.

'We . . .' He plunged in, making a feeble waving gesture with his hand which nevertheless encompassed everything around them. 'We're going to have to sell this, I'm afraid.'

At first, Connie doubted her ears. 'Say that again?'

'The bakery . . .' his mouth was dry and he tried to work up some spit, '. . . and the house, all this property down here will have to go.'

She looked about her with quick, sharp movements of her head. 'Jamie . . .' her eyes were wide and horrified, '. . . you can't!'

'It's this or Gardenia Lodge, and Janine won't give that up.'

Janine. Always Janine. First, last, before everything, everyone else. Connie felt a welling of explosive emotions, like too much air over-stretching a balloon. A wild and reeling sensation filled her head, composed of outrage, and fury, and disbelief. For the first time she saw her brother clearly, weak and completely in thrall to Janine.

'And what about me?' she breathed at last.

'Oh, you'll come and live at our place, of course.' A complacent smirk appeared on his face, the self-satisfaction of one playing benefactor. 'We'll take care of you, don't worry. You'll be moving to a far better home than this. Silly, you know, to be sentimental about this old place.'

He had hoped she might be pleased, even thrilled. But she was looking at him now in a way that made him very uncomfortable. Slowly, the smirk disappeared.

'What's wrong? You'd like that, wouldn't you? Anybody would. Don't tell me you'd rather live here?'

Connie contemplated him still longer and with a hardness in her face he had never seen before.

'Let me get this straight,' she said softly, grimly. 'Things are in such a parlous state that you now mean to sell this place we've owned for generations, in order to keep the bank at bay. You would do that, rather than cross Janine?'

'But Connie, it does make sense. I'm simply retaining the best of my property and selling off the poorer part. You wouldn't expect me to give up a smart house to save a shabby little bakery in a scruffy backstreet, would you? That's not the way to move up in the world.'

'Move up in the world,' echoed Connie. 'It's her I hear talking, not you. And it doesn't make the slightest sense. All you're doing is buying a respite. Unless I miss my guess, you'll still be in debt when this place is sold, and she'll still be spending. You can't control her, can you, Jamie? She's more than you can handle, always was. The bakery makes money, whereas Gardenia Lodge just eats it up. Even I can see that. You were always supposed to be the clever one, but what you're proposing is arse-about-face. The rational thing would be to get rid of Gardenia Lodge, but you're not going to do the rational thing, because Janine wouldn't like it. Have you abandoned all common sense? Has she?'

'Now, look, we can use our property any way we see fit. You don't understand . . .'

'Oh yes I do. Your property? This place was at least half mine by every law of decency. The solicitor advised me to contest the will, you know. By God, how I wish I had. Our great-grandparents established this bakery and it's given our family a decent living ever since. It may not be fancy, but it's a reliable source of income.' She cast a distracted look around her. 'I suppose you'll be selling the contents, too? Yes, of course you will. Janine won't want any of this stuff, will she? And we've nowhere else for it to go.'

'I need the money it'll fetch,' confessed her brother.

'Yes.' The word came out a soft hiss. 'Good quality Victorian chattels will resell for an awful lot more than showy modern furniture like hers. Oh, James, if Mam could only have foreseen what you would do with what she gave you. When she died, this place was safe and clear of any debt. My God, if she had known, I do believe she would have left it to me, no matter what she had against me. She never dreamed that you would marry a squanderer.'

She was eyeing him now with the closest thing she had ever felt to hatred for her little brother, and James felt lonely, frightened, aware of what a support she had always been, how bereft he would be if that faithful prop were ever withdrawn. There was no unconditional love to be had from Janine, he knew that now. He could merely buy her affection. Only Connie had given her devotion free of charge, and she seemed set to turn against him now.

'Please,' he quavered, 'let's not quarrel. We never have before.'

'More's the pity, perhaps. But I'm in the mood for it now, James. What a pretty state of affairs this is. All the money I helped you make, she's had the lot, hasn't she? Wasted thousands.'

'Janine worked as well, you know.'

'Hah! Swanning around choosing wallpaper and tablecloths, playing the charming hostess. Call that work? I'm the one who's worked, James. I'm the fool who rose at five every morning for years and sweated all day in the bakery. A month of that would half kill Janine. Yet she's the one who's keeping what matters to her. She still has her fine house and her bloody café! You're sacrificing this good solid business to let her keep them! This will go instead of her car, her clothes, her ornaments. You're mad!'

'See here, we're offering you a lovely home. You'll share that fine house you're sneering at.'

'Oh, yes,' said Connie wryly, 'and what is my role to be?'

'I don't understand.'

'Domestic skivvy, James? Is that what you had in mind? Connie doing what she's best at, what she's always done?'

'No,' he said crisply. 'We have Mrs Coade, remember?'

'Oh? I thought you might be planning to dispense with her. Every little economy helps, after all, when you're in the muck up to your eyebrows.'

'No such thing had crossed my mind – or Janine's. Be fair to her. She always liked you, Connie.'

'Perhaps that's true – but she never offered me a share in the profits, any more than you did. It never used to bother me, idiot that I was, but it rankles now, all right. I've been a poor relation in this house – your house – haven't I, James? Now I'm to play a similar part at Gardenia Lodge. Be your dependant, without any dignity.'

Her brother drew himself up. 'You can get a job and pay for your board and lodging, if you want to be prideful, but Janine and I were going to offer you an easier life. We know how hard you've always worked, how much you deserve a rest.'

Connie snorted. 'You'd have let me go on working till I dropped if you hadn't decided to sell this place. It's only going to stop because soon you'll have no more use here for the old dogs-body.'

'Now, Connie—'

'It's what I am. My own fault, to a large extent, I admit, but you have taken advantage of it, haven't you?'

'I resent that. No one forced you to stay here and work. The bakery's been your retreat since Tansy died. You haven't sought for anything else.'

'And that was convenient for you.'

'All right, there were advantages for both of us, so don't throw all your hard work in my face. I could have sold this house before, if you hadn't been living here, you know.'

That was what Sam had said. Her gaze faltered, dropped.

'It was your choice to hide away here,' continued James, becoming heated. 'You might instead have tried to rebuild your life. There's what's-his-name, that dock-yard man, been chasing you for God knows how long. Why don't you marry him, Connie? If you don't want to come to Gardenia Lodge, why don't you give him a try?'

'You wouldn't say that if you weren't selling up here. You've never pushed me before to accept him. Now you'd be glad for Sam to take me off your hands.'

'I've told you you're welcome at our place!' exploded James.

A slow smile came to Connie's face. 'Yes, well, to be candid, James, I would rather clean for other people and live in a rented room than accept any more of your

299

help. But, as you say, I have an alternative and it's a good one. Sam warned me, you know, that something like this might happen, and I didn't believe him. I couldn't imagine you ever letting the bakery go. Well, I was wrong about that, and perhaps I've been just as wrong to refuse him all this time. As it happens, I've had my doubts lately. I've wondered if I might be doing myself and Sam a disservice. I needed a jolt, a sign to move me and this is it. I shan't be fearful any longer, Jamie, and I won't be your responsibility. In fact, you won't be seeing much of me at all in future. I've had enough of you to last me a lifetime and now it's best we go our separate ways. I'll marry Sam, if he'll still have me. He'll take better care of me than you ever could.'

He stared at her. 'I'm glad, Connie, pleased for you, but you're saying it as if it means we'll never speak again. We'll still be friends, won't we?'

'You have your wife. Let her be your friend.'

'But she's not!' he burst out. 'Janine doesn't love . . . She's . . .' He struggled, then gave up in obvious distress.

Connie studied him for a space, then quietly said it for him.

'Janine doesn't love you the way I always did. She doesn't offer you much solace when you're troubled. She doesn't think you're altogether wonderful. She's a taker, not a giver. Demands, criticisms – all the things you were spared growing up here with Mam and me – you have to face them with Janine. Your welfare is not her prime concern, the way it was always mine. She isn't a comforter like your good old sister.'

He hung his head.

'I'm sorry, Jamie, you won't have me to adore you any more. As Sam said to me, you're a full-grown man.

You've made your own mess and I can't sort it out for you. If I'm going to make a fresh start, I'd better free myself of you and your problems.'

She knelt again in front of the hearth, turning her back to him, and started poking soot down from the chimney. It was her last word. He was dismissed.

After a long, silent pause, he stood up and left.

Twenty-eight

Connie prepared to marry Sam that same November. He almost tripped over himself in his haste to make the arrangements, lest she should have any second thoughts. The bakery was to close down in the New Year. Nell and Harry were given their notice and luckily secured positions at a local biscuit factory, to commence in the middle of January. James had provided them both with excellent references.

As she packed her things the night before her wedding, Connie experienced a deep, calm sadness at the breaking up of what had been so fixed and familiar for so long. Dispersal was taking place and she was the first thing to go. Next would be Harry and Nell, then the property and everything in it.

When she gathered them together, it was telling to see how few were her possessions. They all fitted easily into two trunks. Near midnight, she finally closed the lids and sat on the end of her bed, looking round the room which was now denuded of any sign that it had ever been hers. Nothing remaining but bare furniture ready for sale to some stranger, no trace left of Connie except her wedding clothes hanging up behind the door, all prepared for the morning.

The outfit was rather splendid – a cream-coloured coat, a rose-pink frock in fine wool and a matching silk toque hat with a short net veil in black. Patent leather court shoes, too. For once, she had been extravagant.

At one o'clock, Connie turned out the light and got into bed. The sheets were cold and she almost fancied the chill was a response to her departure, since she and the house were finished with each other. As she lay and tried to sleep, she felt suspended between two lives and was haunted by a terrific sense of waste. Waste of past years, waste of effort, waste of substance. Her memories brought silent, slow-moving tears. The end of something, the beginning of something.

Next morning, putting the past behind her, Connie was happy and optimistic as she went through a civil ceremony with Sam at the registry office. Jack Chope and Nell Colenso were the witnesses, for James and Janine had not been asked to attend.

Afterwards, Connie went directly home with Sam to his cottage and that was that. Everything had been done in a rush, and he had no time off for a honeymoon. He promised her a week or so away the following spring. They went out for dinner in town that evening, with plenty of wine and a huge bowl of flowers at the table. It was all very quiet and easy. The transition from being Connie Sayers to Connie Tucker was a gentle one, but the difference it made to her life was profound.

From the very start, a feeling of peace and well-being enfolded her, a sense that the change of name made her a subtly different person. No longer unlucky Connie Sayers, out on her own. It was no longer 'me', it was 'us'. She was part of the entity called 'the Tuckers', and subject therefore to better treatment by fate. In place of the curse, she fancied around her a kind of protective bubble, very delicate yet proof against all harm. The bubble was a product of belonging, being wanted, being loved, and gave her a balmy, almost physical feeling of being cushioned and safe.

Within a fortnight, Connie transformed Tucker's bleak little dwelling, so that he hardly knew the house or himself. Everywhere, curtains, rugs and cushions appeared, and vases of flowers. The biscuit tin and fruit bowl were always full. Cupboards were properly stocked with foodstuffs, there was a fire in the hearth and everything was kept dusted. The smell of tea and lavender polish, or something savoury on the stove; clean linen, crisply ironed, always ready; naked light bulbs shaded; a warm woman in his bed – as if some engine had begun to throb, the cottage acquired a feeling of life, and a daily rhythm which was Connie's routine. That engine had stalled when his first wife died and only now had it started to thrum again. Sam's grey stone box was a home at last, and he was a contented man.

Connie found the cottage very light work compared to what she was used to. Sam's place was so much smaller than her old home, with only one short flight of stairs. She could clean around it thoroughly in less than a couple of hours, and was never beset by drains that choked. The lavatory in the yard looked like a sentry box and was scarcely bigger. When Connie sat down, her knees were right up against the door, but the pan always flushed without any trouble and that, to her, was luxury.

This relative ease felt unnatural at first. Connie would look around her, wondering how she could have finished so quickly, thinking she must have forgotten some big task, or even two or three. It was weeks before she grew to accept that she had a few hours to fritter away as she pleased each day. Time for herself, to read a book or listen to the wireless, or make herself look nice for Sam when he came home.

A good husband, Sam. Easily pleased, a hard worker, handy about the house. And in the bed. More romp than romance, of course, that was Sam's way. Security and steady affection were what she needed, and what he gave her. Connie's favourite moment of the day was when he came home in the evening, took off his cap and coat and hung them behind the door, sat down to warm his hands and asked her what was for dinner.

The only lingering cloud in her sky was the forthcoming auction of the bakery. The thought of it dredged up a host of confused emotions – some of them crazy, she knew full well. Nothing had been right in that house, yet it would pain her to see it go. It was, she realised, like clinging to an old sorrow simply because it was a part of her. A part, like a gangrenous limb, best amputated, yet clutched and held despite the knowledge that it was past any cure.

It was impossible to watch the day approach without distress. And there would, she knew, be a lot of people gloating.

James had put it about that the Barbican property was merely surplus to requirements. No one in the neighbourhood believed him. And quite a few, like Millie Chope, were filled with glee to see the Sayers taken down a peg, as she viewed it. What a delight that some of the gains were being sliced away. How it soothed the wounded sense of being left behind, surpassed. How it proved the wisdom of knowing one's place and staying in it.

'Did you see the notice in the paper this morning?' she asked Cynthia, as they queued together at the fish market. 'Everything up for auction Saturday next. Told you they'd get in trouble, didn't I? Too ambitious. Big ideas.'

Cynthia eyed her sideways and her big teeth came forth in a sly, knowing grin. She understood Millie very well. Realising it, Millie blushed and fussed with her scarf. She hunched her shoulders and her neck shrank down into the collar of her coat. Both women were bundled up against the January cold, their breath little plumes of white vapour, tattered by the wind. Under the canopy roof of the market, fresh caught fish were laid out on tables and on the ground in boxes. There were still a good many merchants' handcarts on the quay, even though it was past ten o'clock. Men in suits and bowlers, or Guernseys, sou'westers and sea-boots milled around, buying, selling, arguing.

'I see no wrong in people wanting to better themselves,' said Cynthia. 'I think if you have the ability and the go, then you shouldn't hold back for fear of offending those who haven't.'

Millie's mouth tightened and quivered. Her face, beneath her thin fair hair, was very pale and smooth and oval. It always put Cynthia in mind of a boiled egg. Millie bridled, staring straight ahead of her at the fishmonger's stall. A large cod stared balefully back, but it was better than meeting Cynthia's eye.

'Still,' conceded Mrs Hardin, 'making money's one thing, keeping it's another. I said once, didn't I, it had all come too fast and too easy. What's more, Janine's a spendthrift, no two ways about it. Jamie's too weak to control her and so it's come to this.'

Millie leapt in, seeing a chance to put herself in the right. 'Well, that's largely my point. People who've never had money go mad with it when they get some.

They ought to be content, instead of aspiring to things they can't handle. Stick with what you're born to, that's what I always say.'

In fact, it was not at all what she always said. Millie was captivated by rags-to-riches stories, as long as those involved in them were strangers. The idea that someone she knew could succeed was far less palatable. The comparison then became too immediate, too real. If an unknown person was left a fortune, that was a fairy-tale. If it happened to an old schoolmate or the woman two doors down, then she was undeserving and bitterly envied.

'Not exactly back to square one, though, are they?' Cynthia reminded her. 'They still have their lovely house, their café and their car.'

'Give it time,' smirked Millie. 'Those will go too, unless Janine learns a lesson from this – which I doubt.'

Reaching the front of the queue, she bought a pound of whiting. Cynthia purchased a crab.

'Be going to the auction, will you?' Millie asked as they walked away from the stall. 'Might pick up a thing or two nice and cheap.'

For all her other faults, Cynthia Hardin lacked the vulture instinct, and being proud, she thought it beneath her dignity to scavenge for bargains.

'I don't think so. I never buy anything used.'

Stung, Millie cast a baleful look at her – then seized upon Cynthia's nosiness as something with which to fire back.

'Even so, I'd have thought you would welcome a chance to poke around the house, curious as you are. All these years and you've never seen further than their kitchen window. Must have been frustrating, Cynthia.'

Mrs Hardin looked at Millie as if she were a grub she had found in a lettuce. Then, without a farewell, she walked off.

Millie congratulated herself and ambled on her way, thinking now about the booty to be grabbed at the contents auction. She had always coveted the clock in the Sayers' front room, the one in the alcove with the walnut case. And then there was the brass barometer in the hall, Ada's chinese lacquered musical box, the copper warming pan . . .

Greedy Millie hoped the bidding would not go too high.

The house and business premises were sold to a single buyer on Saturday morning. James stayed long enough to hear the hammer go down on a price just above the reserve, and then he left. His wife had not deigned to put in an appearance at all. Very few people, in fact, were there for the property sale – just a handful of genuine bidders and half a dozen mildly interested spectators.

It was the contents auction in the afternoon which drew a crowd. It was this, too, which nearly broke Connie's heart. Morbidly drawn to this final dissolution, she arrived at a quarter to two and found people all over the house, remarking on the décor and fingering all the family possessions, sneering at some things and pouncing avidly on others. Many were prosperous neighbours, come simply to stare and point and comment. Some were hard-up and hopeful of finding a few cheap necessities to help them get by. Others, like Millie, wanted trophies and items to smarten up their homes. Looking at those assembled, Connie could hazard a pretty good guess at who would be bidding for tools, crockery or blankets, and who would be after knick-knacks. The former were interested only in rummaging through the lots on show. The latter, however, took time to ask a few awkward questions of her. Connie tried to be casual and echo her brother's explanation of the sale, but could tell even as she spoke that no one was convinced.

Professional dealers wandered round with lists which gave brief details of each lot. Somehow, it was the number tickets which upset Connie most, the sight of those labels stuck carelessly on all the loved, familiar belongings. It was like seeing friends up for sale.

The bidders knew nothing of that. Lumps of wood and padding, such were the furnishings. Items with resale value, such were the pictures, the ornaments. Salvage, pickings – to be haggled over, purchased cheaply and then dispersed to God knew where. Connie's home for thirty-seven years, being broken, scattered.

The auction commenced at two-thirty. Connie stood in the sitting-room doorway, behind the crowd. Clearly visible above them was the auctioneer, who was standing on Ada's hearth-stool. Connie listened numbly as the bidding began.

'Ladies and gentlemen, lot number one, this fine quality mirror-backed walnut sideboard. Who'll start me off at five pounds? Thank you, sir. Do I hear ten? Ten pounds, ten pounds? There in the corner. Fifteen, fifteen, who'll give me fifteen? Yes, madam! Thank you. Twenty, twenty, twenty pounds? Come along, now, still a bargain at twenty. Yes? Twenty pounds? Good! Twenty-five, twenty-five? Splendid!'

In the end it went for thirty pounds. The men in

overalls slapped a 'sold' ticket on it and took the bid-
der's name, as attention turned to the gateleg table at
the window.

'Lot two, a good, solid oak table, large enough to seat
four when extended. You'll all have noted the heat
damage to the top, I'm sure. Nothing a skilled restorer
can't easily put right.'

Heat damage – where the blazing Christmas tree
had fallen . . .

The auction went racing on. 'So – who'll offer me two
pounds? Thank you, sir. Four? Yes, four pounds, four
pounds. Six, six, do I hear six? Any more, any more?
Six pounds ten shillings? Come along now! Thank you,
sir! Seven pounds, seven pounds? At the back there.
Seven pounds ten . . . I'm selling unless you stop me.
Seven pounds ten! Once, twice . . .'

The hammer went down.

'Lot three, this splendid upright piano.'

An echo sounded in Connie's mind of slow, laborious
musical notes, and with them came an image. Jamie's
fat little six-year-old fingers tapping out 'Ding, dong
bell, pussy's in the well'. Ada, sitting beside him, guid-
ing him. Connie, standing to one side. Apart. Just
watching.

The piano fetched eighteen pounds.

The auctioneer worked speedily, efficiently. Virtually
everything sold. James, in his need for quick money,
had set low reserves. Some things went for shillings,
even mere pennies. The armchairs, four pounds each
because the covers were worn and some of the horse-
hair padding showed. The grandfather clock for
twenty-one pounds. The china dogs off the mantel
for twenty-three shillings. Grandad Sayers' pocket
watch, thirty-two shillings. Ada's sewing basket with

its needlepoint top, one shilling and fourpence. Her matching needlepoint pin-cushion, sixpence. A pair of antimacassars, ninepence. Two framed prints of the battle of Omdurman, seven and six. A box of assorted crockery, three shillings and threepence.

Connie retreated into the kitchen when the sale moved upstairs. Even from there she could hear the auctioneer's gabble and drone and the intermittent crack of the gavel as the rooms were stripped of beds, wardrobes, wash-stands, dressing tables, jugs and basins, rugs, even Ada's chamber-pot. Soon they would come down here and sell off the table at which she sat and the chair out from under her.

Suddenly, it was all too much. Connie's head sank into her hands and she sobbed from the very pit of her stomach.

Our lovely old walnut sideboard, she was thinking. And our beautiful overmantel. Even Dad's old shaving mug . . .

Suddenly, a voice cut briskly through her thoughts.

'I don't know why you had to be here for this.'

Connie raised her head and blinked at her husband. He was standing at the kitchen door, grim-faced and impatient.

'I don't know why you want to watch and listen. I don't know why you want to come here and be humili-ated. It's no good trying to back up Jamie's lies, because people know. They all bloody know what this sale's for. And here you are among them while they tear up the carcase and pick the bones. Your brother's not here, is he? Janine hasn't shown her face? Only you, Connie, only you are daft enough to put yourself through this.'

Snuffling and wiping the wetness from her face, she croaked: 'Stupid as it may seem, I came for one last

311

look, Sam. After today I'll have no right to set foot in this house any more. It's dreadful, Sam, to see it all sold off. It's our family home and all our stuff. I was born here, I can't help being attached to the place.'

'Oh, I know. You carried the millstone so long, it's like a part of your flesh. This is a hard house, my love. It's a back-breaking house, Connie, and you managed it alone for most of your life. You cared too well for this dump you didn't own. Good riddance to it. That furniture you're mourning over never did belong to you, so let's have no more of this nonsense. You have your own house now, your own furniture, because everything that's mine is yours.'

'I'm not saying it isn't, Sam, and I'm happy there.'

'Then come home right now. This is no tragedy, maid, not for you. They're selling off your prison. The doors weren't locked, I admit, but you would never have walked out by yourself. Thank God you were finally shoved.'

He stretched out his arm, and after a last hesitation, Connie stood up. The arm closed firmly around her shoulders and then he was marching her out.

On the way down the passage they met Millie Chope with her spoils. She had the copper warming pan and the barometer.

'Oh, Connie,' she warbled, 'look what I've bought! I always admired these, you know.'

Connie tried to be gracious, but her smile was sickly. 'Then I'm glad you have them, Millie. They'll need a lot of polishing, mind. I should know.'

'Oh, I'll keep them gleaming, my dear! They're going to look so nice in our front room!'

'See?' muttered Sam, as Millie scuttled off. 'You

shouldn't have come here, giving the likes of her a chance to rub your nose in it.'

Connie sighed. 'I don't care about that. I know a lot are sniggering, but not at me. The joke is on Mam, and on James and Janine.'

Twenty-nine

In the sky over Roborough airfield, a small plane was looping the loop. Bridger's camera lens trailed it, the shutter clicked once, then again and again. The little aircraft levelled out, then zoomed away over the club-house roof as two others took off to perform their display of aerobatics. Clive slipped more film in his camera and stalked their movements, clicking, clicking.

'You like planes, don't you?' observed Janine. 'Do you have a hankering to fly, by any chance?'

He lowered the camera, nodding. 'Yes, I've always fancied it. Bit beyond my pocket, though.'

'Damned dangerous, too. I wouldn't like to see you risk your neck.'

Clive did not like it when she said things like that. When a woman showed concern for his welfare, he always suspected a sly attempt to control him. However, as he had said, he could not afford flying lessons anyway, so he let it pass.

He climbed up and perched beside her on the top rail of the low wooden fence which surrounded the airfield. About two hundred people had gathered for Plymouth Aero Club's annual show. There were queues at the clubhouse for refreshments, and people waiting their turn for fifteen-minute 'flips' over the city or glider flights over Dartmoor.

'Coming back to the flat for a while?' he asked,

nibbling her earlobe. 'I've no more appointments today, and you look good enough to eat in that outfit.'

She did – youthful and sporty in a white pleated skirt and white slouch hat, with a cotton jacket printed in narrow vertical stripes of red, white and green. No one would have guessed she was only one year short of forty.

'I have to pop into the café first.' A salacious grin. 'I've a present for you.'

'Another?' His eyebrows lifted, then dropped, and a crease appeared between them. 'Janine, it makes me a bit uncomfortable, you know. I can't reciprocate. I don't make as much as you.'

'Don't be silly, it gives me pleasure. This present, in particular, will. It's a special book.'

His head went back with a jerk of comprehension. 'Ah.'

'Illustrated,' smirked Janine. 'In colour.'

'Will it teach me anything new?'

'It might. It certainly gave me a surprise or two. It's a limited edition, you know. Called *Venus Rising.*'

'Ha, ha,' gurgled Bridger.

'It isn't on sale in the shops. I had to order it direct from the publishers.'

'I'll bet you did.' He glanced at his watch. 'Well, it's ten past twelve. Let's go. Shall I expect you round about two? That'll give us three hours to peruse this educational volume.'

Dropping to the ground, he lifted her down from the fence. An elderly biplane painted piebald and a bright yellow Bristol 'Bulldog' were conducting a mock battle up above as Janine and Bridger crossed the grass towards the place where they had parked the car. The sky was cornflower blue and streaked with horse-tail clouds. In one corner of the field, spectators were clustered round an auto-giro plane, which looked to Janine a ridiculous thing with its huge overhead propellers. Clive, however, had expressed a lot of interest in it and had taken many pictures. He paused before getting into the car, snatching one last look at the stunts going on in the sky. He would have liked to be somehow involved in aviation, he thought. It intrigued him nearly as much as photography and women.

'I'll get us a bottle of something for this afternoon,' he said. 'What would you like?'

'Cherry brandy,' purred Janine, as they pulled away.

They had spent a boisterous afternoon. Now they were mellow with cherry brandy and pleasantly fatigued by rough and tumble. Clive sat on the bed, the sheet bunched up between his legs looking somewhat like a loincloth. Flipping over a page of *Venus Rising*, he chortled.

'Lord, look at this one! Can you do handstands?'

Janine put down her magazine, glanced at the picture and laughed. 'No, and I'd probably dislocate both hips if we tried a position like that.'

Bridger closed the book and put it aside. 'Can't beat the old favourites,' he said.

Janine, in cami-knickers, murmured a contented 'Hmm.' Her attention though was mostly on the article in the magazine she had found on Bridger's bedside table.

'National Socialist Art' was the title. With puckered brow, she scanned the photographs of sculptures and paintings by state-approved German artists. Finally, tapping the page, she said: 'Sinisterly wholesome, don't you think?'

316

He cocked his head to see, then grunted. 'Couldn't have put it better. All those clean and buxom *frauleins* with their flaxen plaits, tossing wheatsheaves about.'

'All those muscular, square-jawed men staring majestically into the distance.'

'Sizing up some neighbouring territory, no doubt.'

'All so earnest, so purposeful.'

'So bloody hearty and vigorous,' Clive agreed. 'Notice they're all physically perfect, all young. Just a bland ideal. Nowhere a blemish or a peculiarity. I don't like it one bit, it isn't quite human.'

Janine chewed her lip. She had seen the news-reels of roaring rallies, heard the ranting speeches, watched the German troops parading.

'Do you think it's true that we're heading for war?'

'I've a nasty feeling we are.'

'Good for trade, I suppose, in a town like this.'

'Won't be good for anything or anybody,' muttered Clive.

She stretched out a hand and stroked his cheek, feeling the gentle scratch of late afternoon bristles. 'If it does come, I hope to God they won't conscript you,' she said worriedly.

'They might, in time. I'm thirty-three, not exactly old. Same goes for your husband, Janine – although they generally take the single men first.'

'Jamie? They wouldn't have him. He's got flat feet.'

Something in her tone when she said that set Bridger's teeth on edge. Lately Janine spoke more and more disdainfully of her husband. As far as Clive could tell, the man was a decent sort, but just no match for the tough character he had married. Bridger had no feeling of being superior to James – no impulse to laugh at him, either. It was rare for Clive to sympathise with a husband, but he sometimes pitied Sayers. Janine was as she was, of course, and her husband could not meet her needs. Clive was a cad and Janine his equivalent. Sayers was an unfortunate dupe. All of them simply followed their natures. Still, Bridger found some of Janine's remarks about James excessively unkind.

After a while, she stretched and sighed. 'Ah well, I suppose I'd better go. Doris will be ready to close in half an hour.' Reluctantly, she slid off the bed. 'God, how I wish I could stay and spend the evening with you.'

She was full of warmth walking back to the café that day; the warmth of cherry brandy in her stomach and her blood, the warmth of mildly abraded skin on her face from his stubble, the tingle of a pleasant soreness where he had been. Bouncing into 'Janine's' at twenty past five, she asked: 'How was trade today?'

'Steady, Mrs Sayers,' Doris said. 'Quite good, all told.'

Her look was curious. Where have you been? it wondered. I've hardly seen you since ten o'clock.

'Off you go, then,' beamed Janine. 'Thank you, Doris. See you in the morning.'

The woman left and Janine locked the door after her. Going to the till with her banking bag, she started scooping out the money.

Suddenly, half-way through the task, she hesitated, staring at the notes and coins.

She was used by now to taking out sums to pay for presents she bought Clive. A fiver here, ten pounds there – it had grown into quite a habit. Thinking about the bakery sale, and the risk she was running with her affair, it came to Janine all at once that raiding the till could serve another purpose.

Would it not be wise to have a contingency fund? A little store of money of which her husband would know

318

nothing? Something to fall back on if ever James found out about Clive, if he threw her out, divorced her? The longer her association with Bridger continued, the shorter the odds against being caught. And she could not, could not, give him up. Such had the passion become that she would rather risk losing Gardenia Lodge and her business than call a halt.

Her hand moved slowly, tentatively, at first. Then quickly she grabbed ten pounds and stuffed it into her jacket pocket. Ten pounds, for a start.

Ten pounds, fifty pounds, a hundred – the cache of money steadily grew, and finally the time arrived when Janine perceived a need for a special hiding place. A pocket in her handbag was already bulging with notes and they could not stay there. A locked desk or table drawer would elicit questions. And where in the house was safe from Mrs Coade, thorough cleaner that she was? Janine ruled out a bank account or anything of that sort. This money had to disappear from the knowledge of everyone but herself.

She thought about it for days before she hit upon what seemed a good solution.

One morning, Janine locked herself in the bathroom. She had with her a screwdriver and an old leather satchel kept as a memento of her days at Mannamead school. The bag was scuffed and had a flap at the front with a small round lock. Inside was the loot from three months of dipping into the café till.

Janine knelt down and began to unscrew the wooden panel at the end of the bath. Three screws down either side secured it. At the outer edge was a right-angled corner piece in bronze-coloured metal. This came off first, then the three inner screws. She lifted away the square of polished wood and looked with satisfaction at the space beneath the bath.

It was perfect. Barring some desperate problem with the plumbing, what reason could anyone ever have to look there? Why would anyone go to the trouble of taking the bath panel off? Certainly, Mrs Coade would not, and James was no handyman. Such places remained undisturbed for years. And where else could a person lock herself in without arousing curiosity? Whenever she wanted to add to her store, Janine could simply shut herself in the bathroom and do it at her leisure.

Gleefully, she thrust the satchel into the shadowy cavity and fastened the panel back. Easy. So easy. Ideal. Oh, how clever she was.

She had not bothered to count the money, but knew there was already quite a lot. As she stood up, she caught a glimpse of herself in one of the bathroom mirrors and saw she was grinning. Just for a moment, the sight of that grin gave her pause and it melted away.

This was illegal, she knew it. This was an offence against the bank, the Inland Revenue and, of course, she was robbing her husband in a way. She stared at herself and wondered – when had she lost all scruples? When had her conscience left her completely? Was it since she met Clive, since the threat of money trouble had appeared on the Sayers' horizon? Both were involved, perhaps. She so wanted Bridger, so dreaded poverty.

Janine shook herself. To hell with it. The ruthless survived. Anyway, the cash was hidden 'just in case'. She might never need to use it. Who knew what circumstances lay ahead? One day she might quietly feed it back into the business, if the situation indicated such a course. In the meantime, though, it was nice to know it was there beneath the bath, available to her if she should need it.

A year went by. James rarely saw his sister any more. Since their marriage, Connie and Sam had twice been asked to lunch at Gardenia Lodge and had twice refused. Jamie missed her acutely, as he had known that he would. He felt terribly alone and lost these days. He was very much at a loose end without the bakery. There was almost nothing to do all day except keep the café's accounts – and they were a source of distress in themselves.

The takings were mysteriously short of what they should be when set against the quantity of food being consumed. Try as he might, James could not reconcile the two. The goods bought in were not yielding the profits they should. He went over and over the costings, the planned profit margins, the system of measuring and controlling portions, but still there was a discrepancy. The fear of pilfering haunted his mind, yet he could not bring himself to believe it of Doris. In the fifteen years since the café opened, she had been a first-class, trusted employee, and only within the past eighteen months had this shortfall come about. Only since the bakery was sold. James focused on that in his search for a reason. Perhaps they were being invoiced for more goods than they received. He asked Janine if she made a thorough check of each delivery and she swore that she did. She also insisted that errors must lie somewhere in his figurework and scorned the suggestion that anything else was amiss. She became very irritable if he harped on about it too much.

As for his marriage, nothing had been the same since

that morning in the car when James returned from seeing the bank manager. Happy illusions of being loved had evaporated that day. He was left with a marital bargain, a mere contract, and yet it was all he now had, especially since Connie had turned her back on him. He clung to Janine because she was still there, still his wife, sharer of his house, his bed. But not of his soul, he knew that. There was no rapport, no communion between them. She chattered and smiled as brightly as ever, but he recognised this now as the same vivacity she put on at the café. Janine's public face, worn for customers and husband alike. Janine's private self, Janine's heart – he was not sure what they were like or where they dwelt, but he knew they were not with him.

How he needed Connie now, but his old reliable comforter had withdrawn her affection. On one pretext or another, James had gone round to her cottage a few times during the daytime when Sam was out. She never offered him tea or even asked him in. She was always busy or just going out. In the end he had ceased trying and left her alone. It felt like being shut out of a warm room and left in a freezing corridor.

Absorbed as he was in these personal troubles, James paid scant attention to the wider world these days. At the edge of his awareness was the menacing news from Europe, but that was all far off, like some other region's bad weather. He had his own drizzle of depression with which to contend, and it kept his thoughts close to home. As Austria fell under Nazi rule and Czechoslovakia was sold out, James puzzled over the missing profits and lamented his loneliness.

Thirty

Connie had been glad to hear and believe the soothing noises the Government made while Germany encroached, defying treaties, growing ever stronger and pushing, pushing, pushing. She did not perceive or understand the diplomatic bunglings and scurryings, the significance of pacts and new alliances, the complacency, the dithering, the misjudgement. It was sad and vaguely disturbing to read about Czechoslovakia, but she supposed there must be good reasons for what had been done. What did the ordinary citizen know of the great never-ending chess game? Only the country's leaders had a proper view of the board.

Not until late summer of 1939, with Poland the latest bone of contention, did she wake up to what was coming. It hit her when the first bus-loads of evacuees rolled into the city one Sunday morning at the end of August. London children, hundreds of them, the lunch-time edition of the local paper said next day, sent down to the West Country just as as precaution. Because, of course, it was safe down here.

'A mere precaution,' echoed Sam with a grunt, as he folded the paper. 'Takes more than a bit of unease to scare the Government into something like this, bearing in mind how slow they are to react in other ways.'

Connie took two pasties from the oven and turned them onto plates. 'What will they do with them all?' she asked, sitting down and reaching for the jar of pickled onions.

'Place them wherever they can. Farmers will take some of them, especially strong boys. A lot of young girls will go to families who want a bit of unpaid help about the house. Some will be lucky and find a good billet, others will have a rough ride, I'm afraid. I don't suppose the authorities have the time or the means to seek out character references on the hosts. It's the very little ones I feel most sorry for. They won't really understand what's happening to them, or why they've been sent away. Mind you, some are sure to be slum kids. They'll be better off here than they were at home.'

Connie thoughtfully cut her pasty into three and took a few bites from the middle section. Then she said: 'There'll be more, I suppose, if war's declared?'

'Mmph,' agreed her husband. 'Tens of thousands, I don't doubt.'

She stared at him for a moment, then looked down at her plate. 'It's really going to happen, isn't it, Sam?'

'I'm afraid it is. We shamed ourselves over Czechoslovakia. Now we've made a pledge to Poland and we're going to have to honour it. We've played for time and tried to avoid a fight, but we can't dodge this one.'

Putting down her knife and fork, she rubbed her eyes with the heel of her hand. 'I suppose there's still some chance Hitler will back down,' she said, adding with a nervous smile, 'after all, who'd want to take on the whole British Empire?'

Sam returned the smile, but it was less than reassuring. For a while they ate in silence.

Then Connie ventured: 'I suppose we could have one, couldn't we, Sam? If the worst does happen. We've room enough.'

He blinked at her, perplexed for a moment. 'What? Room, did you say?'

'For one of those children.'

He paused in his chewing a second or two, and then rapidly swallowed.

'It said in the paper there's an allowance for people who take them in,' she pressed.

'Oh yes, I know. I wasn't thinking about the expense.'

'Of course, if you wouldn't like it . . .'

'Suppose it wouldn't hurt,' he said slowly. 'Can't do less than other people, can we?'

'Mm,' said Connie, smiling. 'Well, it's something to think about, anyway. And of course, it's all speculation still. Perhaps everything's going to be all right in the end. I mean, we're not at war yet.'

'No . . .' He kept his eyes on his pasty. 'It hasn't happened yet.'

But even as he spoke he was thinking he would have to clear out the box room. There was nowhere else to put a child.

A few days later, the last frail hopes were extinguished. On the morning after Chamberlain's broadcast, Connie went round to the shops as usual, and no one could talk about anything else. In Cynthia Hardin's dairy she met Jack and Millie Chope. Millie, being her usual feather-brained self, was quite excited about it all.

'I wonder if we'll get Yanks here again,' she piped. 'Oh, I hope we do, I like the Yanks!' She rolled her eyes, then playfully poked at Connie's arm. 'Wouldn't do your brother's café any harm, I can tell you. They don't half spend, the Yanks.'

'God's truth,' tutted Jack to no one in particular. 'To

listen to her, you'd think it was a party coming up, instead of something bloody awful.'

'Oh, get away,' scoffed Millie. 'I'll bet it won't be anything like as bad as the last one.'

Irritated, Chope turned to Connie. 'She just hasn't got the sense to be scared of what we're up against.'

'Germans, like before,' said Millie tartly.

'Germans, yes, but not like before. There's something new in that nation now, something fearsome, as if they're possessed. They were never like that before the Great War. We're facing something different this time.'

'Oh, Jack! My dear life!' exclaimed Millie. 'He gets fanciful sometimes, Connie,' she confided.

Behind her counter, Cynthia sniffed. 'I dare say this'll mean rationing again. I'm just thankful I don't have children to feed.'

'You won't be taking any evacuees, then?' Millie asked. 'We're going to, aren't we, Jack?'

'If you say so, I suppose we shall.'

'Sam and I have decided we will too,' agreed Connie.

Cynthia wrinkled her nose. 'Well, do choose carefully, won't you? Some of them are certain to come from terrible backgrounds, you know. Dirt, lice, filthy habits and foul manners. Don't want that sort of thing in your home, do you? Don't let them simply assign you a child at random, if you can help it. I must say, I wouldn't want to take one myself.'

'No,' murmured Chope, with a curl of his lip.

'Of course, I've every admiration for you,' Cynthia went on, 'but I don't know why they must dump so many of them down here.'

'No wonder they call you the dairy cow,' Jack muttered under his breath.

'What was that?' asked Cynthia sharply.

'Cream,' he grunted. 'Give us half a pound.'

'Go on home, Jack,' Millie hissed, 'before you start a row.'

He shambled off, Cynthia's ice-pick glare following him to the door.

'If they accept a rough child, it certainly won't learn any manners from Mr Chope,' she said to Connie, when Millie too had left.

'It won't learn snobbery, either,' retorted Connie, amazing herself. 'Six duck eggs, please.'

On a Friday evening not long after, yet another evacuee train pulled into North Road Station, and soon the nigh-deserted platform became a scene of noisy confusion, crowded with pregnant women, schoolteachers, blind and disabled people, and children by the hundred. Wailing, whimpering, tearful children, others wide-eyed and apparently dazed, some quite calm and curious, staring alertly round them, a few very angry and screaming to go back home. Every age and every size, some well-dressed and others ragged, all with labels on their coats as if they were parcels, clutching gas masks and a few belongings. The chaperoning adults moved among them, harassed and tired, trying to round up strays, comforting the frightened and wiping runny noses. The hubbub was terrific in the shade of the station canopy. Children packed the platform benches and the luggage trolleys, while civic officials shouted instructions and generally tried to keep order.

At the far end of the platform, away from the throng, a small boy stood with his hands in his pockets, gazing up at the engine.

'Cornish Riviera' said the name plate on the side.

Such an engine, black as jet, adorned with brightly polished brass, the wheel-spokes painted red. There was still a quiet whisper of steam, a contented dragon's hiss.

The boy had enjoyed the ride from London. He had never been on a train before. He carried no belongings because he had none, save the clothes he wore, and very ragged they were, not to mention unclean. He had even lost his gas mask, but he didn't care about that. He didn't care about anything much, least of all leaving his home and his parents, for they were no great loss. He was grimy, nine years old and hard as nails, and his name was Albert Plumb.

No one came to look for him – but then, Albert was not the sort to need shepherding. After a while he glanced down the platform and saw that the crowd was gradually funnelling out through the ticket hall. In his own sweet time, he dawdled along and joined them.

A fleet of buses waited outside and he climbed aboard the nearest. There followed a ten-minute ride through the city. Albert peered through the window and noted without emotion that it wasn't much like London. At least, not the part of London he knew. It wasn't bad, he decided. There was a brightness about it, a friendly feel.

Soon they were all unloaded again and directed into some sort of public hall. 'Reception Centre' said the placard by the door. Albert mooched inside along with the others and wondered if he would be chosen, and if so, by whom. Those who were not picked out by hosts were simply allocated. It was all the same to Albert. Whoever claimed him could hardly be worse than his parents, he reckoned.

It was, in fact, a church hall in Bretonside, and most

of the people who came there that day for a child were from the Barbican. Among them were Jack and Millie Chope, and Connie and Sam Tucker.

The Chopes soon picked out two five-year-old girls, twin sisters. For Connie and Sam the decision was less easy. So many bewildered faces, so many tiny waifs. Connie found the business quite distressing and wished that she owned a hotel and could take them all home. She spoke kindly to this one and that one and agonised over a choice. Susceptible as she was to the helpless, she would not have chosen Albert Plumb. She didn't even notice him, for he sat on a bench at the back of the hall, looking self-sufficient and bored.

However, he caught Sam Tucker's eye and aroused his interest. Sam observed him for a while before he made an approach. A slum-child, that was clear at once, and a tough customer, too. But intelligent, Sam guessed. You could usually tell – it was in the eyes. This one was 'all about', as the local expression went. Although a bit blunt-featured, he would not be a bad-looking lad if his spiky hair were properly cut.

Sam debated briefly, then went and sat beside him.

'Not placed yet?'

'Nope,' said Albert, scratching.

'On your own?'

'That's right.'

'Ever been down here before?'

A shake of the head, and then an appraising look from sharp grey eyes. 'Seems nice enough,' was Albert's verdict. 'Are we near the sea?'

'Harbour's just down the road.'

'Oh.' A glimmer of interest now. Albert scratched again. He scratched a lot, and smelt unsavoury.

'Feeling a bit lost, I expect?'

'Not specially,' shrugged Albert.

'Weren't you sorry to leave home?'

'Couldn't care less.'

'Why's that, then? What was it like?'

'Proper dump,' said Albert.

Sam grinned and looked around for Connie, beckoned her over.

'This is, um – what's your name, boy?'

'Albert Plumb.'

Connie looked from the child to her husband and back again.

'Well, I'm Sam Tucker and this is my missis, Connie.'

'Evenin',' said the boy.

'Hello, Albert.' Connie glanced once more at her husband, questioning. By now she was more than ready to let him make the choice. Although – well, this was not the evacuee she had imagined. Not this self-possessed little being with his strangely adult air and cynical face. And stale odour.

Giving a barely perceptible nod, Sam winked at her. The decision was made.

'Fancy coming to stay with us, then, Albert?'

The child surveyed them briefly, assessing this chubby, smiling man and his gentle-faced wife. After a moment, he graciously accepted. 'I don't mind if you don't.'

'Wouldn't you like to know a bit more about us first?' queried Connie.

He would have to be bathed, and straight away, she was thinking. His clothes were fit only for burning.

'You seem all right to me.'

'And where you're going to live?'

"Spect that's all right too.' His gaze fixed on her, bright and shrewd. 'You must be good sorts,' he explained. 'I know I'm not the pick of the bunch. No oil painting, as me old man always says.' Turning to Sam, he added: 'I don't know what you work at, but if you treat me well I'll help you if I can. Fair enough?'

'Is that a fact? And if I don't treat you well?'

'I'll bugger off,' said Albert.

A snort of laughter escaped Connie and she smothered it with her hand. Sam was tickled by him, she could see. Certainly, the boy had character; there was something oddly engaging about his dead pan manner. She guessed he was not a child who would welcome cuddling. Nevertheless, his neglected condition assured her that much could be done for him. For Connie the nurturer, Albert was a splendid opportunity.

'Shall we go, then?' prompted the lad. 'I suppose you'll have to sign for me, or something.'

'I ain't having no bath.'

'Oh yes you are, my son.' Tucker looked down at the boy standing, arms akimbo, in front of him. Glancing to Connie, he instructed: 'Put some water on to heat, and plenty of it.'

'She ain't giving me no bath, not a strange woman.'

'I didn't say she was,' replied Sam. 'I'll do it, and don't you give me any trouble, either.'

Albert scowled. But then he looked around the Tuckers' little parlour and admitted to himself that this was a really fine place and he could have fared a lot worse, so he'd better comply. He blew a snorting sigh down his nose and said no more. A wash wouldn't kill him, he supposed.

Sam followed Connie into the kitchen. 'Have we any carbolic?' he whispered.

'Yes, and by God, he needs it. I think he's got head-lice. I know he has fleas. I've never seen a child in such a state. I'll bet he was the grubbiest one on the train.'

'Well, nobody's going to accuse us of taking a soft option, are they? Where's the nail-brush and the pumice stone?'

Stoically, Albert Plumb endured his bath and emerged as sweet as a daisy. The scent of cleansing chemicals wafted through the house and hung around for quite some time. While he was being scrubbed, Connie rammed his fetid garments into the kitchen stove with a poker and watched with satisfaction as they burned. So it was that Albert found himself naked in the world that night, save for a chopped-off cotton night-shirt which he rightly assumed had belonged to Connie. He was mightily humiliated and said so. The Tuckers soothed him with a cup of cocoa and a promise to buy him some new clothes next day.

Albert could scarcely believe that. He had never had anything new from a shop. A whole set of clothes? A titanic expense. Of course, they were having him on. He was doomed, he was sure, to spend the rest of the war indoors in a night-shirt. For the first time since leaving home, he felt depressed.

The cocoa was good, though, a treat, and when he was taken upstairs and shown his room the clouds rolled back. Albert could hardly get over it – a bed to himself, rugs on the floor, a tallboy in which to put his clothes . . . And there would be clothes, he knew now that there would. These people were truly going to lay on everything he needed.

Looking round at Connie and Sam, he gave a breath-less exclamation.

'Cor!'

Connie went straight out after breakfast next morning. She was back by ten with assorted underwear, two pairs of short grey trousers, two shirts, two jumpers, and a pair of black lace-ups. The shoes were a bit on the big side, but Connie decided that was all to the good. Boys grew fast. This one, in particular, had a lot of growing to do and she meant to feed him up.

'Very thin, aren't you?' she remarked when she saw him in his vest. 'Proper little tin-ribs. Didn't they give you much to eat at home?'

'All I wanted,' said Albert, out of pride.

'Well, I think you'll fill out a bit on my dinners. We're having stew today, and baked apples after.'

She had thought he would be pleased about that, but Albert frowned and looked troubled. Connie soon discovered why.

His eating habits were very poor and very hard to change. He turned up his nose at green vegetables and regarded salads with contempt. Cheese or eggs, roast meats or chicken were foreign or distasteful to him. Only sweet puddings and custard found favour with Albert. He had been raised on fish and chips or, more often, just chips. Bread and jam was his ultimate staple, like rice to the Chinese. He liked to eat it outdoors, what was more, as long as the weather was fine. Completely unskilled with a knife and fork, he hated sitting at table.

As for writing home to his parents, as evacuees were expected to do, Albert stoutly declined.

'Can't write much, never learned,' he told Connie dourly.

'I'll do it for you, if you tell me what to say.'

'Nah. They wouldn't be interested. They were glad to get rid of me.'

'You can't mean that! Your mum and dad?'

'Rotten pair of buggers.'

Connie's mouth dropped open.

'They spend every minute they can down the pub,' enlarged Albert. 'He's been in prison five times – burglary. And she's a bad-tempered cow, always hitting me around.'

'I've never heard anything like it,' Connie said to her husband in bed that night. 'It isn't just that his people are poor, they're bad lots into the bargain. Apparently he's used to roaming the streets until midnight, almost never sets foot in school, and sleeps underneath his parents' bed, so he must hear them while they're – you know.'

Tucker grunted. 'Yes, well that's the way it is for some.'

He says they haven't got a privy of their own. They share one with three other houses and no one ever cleans it. He just accepts squalor and dirt, nothing repels him at all. Yesterday I caught him in the courtyard playing with a dead rat. He'd tied a string to its tail and he was swinging it around his head. I nearly had a fit – and Albert thought that was a huge joke. I took it away from him and then he asked me why we didn't have any bugs in the house like normal people. That's what shocks me, really, what he sees as normal. Believe it or not, he considers us a bit "posh". That was the word he used to me – posh. Can you credit it? And there was I, thinking we were nobody special.'

Thirty-one

At first it hardly felt like a war at all. Barrage balloons
went up around the city, a few anti-aircraft guns were
sited, people observed the black-out and took their gas
masks everywhere, as ordered. The city museum
became a recruiting office, but otherwise nothing happened for a fortnight.

Then an aircraft carrier left the Sound and put to
sea. *Courageous*, manned by a Devonport crew, got as
far as Land's End and caught a torpedo. More than five
hundred men were lost, the city had its first deep
wound and a new crop of Navy widows.

Over a score of merchant ships were also sunk that
month, but for those who had no man at sea, the war
still seemed unreal. It was always 'out there' somewhere, on the ocean or in other countries. To some the
situation felt eerie, to others it was a farce.

From half a world away came news of another skir-
mish in December. Another Plymouth ship, the cruiser
Exeter, well-nigh pulverised after her encounter with
the *Graf Spee*. On the wireless, Lord Haw-Haw crowed
that the *Exeter* had sunk. Later he revised his boast,
admitting she was still afloat but confident she would
never reach home.

Already certain goods were becoming short. In spite
of this, the Tuckers had a good Christmas. Food was
not officially rationed yet. With patience and persist-
ence, Connie managed to store up a few nice things.

Most of the local shopkeepers saved her special items under the counter. Sam bought Albert a couple of Dinky toys for Christmas – a double-decker bus and a racing car. The boy was speechless with gratitude. Connie added two aeroplane pictures to hang on the walls of his room – a fighter and a bomber. Albert would lie in bed and gaze at them each night, and imagine he was attacking Berlin all by himself.

Nineteen forty came in and *Exeter* returned home in a February blizzard, escorted by a small fleet of destroyers, minesweepers and other cruisers. Churchill was there to greet her and so was half the town. Before a roaring crowd, she struggled past the Hoe and up the river past the yard where she was built, to moor at Keyham. The noise resounded all over the city, the dockers were beside themselves with pride. There were speeches and delirious welcomes. Everyone felt good that day.

And some people were still flippantly calling it the 'Bore War'.

Janine, for one, was bored with it, and nettled by certain new expectations of her.

'Think you'll be accepting a kiddie or two, Mrs Sayers? They keep on coming, don't they?' said Mrs Coade. 'Poor mites. Be a treat for some of them to stay in a lovely house like this.' Smirking, she folded her duster into a pad with which to work beeswax over the rosewood bureau.

You aggravating old witch, thought Janine, eyeing her housekeeper sideways with a smile that was tight and cold.

'Think what a lot of labour it would make for you, Mrs Coade.'

'Oh, I shouldn't mind too much – for kiddies.'

Janine went on filing her nails. 'I don't think it would be a good idea.'

'Why's that?'

'I have my reasons – not that I need explain them to you,' ended Janine with quiet severity.

'I was only asking,' sniffed Mrs Coade. 'After all, the lady next door's taken two. And her across the road – she's got one. Half the people in the avenue have opened their doors. Makes it look bad if you don't do the same. I said as much to Mr Sayers this morning.'

'Did you indeed?'

'Made him think, I reckon.' Mrs Coade rubbed busily at the bureau. 'Be awful if people got the wrong idea, I told him. If they thought he was heartless or un-patriotic. Nice man like him – make a good host for a kiddie, I said. Probably enjoy it, too. Hasn't got a lot to occupy him, has he?'

'Mrs Coade,' Janine said acidly, 'don't meddle. Don't try to start any arguments between my husband and me.'

The older woman straightened up with a fresh dollop of wax poised on top of her cloth. 'I take exception to that, Mrs Sayers. I meant well.'

'I can tell mischief-making from good intent, believe me.'

The wax was slapped onto the bureau and vigorously spread. 'I'm sorry, I'm sure, if you see it that way. But then, when I spoke to him I had no idea you'd be so set against the suggestion.'

Oh yes you did, thought Janine. You know me. And I know you.

Wryly, she smiled. 'You won't beat me at man-oeuvres, Mrs Coade, so stick to your housework.'

The housekeeper paused, surveyed her, nodded, one hard woman acknowledging another. 'Oh, I know I'm an amateur compared to you,' she answered softly.

Janine grinned. Then she asked mildly: 'Why do you so dislike me? I haven't been a harsh employer, have I?'

The woman's gaze dropped. She debated, then was brave enough to answer bluntly.

'You're not good for Mr Sayers. I've grown to like him very much. You're not the sort he needs. You'll break him one of these days.'

Janine's eyebrows twitched. 'Well – I appreciate your candour, and you are entitled to your opinion, of course. Just don't act on it, Mrs Coade, don't try to change anything in this house, and we can still get along passably well.'

'I'm surprised you don't sack me for what I've just said.'

'I'm not thin-skinned, and your work is very satisfactory. But I warn you again, don't cause any ripples in my little pond, there's a dear.'

'Shan't say another word,' came the grunt.

She had already said enough, though, to cause a nuisance. That evening James brought up the subject and Janine had to parry his hopeful suggestion that they might take in an evacuee.

'Don't think it hasn't crossed my mind, Jamie,' she said. 'I read the papers too, you know. But it would only remind me of the fact we have no family of our own. I don't want any old wounds re-opened. What's worse, I'm afraid I might grow too fond of the child – and so might you. Imagine the wrench when we had to send him or her home at the end of the war. I really don't want any upsets of that sort. I don't want to suffer the way poor Connie did when she lost her little girl.'

You're not capable of that, thought James, with his new and greater knowledge of Janine. Still, he did not press the matter, fearful of a row.

If anybody risked a painful parting, it was Connie once again. Sam had thought when first he spotted him that a lad like Albert Plumb was less likely than most to embed himself deeply in Connie's affections, and would not be too difficult to give up when the time came. Unlike the pretty, polite little girls selected by the Chopes, Albert had no winsome appeal. Tucker had not foreseen that his wife might view the boy as a challenge and mount a campaign to improve him.

'He deserves better things,' she often said, 'because he's bright, you know, and his nature's good. There's nothing sly or vicious about him. Given a decent chance in life, who knows what he could become?'

'You won't get carried away now, Connie, will you?' Sam would caution. 'In the end he'll go back where he came from, don't lose sight of that. Don't grow too attached or make any plans, or you might finish up being hurt.'

'Oh, give me credit for a bit of sense. I'm well aware we can't keep him, but while he's here we should give him a will to pull himself up, let him see the doors aren't closed to him. That's half the reason the poor and ignorant stay that way – they accept their "place". They look up to others who are simply luckier – or craftier – and think they're a higher breed.'

'Why, Connie, you sound almost like Janine.'

'She isn't wrong about everything.'

So Connie set about reforming Albert, in hopes of equipping him for advancement in later years. Eventually she managed to bribe him with comics into eating proper meals at the table every day. Habits of cleanliness were enforced by Sam. This required the occasional clout – which Albert never seemed to resent. He would yelp and then grin and then do as ordered. Being 'belted' was something he readily understood, and though it discomfited Sam and Connie, Albert took it lightly.

The matter on which the Tuckers expected most trouble was schooling. In the event, however, Albert took to it fairly well. Connie marched him to the local junior school one Monday morning and registered him. She left instructions that she should be informed of days when he dodged off. Thereafter, reports of absence did arrive from the school, but they were surprisingly few.

'Albert,' one of the teachers dryly observed, 'does not find his lessons an ordeal. He is quicker than most of his classmates and likes to show off his cleverness. He can read quite well now, given something which interests him. It is noticeable how well he fares with *Ivanhoe* or *Treasure Island*. Presented with something which bores him, he becomes conveniently unable to read at all. His writing remains deplorable, but gradual progress can be detected. He draws extremely well, particularly diagrams.'

Albert said the school was nice and warm and he'd made a few pals. He doggedly denied enjoying the lessons.

'Don't play truant much, though, do you?' said Sam.

'When I do, you always find out and go on at me, send me to bed at six for a week. Anyhow,' he added, colouring up and bashfully looking away, 'it pleases you, I know, and you have been good to me.'

Well, well, thought Sam – a noble response from such

a formerly wayward lad. Of course, the early-to-bed punishment played a part as well. Sam found it more effective than a hiding, which Albert would simply shrug off. Early-to-bed was a better deterrent altogether. Albert incurred a sentence according to his crime – three days, a week, a fortnight for something dire. If the offence was truly unspeakable, his comics were taken away as well, so he had to lie in bed with nothing to do, while Connie and Sam were downstairs listening to Albert's favourite programmes on the wireless.

The boy's misdeeds were mostly committed against the neighbours. The Tuckers' courtyard, being shared with the two other cottages, was usually hung about with washing. Albert took a fancy one day to an old lady's drawers, grabbed them off the line and wore them out into the street, telling everyone whose they were. On another occasion he cut the rubber buttons off a suspender belt to use as Ludo counters. Sam stopped his Saturday matinée money for that, which Albert thought mighty unjust, since the girdle's owner wore ankle socks nowadays anyway.

Sometimes he earned a cuff for tormenting Cynthia Hardin's terrier, Dermot. The boy had decided from the start that Dermot was a nasty, yipping, scurrying little beast. He liked to sneak up the alley beside the dairy, climb onto her backyard wall and provoke the little dog, blowing raspberries while Dermot dashed back and forth below, jumping and snapping with helpless rage. Many a time had Cynthia caught Albert at it and shooed him off. She called him a horrible little tyke and complained to Connie whenever she saw her.

Often, when he had been to see Flash Gordon at the pictures, Albert startled people in the street by jumping out of shop doorways and blasting them with his 'ray gun'. When they cursed him, Albert swore back and pulled faces. He drew rude pictures on people's walls, hurled the occasional mud pie, pushed the odd dead fish through someone's letter-box. He was Lancelot, Geronimo, Captain Kidd and Ming the Merciless — in short, a normal, noisy, messy little boy. Sam and Connie grew to love him, even if the neighbours did not. It was going to be hard, thought Tucker, seeing him go at the end of the war.

Thirty-two

By April of 1940, food was well and truly rationed.
Butter and sugar and cooking fat were no longer freely
available, a problem especially galling to Janine. The
bakeries could not supply the elaborate confections she
required. The goods were simpler these days and had
to be sold at more sensible prices.

'God, this whole damned business is getting me
down,' she complained to Clive. 'I can't even replace
my crockery – not with matching pieces. Every time
something is broken I have to use some awful oddment
in its place. Everything's deteriorating. And people
have started stealing the teaspoons, you know. It's just
too bad.'

She was lying in Bridger's bath, her head on a small
silk cushion. He, at the other end, had his back to the
taps. He lifted up a foot and teased her nipples with his
toe.

'Trivialities,' he said lazily. 'Have another drink.'
Draping an arm over the side of the bath, he groped for
the bottle of gin. Janine held out her glass and he
leaned forward to fill it.

'Jamie's volunteered for the ARP or some such thing,'
she sniffed. 'He seems to think we're in danger here.'

'He's right.'

'Then why's the city full of evacuees?'

'Good question. I think it's mad to send them here.

343

How safe is the city with the biggest naval dockyard in Europe?'

'Plymouth wasn't touched in the last war. They can't reach us this far west.'

Not yet they can't, he thought, but decided not to say so.

'They won't come any further now,' continued Janine. 'Our troops and the French will drive them back.'

Bridger, not at all sure of that, changed the subject. 'Cornwall next weekend? Can you slip away?'

Janine scowled into her glass, then took a gulp. 'How?' she demanded, flicking soapsuds at him. 'No petrol for your car or mine.'

'We'll go on the train.'

'All right. Suppose there's no choice. I daren't be seen coming here too often.' Perching her gin on the shelf above the bath, she smiled slyly. 'Let's dry off now and go to bed.'

Lasciviously, he cocked an eyebrow. 'No, I've a better idea. As they say in the corniest musicals, why don't we put on the show right here?'

'You're joking! You couldn't!' cackled Janine.

'Oh, but I can. I've done it before.'

A darkness crossed her face. 'I don't want to hear about that.'

'No? You used to laugh when I told you . . .'

'I'm not interested in what you did with the others.'

No indeed, it displeased her now to hear of his adventures – which he knew was not a good sign. Suddenly, however, Janine was smiling again.

'Just give me a demonstration.'

'Certainly, madam.'

There followed a very slippery, soapy coupling. One leg flung over each side of the tub, bosoms bobbing in the bubbles, Janine uttered shrieks of excitement and mirth, while Clive, with buttocks clenched, soon had the bathroom floor awash in his efforts to do her justice. With every thrust, a mighty splosh. The air was full of steam and grunts.

At last they arose, dripping, and started towelling one another, lingering lewdly here and there. By the time they were dry he was able once more, and so they rushed into the bedroom and did it all over again. There was nothing quite like sex for helping Janine forget the war.

Only five weeks later came the panic of Dunkirk. Early June saw the city suddenly full of evacuated French troops. They came in by train, dirty, dishevelled and weary. Most of their kit had been lost in the scramble to escape. For several days they could be seen wandering around the city centre. Tens of thousands of them came and went within a week. Then, refreshed and re-equipped, they were all shipped back to Brittany.

Within a fortnight they had lost their fight. Sam heard over the wireless during his tea-break at work that the Germans were in Paris.

'They're on our bloody doorstep now,' he said to Connie that evening. 'They're bound to come after the dockyard, and it's my guess we shan't have to wait very long. Makes me wish we didn't live so close to the waterfront. They're bound to aim for the flying boats at Mount Batten.'

Connie went on knitting. 'We'll just have to hope for the best. Poor Albert – this is no safe refuge after all.'

Her husband glanced at her. 'Well,' he said, 'there is somewhere else for you and the boy to go.'

Her fingers stopped working. She looked at him.

'Your brother's place, Connie.'

The fingers flicked again at a furious pace. 'I don't want anything more to do with those two.'

'Not even at the risk of life and limb?'

'That's how it is. Anyway, we're getting a shelter.'

'Connie, I think you're being too hard on James. You've snubbed him these past three years or more. Isn't that enough? I know he's a misfit, they both are, but . . .'

'I'm not going to them to beg for anything.'

'Who's talking of begging? He'd be more than glad to put you up if the bombing is bad. In times like these it's not good to be proud.'

'I don't think Janine would care for Albert.'

'Oh, I don't know. I gather she's not without a sense of humour.'

The ball of wool spun as she pulled a length loose. 'They'd upset me more than the war. I dread to think what sort of pickle they're in by now. The minute I soften, James will take it as a chance to cry on my shoulder, I don't doubt. I don't want to know how she's treating him or how he feels. It's up to him to deal with her. I can't help it if he won't. The whole thing makes me sick. As for Janine, I couldn't be civil to her. I used to admire her; now I'd like to kick her backside black and blue.'

'Connie, you know, you helped to make Jamie the way he is. You loved him too well.'

She lowered the knitting to her lap. 'Yes, I did, didn't I? Still, it was you who said to me that he's a grown man now.'

'I didn't think you would ever shun him the way you do.'

'You're saying I've gone from one extreme to the other.'

'That's a fact. You're being harsh now, Connie. He's your only blood relation, don't forget. How long will you keep this up? Until one of you dies?'

She wrapped some yarn around the needles and stabbed them through the ball of wool.

'I don't know, I don't know. But I'm not ready to bother with him again yet. I'm half afraid I might fall back into my silly old ways and start feeling sorry for him.'

'How about feeling concerned for yourself and Albert? When the air raids come, as they surely will, it'll be the poorer parts that catch it, mark my words. It'll be us – the alleys and the terraces huddled round the docks and quays. It won't be the big houses and gardens on the outskirts.'

'We'll wait and see what comes,' said Connie stoutly. 'It'll have to be pretty dreadful, let me tell you, before I'll go seeking a billet with James and Janine. Anyway,' she muttered, 'sometimes when you try to run away from something, you run right into it.'

'Now Connie, I don't see a lot of sense in that. I reckon the further away from here, the safer you would be.'

The smart suburbs might contain no obvious targets, but James was taking no chances. The windows at Gardenia Lodge were criss-crossed with brown sticky tape. Some of them were sandbagged too, and he had turned his study into a refuge room which could be made airtight in the event of a gas attack. It was all extremely unsightly, of course, and filled Janine with wrath. The black-out screens by themselves were bad enough, but when he got busy with hammer and nails, sealing the study door and windows with bits of old carpet, she was enraged.

As for the Anderson shelter, she loathed it and vowed she would never spend a night inside. There it crouched, a dank, beetle-ridden hump in her front lawn. When she looked out of the sitting-room window, the shelter's dark entrance could just be seen. It resembled a mud-encrusted head emerging from the ground and peeping at her, like Chad over the wall.

James had enrolled for the First Aid and Medical Services, and was attending classes four nights a week. It gave him a sense of importance and purpose he had lacked for many years. The war seemed to have bestowed on him a brand new decisiveness which Janine found irritating.

'You're like a jumping bean,' she snapped one evening, as he ran around the house fussing with the black-outs and the curtains. 'I could almost swear you're enjoying all this.'

'I take every precaution to safeguard your beloved house. Why complain about that?' Turning, he glanced reprovingly at her. 'Why don't you volunteer for something? It wouldn't hurt you. You've plenty of time to spare, and you love organising, being in charge.'

'Only of what's my own, Jamie dear. My business, my home.'

His gaze travelled over her. She sat, legs crossed, leafing through a magazine. In her right hand was a cigarette and she drew on it with unconscious regularity every twenty seconds or so. Janine favoured slacks a lot these days, since stockings were hard to come by. Beneath a jacket of herring-bone tweed, she wore a fine-knit fawn jersey, and about her neck was a string of pearls. Her hair was shoulder-length now, rolled back above her temples and caught with combs. Whatever the style of the day, it seemed she could wear it. He frowned that she should sit there so calmly while he bustled about. So unconcerned, as if she were the only one in the world not involved.

She caught his expression. 'Don't give me that sanctimonious look, James. I know what you're thinking about – the ATS or something of the sort. Believe me, I wouldn't fit in, I've no team spirit.'

'People will notice if you don't do your bit.'

Her only answer to that was a scornful little smile.

'Mrs Pope next door has joined the WVS.'

Pointedly, Janine switched on the wireless and turned it up loud. There was a depressing bulletin about Belgium, so she quickly twiddled the dial. A whistle, a crackle, a whine, and she was rewarded with a religious broadcast.

'Whenever I tune in these days, it's either battles or the Bible.'

Irritably, she spun the knob and finally found a music programme. She began to swing her foot in time to it, and fixed her eyes intently on the magazine.

James knew there was no point in saying any more. He glanced at the clock and saw it was time to leave for his first-aid class. He went to fetch his coat and hat, and quit the house without even calling goodbye.

Another wave of men in transit passed through Plymouth after France fell. British troops this time, arriving at Millbay docks in their thousands by liners, fishing boats, hospital ships. Exhausted, unkempt and unshaven, they disembarked to be fed, revived with tea and cigarettes, and sent back up-country on the train.

349

For days the Sound was packed with crowded vessels. It was almost like Dunkirk all over again, huge numbers of tattered soldiers suddenly here and just as suddenly gone.

Just a couple of days after that, the first bombs fell. Three bombs, three people killed in Devonport. And next day, at tea-time, there came another blast.

Connie was setting the table, expecting Sam any minute. On the floor beside the fire, Albert was playing with his racing car. The explosion nearly caused Connie to drop a kettle of boiling water. She had only just taken it off the hob and was poised to fill the teapot. Albert froze for a second or two, and they stared at each other in fright. Then the boy leapt to his feet and rushed outside. Connie followed him down to the quay.

To the east, over Cattedown, there rose a column of smoke. The plane had already gone. Other people were coming out of their houses, pointing, murmuring.

Closer this time. Connie's hand crept up to her throat. Just across the water this time, only a mile off. She clutched Albert, urging him: 'Come away.'

Five more dead, the paper said next morning. The street was called 'Home Sweet Home Terrace'.

It seemed that Sam had been right. The waterfront and dockland areas were going to take the brunt. More attacks followed, small to begin with, a single strike from a single plane, streaking in to drop a stick of bombs and then beat a hasty retreat. The targets were certainly military ones – the RAF base, the shipyard – but it was in the close-packed streets round about that people died. Half a dozen here, a dozen there, a steadily increasing toll throughout August and September.

Thirty-three

Clive Bridger stood with his hands in his pockets, studying the photograph clipped to the wire strung across one corner of his dark-room. It was surely the best he had ever taken. Lord, it was good, in perfect focus despite the speed with which the whole event had occurred. It was luck that he had been on the spot at all, but sheer expertise accounted for the rest.

A Heinkel, in an attack on a battleship anchored in the bay. He had captured the bombs in mid-air just after release. Every detail was sharp and clear; you could see the gunner in the nose, the swastika painted on the tail, the men on the ship scrambling for their own guns. There was a second picture too, only slightly inferior; the bomber wheeling away in a broad arc, while a great white plume of water rose over the bow of the ship. It had been a very near miss.

He would sell them to the local papers, of course. He had done very well out of freelancing since the war started. Still, opportunities for shots like that were very rare as yet. The artist in him felt a stir of discontent. Clive had always taken a pride in his work, always been concerned for quality, but never before had it given him real excitement. Those moments on the Hoe had been a greater sensation than sex, and now he looked with quiet satisfaction on these tributes to his skill in glossy black and white.

Clive left the pictures to dry and went upstairs to his

sitting room. From the packet on the coffee table, he pulled a cigarette, lit it and stood at the window a while, looking down into the street. Life still went on for him in much the usual way, despite the war. Dogs, brides and babies were still the bulk of his work. But every so often now there would be something different, some drama – a shattered house, a couple of bodies on stretchers, a movement of men through the city like a passing gust of wind.

He drew long and hard on his cigarette, inhaling deeply. There was, he had to admit, a dreadful thrill in it all sometimes. It might be ghastly, but it was stimulating. Lately he found himself less and less patient with the bland assignments which earned him his daily bread.

He sighed a stream of smoke and his forehead creased. He had another one of those in half an hour, some wretched woman and her awful offspring. The thought of wheedling some fractious toddler into a pose was exceedingly vexing to Clive today. He resented the necessity to bother with such things, and he could not get his mind off those splendid photos hanging in the dark-room.

Down in the street, among the passers-by, were many uniforms. Most of them naval, but there were men in khaki too, and occasional glimpses of air-force blue.

The dull glow of the cigarette end brightened and ate its way down a quarter inch towards the filter as he sucked in another pull of smoke.

The RAF – they might be glad of a man like him. For photo-reconnaissance, perhaps, or something connected with it. Anything would do, as long as it gave him a chance to get in the air.

Then he expelled the smoke with a snort. Him? Clive

Bridger, volunteer? He who had never done anything much for anyone? Although, of course, even this would be for himself, to satisfy his new yearning for excitement. Bridger flicked the ash off his cigarette. Anyway, it might not be long now before he received call-up papers.

Janine would call him a bloody fool to go before he had to. Not that Janine's opinion should matter at all. Not that she should have any influence over Clive and what he did. Again his forehead crinkled. She seemed to feel entitled nowadays to advise him, argue with him. He didn't like that. It had taken her years to grow possessive, but finally she was becoming like all the others. He had let the affair carry on for far too long, if the truth were told. Because she was so good in bed, and because she had been so sensible, so casual about it for such a long time. Feeling safe, he had dropped his guard while slowly, inevitably, Janine changed into another clinging woman. More subtle than the others, true, but the instinct was the same. He was fond of her, he had to confess. He had never been fond of anyone else. After so many years he supposed he was bound to feel something extra for Janine.

But that scared him, too. It might be just as well, he reflected, to get right away from her before he found himself becoming – God forbid – really attached.

Troubled, he stared down into the street for a long time. A couple of passing WAAFs caught his notice and he watched them thoughtfully until they were out of sight.

The lady and toddler duly arrived for their sitting, and a very trying exercise it was. Clive conducted it with gritted teeth and went back upstairs in a bad temper when they had gone. Slumping in his armchair,

353

he poured himself a whisky and fell again to thinking about his life, about making some changes.

He was still there when Janine let herself in at seven that evening. She failed to notice at first that his greeting was very subdued. He was not in a mood to see her just then, and he felt he had been wrong to give her a key. She had made his flat her second home, coming and going as she pleased. He should have protected his privacy, but there it was – another sign that he was slipping, too involved.

'Jamie has a class tonight and some sort of meeting afterwards,' she told him brightly. 'I shouldn't think he'll be home before ten. Listen, Clive, I've managed to get a couple of gallons of petrol. Why don't we go somewhere for a drink? Find some nice little pub out on the moor? It's such a lovely evening, I'd enjoy the drive. And then . . .' she came and knelt beside his chair, undoing his shirt and sliding a hand inside, '. . . then I'd like to find some pretty place and make love al fresco. How about it?'

He turned his head, looked down at her. She was forty-two but very well preserved. Only the faintest lines beneath her eyes, only two tiny grooves, like brackets, either side of her mouth, etched there by years of satisfied smiles.

The smile, however, faltered now.

'What's the matter, Clive? I don't mind staying in, if you'd prefer.'

For a moment he was silent, pondering. He had been brooding for hours and had reached a decision late in the afternoon. Now, suddenly, the room oppressed him and so did her searching face. Too close. He had let her grow too close. He wanted to pull right away, pull back

354

and put some distance between them. He was going to do so, too, and she would have to be told without delay. No sense in putting it off, now that his mind was made up. He thought about the moor, the space, the emptiness. Yes, he too would like that. His desire was all for wide horizons now.

'No,' he said, 'I think you're right. We ought to have a spin out in the country. There's a very nice pub at Meavy, and then perhaps we'll drive on up to Wistman's Wood.'

'Oh, splendid!' laughed Janine. 'It's supposed to be a very creepy place at dusk.'

They drove out through the city in rich evening sunlight, up onto Dartmoor and along to the village of Meavy with its ancient pub, the Royal Oak. Locals in the little bar eyed them with mild curiosity – a tall, dark man whose head nearly touched the ceiling beams, and a woman in somewhat dressy clothes, a woman with painted nails and a piquant face. Town people, smart and out of place, sitting at a little wooden table by the chimney. They drank a couple of whiskies, then they left.

By the time they had parked the car and walked up to Wistman's Wood, the setting sun was a crimson disc behind streaks of mushroom-coloured cloud. The wood was a colony of stunted, arthritic-looking oaks, growing among the mossy rocks of a hillside. A lonely, eldritch place, it was said to be haunted by all manner of fearful things.

The red sun sank a little lower down the sky, and tinges of mauve and charcoal darkened the clouds as Janine and Bridger writhed upon the blanket he had spread on a flat patch of ground. There was no breath of wind that evening. The tree above them stood

355

motionless, and theirs was the only movement among the boulders.

The sun was still red when Clive stood up, buttoning his clothes, and walked away a few paces down the hill. Janine sat up on the blanket, watching him, uneasy. It had never been so quick before. She almost fancied he had wished to get it over with.

After a while he heard her step close behind him. Glancing over his shoulder, he said: 'I'm sorry if it wasn't up to standard, but there's something on my mind.'

A pause, and then: 'To do with me?'

'It's going to affect you, yes.'

'What is it, Clive?' Her voice was tense with trepidation.

There was no gentle way, so he plunged straight in. 'I've been thinking I might join up.'

'What?' At first she was relieved, amused. It was too preposterous. 'Oh God, Clive, this can't be conscience, surely? You've always sworn you didn't have one.'

'Not such as you'd notice. But it's not to do with that. I want to go.'

She came round to face him now. The red glare lit their features on one side, shadowing the other.

'Have you lost your mind?'

'Don't think so.'

'Clive, you could be killed.'

'Devil takes care of his own, I'm told.'

'Don't bloodywell joke about it! What's brought all this about? Why this sudden death-wish?'

'It isn't a death-wish. It's not all that sudden, either. I've been restless for a long while, and lately it's come to a head. I want a change, that's all there is to it. I want a different life.'

'Flirting with death is hardly the best way to accomplish that!'

'Look, Janine, I'm bound to be dragooned into something before very long. I'd just as soon volunteer now and have some choice in what I do.'

'And what, pray, is your choice?' Her heart was thumping.

'I've a notion to offer my extraordinary abilities to the RAF,' he said lightly. 'I believe I'd look good in the uniform. You know me, Janine, I'm the glamorous type.'

'I should have known. And what about me?'

He looked at her intently, debating within himself. To be callous, offhand? It had always been easy when he was young. He was finding it more difficult these days. Reassure her, then? Placate her, make promises for 'when it's all over'? He was not prepared to do that, either.

'I told you once, if you recall, that you had no claim on me.'

She barely remembered that. Anyway, their years together should have changed his attitude. At least, she had assumed so.

Almost as if he perceived her train of thought, he added: 'You take too much for granted nowadays. But what's between us is beside the point. I say again, I want to go for other reasons. I've had enough of the routine work I do.'

'Ye Gods,' she breathed, 'I thought you had more sense. Well . . .' she turned and walked away a little, twisting her hands, '. . . at least you're not making any noble noises about serving your country. I couldn't stand that.'

'It would be out of character,' agreed Clive. 'I've no

357

pretensions of that sort – though naturally I'd get a kick if I managed to do something damaging to the other side, even indirectly.'

'Oh, good show,' mocked Janine.

The light on the moor was coppery now, like the glare from a furnace. The evening seemed suddenly much too warm and the sunset, so spectacular, appeared more frightening than beautiful, as if it were the glow of a distant conflagration, vast and growing bigger, heading her way.

'It's no great sorrow to leave me, then?' she asked at length. 'Won't you miss me at all?'

No reply. He remained standing, hands in his pockets, gazing down over the valley. There was a droop to his shoulders, but it might have been just weariness with her questions.

'Well?' she demanded, going back to him, nearly tripping among the rocks. 'You can't pretend it's the same with me as it was with all the others, that I can be dismissed without a second thought. You're only human, Clive.'

'Don't, Janine. Don't start giving me all this tiresome drivel, or you will be placing yourself among the others, behaving the selfsame way.'

'I have a right, after all this time . . .'

'You've no rights whatever. No rights over me, no duty towards me, as I have none towards you. I'm not your husband. Go on back to that poor sod and show him some concern.'

'Oh, you awful hypocrite!'

'Not entirely. I've hatched a certain sympathy for Jamie over the years. Other husbands were only names, unknown men of whom I had to beware for a month or so before I moved on to the next girl. I've learnt a lot about poor old Jamie, though. You make me cringe sometimes, the things you say about him.'

'Well, my, my! Listen to Clive the compassionate! Have you undergone a conversion, seen the light or something? Forget the RAF, Clive, and join the Salvation Army instead. I swear I can already hear the chink of tambourines.'

He eyed her calmly. 'Don't snarl, Janine, it makes you ugly. And don't sneer if I harbour a few decent sentiments, either. You'd be glad enough if I changed my plans out of consideration for you.'

'Please, Clive . . .' she gazed at him now with a helpless misery such as she had never known before, '. . . I'll be terrified every moment you're gone.'

'I can't help that. I'm not going to order my life to save you from worry.'

'But I love you.'

'That's no argument. Anyway, I don't want you to. The very fact we're having this little scene proves just how badly things have got out of hand. Where would it lead if we carried on? Would you start to talk about divorcing Jamie, moving in with me? No fear.'

At that, her pride rose up and flung out a lie. 'Please don't flatter yourself too much. I wouldn't drop my standard of living for you.'

'That's my girl, that's better.' He smiled in the gathering dusk. 'I'd be horribly disappointed, Janine, if you let romance get the best of you. I like you strong and realistic – mercenary. That's why this affair has been so durable. But I fear you are in danger now of sagging into soppiness, and I'd hate to be the cause of that.'

Beaten, she hung her head. 'Will you write to me?'

He hesitated, then said quite gently: 'No.'

'I'll write to you.'

'You won't know where I am.'

'God, you're unbelievable! And are you really so damned tough? You've no one else, Clive, have you? No family left? Parents, brothers, sisters?'

He shrugged.

'There's only me,' she pressed.

'Someone else's wife. Very apt, I suppose.'

'Just a letter now and then? You could send it care of the café. Jamie almost never calls in.'

He argued with himself and then relented. 'Oh, all right. But they'll be rare, I warn you. And they won't be love letters. I couldn't write that stuff.'

'News to a friend, I'll settle for that.'

'I hope so. You know I always wanted it kept that way.'

'It's asking a lot of a woman, Clive. Once we've been to bed with a man . . .'

'Janine, don't give me that. Don't tell me women can't be cold-blooded about it. You've slept with Jamie for twenty years and you don't love him. Now let's be moving, the light is failing fast.'

A fortnight later he was gone, off to train somewhere in Essex. Janine was tearful for several days, going about with swollen eyes and a tight throat, but desperate not to let anyone see. When that phase had passed, she became foul-tempered.

The privations of war, just bearable when she had Clive, were intolerable now. Ordinarily she would have consoled herself by spending, but these days she was curbed by the points system – not that there was very much to buy, in any case. Goods were dull and functional, and as for choice, there was next to none. Thanks to the shortages, her appearance was starting to suffer. Her favourite cosmetics were difficult to obtain now, and she had to make do with whatever inferior stuff she could find. Even a decent soak in the bath was too much to ask, it seemed. No more steamy, dreamy hours in her beautiful bathroom with its mirrors and pretty tiles and jars of perfumed oil. A quick splash with five inches of tepid water and a bar of oatmeal soap were now the rule.

She was quietly persecuted, too, by Mrs Coade, who constantly reminded Janine of regulations, enforcing all the petty austerities with gleeful zeal, saying over and over again, 'We're all in this together, don't forget.'

In the kitchen, Mrs Coade weighed everything with precision, and served out portions in strict measures – an exact two ounces of this, a careful quarter pound of that. She resurrected leftovers, turning them into something else next day and serving them up with triumph, knowing that Janine could not abide warmed-over food. Mrs Coade also invented frugal dishes of her own – soups made up of vegetable water and boiled bones, purées of peelings mixed with rice and so forth, then tutted and shook her head and looked aggrieved when Janine had no appetite for the stuff.

James was full of admiration for Mrs Coade. He thought she was doing a wonderful job, and getting right into the spirit of things. She had the proper attitude, he said.

Mrs Coade economised in every possible way. She went around the house extinguishing lights. She washed the dishes in cold water, thereby leaving them faintly greasy, and declined to do the laundry more than once a fortnight. Mrs Coade was not going to wash until every shirt, blouse and item of household linen was well and truly soiled and worth boiling. It was extravagant, she declared, to be always washing things that were scarcely worn or used, just because madam liked to be dainty. Didn't she know there was a war on? she would ask, to Janine's utter fury.

Thus, she was having her revenge, with righteousness to back her up and quash Janine's objections. Patriotism and the Government were on Mrs Coade's side, so she felt very powerful indeed, not so much a servant now as a watch-dog.

Janine grumbled and muttered a lot about dismissing her, but with so many women doing war work or filling the jobs of absent men, she knew it would be tricky to replace her. Whatever Mrs Coade's shortcomings, Janine would not care to do the work herself. Mrs Coade was aware of that and played upon it with ill-concealed delight. She always had her ace card ready, she could always quit.

Finally, one day, there came a clash and she laid that card on the table with a flourish.

'Mutton again?' snapped Janine at lunch. 'Could you not serve something – anything – else?'

'There was no beef left. You don't like kidneys, don't like rabbit, don't like stew. I'm at my wits' end, Mrs Sayers. I can't help the shortages, can I? I do my best . . .'

'Of course you do,' said James hastily. 'Janine, it's very good. We mustn't complain.'

'Mutton,' seethed Janine through her teeth. 'Carrots. God, I'm sick of carrots. And why must we always have jacket potatoes these days? Can't we have them cooked some other way?'

'They're very nutritious,' bridled Mrs Coade, 'and very filling.'

'And don't involve much effort,' grumbled Janine.

'Well, that's all to the good.' James smiled appeasement at Mrs Coade. 'What are we having for dessert?' he asked, in hopes of something his wife would enjoy.

'Prunes. Or else there's cheese.'

Oh, the monotony of it. Janine closed her eyes and muttered: 'God!'

'It's better than some poor devils get,' said Mrs Coade, attempting to shame her. 'There's a lot of hungry people in this world.'

'Don't lecture me!' Janine had not meant to shout. It was out before she could stop it.

Mrs Coade drew herself up. A decisive moment, this, she realised. Did she care to carry on here, or had she had enough? Her sister in the Cotswolds kept inviting her to stay, and lately she had been giving it consideration. After all, the bombings were growing steadily worse. She pursed her lips, then took the step.

'Spoilt, that's what you are.'

James felt he had to protest. 'Now, wait a minute . . .'

'I'm sorry, Mr Sayers, but you know it's true. And I've had my fill, I really have.' She was taking off her apron as she spoke. 'Moaning, moaning, moaning, all the time. I can't stick any more of it, I'm leaving.'

She glanced at Janine in hopes of seeing dismay, but was disappointed.

'Fine, go on,' Janine hissed, too angry just then to care. 'Pay her what we owe her, Jamie. I couldn't give a toss.'

'Ladies, there's no need for this.'

'It had to come,' said Mrs Coade, 'and now she can just get on with it. I'm off.'

She'll be sorry, she thought, as she sailed out. Madam'll have one hell of a job to cope – got no idea.

And that was the truth. Janine had forgotten what it

was to carry heavy shopping, to queue and to struggle onto a crowded bus after waiting forty minutes or more. Fetching groceries, that special form of hard labour which was almost every woman's lot, was a chore she had escaped for many years. The burden was very hard to take up again. In the weeks after Mrs Coade's departure, Janine learned to hurry, get up early and be first at the greengrocer's or the fishmonger's or the butcher's. She now had to traipse for miles in search of scarce commodities, and very soon gave up her heels in favour of comfortable shoes. It would not have been so bad if her expeditions into town had produced a good haul, but many times she returned with her bag half empty, or stocked with foods she hated because there was simply nothing else. At the end of a morning's foraging, she would come home unkempt and exhausted – soaked if it had rained. And then, on the kitchen table, she would lay out her pitiful supplies, look at them in despair and wonder what she might make of them. Small pats of butter and cheese. A tin of corned beef, one of pilchards. A packet of tapioca, some dried peas, a few biscuits. Spinach, turnips, kale, marmite, fish paste. A bit of beef if she was lucky. Such was a typical load.

And carrots, mutton, prunes – all the same things of which she had complained to Mrs Coade. Furthermore, she ended up producing the very same meals as Mrs Coade, despite her best efforts at ingenuity.

As for the laundry, well, Janine discovered that once a fortnight was quite enough when soap was short. So, all in all, she could do no better than Mrs Coade and was saddled with the slog as well. More and more crabby, she wrote regular, woe-filled letters to Clive and waited in vain for replies.

Thirty-four

Another alert. At the first groan of the siren, Connie echoed it with one of her own and then swore.

The dinner was almost ready – liver and bacon in the oven, along with a rhubarb crumble. Cauliflower and boiled potatoes were bubbling on top of the stove. Well, she was not going to leave it this time. The Tuckers had already eaten too many warmed-over suppers following false alarms.

'Take the bedding and get on down to the shelter,' she ordered Albert. 'Where's Sam?'

'In the lav. I hope he can do it quick.'

'Don't be vulgar. Here, fill up the tea flasks before you go.'

Hurriedly draining the vegetables, Connie seized the largest saucepan she could find and tipped them in. Then, pulling the liver and bacon from the oven, she up-ended the dish, throwing the meat in on top of the vegetables. As Sam came in, she tossed him a cloth.

'Bring the rhubarb,' she told him, grabbing a handful of assorted cutlery. 'And mind you turn off the gas.'

It was the end of November, and chilly. The shelter was hardly a welcoming place as the Tuckers crowded inside and lit a candle. Wrapping up in eiderdowns, they perched on the narrow wooden benches and waited, listening. Shortly, they heard a distant thudding sound, and then a couple more. From high above there came the drone of engines, and everyone looked up as if they could see through corrugated steel and earth.

'They're here,' breathed Connie. 'It's a real one, all right.'

'There's a lot of them this time,' whispered Albert after a pause. 'One wave passes, then another.'

'I think you're right,' said Sam. 'This could be the biggest we've had so far.'

'Dinner,' said Connie, with a lightness she did not feel. 'Come on, before it goes cold.'

Handing out the forks, she found they were one short.

'I'll use me fingers,' offered Albert.

'No, you won't, they're filthy. I'll use mine.'

More thuds outside, becoming bangs, then trembling crashes. The Tuckers scrummed down over their food, heads together and hearts pounding, nervously eating too fast.

For a while the noise receded, diminishing to booms and dull thumps, mixed with the spluttering of anti-aircraft. It was always queer to be enclosed in this cramped metal shell by candle-light, guessing at what was going on outside, guessing from the sound and vibration just where and how bad the mayhem might be. Sometimes it moved far away and then came back, like a monster trampling to and fro, searching specially for the Tuckers. It made Connie feel like a mouse in a hole, with some larger animal trying to get at her.

Having emptied the saucepan, they turned to the rhubarb crumble. The roar in the sky kept on and on as they ate.

When the meal was gone they played snap for a while, but only Albert could concentrate on the game. There were lulls in the bombing and then fresh outbursts of fury. They all grew very cold, despite the eiderdowns.

After a time the shrill of a fire engine's bell approached, swelled loud, then shrank away as it passed on. A minute later came another one. Connie's imagination ran riot. She pictured the shelter, alone intact, amid an inferno.

Sam had heard the tinny sound of incendiaries falling. He was worried about the cottage. He fidgeted, hard put to stay where he was.

'I'm going to have a quick glance outside,' he said at last.

'No, you're not!' Connie grasped his wrist, her fingers digging in. And even as she spoke there came another series of explosions, rhythmic and coming ever closer. From a rumble to a cymbal-crash, and finally that dreaded thin scream, falling down the scale. Connie seized the boy and her husband, hugging both as she heard it coming. Albert, for once, was rigid with fright.

'It isn't us,' Sam cried in the last few seconds before it hit. 'It's very near, but it's not us.' Against Connie's back, he had his fingers crossed.

The impact was deafening, a sound made up of high explosive, shattering glass and the tumbling of smashed masonry. The ground beneath the shelter seemed to rock, a shiver crossed the muddy puddle at their feet, and a fierce wind blew in through the entrance. A rattle of falling debris slowly tailed away, and then there was an awful quiet. The ack-ack and far-off blasts seemed merely muffled murmurs now.

'Somewhere further down the road,' said Sam at last. 'Or it might have been Southside Street.'

'Oh God, we haven't had one like this before,' Connie

said with a quaver. 'It's very bad tonight. I'm afraid they're going to hit us as hard as London.'

Harder, I'll bet, her husband thought. He glanced soberly at Albert, thinking the boy had been pushed from the frying pan into the fire.

Albert, the immediate peril passed, was quite composed again. He watched a black beetle crawling up the wall above Sam's head. After a while he plucked it off and dropped it into the saucepan, thinking he would keep it for a pet.

A couple of hours ticked past. There were no more blasts nearby, but after a time there came an impact some way off, followed by a dull bellowing unlike anything they had heard before.

'What the hell was that, I wonder?' muttered Sam.

They listened and at length Connie said: 'What's that smell?'

'Smoke, of course,' piped Albert.

Sam's nostrils flared. It was a filthy smell, thicker, more pungent than the smoke of any normal fire.

'Oil,' he said, 'that's what it is. Burning oil. I think they've hit the tanks across the water.'

'Oh my Lord,' sighed Connie, taking up her knitting. 'It'll take a week to put that out. What's the poor old city going to look like in the morning?'

She was frightened and sad when she saw it next day. There had been fires all over town, and the smoke of them mixed with the vast black pall that issued from the blazing oil tanks at Turnchapel. It darkened the morning and made Connie cough from time to time as she trudged up to the city centre with her basket over her arm. She had barely slept a wink all night and her head was aching. Still, the Tuckers had been lucky, their home was intact.

On her way she passed many less fortunate houses, burnt-out, smashed to rubble or, as in one case, cut raggedly in half. Pathetic ruins with charred roof beams, layers of soot round window-holes, bedroom floors hanging and timbers in heaps. Everywhere people stood about in little groups, staring, shaking their heads, or comforting some sobbing householder who had lost everything. So much dust and broken glass, so many bits of things strewn about the streets. A swatch of curtain, part of a teacup, the seat of a cane chair, a man's boot, a half-burnt book. Never anything in one piece.

Any of them could have been her house. Indeed, disaster had come very close. Two incendiaries had dropped in the courtyard. Three others had ignited fires not fifty yards down the street. On the whole, the Barbican had escaped without very much damage, but it had been pure luck and who knew how long that could last? Connie thought she could not bear to lose another home, to be forced again from a place where she was settled.

James Sayers had a harrowing day in the aftermath of that raid. Some of the blast injuries made him physically sick. He would see to them, smiling and joking or matter-of-factly reassuring, then go away behind a wall somewhere and vomit. In the course of that day he attended a score of people. One old woman suffered a stroke as she was pulled out of the rubble and died in his arms. He treated a youth who had lost a foot but was simply too dazed to know it. And in one brief period of light relief, he bandaged the leg of a toy giraffe for its anxious five-year-old owner. James was very good with splints and dressings and shock and breathing problems, but he rarely dealt with burns. It was partly because it upset him too much, but more because it was felt that the sight of his scar could distress the victims. The other members of his party usually treated the burn cases.

Urged by the viciousness of the raid, he determined to call on his sister that evening, no matter how little she wished to see him. He wanted to offer the Tuckers a place of refuge.

Sayers needed no torch that night as he walked along the Barbican quays. Across the harbour the oil tanks were still blazing, billows of fire blooming and melting into the air, forever renewing themselves. The sky was lit a lurid, wavering red, the stink was heavy and fumes stung his throat. Every so often he wiped his eyes and spat. The water mirrored the glare, a crimson stain seeming to lie upon it, looking to James almost like a stream of lava. If the bombers came again tonight, the city would be a floodlit target.

As he turned up New Street, his fingers tightened on the paper bag in his right hand. Inside were two eggs, a packet of tea and a saffron cake. A present for Connie and Sam.

To his great surprise, the door was opened by a small boy, who looked him up and down and suspiciously asked: 'Yes?'

'Mrs Tucker . . .?' asked James hesitantly. 'Doesn't she live here . . .?'

'She does. Who are you?'

'I'm her brother.'

'Didn't know she had one.'

James flinched. Did they never speak of him at all?

'Well, she has, and here I am.'

Turning, Albert shouted back into the house. 'Missis? Here a minute. There's a man.'

James stared at the boy as he waited. The London accent told him this was an evacuee.

Connie came to the door, wiping dish-water from her hands. Halting at the sight of James, she said: 'Oh.'

Quickly he thrust out the paper bag. 'I had to pass this way. I thought you might be glad of a thing or two.'

Her eyes seemed to linger for ages on the paper bag. He guessed it was because she was making her mind up and would rather stare at the bag than stare at him. At last, slowly, she took it.

'Well, that's . . . Thank you, Jamie.'

He hovered. His eyes were pleading now. She fought with herself.

Albert, still holding the door, was boldly studying James. 'Bloke says he's your brother,' he told Connie, breaking a dreadful, strung-out pause.

Finally, quietly: 'Yes, he is.' Standing back, she opened the door wide.

Albert whistled as Sayers stepped into the light. 'Must have been some fight,' he remarked, pointing at the scar.

'It was an accident, Albert,' reproved Connie. 'Not everyone goes around brawling, you know. There are other ways to get hurt.'

'It's usually a fight where I come from,' said Albert dourly.

One last hesitation, then Connie nodded towards the kitchen. 'Go and say hello to Sam,' she instructed James. 'I'll make you some tea.'

Tucker was having his dinner – sausage toad-in-the-hole. He blinked at Sayers in disbelief, then cocked an eyebrow at Connie.

'He, um, brought us a few extra supplies, Sam.'

Her husband smiled and went on eating. 'Well, that's good of him, isn't it?'

'Mm,' she said awkwardly. Just now she had a feeling similar to those she had known on bygone Christmas days, when some disliked relation had bestowed a gift upon her – especially when it was a nice gift. The same embarrassment and shame, the same sense of obligation to be grateful. She was both annoyed with James and tempted to forgive him everything.

He stood uncertainly in the centre of the room.

'Sit down, then,' she told him, unsmiling. James sat down before the kitchen range and she went to the cupboard, brusquely rattling cups and clanking the tea caddy. Albert seated himself beside Sam, chin on hand, surveying the visitor. He caught sight of the civil defence badge on Sayers's coat.

'What branch you in?' asked Albert.

'First aid.'

'Were you out last night?'

'And all day today. I'm pretty tired.'

Connie handed her brother his tea, thinking he did indeed look exhausted. Never before had she seen him like that, pale with the kind of fatigue she had once known so well.

'First aid,' she murmured, surprised. 'How long have you been doing that?'

'Almost since the start.'

'I suppose you've seen some nasty sights?'

'Yes, and today was the worst so far.' His voice was haunted.

'All right up your way, is it?' Tucker asked, cleaning his plate of the morsel of sausage kept for last.

'Nothing fell anywhere near us. The suburbs are fairly safe, I think. So . . .' he moistened his lips, '. . . if you get bombed out, or if it just becomes too much for you, you know where to come. That's partly the reason I've called, to tell you the truth. I want you to know you're welcome to stay at Gardenia Lodge while this goes on. This area's very vulnerable and I don't like to think of you here in the thick of it all.'

'Hmm, but there are three of us now, as you see,' said Connie coolly.

'No matter.'

'Janine would love that – I don't think.'

'It wouldn't be up to her.'

'My, how things must have changed.'

'Connie, please, I haven't come here to quarrel. I've made the offer and it will stand. You can take it up whenever you like. It'll be a big weight off my mind if you do.'

'We appreciate it, James,' said Tucker with a frowning glance at his wife. 'Let's just hope it doesn't come to that.'

'Amen,' said Connie. She managed a smile. 'We're very fond of this little house.'

Sam pushed his plate aside. 'How's Janine coping? Finding life a bit harder these days?'

Sayers recognised the cue and took it. He could see Connie softening, loosening up, as he related all Janine's frustrations.

'She'd half forgotten how to do for herself,' he ended. 'In some ways she's having a tougher time now than you are. It's a come-down for her, and sheer hard work plays hell with a person after years of ease. I'm sure she has all your sympathy, Connie,' he added knowingly.

'Oh dear, does it show that much?'

'Business all right?' enquired Sam.

'Plodding along,' James perceived the question in Connie's eyes and admitted: 'We're still in debt.'

'Very much?'

'I'm afraid so. It's not that Janine is spending, mind you – there's nothing these days to buy – but the money we bank just isn't enough to keep us out of trouble. We're past the point of no return, I fear, and the end of it all is going to be bankruptcy.'

There was a momentary silence. Sayers looked helpless, resigned. Tucker felt sorry for him, however great a fool he had been, and from Connie all the remaining rancour dropped away. He was going to pay the penalty. What need had she to add to his misery?

'Would you like some supper, Jamie?' she asked gently. 'I'll do you something on toast.'

'No,' he said, 'thanks, but I'd best get home. I'm longing for my bed.'

'Thanks for the eggs and stuff. It's difficult to manage, especially feeding a kid.'

He stood up. 'If I'd known about him, I'd have brought another egg. Still, I'll get you some more. I'll bring you some butter and sugar from the café.'

'That would be a big help, Jamie.'

'Perhaps I'll call round on a regular day?' he suggested hopefully.

'Come whenever you like, my dear. A lot of water's gone under the bridge, after all.'

Thirty-five

The more he saw of disaster, the less patience James had with his wife. The war had forced changes of circumstances upon her, but made no difference to the way she was. In James it had wrought a personal alteration. A stronger, less self-centred man was emerging, one with diminishing tolerance for Janine and her petty complaints. Returning home to Gardenia Lodge, he would find her whining and sullen, or snappish amongst her plush furniture and knick-knacks. This, when he had spent dreadful hours attending the injured. It made him every bit as short-tempered as she was.

After Christmas that year the bombs grew bigger, and destruction spread accordingly. He was weary of grief – hysterical or stoically silent, it made no difference. And he always felt ashamed of Gardenia Lodge, so smart and untouched, after watching a family tramp away from the ruins of a terraced cottage, to swell the numbers at some cram-packed rest centre.

There were arguments when James suggested billeting a few of these unfortunates. Janine said point blank that she would not take anyone in unless ordered by the local authority. Well, sooner or later she probably would be so ordered, thought James, and might find herself landed with people she loathed, which would serve her right.

Worn out and depressed by what he witnessed daily,

he came close to hitting her sometimes when she moaned and drooped. But instead he would set about her with talk of mass burials, mobile canteens, overcrowded hospitals, eclipsing her domestic woes with tales of infinitely greater problems. How to identify the dead who belonged to no one? Where to store possessions rescued from dwellings which were now unstable? He nettled her with praise for the Army and civilian efforts to clear up and keep everything running. He had given up urging her to join in and help, but the implication was always there that she should. That, too, he believed, would be forced upon her in the end.

Then, in January, tragedy finally touched Janine.

On his way to see Connie one morning, James was passing through Bretonside when he halted in his tracks at the sight of a ruined house just ahead.

It was the Jordan place. There was nothing left but two shaky portions of wall and a pile of broken bricks and splintered wood. A couple of demolition men with sledge-hammers were knocking down all that remained standing.

Slowly James walked on down the street and stopped where the front door had been, staring at what was left of Janine's old home. The workmen paused when they saw him and one of them said:

'Not much for us to do here. Direct hit. Whole thing just caved in. These bits of wall are dangerous, though, and you know what kids are, poking about.'

James nodded silently, then steeled himself to ask the question.

'The man who lived here . . .?'

'Killed. Never would go to a shelter, the neighbours

say. Religious type, apparently – left it all up to God's will. Silly so and so.'

Watching Sayers' face, the workman's mate laid a hand on his arm and muttered:

'Shut up.'

Both men looked uneasily at James. The first, slapping dust from his overalls, took off his hat and wiped his grimy forehead.

'Did you know him?' he asked.

'My father-in-law.'

'Aw. I'm sorry.'

'When did it happen?'

'Night before last. How is it you weren't informed?'

James shook his head, at a loss. 'We didn't keep very closely in touch, and what with all the general chaos . . .'

The workmen nodded.

'You don't know where they took the body?'

'Sorry, no,' they said. 'One of the hospitals, maybe. Or the council might have taken charge of it. Better go and ask.'

'Yes,' said James vaguely. 'Yes, well, thank you.'

He turned and walked off, wondering about the funeral arrangements, or whether Jordan might have been buried already. The authorities wasted no time nowadays. He bent his steps towards the council offices to make enquiries.

Janine received the news with the same dull shock her husband had felt. Matthew, her only blood relative, gone. When James went home that day and told her, she felt peculiarly forsaken, as if a gate, left open when she started out and open all the time of her journey, had finally closed behind her for ever. However slight her affection for Matthew, the thought of his dying alone distressed her and the guilt of neglecting her poor old parent weighed heavily for a while. Janine had not paid him a visit in nearly a year.

The Sayers arranged the burial, using the services of a rival undertaker. Quite a number of people attended, mostly from Matthew's church. Some of them looked askance at what they considered his faithless daughter, abandoner of father and religion. One woman was heard to wonder aloud why Janine had bothered to come. They were such a priggish crew that James could well understand his wife's revolt against their sect. Ordinarily, she would have stared them out, but today they upset her. Sayers put a supportive arm around her while the service was read. Among that gathering, she had no other friends.

Janine had never liked herself in black, but was stricken enough to wear it for some weeks afterwards. She might have remained in mourning dress longer, were it not for a happy occurrence in February, which put back the spring in her step and the shine in her eyes.

She received a letter from Clive.

It was there among the bills one morning when she called at the café. Doris saw Mrs Sayers give a start when she spotted it. Then, with a haste a mite undignified and certainly out of keeping with mourning black, Janine scampered off to the toilet with it. Doris frowned. She had been looking at the envelope before Mrs Sayers came in. It was postmarked London, and the handwriting was large, rather spiky. Obviously a very important letter, a letter Mrs Sayers could not wait to read. Fancy taking it into the lavatory. Just the sort of thing a schoolgirl would do. But then, Mrs Sayers had not been herself for many months.

A woman was waving to catch her attention, so Doris went to serve. The customers were a different type these days – a lot more service personnel, and girls who worked on buses and in factories, drove lorries and knew about plumbing. There were fewer now of the middle-aged and middle-class, though the theatre folk still came in. But even they were a different breed, more down to earth, with no pretensions. These people did shows for the troops and the works canteens, shows for audiences in uniform, or overalls and headscarf turbans. The café sold heavier food these days, of course – plain and filling, served from crockery which was mostly unpatterned and thick. Common stodge, Janine called it. In her bad moments, she sometimes wailed that her café was becoming just like a station buffet. Doris didn't mind. She liked the new variety of customer. They were people with whom she could joke and be at ease. No need to kowtow to a soldier, or 'madam' a couple of jolly ATS girls.

Janine was in the lavatory quite a long time, for she read the letter thoroughly three times over. When at last she reappeared, her face was radiant.

'Had a bit of good news, Mrs Sayers?' Doris ventured.

'Yes, as a matter of fact, I have,' said Janine, pink-cheeked.

'Oh, I am glad!' Doris waited hopefully, but Janine was not going to confide.

'Thank you. Well now, any problems? Do you need me here for anything?'

'Don't think so,' Doris said.

'Then I'll leave everything in your capable hands, dear. There's so much else I have to do today.'

She was stuffing the letter into her handbag and looking very abstracted too, as if she were planning something.

'Will Mr Sayers be pleased at your news?'

It was asked in innocence, but it made Janine's smile snap off. Then, swiftly, it clicked on again.

'Mustn't mention it to him, Doris. I'm arranging a surprise for him, you see.'

'Oh,' said Doris, beaming. 'Isn't that nice? Can I be of any help?'

'No, dear, thank you, and remember, mum's the word. Now, I must be off. I'll be in for the takings at half past five as usual.'

So she was, but a very different Janine came back to lock up that night. The mourning dress had been shed and put away. She was wearing a blue silk blouse with a beige skirt and coat. She was chatty and buoyant again, as if some mysterious switch had been thrown to turn on all the lights in her soul. Such a rapid transformation – Doris was utterly bemused. But then, Doris did not even know that Clive Bridger existed, let alone that he was coming home on leave.

Thirty-six

Sadly, it wasn't quite like old times. Nothing was the same at their favourite hotel.

'Most of the staff we knew have gone. I hardly saw a familiar face. No special welcome for us this time, Clive.'

Kicking lightly at the sand, Janine linked an arm with him as they walked along the deserted beach below the golf course. The morning was dull but not especially cold – the kind of neutral day that typified a Cornish winter, with white sky, grey sea, and little waves flopping idly up to the tide-line. Janine's wine-red coat and his blue uniform were the brightest things in a world that seemed bled of colour.

'I suppose we should have expected a change for the worse,' he said. 'I'll check out tomorrow and take a room in Plymouth for the rest of my leave.'

'I hoped you'd have more than four days,' sighed Janine. 'After all this time, I thought they might give you a week.'

Bridger merely shook his head.

'What's it like? Are you glad you went?'

'It's as I expected. And yes, I am.'

'Is it dangerous, what you do?'

'Sometimes.'

'Oh God,' she muttered.

'Don't let your imagination run wild. I spend ninety per cent of my time on the ground.'

Janine took little comfort from that. She was silent for a short while, then she said: 'You didn't answer my letters, you brute. Long silences worry me, Clive.'

'No news is good news, believe me. If anything happened to me, you would be notified.' Pausing, he added with a half-embarrassed smile: 'I gave your name as the person to contact, since I don't have any next of kin. I take it that's all right? Or might it cause trouble with your husband? I said I was a distant cousin. He wouldn't know any different, would he?'

'Probably not. Jamie really isn't very sharp. All these years – he's never suspected, you know.' She glanced at him sideways as they walked on. 'You haven't fallen for some little WAAF, then? You're not seriously involved with anyone else?'

'I'm never serious, Janine, not even with you.'

'I'm just your long-standing friend, I know. But you have come back to spend your leave with me, and I'm sure you could have gone elsewhere, in other company.'

He had no way to parry that, and he hated to talk about feelings. Picking up a handful of pebbles, he stopped and shied them out into the sea.

'City's looking battered,' he said. 'Patches of destruction everywhere, like canker sores. You really ought to get out, Janine. You can bet there's more to come, and probably worse.'

'I'm not leaving my house. Jamie won't quit town, of course, he's needed by civil defence – but that means he's often out during the evenings and at night. If Gardenia Lodge should catch an incendiary bomb, there would be no one there to prevent the fire if I were away.'

'Are you telling me you stay indoors during air raids?' he asked, walking on.

'Certainly I do. I go and sit under the stairs.'

'Haven't you a shelter?'

'Hmph, to hell with that. Filthy wet hole in the ground.'

'That's just what you'll end up in – six feet deep – if you don't watch out. You may be able to douse an incendiary, Janine, but you could just as easily catch a five-hundred pounder. Good God, see what happened to your father.'

'Don't nag me, Clive. It makes you sound like Jamie.'

They had reached the cliffs at the end of the beach, so they turned to begin to walk back. Ahead in the distance the hotel squatted drably on the cliff-top, no longer sparkling white for want of paint.

Looking up, surveying Bridger, she smiled. 'You do look good in the uniform, I must say.'

'Making your heart race, is it?'

'You are. You always have, as well you know.'

He stopped again and grinned at her. 'Funny, isn't it, how bad lots are attractive, even to each other? If I'd ever felt disposed to marry, you're the woman I would have wanted, Janine.'

'Such a compliment.'

'I mean it. You're the only female who's never got on my nerves – well, hardly ever.'

'Oh, you and your silver tongue.'

They walked the rest of the way in companionable silence. But as she thought over what he had told her, Janine found herself growing melancholy. Her Clive could be dead in a month, a fortnight, even next week. She dared not imagine how she would feel or what the rest of her life would be like in that event. For the first time, she realised she was in a bit of a mess, crazy for a man who might be killed at any time or simply drop her if he thought it the wisest course; sick of her husband; bored with her business; financially rocky and no longer young. Her only consolation – her only life-raft if everything fell apart – was the satchel stuffed full of money and hidden under the bath at home.

When they reached the hotel, Bridger paused at reception to look at the day's menus. But she grasped his arm tightly and urged:

'Let's forget about lunch. Just take me to bed.'

It was the first time she had ever wanted it for solace.

Janine sat up in bed in the cold, staring out of the window. It was now just after three in the afternoon. Beside her, Bridger was sleeping, but he was not quite the same old Clive, she knew that now.

It was the sex that gave the game away – lovemaking far more emotional and affectionate than she had ever experienced from him before. He did have nerves, and this was where he showed them. Tough, self-centred Clive, whose way of life had left him close to no one but her, cynical Clive had wanted comfort just as much as she did.

Was he really so glad he had gone? she wondered. Perhaps he had mixed feelings, now that he had sampled the reality. How many narrow escapes had there been? What awful things had he witnessed? What might have befallen men who were his friends? She wouldn't ask him, knew he wouldn't like it. He would turn on the old bravado and caustically dismiss it all as her imagination. Men and their pride. She guessed, and rightly, that he had no idea what his body betrayed.

Janine looked out at the sky and shivered, thinking of planes going down. The grimness of the war was all too much for her, really. She had none of the right kind of strength for this. Oh, she was determined and effective at getting her way. But fortitude? Janine was not equipped with that. Clive had more of it than she did, she acknowledged. They had always been such a shallow pair, just out for fun. Wasters, users, deceivers, tares among the wheat. But he, at least, was displaying some guts and not whining about the hardships. It made her feel ashamed. James had never succeeded in doing that. But Clive? He was her counterpart, her fellow sinner, and even he was making his contribution.

Fearful and dejected, she watched him sleeping, wishing he had never shown that better side. Guiltily, she hoped he might sustain some minor injury – just enough to get him discharged and sent home to her. How she yearned to have everything back the way it used to be before the war, when life was just as she liked it.

She saw him off three days later at North Road station, not caring very much about who might see. She was only one of many women kissing servicemen goodbye, and most had eyes for no one but their own.

Clive seemed entirely his confident self again, joking over stewed tea in the buffet. He was full of breeziness now, his cap at a jaunty angle, and he swaggered down the platform when the train came in, swinging his bag as if he were off on holiday.

He found a compartment half empty and jumped in. Leaning out of the window, he said: 'Think about what I told you, Janine. Move out of town.'

'Go to some funkhole? Not on your life.' She reached up, fiercely gripping his hands in hers. 'You be careful,

Clive, you promise me. I know you must do as you're ordered, but let that be enough. Don't you volunteer for anything rash.'

Scoffing, he said: 'Clive the hero? Don't make me laugh. You know how much regard I have for my own precious skin.'

She could only smile weakly.

'You mustn't fret,' he said.

'How can I not? Mind – it will help if you don't make me wait so long for a letter this time.'

'I'll write you within the month, I promise.'

Dropping the window a little more, he stretched down to kiss her as the whistle blew. Then, as the train began to move, he muttered: 'Damn – I nearly forgot!'

From his trouser pocket he pulled a tiny box and pressed it into her hand. 'I thought it was high time I bought you something,' he said.

She was trotting as the carriage moved, her gaze dipping from his face to the red plush box in her hand.

'What . . .?' she began. 'Oh Clive, I . . .'

'Hope you like it.'

'I'll adore it, whatever . . .'

She was running now, and bumping into people on the platform, losing ground fast as the great wheels rolled and the sound of steam and thunder drowned their voices. Then Clive was drawing swiftly away, and soon he became just one of a long, long row of heads and waving arms.

The train sped on and dwindled from sight, leaving behind it a strange, charged silence. Turning, Janine saw other women standing stock-still, staring down the track. After a while they seemed to come slowly to life and they drifted away.

Janine walked back to the buffet. Over another awful cup of tea, she opened the box.

A necklet on a fine gold chain, a flower set with diamonds. A gardenia.

Janine had rarely wept in her life, and never so hard as now.

Thirty-seven

Albert Plumb was engaged in a spot of demolition. Picking up a chunk of brick, he hurled it at a window. With a glorious crash, the glass shattered. The boy selected a lump of concrete and flung it expertly at a second pane. The shards hit the ground with a musical tinkle.

There was nothing Albert loved more than a bombsite with a few windows left to break. He stood amid a hundred square yards of rubble, looking for all the world as if he had knocked down the houses single-handed. He was dusty and his knees had been scraped in clambering around, but he was happy. Kicking his way through broken masonry, he spotted another window to smash and was poised to throw his stone when a voice commanded:

'Albert! Stop that! Come on home, I've been looking for you everywhere. The King and Queen are coming to town today, and we're going to see them.'

Albert groaned. Turning, he gave Connie a look which was both a frown and a plea. 'Oh, what for, missis? I don't want to.'

'Of course you do.'

'I've seen him before. He came round our way once to open a new hospital.'

'Well, you're going to see him again. I hear he's to meet a few of the civil defence volunteers. He might speak to my brother Jamie. Imagine that.'

Albert failed to see why that should interest him, and still he hung back.

'Come home and get washed.'

Remaining defiant, the boy loitered, kicking at rubble. He and Connie eyed each other stubbornly across the devastation. She looked almost as scruffy as he did, an old coat thrown over her pinafore, flat shoes and ankle socks on her feet.

'I'll tell Sam,' she warned.

That did it. Grumbling, he slouched towards her.

'Hurry up, we both have to change. And don't look so wretched. The bomb-site will still be here tomorrow.'

It was the twentieth of March, 1941.

The town was looking as festive as it could under the circumstances, aided by bright sunshine and the first green of spring. People had been clearing up the streets, sweeping away ashes, broken glass and the spillage from ripped and rotten sandbags. Albert remarked that he couldn't see why they bothered. Since the royal couple were coming to inspect the damage, why not let them see it at its worst? Connie had to admit he had a point.

Everywhere Union Jacks hung from public buildings. The population turned out in their Sunday clothes, the town dignitaries in their chains of office, and crowds built up along the expected route. Albert and Connie joined the multitude in Cornwall Street and knew by the sound of rising cheers when the party was heading their way.

The sovereigns passed by in an open car. The Queen, swathed in a fur stole, bedecked with pearls and crowned with the usual musketeer-style hat, was smiling, smiling all the time at everyone amid a storm of

389

clapping and whistling. So unruffled, so confident – don't worry, said the smile, it'll be all right.

Connie had a close view of King George as he passed within ten feet of her. A man in simple naval uniform. The wealth of gold braid on the peak of his cap was the only touch of glamour. His smiles and waves were more restrained, more solemn. Connie thought he looked tired and troubled.

The effect on the people, though, was magical. The visit was meant to give heart to a weary town, and it succeeded. The couple spent some hours visiting the worst of the bomb sites, then the hospitals and the refuge centres, listening to the dispossessed and the bereaved. In the city centre, a party atmosphere could be felt. Bands played on the Hoe and people danced. Speakers exhorted everyone to bear up and carry on, reminding them of Plymouth's history. And during the afternoon, outside the Guildhall, certain of the voluntary workers assembled for a handshake.

'There he is, there's Jamie,' Connie said excitedly.

She and Albert watched from the front of the crowd confined to the pavement across the road, as the King and Queen walked slowly along the line of firemen, first-aid workers, wardens, rescue and demolition men. James Sayers was the fifth from the end, and Connie was enraptured to see the figure in naval uniform stop and clasp his hand and exchange a few words with him.

Albert yawned and wished he were back on the bomb-site. He was tired of all the waiting around and the pushing and shoving. Beside him, a little girl was fluttering a paper flag right next to his ear. He slapped it away, then dug his hands in his pockets, fed up.

After a time the royal couple returned to their car and moved off, *en route* for some inspection on the Hoe.

More cheers arose and massed ranks of school-children flapped Union Jacks they had made with red and blue crayons. Connie took Albert by the hand and hurried across to her brother.

'We were watching, Jamie, we saw it all. What did he say to you?'

'Oh, what you'd expect. Well done and so on. Asked me what I did for a living. Remarked on how bad some of the injuries were.'

'You must be proud.'

He nodded, beaming, shyly pleased that he had been chosen.

'But where's Janine? Why isn't she here? Don't tell me she wasn't interested?'

His smile dropped. 'Oh, well, she said she woke up with a headache this morning. Probably had a gin too many last night before bed. She's staying at home today.'

Connie thought it rotten of her sister-in-law. James had become a better man since the war began, something Janine did not appreciate at all. His moment to shine, and she could not be bothered to watch, excusing herself with a trifling pain. Nothing showed more clearly how little she cared for him.

'No headache would have stopped me coming,' Connie said.

He waved it away. 'It really doesn't matter. Whole thing only lasted a minute, after all.'

'That's not the point.' She kissed his cheek. 'You looked very smart and poised,' she told him. 'Can you imagine how Mam would have felt to see this?'

'Oh, cock-a-hoop. She would have been insufferable ever after,' chuckled James.

'Like to come back to our place for tea, Jamie? Come and tell Sam all about it.'

'I would, but poor old Doris is stuck at the café on her own. I thought I'd go down and let her have the last two hours off. I'll come round in a day or two, all right?'

'All right, Jamie. Take care of yourself.'

Sayers looked down at Albert, winked and ruffled the boy's hair.

'Bye,' he said to Connie, and went on his way.

There was no one in the café. Doris sat in the kitchen, morosely eating cake. She had not seen the King and Queen at all, since their route had taken them another way. Forced to hold the fort at 'Janine's', she felt more than a little peeved. It was not as if she had had many customers in – only nine all morning, ten at lunch-time. Nobody at all this afternoon.

Doris loved parades and ceremonies, especially if royalty were there. She always watched them avidly on the newsreels at the pictures. Just now, she sourly imagined she must be the only person in town to be missing them.

Hearing the doorbell tinkle, Doris muttered an ill-tempered 'Hmph' and heaved herself to her feet. But instead of a customer, she found Mr Sayers in the café, hanging up his hat and coat.

'Like to go now, Doris? The King and Queen are still up on the Hoe.'

'Ooh! I would – oh yes, I would!'

'I'll stay here, then. Take the rest of the day.'

'Oh, that's . . . Oh, you are good! Thank you!' She was pulling off her apron, tidying her hair.

'Better hurry, I think they're going off to tea with the Astors soon.'

Doris went puffing out the door, dragging on her coat.

James wandered out into the kitchen and poured himself some coffee, thinking over his brief meeting with the monarch. Despite what he had said to Connie, he was wounded and disappointed that his wife had not been there. James still craved her admiration and respect, but it seemed that nothing he did could impress or interest her.

He had been sitting for perhaps twenty minutes when the doorbell rang again. Going out into the café he found a young lad in a postal uniform. Soberly, the boy looked at James and asked:

'Is your name Sayers?'

'Yes.'

'J. Sayers?'

James nodded, his eyes fixed on the telegram the boy held in his hand. He was more puzzled than anything else. He had no family outside Plymouth, no one in the forces, and all Janine's relations were already dead.

He reached out, took the telegram. The boy hovered.

'Want me to wait?'

'Hmm – no. No, thank you.'

Alone again, James delayed for several minutes, debating with himself.

'J. Sayers.'

For him? Or Janine? Well, either way, James considered it his business. He opened it.

Thirty-eight

Janine's headache, quite genuine, had led her to take a nap that afternoon. She lay beneath the counterpane, clad in jade silk pyjamas, peacefully snoozing. Gardenia Lodge was silent save for the ticking of clocks, and when her husband let himself in he did so very quietly. She was not aware of him in the house, looking for her downstairs, going from room to room, or finally, just as softly, coming up to the bedroom.

Then, as if from a distance, she heard someone speak to her.

'Janine . . .' The voice was low and yet strained.

She stirred, but sleep held onto her.

'Janine.' The voice was louder now. The tone of it conveyed alarm and pulled her out of drowsiness. She opened her eyes and focused them on her husband.

He was standing just inside the bedroom door, his coat undone and his hair blown about. She had never seen him dishevelled before. The knot of his tie was all to one side and his eyes were unnaturally bright.

Slowly she raised herself on one elbow. 'Jamie? You're back early. Is something wrong . . .?'

Then she saw that he clutched a piece of paper. He held it out towards her and his hand shook.

'What is this?'

She blinked at it, pushing back the hair from her face. 'I can't see it, bring it here.'

James didn't move. 'Bridger,' he said levelly. 'Who is this man, Bridger?'

Her heart seemed to bounce like a yo-yo. It was the letter Clive had promised her! The remaining stupor of sleep dropped away and suddenly she was alert, on guard. Peeling back the bedspread, she sat up.

'How did you come by that?' Her gaze was on him, wary but steady.

'I was at the café this afternoon when it came.'

'Since when do you open correspondence addressed to me?'

'J. Sayers, it said on the envelope.'

'I see.'

He noted the tightened muscles at her throat. She hadn't realised what it was, he could tell. Her correspondence, she'd said.

'Well,' Janine prompted, 'since it's mine, may I have it, please?'

Folding it in half, he slipped it in his pocket. 'I asked you a question. Who is he?'

Computing possibilities, she stalled. It was clearly not a very long letter. Only a small piece of paper, she had observed. And Clive was never romantic. There was probably nothing too incriminating in it. Still, she didn't know precisely what the contents were and doubted she would be wise to try and pass Bridger off as a cousin.

'Oh . . .' her laugh was light and easy, '. . . he's just an acquaintance. Someone who used to come to the café a lot before the war. I think he had a crush on me, silly man.'

'Ah. Writes to you often, does he?'

'Now and again.' She was dismissive. 'I don't think he has anyone else, poor soul. Sad, isn't it, when

395

servicemen have no one at home? Post from friends and family must be so important, such a comfort in wartime.'

'Hmm.' James sat down in the oyster chair. 'I take it, then, that you've been writing back – out of the goodness of your heart?'

Something gleamed in her eyes, stiletto points of anger in their darkness.

'I did answer him, yes. I found it a bit of a nuisance, but it seemed unkind to ignore his notes. I wrote and told him what it's been like here. Nothing he couldn't have read in the papers, really.'

Her husband nodded. 'Newsy stuff, eh? Nothing – personal?'

'Not on my part.' Janine stood up, went to the dressing table where her cigarettes lay. Between the puffs as she lit one, she mumbled: 'As I said, he seems to have a soft spot for me, but I don't encourage that.'

'Your little contribution to the war effort, is it? Penfriend to a lonely serviceman?'

She didn't like his grin. Twin streams of tobacco smoke issued from her nostrils and she took another, rather abrupt drag at the cigarette.

'Please don't be sarcastic, James.' Her glance fluttered back and forth from his face to his coat pocket. She could see a corner of the paper peeping out. 'What does he have to say, anyway?' Her voice was a little high, with a quaver she couldn't quite control.

'It's – a bit of news, nothing else.' His grin had vanished. His face was utterly straight.

Janine looked relieved. 'There, you see? Good heavens – did you think I was carrying on?'

'Well, you've never mentioned him to me.'

'That's how unimportant it was, my sweetheart.'

'He always sent his letters to the café, then?'

'I don't give my home address to casual acquaintances.'

James leaned back in his chair, clasping his hands across his midriff, pondering. He still seemed troubled and she supposed he wasn't yet quite convinced.

'Oh, Jamie.' She crossed the room, knelt down beside the chair and started fondly smoothing strands of his windblown hair into place. 'I hope you haven't upset yourself by imagining things. Good God, I'm not the sort to have affairs! Anyway, even if I were, he wouldn't be my type. He's much younger than I am, you know, and not a bit attractive. Lord, if I'd ever thought those silly letters could upset you, I'd have told the wretched chap to leave me alone.'

Her face was near to his, calm and smiling now. This Bridger, she claimed, was nothing to her. Well, now he would see. He took a moment to prepare and then said softly: 'I'm glad you're not involved with him in any close sense, Janine.'

She dealt him a peck of a kiss. The gardenia necklet sparkled at her throat and she fingered it unthinkingly. 'Of course not! What a notion!'

'Because you are mistaken about one thing.' His gaze trapped hers, blue eyes holding black. Her smile faded.

'You see, it's not a letter this time. It's a telegram.'

Slowly the face before him changed, growing very white and very rigid. It drew away from him, a frightened mask.

Reaching into his pocket, he gave her the paper at last.

In her shock, she had to go over the wording several times to absorb the message. James saw her fingers loosen as she read, and he took the cigarette before she dropped it.

Janine hardly noticed that. For her, the world had narrowed down to a little rectangle of buff-coloured paper, half a dozen devastating words.

'. . . deep regret . . . killed early this morning . . . condolences.'

She shivered like an aspen leaf and her eyes grew glassy, distracted. Dizziness swept over her, she swayed and James thought she was going to faint. But instead, a hollow sound came up from her throat, followed by a series of formless noises, like the first struggling efforts of a dumb person to shape a word.

'Uh, uh, uh . . .' The gasps grew faster as horror seized her. All pretence of innocence forgotten, she stumbled backwards to her feet and uttered a wail. Both hands were pressed over her mouth, but the sound still tore out raw and frightful, agonised. She was hunched as if she'd been thumped in the stomach and her stare remained fixed on the telegram, lying now on the carpet.

It was James who shed tears first. They swelled up, glistening, in his eyes and spilled out in misery at the betrayal.

Janine, however, was scarcely aware of him, not even his physical presence, let alone his feelings. Bridger was gone, her one great passion, that was all she could think of. Everything else lost importance. What matter if the truth were out? What matter how her husband suffered or what reprisals he took? She cared about nothing outside her grief, least of all the man who sat alive and safe in the satin chair, while her lover's body was somewhere at the bottom of the English Channel.

Raking her fingers through her hair, she clawed at her scalp, sobbing dryly.

'My . . .' James's voice was trembling, '. . . what a display for a mere acquaintance. It's not so long since your father died. There was no such reaction then.' He shook his head, still half incredulous. 'You deceitful, immoral, treacherous . . . Oh, you rotten little bitch!' The last word dissolved, becoming a sob. 'Dear God, I did all I could to please you, arranged for you to keep your house, and still you betrayed me. I thought you had honour enough to be faithful after that.'

Her head jerked up and her expression changed abruptly, desolation turning into sudden viciousness. Anguished and reckless, helpless to punish anyone else for Bridger's death, she struck at the nearest – only – target.

'Well, you thought wrong! In fact, I was already seeing Clive when you sold the bakery. He was my kind, which you're not. I never had a thing in common with you, James, and I realised years ago that we weren't going to grow any more alike. We have different natures altogether. You never were the sort of man I needed.'

In a trice he was up and out of the chair, and his tears ran down to a mouth that was snarling. Fiercely he rubbed them away and the blue eyes were red-rimmed, glaring.

'I was a man who gave you everything you asked for – the café, this house and all that's in it, clothes, a car, a woman to do the household work . . .'

'Gave?' yelled Janine. 'You gave? Hah! What created our success, may I ask? My ideas, my style.'

'Who put up the money, tell me that?'

She was standing before him very upright now, the

look on her face almost challenging him to knock her down. 'I don't have to thank you for anything, James. Without me, you'd be down on the Barbican still, in that dreary little bakery.'

'I'd be bloody glad to have the bakery back,' he bawled. 'Moved us up in the world, did you? Improved our social standing, did you? Made us the envy of all our old neighbours? You've ruined me, you stupid, selfish, extravagant no-good. We were merely prosperous, but you want to live like the rich. If you wish to take the credit for making the money, Janine, then be prepared to take the blame for losing it as well, because that's what you've done. We won't even end up where we started. We'll have nothing. Understand?'

So distraught was she that insolvency seemed like a trivial matter just then.

'I suppose you've been too absorbed to keep an eye on the accounts,' continued James, 'but I assure you we're in deep, deep trouble.'

'I don't bloody care!' she screamed, weeping again. 'Now, he's gone, I don't want any of it.'

'I never wanted Gardenia Lodge or the café in the first place, Janine. I'd give a lot for the simple life I had before I met you. Right now, my greatest regret is that I ever set eyes on you. The bakery might have been humble, but it was safe. I admit I had no ambition, and I'm sorry I pretended otherwise when we were courting. I never had your energy – or your greed. I would have been content in my little rut, and you despise me for knowing my limitations.'

'And for your dullness, James, your damned reclusive shyness. If only you'd taken me out sometimes, or let me entertain. Until I met Clive, the only excitement I had was spending money.'

'Meeting him didn't stop you, though, did it? Not if the bank statements are anything to go by. Quite the reverse.' His pupils contracted to pinpoints. 'Who's been footing the bill for this affair? I assume there were hotel rooms to pay for, lunches and so forth?'

'Sometimes he paid, sometimes I did. And we bought each other presents, as lovers do,' she retorted.

'Yes, I see. I begin to understand why the takings have been short. I suppose that was one of his gifts, that thing around your neck?'

He took a step towards her and Janine's hand closed protectively over the golden gardenia.

'That's right. That's why I never take it off.'

Turning away, she crumpled again, slumping onto the bed and curling up in a ball.

He stared at the curve of her back. 'When did it start – five years ago?'

'Six.'

'Yes,' he breathed, 'now I think of it, that was when I came to realise you didn't love me. That was when I really began to feel the chill, but I never guessed there was already another man around. Very careful, weren't you, Janine? What a liar, what a planner. Did you laugh at me when you were with him? Why didn't you just run off with him? Was he already married, or didn't he have a nice enough place to offer you?'

Her only reply was a rattling sniff. Her eyes were stinging, her throat was aching. She desperately wished she had a bottle of Scotch.

'Well, like it or not, I'm still your husband . . .'

A sullen mutter. 'I don't want you.'

At that, he pounced and seized her, hauled her off the bed and held her by her upper arms, squeezing brutally. 'He's dead,' he hissed, 'your precious Clive is dead, but I'm still here and you're stuck with me. Me, and whatever kind of shabby life we have to live when the property goes. Me, and this . . .' He ran his forefinger over the scar. 'Me, and the very short leash on which I'm going to keep you from now on.'

Briefly, Janine considered that, and then a strange smile crossed her face. No matter what it cost her, she was not going to be humbled like that. She, who had always been in charge, was not about to submit to Jamie's control.

'I fear you're wrong.'

'Oh? Am I indeed?'

'I'm not staying with you, James. You can't play masterful with me, it's just not in you. You wouldn't enjoy it, even if you could. It's better that we go our separate ways.'

'And where would you go, I'd like to know? There isn't any Clive to run to, no father to take you in. What are you going to do? Camp out in the shelters with the homeless? Oh, not you. You won't have any money, Janine. None at all – imagine that.'

She produced her trump card and laid it down triumphantly. 'Ah, but I do have a little money, James – enough to give me a fresh start, anyway. You could call it my emergency fund. I've been amassing it these past four years. You were only partially right about the takings. What I spent on Clive was merely a quarter of it. The rest was for me. I firmly believe a girl should have a safety net.'

His hands dropped away. He stared at her.

'You've been stashing money away for yourself?' He sounded dazed.

'Seemed like a wise precaution. I thought if you found out about Clive you might divorce me. Now you're threatening something worse, so I'm doubly thankful I have a means of escape.'

Sheer disgust replaced the amazement on his face. She realised at once that she had made a grave mistake in blurting that out. Too late now to retract it, though, or pretend it was only a bluff.

His voice dropped almost to a whisper, he was so appalled. 'My God, you're worse than rotten, you're evil.'

She licked her lips and her gaze flickered nervously. His use of a word so strong disturbed her. But she told herself now, as she had before, that she had merely acted in self-preservation.

'You're a man,' she retorted hotly. 'And you're younger than me. You can always make a living more easily than I can.'

'The bakery was my living, the only thing I knew.'

'Well, learn something else, don't be so . . .'

She had no chance to finish. Rage engulfed him utterly, with violent results.

The blow was so hard and unexpected that it sent her reeling, a sudden curving swing of his arm and a dizzying smack across her face. With a shriek, she tottered, fell upon the bed, and the room seemed to do a half-turn. Astonished, she clamped a hand to her nose and found it bleeding.

He had hit her! Soft old James had actually hit her! And what a wallop, too! Pain and amazement half stunned her.

He came towards her. 'Tell me where you've put that cash, Janine. You're not tripping off with that and leaving me to lose my shirt.'

Licking the salty red trickle off her upper lip, she panted: 'It wouldn't save you from the bank.'

'I didn't say it would. I've a fair idea of how much you've taken. I know what the shortfall is. But I'm not about to let you keep that money. You're not coming out of this with any advantage. I don't intend to be the sole loser, my dear. Did you never think about the taxman, by the way, how much trouble there could be – for both of us – if ever he smelt a rat?'

She squirmed off the bed and backed away, although there was nowhere to retreat, since he kept himself firmly between her and the door. She had never thought it would be like this. She had thought she would have a cool head, if and when the confrontation over Bridger came. She had never dreamed it would come to light in this particular way. The shock of his death had robbed her of her wits. She had said too much, and it would not be simple now to slip away with the money.

As James advanced upon her she shrank into a corner, then began sliding along the wall, her back flattened against it.

'Let me get my suitcase, James, and pack. You won't see me again. In time you can divorce me automatically. Just leave me alone, just give me an hour to collect my things and I'll clear out.'

'Oh no, Janine.' He grinned at her. 'I don't want that. You're not going anywhere. I want you to remain and reap what you've sown.'

'We'd be miserable together. There isn't any point in that.'

'It's precisely the point. I want company in my misery.'

He was coming round the foot of the bed. Fearing another blow, she made a sudden dive, rolled across the

404

bed and off the other side, ran for the door and fumbled to pull it open.

Just as fast, he lunged towards her and slammed it shut again, hauling her away by the collar of her pyjama top. He swung her sideways and she crashed against the dressing table. Thoroughly scared now, she sidled away from him.

'Now, about the money, dearest . . .'

'It's in a deposit account.'

'Indeed? Then you have a passbook?'

Janine was silent.

'No, I thought not. You've hidden it somewhere – probably in this house.'

She was circling him, inching round towards the door, and once again she tried to bolt. This time she managed to fling it open, and fled half-way to the top of the stairs before he caught her.

Reason and self-control abandoned him completely now, as if her bid for escape had pushed him off the edge. He slapped her over and over and over, swiping her head from side to side until her knees began to buckle and slowly she sagged to the floor. James let go of her at last and Janine collapsed in a heap. For a minute he stood over her, watching her body shake with silent sobs. Then all at once, the anger purged, James felt weary and ashamed, utterly depleted. Moving away from her, he leaned upon the landing banister, hanging his head. The geometric tiles in the hall below seemed to move and change, as if he were drunk. He closed his eyes and hot tears once more started down his face.

He did not feel like the same man who had shaken hands with the King a few hours before. That had been another James, one who did not know the half of what his wife had done. Even if she gave back the money, the damage done between them was far too much to mend. He hated her now and revenge would be the only thing to savour in years to come. But then, the alternative, letting her go and being alone, dismayed him too. He rocked himself helplessly, wanting Ada, wanting Connie. And yet, was it not their devotion which had left him so ill-equipped to handle a woman like Janine? Vaguely, he began to perceive his mother's pernicious influence for what it was. Another illusion breaking up.

Suddenly a movement caught his eye, alerted him. His wife had scrambled to her feet, she was starting down the stairs.

'Janine!'

She looked round fearfully, panicking at the thought of further beating – and missed her footing. A single startled cry, a flurry of limbs, a series of thuds, and she was at the bottom, groaning, stirring weakly.

Slowly James went down the stairs. Her head snapped up and she glared at him through her tangled hair. Grasping the stairpost, she started pulling herself to her feet. As soon as she put weight on her right leg, however, she emitted a squeal of pain and slid once more to her knees. When her husband reached her, she swung her right fist at him, as much in rage as in self-defence.

He caught it easily, gripping the slender wrist and forcing it down. Kneeling, he pushed his face right up to hers.

'As I said, you're not going anywhere. Now let me see that leg.'

Quivering, flinching, she waited while he made a quick examination. He did it with frosty efficiency, as he might for an injured enemy.

'Not broken,' he muttered. 'I should think you've torn a ligament. It may need a plaster cast, I don't know. That'll slow you down a bit, won't it, dearest? So come along now, back to your room.'

Her hold upon the newel tightened in resistance. Then she caught sight of herself in the big hall mirror, saw a wild-haired woman with smeared make-up, a middle-aged woman in silk pyjamas sprawled with one leg out in front of her, the other resting on the bottom stair, her arms wrapped fiercely round the stairpost. She looked so helpless, ludicrous. Janine wept distractedly, shaking her head.

James stood up and his voice came coldly from above her.

'You can either let me carry you or else be dragged, I don't mind which. Needless to say, if I have to pull you, it'll hurt.'

He took her silence for surrender, crouched and lifted her.

'By God,' he muttered as they went upstairs. 'I've put you in front of everything and everybody all these years. Well, I was always selfish, so perhaps you're just what I deserve. I'm only sorry I didn't do the decent thing by Connie long ago. That's the worst of it. I gave you her rightful share as well as my own and I've always known it.'

Surly, silent, she wouldn't look at him. He dumped her none too gently on the bed. Then, turning, he took the key from the inside lock and changed it to the outside.

'What are you doing?' she gasped.

'I'm locking you in, Janine. Don't want you crawling off anywhere.'

'My leg – you're going to strap it up or something?'

407

'All in good time. It isn't going to kill you, it can wait. It'll suit me very well if you're disabled for a while. I'll get you down to the hospital later on. Meanwhile, I suggest you lie quiet, seeing I've nothing to give you for the pain.'

'But where are you going?'

'Out for a while. Just out, to think things over. So much dirt has shown up today that I hardly know where to begin.'

With that he left and she heard the key turn in the lock, heard it taken out. His footsteps receded down the stairs and then the front door slammed. Slowly Janine subsided onto her back. She gazed at the ceiling and felt the anguish well up again. A shudder went through her from head to foot, her chest heaved with a massive sob, and a cry for Bridger went echoing through the house.

Thirty-nine

Half past five. The shops were closing as James walked
down Bedford Street. People were going home to tea,
still talking about the King and Queen. Paper Union
Jacks were blowing about in the gutters and a festive
atmosphere still lingered, as if the echo of brass bands
and cheering had not quite died away. The city felt
mellow, happy, basking in the evening sun. The mood of
it reached him even through his turmoil and stirred
a peculiarly keen affection for his town. His friendly,
familiar town. He stopped once or twice on his way to
the Hoe, possessed by an inexplicable urge to look and
look and look, take the image of Plymouth into his
mind and preserve it there. He was needing a hold on
something solid, perhaps, something real, dependable.

He walked across the promenade, down to a shelter
lined with green-painted benches near the sea. Grateful to find it empty, James sat down. The Sound
stretched away before him, glittering blue and
tranquil.

He wished his mind were in a similar state. He
wished he could organise his thoughts, go through
them in some orderly way, resolving questions and
placing them aside in a neat row labelled 'settled'. But
every matter over-lapped with another and his mind
kept scurrying back and forth, leaving arguments
unfinished, distracted by new aspects, fresh consider-
ations. He couldn't concentrate at all and emotion

overwhelmed him constantly, so that all he could do was silently rail against his wife. Somehow, he hardly gave Clive Bridger a thought. The other man was just a name, faceless, dead and gone.

At six o'clock the air raid siren sounded. James took no notice and nothing came of it. The sun began to set and still he remained, a solitary figure, hands sunk in his overcoat pockets. For the first time ever, he had come out without his hat.

Daylight ebbed away, the old familiar landmarks faded from sight and darkness closed around him. He realised he hadn't brought a torch and would have the devil's own job to find his way anywhere now in the blacked-out town. He kept thinking he ought to make a move, go and see Connie, perhaps, seek comfort from the one reliable source. Yet he remained as if anchored, delaying like one who had a raging headache but felt too wrung out and wretched to make an effort and take a powder.

Somewhere below he could hear the sea lapping round the rocks. In the pitch dark he had almost a blind person's perception of scent and touch and sound – the smell of brine and seaweed pricked his nostrils, and the breeze brushed over his face like a fluttering cold silken scarf. He felt suspended in a void containing nothing solid except the bench on which he sat. Moving along the wooden slats, his fingers traced some scratches in the paint, read them like braille, the names 'Mary' and 'Alf'. Probably a married couple now. Was Mary a good woman, he wondered? Did he have the only bad one in town? Funny the way one always imagined one's trouble to be unique. Logically, it couldn't be so. Still, he doubted there were many around like Janine.

He had loved her so much – still did, if he were honest. It was perfectly possible to hate her as well, he realised. The two extremes of emotion were bent together, ever face-to-face, like the ends of a copper bangle. Only a token gap lay between them, and precisely because they were so close, both could be touched, experienced at once. He had thought, as she tumbled down those stairs, that she deserved to break her neck, that he hoped she would. Yet, he had felt relief to see her moving, trying to stand. He was glad that she'd hurt her leg, that it gave her pain. At the same time he was thankful that the injury wasn't worse. Half of him wanted, even now, to go back home and kill her. The other half wanted to make excuses for her, pretend that there was still a chance of patching things up.

It was all speculation, of course, because James could do neither. All a helpless, hopeless fantasy, veering over and over from murder to reconciliation and back again.

He might have sat there all night in his turmoil, but for the greater crisis which came to overtake him. At just after half past eight a genuine choice was put before him, heralded by a dread, familiar sound.

Winding up from a groan, the sirens brayed.

James looked up in response, staring into the night. It was probably real this time, now it was dark. Slowly he stood up, thinking that he should go and make himself available for duty – purely a reflex now whenever the alert began.

Then he thought about Janine. He had quite forgotten the chance of an air raid when he locked her in. At the time the war had seemed unreal compared to his personal disaster. Now, in some confusion, he argued with himself.

She never used the shelter anyway, and he would be needed by civil defence. To hell with her, she'd be all right.

But then, he hadn't left her the choice to use the shelter, had he? Not even to hide beneath the kitchen table or in the cupboard under the stairs. The first-aid branch had other men, and he had already done more than his share for the service.

Janine was a bitch. She deserved to die. Not that she would – no bombs ever fell in that part of town.

Tonight could be the exception, though. A plane off course, a stray stick dropped wide of its target area . . .

Oh, what was the use? The raid would probably be over before he reached home, and better people than Janine might die for want of his help.

He debated and dithered for several minutes – until his ears picked up another sound. A droning he knew all too well, monotonous and very heavy. Stronger than he'd ever heard before.

Stripes of white light shot skywards, waving this way, that way, in great arcs. Picked out in their brightness, James saw aircraft – and his mouth went dry. Bombers without number, it seemed to him, countless orderly ranks coming in from the sea. Wherever the swinging, questing searchlights probed there were more of them, a buzzing host that made him think of monstrous, evil house-flies.

No limits this time, no half measures. An example was to be made of Plymouth and he knew beyond the slightest doubt that it wouldn't matter tonight what part of town his wife was in.

The pumping boom of the anti-aircraft had started

412

now, regular piston-thuds from sites all over the city. It wasn't so dark now, either, because fires were flaring everywhere as incendiaries showered down. Already the glare of flames from Cattedown threw a sullen amber light across the harbour.

Dashing up the steps from the shelter, James tore up the slipway cutting through the grassy bank to reach the promenade. Looking up as he ran, he saw the sky flushed ugly orange over the city centre, the colour diffusing into a dirty smoke which hung down low. Above him the dull roar of engines was unrelenting, and as he gained the top of the slipway and sprinted across the asphalt, he heard a metallic clatter, like a rain of scrap metal close by, saw three magnesium bombs go scudding harmlessly across the ground. The rest of the batch found a target, though. Seconds later there came a brittle sound of shattering slates and a tinkling of broken glass from a house in Holyrood Place. Fire broke out in the upper storey almost at once and blossomed swiftly.

James paused, panting, staring at it, seeing ghastly possibilities. Imagine someone trapped in an upstairs room. Imagine someone locked in, like Janine.

His Janine. No matter what she had done, no matter what she had cost him. Leave her without the option of saving herself? Because she had been unfaithful, spent his money? They simply weren't reasons enough, and if the worst befell her he knew his conscience would drive him mad.

He gazed down the hill, heart thumping. He had to get home, take her down to the shelter. He had to go the quickest way – through the shopping centre, which was fast becoming a furnace. Laid out below him in its basin of land, the city already burned ferociously.

413

Spooner's department store had become a vast inferno. Right down the road in front of him, the Royal Hotel was a thundering pyre. Lesser blazes everywhere were merging into one another, combining into great ones. An excited crackle filled the air, seeming to carry a note of delight. Columns of flame reared up between rows of buildings, making the city centre look like a griddle. Far beyond it, the glow extended well out into the suburbs.

Such a long way to Gardenia Lodge. Such a long way to run.

The noise of the barrage was pitted against the shriek of diving planes and the crash of high explosives as James started down the hill. The heat from the blazing Royal Hotel struck him like a gale from hell as he reached the bottom. Flames were gushing from the upper windows and through the roof, while firemen nearby struggled to lay hoses. James heard one of them curse and fling his arms wide in frustration, yelling to his mates that the hydrant nozzle wouldn't fit.

A moment later they all abruptly scattered, flinging themselves into doorways at the whistle of a stick of bombs. James sped on up George Street. From behind him came a series of blasts, evenly spaced but swelling in power and sound and heading his way. It felt for all the world as if they were chasing him, and the last one all but caught him. At the noise and shock of the impact he let out a scream of fright, and a fast-moving wall of hot air knocked him flat on his face in the road. Chunks of masonry rained around him and he threw both arms over his head. Something hit him between the shoulder-blades and he grunted with pain. A cloud of dust blew over him and he felt the prickle of grit bouncing off the backs of his hands. Winded, he lay for

414

some seconds, then raised his head and looked around. The bomb had struck a shop some way behind him. And now, before his eyes, the whole building came down, four storeys subsiding with a rattle of broken stone and a whoosh of powdered plaster. A leisurely, almost languid collapse, it somehow reminded James of a woman fainting.

He scrambled to his feet and pounded on. Around him the street was a tunnel of dark façades from which shot claws and fans of fire, blown over like cresting waves in the wind. The café was a hideous cavern of red. The window had shattered and what remained of the glass was dripping, molten, onto the ground, the golden letters of the name 'Janine's' dissolving and sliding away. Tram-wires dangled everywhere, and in dress-shop windows dummies burned like victims at the stake.

Far overhead, the coughing and droning of engines went on and on. There were constant concussions all around, and the desperate response of anti-aircraft guns. On every side of him the city was being cremated, pulverised. Favourite stores, familiar haunts, all the mellow old streets of the centre with their comfortable atmosphere. Such a small city – so compact and cosy. Piteous to see it now, incinerated, smashed, bathed in this infernal glare and wrapped in stinking smoke.

In Cornwall Street he found a fissure in the road and a crater where a bus stop used to be. From end to end the buildings spewed out banners of flame which swirled and lashed in the wind. Here, too, were firemen, overwhelmed and frantic, able to contain small blazes only, while the greater ones burned unchecked. One of them saw James and bawled at him to get away,

415

waving him to stop and take a different direction. Sayers heard him shout out:

'. . . bloody fool . . . can't go up there . . .'

But James ignored him, shrugged off his coat as he ran and held it over his head, for in front of him for fifty yards the fires were rampant on either side and the road between them was sticky with melting tarmac. He felt his feet slip on it, felt it clinging to his shoes and slowing him. In the lurid light it shone wet-black and the smell of it mingled sickeningly with the stench of fat and roasting meat from a blazing butcher's shop, and the whiff of his own clothes singeing. Despite the coat his face was scorched and he winced at the sting of blistering skin on his hands. His eyes were streaming with the smoke and his throat felt seared as if he had drunk scalding water. Within him, 'little Jamie' wailed in terror. Fire again, and this time nobody was going to come and rescue him. This time he was going to cook.

But suddenly he was through it, out, and racing for the foot of Tavistock Road. There he paused, his breathing racked, a high-pitched sob. He would have to take a moment's rest, for the next leg was all uphill. Pulling on his coat, he sank onto a doorstep and closed his eyes.

The noise was relentless, merciless, crash after crash of explosions and the screech of planes diving, one after another. Quite precise and orderly, while pandemonium reigned on the ground. Twice he caught the tinny sound of a fire-engine's bell in the distance. It sounded so feeble – he let out a croak of laughter and shook his head. They hadn't bargained for this, the bloody authorities. No one had bargained for anything like this, for total destruction, catastrophe.

No point in worrying now about the property they

had lost. 'Janine's' was finished. For all he knew, the bakery had gone, too. It was only Gardenia Lodge which mattered now, and once he had got his wife out that could burn as well for all he cared. After all, it as good as belonged to the bank already.

After a short while he got to his feet and started up the hill at a trot. He kept to the right hand side of the street, for on the left were many more fires. Still, the road was broad and the heat was bearable. Partway up, he halted, looking back. The town below was a vista of mottled red and black, overlaid with a haze of smoke. Spooner's store was a vast conflagration, fed by tons of clothing and soft furnishings. In parts of the city great spurts of flame towered up above the pall, and in the flash of a detonation, James saw another tall building disintegrate, giant slabs of stonework flying.

He laboured on, wishing he were younger, far more fit, and cursing himself for turning that key in the lock. If Janine were dead, then he would have killed her, and he didn't know how he would ever live with that.

After what seemed an age, he reached the turning. Only half a mile now, half a mile. He struggled on.

Fortune was cruel that night, allowing him to make his pointless run and get so close before it felled him. He was nearing the junction with the avenue when he heard a whining cadence from above. A second after he passed by, a terraced house was hit. Glass and slates and brickwork sprayed far and wide. Briefly, the walls appeared to bulge out and then the whole structure slumped.

James Sayers' body ended up in a doorway across the street, surrounded by rubble. Janine had finally, literally, cost him everything.

*

She hadn't stirred when first she heard the siren. She had lain in the dark, still sobbing for Bridger, indifferent to everything else.

Another raid, a bit more patchy damage, a few more deaths. Well, what the hell, even if one of those deaths should be her own? Extinction had never been a thing Janine especially feared, or so she believed. The prospect of reaching the end without tasting life – that was what had always appalled her. Missing her share and knowing it, still wanting when it was far too late. That was what she had striven to avoid, what in the end had made her so dishonourable. Although – there had also been frustration and a mite of desperation, when she discovered that nothing she bought was ever enough and that nothing she tried was quite so wonderful after all.

Except for Bridger, of course.

Janine had always been loudly sceptical regarding any sort of hereafter. Yet old religious promises came creeping back to her now, echoes from Matthew's nightly Bible readings, from prayers around the Jordan family table, from the burial service, and all the platitudes Mr Jordan had always offered to the bereaved. Hoary old lies, she had called them then. Words about meeting again, being reunited in death, together for ever and so on. Now she yielded to hopes that there might be some truth in them after all, so that if she died tonight she would be going to join her lover, wherever he was.

Outside she heard voices, doors banging. The neighbours running to their shelters. Well, she had never deigned to use her own, even when she could, and tonight she was trapped in the house anyway. Tonight it was a matter entirely of fate, which seemed very right and proper somehow.

Between her swollen, sticky eyelids oozed a few more tears. Her headache was back with a vengeance and her fingers squeezed convulsively at the screwed-up, sopping handkerchief in her palm. If she didn't move, her leg just throbbed. To shift her position at all sent a hot pain slicing from the heel to the back of her knee, and so she lay motionless on her side, exhausted with weeping.

She heard the bombers coming in, and the clacking of the barrage, but all of it was just a backdrop to her own emotional uproar – until the noise from overhead became so uncommonly loud that it forced itself to her attention. An unremitting thunder filled her ears, filled the room, so low and close that it seemed to come from the very ceiling.

Her shuddering sobs trailed off. She blinked. She listened.

There didn't seem to be any explosions at first, just that ceaseless, heavy hum. She had heard it many times before, of course, but never at such volume. Rolling her head on the pillow, Janine stared upwards in the darkness, holding her breath. Then she turned further to look through the window and saw the night sky, lurid red.

Not a few scattered fires this time, but something huge, a conflagration so immense that it shed its awful light for miles around.

Stiffly, wincing, she eased herself out of the bed and hobbled to the window. Beyond the trees at the end of the road, she saw a fountain of flame engulfing the steeple of a nearby church. In every direction glowed a ruddy light, as if from the ember bed of a mighty bonfire. A thin veil of yellow-grey smoke was drifting round the house.

Janine backed away from the window, fatalism giving way to fear. She knew what this was – 'coventration', as the Germans laughingly called it. No aiming for military targets tonight, the town itself was going to be razed.

And suddenly, dying, following Bridger, did not seem so attractive after all. Animal instinct asserted itself, throwing romantic tragedy to the wind. With the threat of death came clarity regarding less important matters. Insight informed her coldly that if Clive had not kept his detachment, if he had fallen at her feet, she would very soon have tired of him. For something so false, she had landed herself in this awful predicament. Terror started bubbling up and she tried to clamp it down.

Where was Jamie? Janine didn't know what time it was, but she guessed several hours had passed since he went out. He might have come home, she might not have heard him. Perhaps he was downstairs even now, deliberately allowing her to stew.

She stumbled to the door, crying out as her leg responded with stabs of pain. Seizing the door-knob with both hands, she pulled and twisted it, frantically rattling it, but to no avail. In frustration, she beat upon the wood, pounding her fists at two inches of oak and shouting for James.

There was no response. He could be out with the first-aid party, too angry to care what happened to her. Janine put the light on, knowing the black-out was less than useless now, for the night was illumined as if by a rosy dawn. Returning to the window, she threw up the sash and yelled for help. No good – the avenue was deserted, all her neighbours were underground. She called until her throat was sore and then gave up.

Spotting a hat-pin on her dressing table, she grabbed it, bent it into a hook and hurried again to the door. Stabbing it into the lock, she jiggled it. It seemed to work in books and films, but it would not work for her. After a time she flung the hat-pin furiously aside and flopped once more upon the bed to ease her leg.

Soon she heard the first crashes and blasts of high explosives coming down. Distant, then drawing nearer, receding, coming back again.

Coming . . .

She stiffened, eyes straining wide. A descending screech, the dreaded glissando of a stick of bombs sent her thudding to the floor and squirming madly under the bed. The explosions seemed to march toward her, the furthest a deep bass drum-beat, the nearest an indescribable shock of sound. Even though she covered her ears, her ear-drums nearly burst and she shrieked with all her might. The house quaked and the windows caved in, broken glass and sticking paper sagging from the frames. The air in the room seemed to flick like a whip, and the ceiling opened as two slabs of plaster swung down like trapdoors.

Janine lay shivering until once again the bombing moved away. Finally, hesitantly, she emerged and crawled to the shattered window. Across the road, not forty yards down, was a mound of smoking rubble where only minutes before had stood a large house.

Yards. Just yards. It could so easily have been Gardenia Lodge.

The shelter, that dank, despised little hole, looked very inviting now. She could see it out there in the garden, a dark hump in the lawn.

'Here I am,' it seemed to say, 'but you can't have me. Like all the other things you took for granted, scorned and squandered, you've forfeited me.'

She ripped away a swathe of sticking paper, heedless of the glass which cut her hands. Leaning from the window, Janine looked down on the concrete walkway running round the house. Jump twenty feet onto that? She could break her neck, her back, at the very least knock herself out.

Then she recalled another time-honoured method of escape. Stripping the bed, Janine began to knot the sheets together.

She had time to join them but none of her modern furniture offered an anchoring point. All of it was curved or streamlined, most of it too light to hold a person's weight. She looked around her helplessly and panic began to take over.

Soon would come another rain of bombs, and this was the day her luck had run out. That near miss had been the last of it. She knew, she simply knew, and ...

Here it came.

Three more blasts in quick succession rocked the avenue, robbing her of all remaining power to think. Half-crazy with fright, she dropped the sheets and hurled herself back to the door. In the bathroom across the landing, out of reach, was her money, a thing of no consequence now. She would have given the lot in exchange for a key. She scrabbled madly at the wood, thumping on it, howling.

And then from the sky came the answering howl of a plane in headlong descent. Petrified, Janine looked up, her face a caricature of itself, piteously comical in its terror. Nemesis was on its way and it told her so. High up in the night above the house, a thin, shrill note announced it, filling out, becoming raucous and louder, louder, louder . . .

She sank to her knees, hands over her ears, whimpering in despair. Before her eyes was the lush mauve carpet and the shining jade-green silk of her pyjamas. In a series of flashes, her mind's eye also saw the rest of the house. This pretty house and all her pretty things, awaiting destruction with her. The pierrots in the hall, wide-eyed as if with horror; the harlequins in the dining room, grinning beneath their masks; the odalisques in the bathroom, inscrutably calm; the bronze and ivory dancing sylphs poised on the drawing room mantelpiece; the mirrors, lamps and cushions which were all an expression of her; the expectant stillness in every room as Gardenia Lodge lived its final seconds.

Her whimpering stopped. She closed her eyes. All over in another instant now.

When the house came down around her, she scarcely knew a thing.

Forty

Smoke, a stench of burning, and silence. It was dawn. Sam Tucker stood in the courtyard, looking round him. The cottages were all untouched. The neighbouring houses of New Street also appeared undamaged. He walked to the courtyard gate, went out into the street and looked to left and right. Further down towards the quay, he could see a roof smashed in, so he went that way. Yes, a couple of houses gone here, nothing left but wreckage and fissured walls. No sign of any people. These dwellings, having no back yards, had no shelters either, so the occupants went to some communal bolt-hole provided by the city council.

Sam walked on. Southside Street appeared to be all right, apart from a strike near the waterfront. Wandering around, he saw evidence of a few small fires in nearby streets, and found a couple more properties quite demolished by heavy explosions. Apart from that, the Barbican had not been badly hit.

Across the water at Cattedown, however, it was a different story. Over there, fires could still be seen burning and many familiar structures had vanished. He squinted, searching for shapes which belonged to that skyline and were no longer there.

He started to walk again, doubling back towards the city centre. Now he began to encounter people – firemen, wardens, first-aid workers, families returning home from public shelters. All were shocked, exhausted, very quiet as if words failed them.

Sam could hardly credit what he saw when he reached St Andrew's Cross. Countless hollow husks and skeletons of buildings, rising gaunt and scorched above flat expanses of débris. Much of the city centre had become an open space, resembling a builder's rubbish dump. What remained standing amid the waste were odd walls, iron girders, mere shells of shops and offices.

Tucker ventured down George Street as far as the café – at least, to where he calculated the café had been. The precise spot was hard to pinpoint. The rubble of 'Janine's' was mixed with that of neighbouring businesses and all was strewn far and wide by the force of blast. In reality, George Street was now little more than an open track.

In a landscape so terribly changed, one could easily lose one's bearings, and after wandering around for a while, Sam found himself bewildered. Nothing appeared to be quite where it should be. Surviving buildings reared up in what seemed the wrong place, because they were visible now from points where they could not be seen before. Lonely façades, bereft of their neighbours on either side, were just as confusing. Used to seeing a certain frontage as part of a row, Sam was often hard put to recognise it as the watchmaker's place, the bookshop, or whatever else it was. Everywhere, things still smouldered and little flames like dancing sprites capered along charred timbers. Many fire crews were still dampening down and hoses trailed hither and thither across the ground.

More and more people began to appear as the time neared seven o'clock. Looking as lost as strangers, they stared about them in mute disbelief as they picked their way along. The city which had stood here yesterday was all but gone. Charcoal and ash, broken stone and melted, twisted metal were left, but not much else.

Eventually, Sam went home. Connie was still asleep and so was Albert. They had not emerged from their shelter until nearly four. Tucker made his own breakfast and left them undisturbed. He had to settle for bread, cheese and no tea, for there was neither electricity nor gas to heat anything. He would have to get Connie and Albert away, he decided as he ate. He would have to send them up to Gardenia Lodge pretty soon. One more night like that one and even he would be ready to clear out.

Later he made his way to work on foot, for no bus turned up. He guessed, correctly, that the depot had been hit. Sam half expected to find the dockyard wrecked, but Devonport's destruction was not to be for another month. Work went on and he did his shift as usual, in company with a very jittery Jack Chope. Millie, confided Jack, had been so scared last night that she had wet herself.

Connie kept Albert home from school that day. She wanted him with her in case of a daylight raid, however unlikely. She could not stop shaking and found herself jumping at every little noise. The banging of a door or even the sound of a chiming clock made her heart lurch, and all the time she watched the dial, fearfully counting the hours until dark, when 'they' might come again.

When she thought of her brother, she felt relief that he lived well out of the centre and therefore was probably safe. He would be stretched, no doubt, with his first-aid work, but she hoped he might find some time to call round. All day she half expected his tap at the door. After all, he would want to check and see that she was all right.

But the day passed and James did not come. 'They' did, however, when night fell. They returned to finish the job.

After that second terrible night, Connie set off for Gardenia Lodge to seek her brother. By now there were well over three hundred dead and she was more than ready to take up his offer of shelter.

Among the ruins everywhere she saw demolition squads and salvage teams. Even women worked with picks and shovels, and half the population seemed to be on the move, carrying bedding and personal effects. They wheeled their belongings in prams and handcarts or anything else which would serve. Some were going to stay with friends or relatives, or else to refuges in church halls, even schools. Others were moving out to the country, preferring to sleep in a tent or a barn, even under a hedge, rather than risk another night in town.

Many business people whose premises were gone had returned to trading like barrow boys from temporary stalls which sprang up in the morning and vanished again by dark. As she trudged towards Gardenia Lodge, Connie passed through little shanty markets set up in the open air. Some of them were bizarrely cheerful, selling bright fabrics or toys.

She passed the place where James had been killed and turned left into the avenue. Within another three hundred yards, she reached Gardenia Lodge.

The sight of it transfixed her in the gateway. The house was split in half and the front had collapsed into the garden, burying even the Anderson shelter. The upstairs floors were hanging and the roof sagged over the cavity of a bedroom like the peak of a cap pulled down over one eye.

Connie stood there aghast for she knew not how long. With foreboding she was recalling that Jamie had not been to see her the day before. She had told herself he was simply too busy. But now . . .

After a time she heard footsteps behind her, and a woman's kindly voice.

'My dear, I saw you from my window. Did you know the Sayers?'

She had used the past tense and said 'the Sayers'. Both of them. Slowly Connie turned and looked at her.

'I'm Jamie's sister,' she said in a very small voice.

The lady blinked. She was plump, with grey hair. Sympathy was in her eyes.

'Yes,' she said, 'I remember now. I used to see you come and go, but you haven't been here for some time. My name is Mrs Pope. I live next door.' Taking Connie by the arm, she gently urged: 'Come with me. Come into my house and I'll give you some tea.'

Connie knew without further telling that James and Janine were dead. The only surprise lay in hearing that they had not died together.

'I don't know whether James was coming home or if he had just left,' said Mrs Pope, as she sat down on the sofa with Connie and poured her tea. 'It seems he often took that route as a short-cut into town. People in that street knew him by sight and knew that he came from the avenue. Janine was brought out of the house yesterday morning. When the rescuers came, I told them she must be trapped in the shelter, so they dug that out first, but she wasn't there. Then they started excavating back further into the house and found her.' Mrs

Pope squeezed Connie's hand. 'It's thought that they both died more or less instantly, which should be of some comfort to you.'

Connie wiped her eyes and sniffed. 'I can't believe it, not here. I thought it was safe this far out of the centre. I was coming today to ask Jamie if we could stay while these heavy raids keep on. I didn't expect to see so much damage hereabouts.' She emitted a soft, hoarse laugh. 'You know, the Barbican's almost untouched compared to the rest of the town. I was in the safest place all along. Isn't that ironic? Of course,' she ended shakily, 'they may not have finished yet.'

'There's still the dockyard,' said Mrs Pope. 'God help Devonport.'

'My husband works there,' nodded Connie.

'At the docks?' The lady's forehead creased. 'It would seem that you and your brother led very different lives.'

'Oh . . .' another tearful laugh, '. . . I've never had money like Jamie and Janine did. She was very – ambitious.'

'Yes, I don't doubt it. Rather a modern woman,' observed Mrs Pope thoughtfully. 'A bit of a handful, I should imagine. Still, one couldn't help liking her.'

'I used, once, to like her very much. My brother adored her,' mused Connie. 'He would never have ended up here if not for Janine. He'd be living on the Barbican still . . .' Her voice trailed off. For a moment she seemed far away, then abruptly she gulped another mouthful of tea. 'It's all a roll of the dice, isn't it, who catches it and who escapes?'

'Everything's turned upside down in time of war. I don't mean just in the obvious way. It's when fortune often changes its favourites, I believe.'

429

The remark made Connie look at her. Kindly eyes smiled back.

'I do feel for you,' said Mrs Pope. 'There's little else one can ever say. If there's any small thing I can do to help . . .?'

'Bless you, I'm grateful, but I don't think so.'

'By the way,' said Mrs Pope after a moment's pause, 'there's been a spot of looting, I'm afraid. Some people are dreadful, aren't they? Vultures and ghouls on the look-out for an opportunity. When the workmen arrived, they drove off a couple of young louts who were picking over the wreckage of your brother's house. It seems they ran off with a thing or two.'

Connie shrugged.

'Of course, almost everything was ruined, but while they were digging, the men did salvage a number of items. They brought them in to me for safe keeping. If you're the Sayers' only remaining kin, I dare say they belong to you. Do you know who your brother's solicitor is? You must see if there's a will.'

Of course, thought Connie, Mrs Pope was unlikely to know that James was nearly bankrupt. She doubted very much that he could have left her anything.

'Hmm,' was all she said.

'I'll show you what the men recovered,' said Mrs Pope. 'Just a few pitiful remnants, I'm afraid. Such a lovely home, too. Janine had such charming taste.'

She went off to some other room and Connie finished up her tea. She did not really want any of Janine's things, but she did hope for something personal of Jamie's. The only memento she had of him was a photo, taken when he was small, the year before the fire.

Mrs Pope returned with a large cardboard box and put it down beside Connie on the settee.

'There you are, dear, have a look through.'

One by one, Connie lifted out dust-covered oddments and brushed them off. A small bronze figurine – Salome. A green-glass perfume bottle etched with Egyptian eyes. The stopper was missing and the neck was chipped. A scent of jasmine still lingered inside. There were several books, and a jewel box containing mostly paste. A brown envelope from the hospital held the Sayers' wedding rings, and a delicate flower-shaped necklet. Connie held it up to the light and the tiny diamonds sparkled.

'Apparently Janine was wearing that when she died,' said Mrs Pope. 'Beautiful, isn't it? Certainly real, you can tell.'

Laying aside the gardenia, Connie turned back to the box. Jamie's razor and pocket watch pleased her more than anything. There was also a marble paper weight and a fountain pen which she recognised as his.

'There's some clothing as well,' said Mrs Pope. 'I'll fetch it in a minute. You'll find little use for it, I fear, it's pretty badly soiled and ripped. Of course, the furniture was quite, quite ruined. I dare say there's more stuff still to be found inside the back of the house, but at present it's just too dangerous to go in and I don't know when the demolition people will get round to it.'

Connie nodded and went on sorting through the box. An evening purse turned up, with just an eyebrow pencil in it. There was a clothes brush, a soap dish, a small oil painting – badly gouged – an embroidered table runner and a copper saucepan. And finally, in the bottom of the box, a leather satchel.

She picked it out, blew the dust off it and tried the catch.

'It's locked,' said Mrs Pope, stating the obvious.

'There seems to be something in it – probably papers. The workmen nearly missed it. They said they found it when they moved the bath. I imagine it may have been in the drawing room. I suppose the bath fell down through the floor above and landed on top of it. Anyway, perhaps you can find some means to open it.'

Connie dropped the satchel back in the box. 'I can't carry all this now,' she said. 'I'll take a few things with me and I'll ask my husband to call for the rest, if I may.'

'Yes, quite all right. I'm at home every morning.'

'Could I borrow a shopping bag or something?'

'Certainly dear.'

Connie took the small things, the personal ones, and left the heavier items. Almost as an afterthought, she put the satchel in the bag. It might contain something of sentimental value.

As she was leaving, the tears returned. 'More funerals,' she told Mrs Pope. 'I've seen too many in my time.'

It was several days before Sam and Connie tried to open the satchel. Late one evening, Tucker had a stab at picking the lock, but to no avail. In the end he cut the stitching which joined the leather.

What fell out on the kitchen table rendered both of them speechless. Banknotes, bundled up in wads and tied with string. Hundreds and hundreds of pounds – possibly more than a thousand.

Connie stood staring, rubbing her palms on her apron in the way she always did when she was nonplussed. Sam kept opening his mouth to speak, then closing it again, as if no words were adequate or he had a thousand questions and could not think which to ask first. The kettle sang on the hob, then shrieked to the boil, emitting clouds of steam while the Tuckers gazed from each other to the money and back again.

'My dear God.' Connie's hand crept up to her throat. 'Is it genuine, Sam?'

'I don't think James was any forger, maid.'

'But he had no spare cash. He was going broke. If this was from the business, why didn't he bank it? It could have bought him some time.'

Frowning, Tucker shook his head.

'Where else could it have come from?' Connie asked. 'Did he win it, find it, steal it?'

Sam was silent, thinking. Then: 'You keep saying "he". What about Janine? She was the one with all the ingenuity.'

'That doesn't answer the question.'

Pursing his mouth, he sat down and took up a bundle, flipping through it.

'Win it?' he murmured. 'How? On the horses? This much? Never. And what else could he gamble at around here? This isn't Monte Carlo. Could he have found it? Pretty unlikely. Would he have kept it if he had?'

'Jamie was honest.'

'I agree, which rules out stealing. Anyway – from where?' He dropped the bundle, spreading his hands.

'Janine – could she have done those things, any of them?'

'I don't see how.' He looked up at her. 'This is from the business, Connie. It has to be. You said it might have staved off bankruptcy for a while – but it wouldn't have been enough to save him in the end. Now, we've said James was honest – but was she? Perhaps your sister-in-law was salting a little away, so she wouldn't be left with absolutely nothing. Do you think Janine was capable of that?'

Connie sank down opposite her husband, considered long and carefully, then decided: 'It's possible. Yes, she might have been. Money was always so important to her. And she would dare, illegal or not, if she felt hard-pressed. Janine would have had the guts and the gall.' She looked at the heap of notes. 'If you're right, then this belongs to the bank.'

Tucker's mouth clamped tighter, twisted sideways. His eyes darted back and forth across the pile of money.

'Does it?'

'Well, who else?'

'How about you?'

'Sam! I couldn't! Not if . . .'

'They don't know this exists. Nobody does, unless I miss my guess. Who's going to come back on us, Connie? The business was nothing to do with you. It belonged to James and Janine and they're both dead. You were never made any sort of partner. Little more than a live-in employee, that's what you were. And that ended more than four years ago.'

'You're telling me to do something criminal, keep money on which the bank has a prior claim!'

'Lower your voice, you'll wake Albert. Now listen to me. I don't care about the bloody bank. It's rich as Croesus and over the years it's had its pound of flesh. It's had the bakery and coming on for twenty years of interest. It'll have the site value of Gardenia Lodge, no doubt. Perhaps it'll get some sort of insurance payment too. I don't know. What I'm sure of is this – you put more than a decade of toil into that business and were poorly rewarded for it. James and Janine reaped the benefits. She lived in comfort and spent, while you slogged. She spent and James let her. She spent until she lost all they had behind them. But this is yours.' He tapped his forefinger sharply on a wad of fivers. 'This is some, at least, of what you should have had if they – and your mother – had played fair with you. Don't be a mug again, Connie. Don't be a fool this time, grab what you're entitled to. It's come to you as if God himself wants it that way. It could have happened otherwise, you know. The looters might have found it first, the workmen might have missed it, or thrown it away because it was just a scruffy old leather bag. But no – it was meant for you. It's fallen into the hands of the one who deserves it most. Don't you dare think of passing this to the bank!'

'I'd feel like a thief, I'd be no better than Janine! I wouldn't be able to sleep for worrying.'

'You'll get over that.' A glint appeared in Tucker's eyes. 'I'm your husband, and I'm asserting my rights as head of this household now. I'm giving an order and you'll just be doing as I tell you, Connie. If there's any guilt involved, it's on my head. That ought to make you feel better.'

There followed a lengthy silence. Then: 'What would we do with it all?'

'Nothing to attract notice. We can have little holidays away, the odd night out, a few nice things for the house. We can have a nest-egg and be secure. We can spend it slowly over the years.'

'If we live that long. I'm afraid there will be a thunderbolt – delivered by Goering, probably.'

Tucker's round face relaxed into a smile. 'Somehow, maid, I think luck is with us.'

Her voice became panicky. 'No, we'll be punished. Something will happen. Oh, Sam . . .'

'There you go again. For most of your life you've been

good and down-trodden. It's time you learnt to be a little wicked and enjoy it.'

Could he be right? Did she dare? Was the money a gift, or a test of scruples? Connie agonised for a while. But then she remembered Mrs Pope, something the lady had said. What was it – words about fortune changing favourites?

Gingerly, Connie fingered the money, then clasped a handful of it. And all at once she began to shake with laughter, both frightened and excited.

'Oh, dear Lord! Oh, Sam,' she said. 'We'd better think about where we're going to hide it.'

Thank God, thought Tucker. Sense at last.

Connie sighed. 'This makes me wish so much we had a child. I suppose it's too late now, I'm forty-two. We've been married four years and nothing's happened. I think more and more often how much I would love to keep Albert . . .'

He cut in gently. 'Now, don't ask too much. Be content to give him some happy times while he's here. We can certainly afford to now.' Wryly, he added: 'The way this war looks set to drag on, he'll be with us for a long while yet, I reckon. He may not be a child any more by the time it's over.'

Forty-one

One fine evening that September, a head appeared over Cynthia Hardin's back wall. Dermot the terrier started and growled. Shoulders followed the head, and there was Albert Plumb, arms folded atop the wall.

Dermot raised a quivering lip to show his teeth. He skittered into his kennel, then poked his head out again, angry little eyes watching Albert through a fringe of wiry hair.

Albert grinned and looked down at the bone which lay between Dermot's front paws. From the very start, the boy had thrown himself whole-heartedly into the salvage effort. He went around collecting tins in a cardboard box mounted on a pair of old pram wheels. It made a terrible clatter on the cobbles, especially when it was full of empty cans. So dedicated was Albert that he made a perfect nuisance of himself by rifling through people's dustbins or knocking daily on their doors demanding waste paper and rags.

Bones were also useful items for the cause, and Dermot had a fine one. It was half as big as he was, and still bore a few shreds of meat. Albert eyed it keenly. His makeshift cart was half empty today. The bone would be a valuable addition to his haul, so Albert decided to confiscate it.

He was standing on an upturned dustbin. Bending his knees, he thrust himself up onto the wall, scrambled over it and dropped down into Cynthia's yard.

Dermot stepped forward, snarling, then retreated to stand guard over his bone. Albert advanced and pounced, and a struggle ensued.

At length the noise brought Cynthia rushing out. She seized the boy by the shoulder of his jersey, violently shook him and boxed his ears. Then she opened the yard gate and shoved him out into the alley, chittering threats and abuse.

Albert headed homeward, muttering darkly. He suspected she must be a fifth columnist, or else she would have gladly donated the bone. He tramped down the street, rattled across the courtyard with his cart and went into the house. It was twenty past six and he was hungry, thinking only of hotpot and currant pudding.

As yet, he did not know that this day was a turning point in his life.

The smell of dinner greeted him as he walked in, but Connie's usual smiling welcome did not. When she heard the front door she came out of the kitchen, but a tense expression was on her face.

She said: 'Albert, where have you been all these hours?'

'Went scrap collecting straight from school.'

'Oh, I see. I've been waiting for you.'

Something was up, he could tell at once. She was looking at him in a very odd way, both pitying and eager. His canny eyes studied her.

'Something the matter, missis?'

She regarded him a moment longer in that same peculiar manner. Then she put an arm around his shoulders.

'Come in here.'

He was ushered into the sitting room. Sam was home, but he had not taken off his cap and jacket. Like

Connie, he seemed on edge, standing before the fire instead of relaxing in his chair.

Albert looked from one to the other. 'What have I done?'

'Nothing, son,' said Tucker. 'Don't worry, you're not in the doghouse.'

Albert breathed more easily. He had feared some dire complaint had been made about him.

'What is it, then? Have I got to go or something?'

Connie looked a question at Sam, who made a small gesture which said: You tell him.

She squatted down to bring her face on a level with that of the child.

'Albert . . .' she cleared her throat, '. . . now listen. There's something you have to know. A letter came today in the afternoon post. It was from London.'

'Gawd,' said Albert. 'Don't tell me they want me back?'

'It wasn't from your parents,' said Connie gently. She brushed back his hair from his forehead. 'It was about them, though.'

The boy looked at Sam, then back to her.

'They've been bombed?'

'No,' said Connie, 'it's something else.'

'He's in jail again? They both are?'

'Nothing like that. There's been an accident, my dear.'

The child regarded her silently.

'No one's quite sure how it happened, but the guess is that one of your parents may have been smoking in bed. At any rate, the house burned down. Apparently both of them left the pub very drunk that night.'

Albert had been holding his breath, and now he let it out slowly.

439

'Oh,' was all he said. He seemed astounded.

'Are you upset?' asked Connie, stroking his face. 'I know you didn't care for them, or they for you, but they were your mum and dad, weren't they?'

'Crikey,' breathed Albert, then swallowed hard. 'The poor, silly sods.'

Connie glanced up at her husband. Sam smiled wanly. It was obvious the boy was shocked. However little love he had felt for them, the Plumbs had been his kin, and all he had known for most of his short life. His toughness seemed for the moment to desert him.

Looking at Tucker, he gasped: 'Oh, my Gawd, I'm a horphan.'

'Come here, boy,' said Sam.

He sat down, knees apart, in his chair and leaned forward. The boy stood in front of him, pale and still skinny despite Connie's efforts to fatten him.

'You're nearly eleven now, aren't you, Albert?'

A nod.

'This war's going to last a long time, I'm afraid. Even before this letter came, Connie and I were expecting you to stay with us for a good many years. We were quite happy about that. We still are. In fact, we'd be delighted to have you to stay for good, if you would like that. You're not homeless, Albert. You're not an orphan, either, unless you choose to be.'

'Choose to be? What does that mean?'

Connie answered. 'Sam and I have talked about this on occasion, Albert. We're very fond of you, my dear, and you know we have no children of our own. Are you aware that I once had a little girl, but lost her?'

'Mister told me.'

'Well, we're not exactly young any more. It's not very likely any new babies will come along. So we've plenty of room and time for you, and . . .' she cast a twinkling glance at her husband, '. . . we can well afford it, even when the war is over and the allowance stops. What we're saying, Albert, is we'll adopt you – if you want.'

He needed a moment to take it in. Stay here permanently? Have this good life always? Be Sam and Connie's son?

'Cor!' he exclaimed. 'Proper, like?'

'All legal,' Sam confirmed.

A terrific grin lit Albert's face.

'Would you like that?' Connie asked.

'Gawd's truth, missis! Would I?'

Connie could barely contain her delight. Sam could see she was ready to cry.

'That's settled, then,' he said briskly. Giving the boy a gentle push, he added: 'Go and kiss your new ma. Then get upstairs and have a quick wash. Your dinner's nearly ready.'

When the boy had gone, Sam hugged his wife. 'So, Connie,' he murmured, 'the last need is filled. It seems you weren't asking too much, after all.'

One day in 1942, Connie was walking alone on the Hoe. The pier was gone and some of the elegant houses were in ruins. The bandstand had been dismantled and taken away to be used as scrap metal, and there were craters in the promenade. But the Sound was as blue and calm as ever, and the grass of Hoe Park grew lush and undisturbed.

Near the Naval Memorial, Connie took a seat. Her husband was at the dockyard, and her son, now registered in school as Albert Tucker, was at his lessons. Connie looked down the hill at the wasteland which was once the city centre. She knew they would never

441

rebuild it the way it had been. Plans were already under discussion, though, the newspapers said. Experimental ideas were being put forward. Connie could not imagine what that meant.

Anyway, her own part of town was still surviving. The ancient Barbican streets had been lucky over and over again.

What irony that was, she thought, when Gardenia Lodge had been flattened. How odd and unpredictable, how crazy life could be. And yet it did dispense a measure of justice now and then. Sometimes, in a roundabout fashion, it made things right. And how strange, she thought, that a fire had blighted her early life and another had brought her a blessing, by giving her Albert to adopt. The Tuckers, she supposed, were a family of odds and ends, but they went together well. She had a cautious faith these days, a sense that everything was going to be all right.

Around the bench where she sat, the grass grew thick and uncut. It was starred with daisies and patches of clover. Connie, at peace within herself, sat and watched the flowers dancing in the breeze.